CURSES

CINDY SPENCER PAPE

Dedication

To the best in-laws in the world, Bruce and Judy Pape. Thanks for all the love and support, and for raising my very own hero.

CONTENTS

Chapter One _______________________________________ 7
Chapter Two _______________________________________ 25
Chapter Three _____________________________________ 35
Chapter Four_______________________________________ 51
Chapter Five _______________________________________ 63
Chapter Six ____ 79
Chapter Seven _____________________________________ 89
Chapter Eight ______________________________________ 105
Chapter Nine_______________________________________ 125
Chapter Ten _______________________________________ 145
Chapter Eleven _____________________________________ 161
Chapter Twelve ____________________________________ 175
Chapter Thirteen ___________________________________ 191
Chapter Fourteen___________________________________ 205
Chapter Fifteen ____________________________________ 219
Chapter Sixteen ____________________________________ 233
Chapter Seventeen _________________________________ 245
Chapter Eighteen___________________________________ 255
Chapter Nineteen __________________________________ 263
Chapter Twenty____________________________________ 273
Epilogue ____ 283
A word about the author… ___________________________ 287

CHAPTER ONE

"I do *not* need to get laid!"

"Yes, my friend, you do. Desperately."

Mel's hand stilled on the mortar and pestle she was using, and she glared at her best friend, who was curled up in a chair by the window in Mel's kitchen. "You're nuts! Just because things have been a little off lately…"

"Mel, you're more than just 'a little off. You haven't been yourself in weeks." Karen's voice had taken on its 'don't-mess-with-me-I'm-a-fifth-grade-teacher' tone, so Mel knew there was no use arguing, though she was strongly tempted to stick her tongue out. Instead, she stalled until she could figure out what to say. She nibbled on her lower lip while she dumped the mortar full of herbs into an earthenware mixing bowl and turned off the stove.

"I'm sure it's nothing, Kare." Mel forced her own voice to soften. Karen was going through a rough time herself right now, with a messy divorce and her mother dying of cancer. She didn't need crap from her friends. Determined not to ruin this rare opportunity to spend a sunny Saturday morning with her friend, Mel poured the steeped soapwort leaves through a strainer, allowing a thick, clear fluid to drain into the bowl. The sweet, pungent aroma of steaming herbs filled the room. "So a few plants are wilting; it's nothing to worry about. I've just got a lot on my mind, that's all."

"I know, honey, but for you, wilting plants are a big deal." She gestured around Mel's herb-filled kitchen. Sure enough, there were several brown leaves and dried stalks, something that had never happened to Mel before. Maybe she should move them outside, see if the warm May sunshine could help them out. "I just think you've been neglecting yourself. A few rounds between the sheets would go an awfully long way toward relieving some of that stress."

Mel rolled her eyes. "And, hypothetically, *if* I were to agree with you, where do you suggest I find someone? This is an awfully small town, remember. And everybody in it knows better than to screw around with the local witch." She squeezed the gelatinous sap from a couple aloe vera leaves into the bowl. "Oh, and then again, there's the little matter of a curse."

"Curse, schmurse. I'm not telling you to get married, though that might not be a bad idea eventually." Karen's brown eyes twinkled as she inhaled the fragrance of Mel's concoction. "I'm telling you to have some hot, steamy sex!"

Mel shook her head, refusing to comment. She loved Karen deeply, but sometimes… She gave the bowl a final stir with the plastic spatula, then scraped the viscous liquid through a funnel into a pretty glass bottle. Tiny green flecks floated in a crystal-clear suspension, which glinted brightly in the warm sunlight streaming through the open window.

Karen must have decided it was time to shut up. She rolled her eyes and changed the subject. "Looks pretty. What are you making, anyway? Potion? Healing salve?"

Mel did her best rendition of an evil cackle. "Something for you, my pretty."

Karen laughed. "No, really!"

"Well, it is for you," Mel countered. She'd put a little soothing, relaxing magic into the batch, but her friend would never know. She wedged a cork into the bottle and handed it across the big pine table. "Consider it a Mother's Day present, since you're determined to act like you're mine. Shower gel."

* * * *

Okay, so maybe Karen had been right, Mel admitted a few hours later. Apparently she did need a man, judging by the way her pulse started jumping as she looked up, way up, at the grade A prime specimen of masculinity standing just inside her office door. Well over six foot, with shoulder length black hair and intense amber-gold eyes, her new summer tenant was just about the sexiest thing Mel had ever seen. She supposed dragging him all the way inside for a late afternoon quickie was a bad idea, but for the first time since she'd been running her resort cabins, she actually considered it.

Get a grip, Mel!

She forced her mouth to close and really hoped she wasn't drooling.

"So the cabin is completely isolated?"

Her head went up and down like a bobble-head doll's. "Absolutely. The only road leading back to it is a two-track, and the only way to the two-track is across my property. Even the riding stables and fishing guides don't take tourists that deep into the woods."

"But what about your resort staff?"

"Staff?" Tilting her head, she tried for a moment to figure out what he was asking. "What staff?" Then she laughed, breaking the stupidity spell that his stunning presence had obviously cast on her normally down-to-earth brain. "Oh. Staff. I'm it, I'm afraid, at least for the next few weeks. Whispering Pines isn't exactly the Ritz." She gestured down the gravel drive to where six of her seven rental cabins were clustered in a tidy circle. The hunk—one Mr. Jonas Pierce, according to his registration forms—was renting cabin seven, which was really her great-great-great grandparent's cabin, located about a mile back into the woods. Her own house, though nearly a hundred years old, was actually the new residence on the property.

"If you need something, you can contact me on the two-way radio. There's no phone in that cabin, so you'll be completely on your own."

His deep sigh sounded heartfelt, and his crooked smile made her stomach do cartwheels. "Wonderful!" Tiny lines crinkled at the corners of those unusual golden eyes, and his broad shoulders relaxed.

She couldn't help smiling back. "See if you think so after a week with only yourself for company."

"I assure you, Ms. MacRae, I will. Myself and I get along just fine on our own." Deep lines bracketed his mouth as he smiled, and it was all she could do not to touch them, try to smooth them away. His chiseled cheekbones made her think he had some Native American blood, but whatever his heritage, it had sure come together perfectly.

She wasn't sure if he was making fun of her or not, so she got back to business. "Well, then you've come to the right place. You're paid up in advance, so you're good till Labor Day. I hope you enjoy your summer at Whispering Pines."

"Do you close after Labor Day?" One straight dark eyebrow quirked upward.

"No," she replied. "As soon as the summer vacation season ends, hunting camps begin. Those, followed by ski and snowmobile season, make up the bulk of a Yooper's year." Life in Michigan's Upper Peninsula was still as dependent on the changing seasons as it had been when Mel's ancestors had arrived a hundred and fifty years earlier.

"Yooper?" His amber eyes went blank, and Mel groaned silently. Apparently the stupid spell was back. The New York stud muffin might look like a local in his faded jeans and well-worn hiking boots, but he wasn't likely to know the regional slang.

"A Yooper is a person from the U. P., or Upper Peninsula."

"Right then." He sounded faintly amused, but at least he didn't seem to notice that she still couldn't stop staring. Of course, with his looks, he was probably used to being ogled. A single band of white streaked down from his left temple, punctuating his thick black hair, and she had to fight off the urge to reach out and touch it.

"So how do I find the place?"

Mel handed him a photocopy of the local soil survey map with a trail highlighted in yellow. "I'm glad you have a Jeep," she told him, looking behind him to his vehicle. Judging by the New York plates, it was his own and not a rental. "The two-track gets pretty nasty when it rains." Grabbing her keys off her desk, she motioned him out the door ahead of her onto the wide porch, which wrapped around two sides of her log home. The office had a separate entrance on the side of the house, so she didn't need to use her front door for business. "You can follow me to the cabin."

He nodded, though he'd stiffened again while his lips tightened and his eyebrows drew together. Okay, so he didn't want company even as far as his cabin door. *Fine.* She watched him stride down the driveway to his dented and muddy four-wheeler. That's why she kept the remote cabin, for guests who wanted to commune with nature in privacy.

The drooling problem started to come back, though, as she gazed hungrily at the supple muscles outlined by his close-fitting jeans and snug gray T-shirt. The Jeep and his worn, casual clothing projected the image of a man at home in the wilderness, even though the cabin had been booked by an accounting firm in New York City. After meeting the man, though, Mel had no qualms now about renting him the isolated cabin. Mr. Jonas Pierce definitely looked like he was able to take care of himself.

Realizing that she'd been staring again, Mel shook herself and hurried to her own vehicle. The ancient compact pickup truck sported as much rust as yellow paint these days; it was older than the hills and twice as cranky, but it got her where she needed to go—most of the time.

"Come on, Jezebel, don't let me down, now." She really didn't want to lose face in front of her new tenant, though she tried to tell herself it was just professional pride. She'd never been very good at lying to herself, so she was forced to admit to a more basic reason. In the last five minutes, she'd come to the conclusion that Karen was right. She needed a man, and this man was gorgeous, ostensibly single, and here for just three months. He was the perfect candidate for a hot summer fling, and she didn't want him to think she was an idiot.

After two false starts, Jezebel, as Mel's grandmother had named the truck years earlier, finally started with a sputtering cough. Great. Time for another tune-up. "Thanks Jez." Mel patted the dashboard. She hadn't wanted to ride up and back with her new tenant. Not when she wasn't really sure about her attraction to him and what she wanted to do about it. No, she admitted, again forcing herself to honesty as the truck bumped along the gravel road that led into the Sanctity Area Wildlife Preserve. She knew exactly what she wanted to do with that great looking package of testosterone, and once again, lying to herself wasn't going to do a bit of good. She very much wanted to jump his gorgeous bones.

* * * *

Whispering Pines certainly wasn't what he'd been expecting, Joe mused, following the yellow truck that should have been in a museum—or a junkyard. There were no cheesy gift shops or stuffed deer heads to be found. He banged his head on the ceiling of his Jeep as he hit yet another pothole on the rutted track that passed for a road. He had to admit, he'd gotten what he'd paid for. When he'd had his accountant make the reservations, he'd asked for the most remote cabin available, and judging by this sorry dirt track, he'd gotten it. With her long lean legs and long red curls, Joe's landlady was a whole lot cuter than he'd been expecting, too. He whistled a rusty tune as he got out of the Jeep, and followed her swaying hips up the steps to the cabin porch. This summer suddenly looked far more promising than it had just a few hours earlier.

The cabin was apparently as old as the forest around it, but it was neat and well maintained. The knotty pine porch was smooth and spotless, with vividly colored clumps of spring wildflowers clustered around the foundation.

"Appearances to the contrary, there is running water and electricity," his landlady told him with a cheerful grin as she inserted a large, old-fashioned key into the lock. She had a heart-shaped face and pointed chin that lent a foxy look, and her eyes were downright stunning, a clear aquamarine, almost exactly halfway between blue and green. Joe had to make a conscious effort to look away. "But there's no TV and no phone. If you need anything, you can call me or the sheriff's office on the two-way radio." She handed him the key, then stepped aside so he could precede her through the door.

"Don't sweat it." He'd have to go into town for internet access, but he'd grown used to that as he traveled the world searching out stories. He was a horror novelist. Research in rustic backwaters was part of the job. He tapped the phone clipped to his belt.

"Cell service is iffy out here at best," she warned. "We're too far away from the towers."

"Satellite," he answered, gazing approvingly around the tidy interior of the small building as his eyes adjusted rapidly to the reduced light. "Works anywhere." He traveled to remote areas all over the world in the course of his research. The satellite phone cost a lot more, but it never let him down when he needed it. Somehow, though, he didn't think Sanctity was going to pose the same kind of threats he'd encountered in, say, Transylvania.

"Is the cabin all right?"

"Perfect." It was small, but the single main room was just as meticulously maintained as the exterior, and exuded comfortable charm. The rugged pine dining table would serve for both writing and meals. There were several windows nearby to provide plenty of natural sunlight, and an electrical outlet to plug in his laptop. The appliances, other than the microwave and automatic drip coffee maker, looked to be as old as Joe, but they gleamed and the refrigerator hummed. The polished wooden countertops echoed the yellow pine floor, which was scattered with colorful handmade rugs.

"The bathroom's through there." Mel pointed to a doorway in the rear of the living space with long slender fingers that had short clipped nails and calluses from hard work. "It was added on in the seventies. There's no tub, but the shower works well. You'll have to come up to the main group of cabins for laundry facilities, or else use the Laundromat in town."

He assured her that the arrangements were fine. His eyes took in the pair of overstuffed chairs and leather sofa that surrounded a fieldstone fireplace, and a log ladder that led up to what he assumed was a sleeping loft.

"There are fresh sheets in the cedar chest by the bed," she told him. "Just drop the dirty ones off at my cabin when you want them washed. You're sure you don't want me to clean for you? Not even once a week?"

"No." He didn't want anyone, not even his hostess, walking in on him unannounced. "I live alone. I'm used to cleaning up after myself."

"Okay, then." Melissa gave him a tentative smile. "If you need anything, just call me on the radio, or stop by my cabin." She twisted one silky copper lock between her fingers, then impatiently shoved it behind her ear. Her nervous gesture made him wonder if she was feeling the same attraction he was. "I guess I'll head back then. Enjoy your stay, Mr. Pierce."

"Joe," he corrected. "Or Jonas if you prefer." That was odd; he never let anybody call him Jonas, not since his mother had died. He'd spent so much of his life trying to be "just a regular Joe" that he'd even adopted the name.

Of course, "Mel" seemed a little prosaic for a witch, too. When he'd been told his prospective landlady was a witch, he'd imagined an aging hippy in flowing skirts, who dabbled with herbs and chanted at the moon. Since he'd been investigating the paranormal all his adult life, he really ought to know by now that the stereotypes were seldom, if ever on the money. Melissa was a name better suited to the image he'd carried in his mind. Wasn't it the name of an herb?

He decided he wanted to talk to her. He was here to finish writing one book, and maybe to do research on the next, which he'd pitched to his editor as being about a small-town witch. Getting to know her a little better would kill two birds with one stone. He could begin his research and start to see how deep this attraction between them went. Food. That was a nice, nonthreatening basis for initiating conversation.

"I need to pick up some groceries," Joe called as Mel turned toward the door. "Do I go back past your place, or is there a shortcut to town?" He took a second to admire the long, lean lines of her that even her faded jeans and oversized flannel shirt couldn't disguise.

She paused, and looked back at him. "Past my place. The two-track is the only road in or out of this spot, and it doesn't go anywhere but here."

Joe nodded, as though he hadn't noticed that on the way in.

"Great." He caught up with her in two strides and held the door open with his hand. "I was wondering, though. Since I'm new around here, and don't know any of the local places, perhaps I could buy you dinner in exchange for showing me around a little bit."

Her tilted blue-green eyes widened, and she took a reflexive step back. Joe stifled a predatory grin. It was good to know she felt the chemistry too. "D-dinner?" She shoved her hair back behind her ears again.

"Dinner," he repeated firmly, stepping forward to close the gap between them. "I assume there's some place to eat in Sanctity." There was. He'd checked the town out on the way in, but she didn't need to know that.

"Sure," she breathed. "Of course. There are two." That matched his count: a diner and a McDonalds. Frankly, neither had held too much appeal, but it was late afternoon, he'd had a long drive, and he was hungry. He could live with French fries and a salad for one meal.

"So shall we go get dinner?" he reiterated patiently.

"Sure, I guess." Her eyes widened even further and she looked like a rabbit about to bolt for cover. How could a woman as attractive as Mel be so startled by a guy asking her to dinner? Were all the local men eunuchs? He wondered what she'd look like if—or when—he asked her to go to bed with him.

Closing the door behind them, he pocketed the key to the cabin. "I'll follow you back to your place." He cast a disparaging eye at her battered old truck. "We'll take my car from there."

She nodded in agreement, but didn't say a word. He got her as far as her own cabin door when she stalled him again, though at least she'd led him to the entrance of her living quarters instead of the office. "I've got work to do first. You can wait inside if you want, or follow that path over there down to the lake. It will only take me a few minutes."

Mel's cabin looked almost as old as the one he was renting. It was larger, with two full stories, but built along similar lines, and Joe wouldn't have minded seeing inside it. He was far more interested, however, in exploring the lady herself. "I'll help," he offered. "What do you need?"

Her blush made her look about sixteen, and he felt a small pang of guilt over the lust he'd been feeling. He was thirty-nine years old, and she couldn't be even thirty. He'd never been into robbing the cradle.

"Just got some cleaning in one of the cabins. There's a couple from Grand Rapids arriving first thing tomorrow morning." She rolled her eyes and smiled wryly. "Honeymooners. It won't take me long. You don't need to help."

"I know, but I'm going to anyway." He hadn't gotten where he was in his career by taking no for an answer. He waited while she ducked inside and returned with her equipment. He wrested away the broom and mop she held in one hand, then followed her down the path.

The cabins were all smaller, more modern replicas of Mel's home. Only one cabin of the six had a car pulled up alongside. Unit two was apparently occupied by someone from Wisconsin. Somebody wealthy, judging by the Lexus in the parking spot. Despite the rustic surroundings, Whispering Pines must attract a high-end clientele.

"You're sure you wouldn't prefer one of these cabins?" Mel's movements were swift and deft as he helped her make up the king-sized bed in cabin five, which was off to itself a bit at the end of the lane. He watched those sturdy but graceful hands as they smoothed the crisp cotton sheets, and couldn't help but wonder what they'd feel like on his skin.

Joe hesitated, but not because he was considering switching. Frankly, it was getting damned hard to think about anything other than laying Mel down on the firm, inviting mattress, or trying out the Jacuzzi tub big enough for two in the bathroom he'd just helped her scrub. It had taken all his willpower to keep his hands to himself when she'd bent over the tub, her trim backside pointed up at him.

"So do you want to move?" She tugged a handmade quilt up over the sheets. "It's not a problem. We're not booked up for the summer yet."

"Absolutely not." There was no question of that. His tiny, rustic accommodations suited him perfectly. Aside from enjoying the sense of history at the older cabin, he wanted, needed the isolation it offered.

"Okay, then, if you're sure." They moved out into the living room where she ran a dust cloth across the fireplace mantel while Joe vacuumed the already spotless area rug.

"We're finished!" She must have run out of tasks to delay going to dinner, because she bit her lip and dropped the cloth into her bucket of supplies. "I'll add fresh flowers and a fruit basket first thing in the morning, along with some muffins. I would have done that at your cabin too, but I wasn't expecting you till tomorrow."

"Well, don't worry about the flowers." He followed her back up the path, wondering if he'd ever get tired of watching her walk. "But if the muffins are homemade, I'll take a rain check on those."

"It's a deal." She turned and gave him a shaky smile, but didn't break stride. Then she led the way to her back door this time. The path curved through a colorful, well-tended garden, up onto a wide sunny deck. He followed her through a glass-paned door into a pristine kitchen.

Wow! Joe blinked as he followed her inside. Aged yellow pine blended seamlessly with high-tech stainless steel. Bundles of herbs hung drying in the window, while fresh ones flourished in plain clay pots scattered about the room. A gleaming pot rack hung above a center island, and every surface sparkled. This wasn't the workroom of a witch; it was the domain of a chef!

"Have a seat." Her voice was breathy, and her hands fluttered nervously. She pointed at cushioned wooden chairs surrounding a larger version of the pine table he'd loved up at his place. It bore the scars of decades of use beneath layers of finish, and an earthenware jug holding a haphazard spray of spring wildflowers graced the center of the table. She stood for a second poised in the archway that lead to what he presumed was the living room, and a flight of stairs. She licked her lips. "I'll be ready in five minutes."

Sure, and I'm the Queen of England. He pulled out a chair and sat as he watched her flee. No woman on Earth could get ready for a date in five minutes, but this one just might be worth the wait.

Melissa MacRae, however, turned out to be full of surprises. While Joe had been mentally classifying the various herbs in her window, the woman returned. She still wore the same faded jeans, but a sunny yellow pullover had replaced the flannel shirt, and the soft knit clung snugly to generous curves that the flannel had only hinted at. Leather sandals graced dainty feet instead of the hiking boots she'd sported earlier, and her coppery hair had been freed from its ponytail to bounce gaily about her shoulders.

"Ready?" The slight breathiness in her voice was the only indication that she had rushed to rejoin him. For some reason, that notion pleased him. Standing, he smiled, eyeing this softer, more feminine Mel hungrily.

"We can drive into Escanaba if you want something other than Mickey D's or Rosa's Diner." Unlike the women he knew in New York, she didn't wait for him to open the door and hand her inside. Instead, she bounded ahead and clambered easily into his Jeep. "Sanctity doesn't offer too many options."

"The diner should be fine." He didn't much care what he ate as long as it was filling, and not swimming in bacon grease. It was the company he was interested in.

He ordered onion rings and a meatless chef's salad. After the waitress had left, Mel looked up at him through sooty lashes.

"Rosa does some vegetarian stuff. Why didn't you just say that's what you wanted? Her veggie lasagna is really good."

Busted. He grinned at her perceptiveness. "That's what I had for lunch."

Her tilted eyes crinkled at the corners when she smiled. Tiny lines radiated from them, so she might just be older than he'd thought at first. Maybe even all of thirty. That was good. Now he wouldn't have to feel guilty about his unexpected but powerful interest in getting horizontal with Mel.

"If she gets to know you a little, Rosa will cook to order, even if it's not on the menu," she advised. "She makes a mean wet burrito, too, with or without the green meat."

Green meat? He shuddered at the very thought, and her tinkling laugh let him know she understood.

"The meat is fresh; the tomatillos in the seasoning make it green," Mel explained. "But trust me, what she can do with pinto beans is every bit as good."

"I'll keep it in mind." At least Mel seemed to be open-minded about his lifestyle. He'd worried a little about being a vegetarian in this area populated so heavily by hunters and fishermen.

"So how did you hear about Sanctity?" she asked him later between bites of a thick grilled cheese sandwich. "We don't get a lot of business from New York City, and something tells me you're not here for the fishing."

"Nope." He grinned back. "Though I've tried catch and release a time or two. It never really did much for me."

"So…"

"Truth is I'm a writer." The best cover stories always stuck as closely as possible to the truth. "A friend of mine who *is* a fisherman was here last year. He told me Whispering Pines would be a nice, quiet place to compile my notes and get to work on my manuscript."

"What kind of manuscript?"

"It's a historical piece." Partially true. He'd planned to set his witch story in the eighteen hundreds. "Nothing very interesting, mostly about the impact of the French on the Revolutionary War." Completely false. It was a subject he'd done a major research paper on in college, so he could discuss it in nauseating detail when required. It was also boring enough to circumvent too much attention. He finished off with another truth. "I've got boxes of notes, reams of research material. I just need to put it all together."

Reddish-brown eyebrows scrunched together. "Willoughby. Kent and Nora Willoughby. They're the only guests I had last summer from New York."

"You're good." He raised one eyebrow. Apparently the pixie-like exterior concealed a razor sharp mind. Cool. While that could make his research more difficult, it would sure be a lot more fun. "Kent and I have been friends since college. He knew right away that Sanctity would be the perfect spot for me to hunker down and get to work." Kent had also told him the owner of the resort was a witch, providing the idea for his story. Of course, his friend hadn't bothered to mention that the witch was a young, pretty redhead, and Joe wondered what was up with that.

"I'm glad." She popped a French fry into her inviting mouth. "I'll have to send the Willoughbys a thank-you note for the referral."

They ate quietly for a while, each sneaking guilty glances when they thought the other wasn't looking. Joe felt absurdly like a teenager on a first date—desperate to impress, but at the same time needed to remain cool and inscrutable. Had it been that long since he'd been with a woman? His hormones sure seemed to think so. They hadn't gone this crazy since he *was* sixteen, more than twenty years ago. Maybe she was a witch, he thought wryly, and maybe he was falling under her spell. It would sure explain a lot. His only consolation was that she seemed to be just as nervous as he was. Every time he caught her peeking at him, she ducked her head and blushed.

"So tell me about your research," she said eventually when they were both nearly finished with dinner.

"My what?" Joe jerked himself out of his fantasies, where she'd been asking him an entirely different question.

"Your research. What new and fascinating things do you have to tell the world about the Revolution?"

"Oh." He paused a moment to make sure he remembered what he was supposed to be discussing, then filled her in on the basics, hoping she'd get bored quickly.

"So shouldn't you be in New England? Or even France?"

"That was last summer." In fact he had been in France for a while the previous year, researching the catacombs under Paris. "I've got all the material I need. Now I just need to hibernate somewhere with my computer and write."

"Well." She grinned, again. She seemed to do that a lot, and it did something funny to his stomach each and every time. "You picked the right place. If you don't hunt or fish, Sanctity is ideal for hibernation. There's nothing else to do."

"I don't know," he admitted, eyeing her luscious curves openly. "I'd say the place offers some distinct possibilities."

She blushed again, charming him. He hadn't thought modern women still knew how. He was going to have to play this carefully. He did have a lot of work to do, starting with a rapidly approaching deadline on the Paris manuscript that he needed to finish and submit to his impatient publisher, and ending with an outline for the witch book.

Getting close to the witch, however, had taken on a whole new appeal now that he'd seen her. A brief fling wouldn't hurt his research at all. It would make it easier to discover her secrets, and getting a little action would keep him motivated during those endless, lonely hours of typing. A summer romance was all it could be, of course. Joe Pierce did not make commitments. He wasn't a monk, but he sure as hell wasn't the marrying kind, either. Not in this lifetime.

"When do the tourists arrive?" he asked, breaking the silence that had descended after his suggestive remark. "I noticed most of your cabins are empty."

"In a couple weeks. Memorial Day weekend really kicks off the summer tourist season in Michigan."

"Just like New York." Joe had spent so much more time in Europe and Africa that it was sometimes easy to forget how things worked at home. He'd done some basic research about upper Michigan before coming here, but there was still a lot he didn't know. Intent on learning everything he could as swiftly as possible, he quizzed her about the region.

"The Upper Peninsula is full of wildlife," she informed him. He nodded, encouraging her to continue.

"The people of the U. P. are mostly of Native American and Scandinavian descent, although Sanctity and several other towns were settled by Scottish and Irish immigrants back in the early nineteenth century."

"Most of them came as fur traders?"

"Loggers," she corrected. "The fur traders were earlier, and mainly French. In the nineteenth century, Michigan pine built a lot of the East Coast cities, and factories for the Industrial Revolution. Iron and copper mining came later. Now that the natural resources are all but gone, the U. P. survives mostly on tourism."

"Predominated by hunting and fishing."

"Right. Aside from the lake shore communities, of course. There are summer homes and marinas all around the Great Lakes. Inland, though, it's mainly sportsmen who keep our economy alive. Fishing and hiking in summer, hunting in fall, skiing and snowmobiling in winter." Her voice warmed with enthusiasm as she talked about her home.

"What about the Wildlife Preserve?" Joe asked. "Doesn't having such a huge protected area put a crimp in the hunting and fishing?" The Sanctity Wildlife Preserve was another reason Joe had chosen this town. Five thousand acres of hunter-free wilderness held a huge appeal to someone who needed to spend time running through the woods unseen.

"Not really." She made a quick face, wrinkling her nose before her mouth closed delectably around a French fry, and it was all Joe could do to follow the conversation. He needed the information, but all he really wanted to do was to drag her back to one of her cabins and get naked. The force of his desire was unsettling; he couldn't remember ever wanting a woman, particularly a specific woman, this badly.

"The hunters will always manage to find a way to get their killing fix." Her voice was filled with disdain that almost matched his own, but brightened as she continued. "The Preserve is a draw for some degree of eco-tourism, though. I work with several guides who do photo safaris and catch and release fishing. It's an area of the business that several of us in Sanctity have been trying to develop."

"Photo safaris? This isn't Africa." Teasing Mel was fun. He got a kick out of making her blush.

"Photographic hunting trips if you prefer." She shrugged. "But whatever term you use, the program is gaining in business. Since my property abuts the Preserve, Whispering Pines is ideal for the noninvasive programs."

He had to agree. Her proximity to the preserve, and the strict no-hunting policy on her land certainly made the place ideal for him.

It took effort, but they managed to keep the conversation light for the duration of the meal. Her vivid descriptions and obvious love for the land added depth to the dry facts. He also caught her licking her lips a time or two when she thought he wasn't looking. Oh yeah, she was feeling the heat the same as he was.

When their waitress brought the check, Mel reached for her wallet. The shock that went through his system when he stayed her hand with his was alarming. A light social touch shouldn't send tremors throughout his body. "I asked you to come with me, remember?"

Withdrawing her hand as though she'd burned it, Mel blushed again, and nodded. Her eyes were as round as their dinner plates. "Okay."

At Joe's request, they walked the block to the local grocery store, where she helped him locate the supplies he needed to stock the fridge and cabinets up at his cabin. The prices were higher than he was used to, but money wasn't a problem for Joe. His publisher and agent saw to that very nicely. The selection was a little limited, so he'd have to manage an occasional trip to a larger city.

The store was small, but fairly crowded. Mel smiled and said hello to most of the people they encountered, even stopping to introduce Joe to a few. He shook hands with a pair of elderly ladies and a young couple, even the town mayor. Mel was friendly and open, with a kind word for everyone and usually a question about some mutual friend or a member of their family.

"Well, it was nice to meet you Mr. Pierce." The rangy teenage boy turned back to Joe politely after a quiet conversation with Mel.

"You too, Tom."

"Don't forget to have your mother call me," Mel reminded the boy. "And tell her the chamomile tea should be fine for helping her sleep." Apparently Mel was the local expert on herbal cures, but from what Joe had seen so far, her advice was more common sense than magic. Even Joe's doctor friend acknowledged that chamomile was a mild soporific.

They rounded another corner, encountering yet another older couple. Joe paused, expecting Mel to stop and chat as she had before.

She did make the effort. He saw her square her shoulders and force a smile, but it was wasted. The man just stared at his shoes as the couple pushed by, while the woman narrowed her eyes and sniffed in Mel's direction, her lips curled as if she'd smelled a skunk.

Mel kept the smile up until the couple had continued around another corner, then sagged taking a deep breath. Then she shook her head and looked up at Joe. "Canned soups?"

She lagged behind as Joe approached the check out, and the middle-aged man at the counter gave Joe a wide smile. "Welcome to Sanctity, son. Here to get a head start on some fishing?"

Joe shook his head. "No just here for a while to relax and get some writing done. Name's Joe. Joe Pierce."

"Phil Mercer." The older man reached out a hand for Joe to shake. Joe reached to take it, but the other man suddenly withdrew his hand. "Melissa." He said Mel's name as if it were a curse.

"Hello, Phil."

The grocer ignored her and began to ring up Joe's purchases.

When he was finished, he gave Joe a nod. "I imagine you're staying up at Talcott's. Food in the dining room there is good, so you shouldn't need to cook much."

Joe nodded at Mel. "Actually I'm at Whispering Pines. Ms. MacRae generously agreed to show me around town."

Mercer snorted. "Whatever you say, mister. Have a good night, now." With that, he rang up Mel's order, without so much as another word.

Mel stood in stoic silence, thanking the man politely even though he'd ignored her. Joe's eyes narrowed. There were definitely undercurrents in this town that merited a closer look. All was not sweetness and light in Sanctity, Michigan.

He waited till they were driving back to her cabin to ask her about it. "What's with the cold shoulder?" He hadn't noticed any hostility toward her in Rosa's diner, so the dagger looks she'd gotten in the grocery store troubled him. He wasn't at all comfortable with the rush of protectiveness he'd felt.

"Nothing." She shrugged, tipping her head to stare out the window and avoiding his gaze. They lapsed back into silence.

It wasn't nothing. Joe knew better, and he was going to uncover the truth—eventually. He didn't want to push too hard too fast, giving her an excuse to pull away, so he decided to let it go for tonight, and he kept his eyes on the winding dirt road.

It was nearly twilight when they approached Mel's cabin. Elongated tree shadows transformed the pleasant green forest of the day into a gray, reaching horror-movie set, casting a pall of grimness over the land. Joe loved this time of day.

"So should we try the wet burritos tomorrow night?" He didn't know quite where that question came from as he walked Mel to her door. She sidestepped, avoiding his touch as he reached out to take her elbow. He didn't know why he wanted to touch her so badly, or why she kept backing away. He only knew that he wanted, needed to see her again.

Sensing her hesitation to his dinner invitation, though, he began to reassess the idea. A second meal in as many days could definitely be construed as a date. *It's research. Just business.* He tried to convince himself he wasn't thinking with his glands.

"Okay, I guess," Mel allowed slowly. "If you're sure. You know the place now, you don't really need me to show you around."

"I don't need your company, Mel." He held the screen door while she opened her lock. "I just like it. I'll pick you up at six."

Stepping inside her doorway, she peered up at him through partly closed lashes and cast a tiny, unsteady smile. "That would be great, Jonas. Thanks." She slipped inside and shut her door before he could say another word.

Walking to his Jeep, Joe shook his head. He wasn't sure what he'd gotten himself into this time, but it sure looked like it was going to be an interesting summer.

CHAPTER TWO

"I'm still not sure about this," Mel confessed, sitting across her kitchen table from her grandmother's best friend, Harriette Sharp. This made two days in a row that friends had dropped by for morning visits, and she wondered if there was a conspiracy afoot to meddle with Mel's love life—or lack of one. "There's something different about this guy. His aura's all murky—I can't read him at all."

"Different is good, little girl. If you hadn't been holding out for somebody different, you wouldn't be a thirty-four-year-old virgin. As far as his aura goes, are you sure it's him? You said yourself that your powers have been a little unreliable lately."

"They have been unpredictable," Mel admitted. "That's why I know it's time, but Jonas… I don't know. There's just something about him that's strange. I'm sure of that much." Overnight she had begun to develop cold feet about the idea of having an affair with her summer visitor.

"He's the first man who ever really got your pulse racing, isn't he? Don't you think that's strange enough?" Hattie, as always, went straight for the jugular. "You want him, girl. Stop making excuses and do something about it."

"That's the problem. I do want him." Mel hated to admit it, but

Harriette had a point. The older woman had helped raise Mel, knew her far too well, sometimes better than Mel knew herself. "I've never felt like this before, never been drawn to anyone quite this much. Not even Leo Watson in the tenth grade." Since that unrequited crush had hitherto been the great romance of Mel's life, that was saying something.

"It's time, kiddo." Hattie nodded her silver head sagely. "Your hormones and your powers know it, so you might as well admit it. You need a man."

Mel let out a snort of disgust and regret, even though she'd had exactly the same thought yesterday when she'd first laid eyes on Jonas. "I sure need something."

* * * *

The pungent odor of pine drifted upward from the fallen needles crunching beneath Mel's feet. She loved every season here in the forest, and walking the wooded acres of her property was the best way she knew to clear her head. The dense evergreen canopy shaded her from the afternoon sun as she strolled through the woods, mentally replaying this morning's conversation with Hattie. Try as she might, she couldn't remember a single instance where Harriette had ever steered her wrong. Mel's mother had died when Mel was just a baby, leaving Mel in the care of her grandmother Martha and Martha's boon companion Hattie. It had been Hattie who had provided softness in Mel's existence; Martha had been a terse, no-nonsense woman. Hattie had kissed scraped knuckles and bandaged knees, then later helped Mel through menarche and acne, teenage crushes and eventually the death of her grandmother. No matter how far out Hattie's current advice seemed to be, Mel knew she owed her friend the courtesy of serious consideration.

Furthermore, Hattie was probably the only person in the world who knew as much about the MacRaes as Mel herself. Fully aware of the family history, knowing the challenges Mel faced, the older woman still insisted Mel should let herself get involved with Jonas Pierce.

It wasn't like she could have a real relationship; that was the nature of her family's curse. MacRae women weren't allowed the luxury of happily-ever-after, and in her secret heart, that was what Mel craved most. A real romance, the permanent kind. She'd sacrifice almost everything she had if only she could be normal, if she could someday look forward to having a husband and a half dozen kids to call her own. But that outcome wasn't possible.

After turning thirty-four this spring, Mel had realized something was wrong. Though she argued with her friends, she knew inside that they were right. Her body was crying out for something she'd never yet experienced. She would wake in the night, drenched with sweat, dreaming of hot, steamy sex. Made-for TV movies could bring tears to her eyes, and her special abilities, the ones that comprised the plus side of being a MacRae, had begun to fluctuate wildly. It was time.

Jonas Pierce, she had to admit, was an ideal candidate. He was nice, smart, and gorgeous, and most importantly, he would be gone by September. There would be no temptation to prolong the relationship.

She suppressed a pang of guilt over that last thought. She wasn't going to attack the man, take advantage of him. She'd just let him catch her if he showed an interest in the chase. Nobody would get hurt. So why did it feel so wrong, so cheap? *Get over it*, Mel told herself, over and over. That was the way things had to be. She hopped over a small stream and began her circuitous stroll home.

A movement off to her left caught her eye, drawing her out of her introspection and back into the world around her. Standing stock-still, she scanned the thick undergrowth along the stream bank, then held her breath when she caught sight of the creature. The biggest, most glorious wolf she had ever seen watched her from the brush. His sleek pelt was a dense, pure black, with one distinguishing streak of white running from his left eye to just behind his pointed ear. Strength and power radiated from the animal, and Mel gasped when his brilliant golden gaze connected with hers.

She felt no fear, sensed no threat emanating from the magnificent creature, just an overpowering sense of wonder as she maintained eye contact. Wolves were making a comeback in the Upper Peninsula, but this was the first she'd encountered up close, and she was profoundly grateful for the experience.

"Hunt safely, friend," she whispered. She knew her own aura projected nothing but peace and respect. She believed, knew, that the creatures of the forest could sense such things. "Hope your pack's somewhere nearby." For some reason she didn't like to think of the wolf as being as alone as she was herself.

She delighted in the prospect of a wolf pack making their home in the Preserve, though she knew the hunters who frequented neighboring lands would be less than pleased. Mel and the other environmentalists in the area would have their work cut out for them convincing the hunters to leave the predators alone. Old beliefs died hard out here in the hinterlands.

Turning back to the path, Mel moved steadily toward home. To her surprise, the wolf followed, not on her heels, but off in the brush, trotting parallel to the path. It was almost as though he was watching over her. He stopped at the verge of the woods, just shy of her garden.

"Good-bye," she called softly, mounting the steps to her back porch. "Be safe."

With a motion that bore an uncanny resemblance to a nod, the great wolf turned and faded swiftly into the shadowed wilderness.

The image of the wolf was almost enough to keep Mel at peace through the rest of the afternoon. Almost! Still wrestling mentally with her decision to see Jonas again, she lay on her back under the kitchen sink in cabin one, wrestling physically with a leaky drain.

"If you'd accept our offer, you wouldn't have to do that."

Hearing the oily, familiar voice, Mel sat up so fast she whacked her head on the underside of the steel basin.

"I thought I told you to stay off my property." Her voice was no more than a hiss as she stood, rubbing her head.

"Just keeping an eye on the future site of the Talcott Wilderness Resort." The intruder lounged indolently against the open door frame. Raking a lascivious glance over Mel's figure, he smiled nastily. "Not that there aren't other things around here worth keeping an eye on."

Eyes narrowing, she clutched the pipe wrench tightly and glared back at the tall, slender figure in her doorway. Sean Talcott was a crook, in Mel's opinion, but Nature had camouflaged his internal nastiness with angelic good looks. He was tall and slim, with sapphire-blue eyes and golden-blond hair. He was gorgeous, with his perfectly pressed khakis and a polo shirt that almost exactly matched the shade of his eyes and bore the logo of Talcott Lodge, her more upscale competitor on the other side of town. But underneath the golden exterior, the scion of the Talcott empire was rotten to the core.

"Well, enjoy the view, because you're never going to get your greedy little paws on either one." She didn't feel like playing his game, so she gave it to him straight. "Not on me, or my land. Now take a hike before I call the sheriff."

"Oh, I don't think so, sugar," he drawled softly, moving closer like a wildcat about to pounce. "You'll cave, eventually. They always do. And later, I might not be feeling so generous. Accept our offer now, and I promise you a job at the new resort. Make me wait, and you'll be out in the cold."

"I don't like you, Sean." Mel kept her voice surprisingly level. She tapped the pipe wrench against the palm of her hand. "And I really don't like threats. Now whether you like it or not, this is still my property, and it's going to remain that way. Nobody is putting up a four-story hotel and a golf course on MacRae land."

He'd backed her into a corner of the kitchen area, but he hesitated when she lifted the wrench.

"Now." She poked him with the wrench, pushing him backward, toward the door. "Get your fancy butt into your fancy SUV, and get the hell off my land." She gave him the nastiest grin she could manage. "Then go tell your daddy to back the hell off. Remind him just who he's been threatening. You really don't want to piss me off, do you Sean?"

Sudden comprehension dawned on his sculpted features, and he backed up all the way to the door, then took one hasty step out over the threshold, but he kept his sneer in place and managed a rude little snort. "Fairy tales, Melissa. Nobody with half a brain really believes you have any magical powers."

"But then, nobody ever accused you of having half a brain, did they Sean? Just tell your father that if either of you ever wants to have sex again in this lifetime, you'd better leave me and my property alone." She walked forward to stand in the doorway, then leaned against the sturdy pine trim for support. She was shaking in her boots, but she couldn't let him see it. What was the use of being called the town witch if you couldn't use the occasional threat to defend yourself? "Because if you keep harassing me, there won't be enough Viagra on the planet to help either of you get it up."

For all his protestations of skepticism, Sean Talcott had grown up in Sanctity, after all. He'd known Mel and her grandmother all his life, had heard the stories from before he could walk. There had to be a tiny part of him, deep down inside that really believed Mel was a witch. However small that kernel of belief was, it was apparently enough, and Mel sagged against the doorjamb with relief as he turned and bolted for his Cadillac Escalade. Gravel sprayed and rubber peeled as he spun the SUV around and out of her tiny parking lot.

"You okay, Ms. MacRae?" Startled, she dropped the pipe wrench, just missing her toes. Then she looked up and smiled. It was the honeymooners from Grand Rapids, standing, hands linked, on the front porch of cabin five, with matching expressions of concern on their young, happy faces. They couldn't be more than twenty-two. Mel suppressed a pang of jealousy. She shook her head, feeling suddenly ancient.

"I'm fine, Sherry, but thanks for asking." She sighed, tucking a loose strand of hair back behind her ear. "Just a visit from the neighborhood nuisance. And please, call me Mel."

"Okay, but call us if he bothers you again." The young husband was apparently eager to prove his manhood, and from the glow on his bride's face, it was working. Mel found the whole thing sweet and unexpectedly touching. What she wouldn't give to have someone look at her the way Tom was gazing at Sherry. The bond between them was practically a tangible thing, and once again Mel sighed.

"Thanks, Tom. But now that I've vanquished the sewer rat, I suppose I need to get back to the real plumbing. You two have a nice afternoon." Picking up her wrench, she reentered the vacant cabin. For the rest of the afternoon, she deliberately focused her thoughts on the leaky pipe, excluding Sean Talcott, Jonas Pierce, and the newlyweds from her troubled mind.

* * * *

Joe kept telling himself it wasn't really a date. He was just getting close to a potential source. Yeah, he thought with a mental snort, real close if he were lucky. His professional curiosity was teaming up with his hormones to outvote his sense of self-preservation, which was urging him to pack up his stuff and run. Since Jonas had spent his entire life fine-tuning his self-control, his wild attraction to Mel was more than a little worrisome. He'd glimpsed her walking through the woods this afternoon, looking as comfortable and at home as a dryad in her element. It had taken all of his control not to jump her then and there. Instead, he'd stayed back, simply watching, observing.

He'd be seeing her tonight. That would be time enough if things were going to happen between them.

After showering and shaving, he pulled on a pair of olive drab jeans and a black brushed-cotton shirt. It was still cool up here in the woods, so he tossed a leather bomber jacket over his shoulder as he walked to his Jeep. It isn't really a date, he reminded himself one last time. Too bad his hormones didn't believe it.

* * * *

Shit!

She'd been so determined to put Jonas out of her mind that she'd almost forgotten their date. She glared at her watch, then washed her hands in the now-finished sink of unit one. She barely had time for the usual preparations, let alone the special ones she'd been thinking about. Scooping up her tools, Mel hurried back to her cabin. Fortunately, the herbs she'd left steeping earlier hadn't boiled over, so she strained the liquid into an antique pink glass goblet and carried it up the stairs.

After a ruthlessly fast shower, she rubbed her skin with fragrant body oil, loving the way it soothed her too-quickly-shaved legs. She blended the mixture herself every summer, from roses, lilacs, lavender, and rosemary. It was her personal fragrance, and she infused it into everything from her shampoo to the potpourri that scented her house. She brushed out her hair, then, still naked, she carried the pink goblet into one of the spare bedrooms, placing it carefully on a low dresser, between two thick pillar candles. After lighting the candles, she sat cross-legged on the rug in front of her altar and closed her eyes.

The incantations she used were as old as the MacRae family, older than the town of Sanctity itself. Generations of knowledge had been passed to Mel from her grandmother, knowledge that had come over from Scotland a hundred and fifty years ago, but had been old even then. She had never used her knowledge or her powers to hurt a living soul, and she wasn't starting now. This wasn't a love spell, or a potion to make her irresistible. Jonas would remain entirely in control of his own actions. This spell was all about her.

"Open my mind, my heart to the possibilities of the universe. Let not my doubts or fears constrain me."

Finishing the chant, she took the goblet in both hands, bowing her head in reverence before she drank. There. It was done.

Blowing out the candles, she completed her ritual, then padded back to her bedroom to dress. There was no point in overdressing for Rosa's, so she chose a soft knit top and a pair of skintight jeans. At the last minute, though, she changed her mind. The jeans came off and she slipped into a flowing denim skirt, then, impulsively, she shimmied out of her pink cotton panties, tossing them in the hamper along with her sports bra. She felt daring, a little strange, but exhilarated by the unfamiliar sensations of her clothes sliding against her skin. A cardigan and flat rope sandals completed her outfit, then she headed downstairs to wait for her date.

"So tell me about yourself," Joe began after they'd claimed a corner booth at Rosa's. The drive into town had been accomplished in silence while Mel chewed nervously on her thoughts. One look at Jonas in his soft black shirt had her palms sweaty and her mouth going dry. His long hair was loose and shining, and it was she could do to keep her hands from running through the strands. She sure hoped Hattie's advice had been sound, because otherwise, she was in a whole lot of trouble.

His question caught her by surprise. A man who actually wanted to talk about her? She couldn't tell him everything, of course; she didn't want to scare him off, but she did give him vignettes. Stories about growing up in Sanctity, her college years at Lake Superior State in Sault Ste. Marie, and the trials and tribulations of a wilderness innkeeper. He was a great listener, Mel discovered, and their food was set in front of them before she realized time had passed.

"I spent the afternoon doing plumbing." She showed him her ragged fingernails. "It's not exactly a glamorous life, but I like it. How was your day?" She forked up a bite of Rosa's Mexican specialty, closing her eyes to better enjoy the explosion of flavors.

"I took a walk in the woods." He paused to take a bite of his own meal, then smiled and nodded his approval. "Then did a little shopping here in town, spent some time getting to know the area."

"That should have taken all of five minutes." His white teeth flashed in response to her quip, and she swallowed hard as her stomach fluttered.

"Actually, you'd be surprised how much you can learn about a place chatting at the local hardware store." There was an almost feral gleam in those amber eyes, and Mel suddenly had the sensation of being hunted. She didn't know whether to be thrilled or frightened.

"So did you learn anything interesting?" She licked her suddenly dry lips.

"You could say that." His grin reminded her uncannily of the wolf she'd seen this afternoon. "When I mentioned that I was staying up at Whispering Pines, Jerry at the store felt obligated to warn me about you."

Her fork clattered against her plate as she dropped it. "Really?" She was pretty sure he wasn't buying her feigned nonchalance.

"Umm-hmm." He sipped his coffee slowly, dragging out the suspense.

"Why?"

"Why what?"

"Why did Jerry warn you off?" Jerry Svensen had never much cared for Mel, not since the day she'd trounced his daughter Jenny at the sixth grade spelling bee. Still, he'd never been overtly disparaging to the tourists before, at least not that she knew of. This thing with the Talcotts was apparently stirring up even more dissension than she'd realized.

"Oh, nothing unexpected," Jonas purred, his deep voice sending shivers down Mel's spine. "Rat-trap cabins, overpriced and under-staffed. He even hinted that you might be after my virtue."

"He did?" Ouch! That one hit uncomfortably close to home.

"Yep. I assured him that that wouldn't be a problem."

It wouldn't? Drat!

Joe continued with a twinkle in his eye and a lazy grin. "Of course, there was one more thing he thought I ought to know."

"And what was that?"

"According to the good Mr. Svensen, the lovely Miss Melissa MacRae is a witch."

Chapter Three

He watched her go still, like a rabbit sensing a predator. Damn, that analogy was really annoying. "So. Are you?" He kept both his expression and tone totally neutral.

"Am I what? A witch?" Her voice was high and brittle, her cat's eyes wide.

"Sure. It's a simple enough question. Are you or aren't you a witch?"

While Mel drummed her fingers on the table, Joe let his gaze trail from her sultry mouth down to her sturdy, calloused hands. Odd, he usually liked the refined, perfectly manicured type, but somehow he couldn't resist the image of those strong, supple fingers splaying across his flesh.

"I guess that would depend on how you define the word witch." Her shrug almost managed to convey the nonchalance she was obviously striving for. Joe had to grant her points for trying.

"I think the more important question would be, how *you* define it. Tell me, Melissa. By your own definition, are you a witch?"

He watched with preternatural intensity as she inhaled deeply, gathering her courage. Then she looked up from under her thick fringe of lashes to gaze directly into his eyes.

"Yes. By my definition, and probably most others, I am definitely a witch."

Her honesty was unexpected. "You mean you're a Wiccan, right?" That would mean she practiced the ancient religion of witchcraft, without implying she had any actual powers. It seemed like the obvious explanation and had been what he'd expected to discover here in Sanctity.

"No." Once again, her answer took him by surprise. "I've never been into organized religion."

He suppressed a laugh, wishing once again that his research subject wasn't so appealing on so many levels. He needed to keep her talking. "So then, what makes you a witch?"

"Magic of course."

Joe managed not to choke on his burrito. Barely. The heavenly taste in his mouth had suddenly turned to sawdust. "Magic?"

"Umm-hmm. Spells, potions, visions. About what you'd expect." She calmly forked up another bite of Spanish rice.

Spells? He swallowed forcibly. Potions? This was perfect. Not only did the woman admit to thinking she was a witch, she actually admitted using spells and potions, and to a virtual stranger. This was going to be the easiest research of his career if a little disappointing in the personal arena. Obviously she was flakier than he'd thought.

"I wasn't going to say anything, because I know it sounds crazy, but I'd rather you heard it from me than from Phil Mercer at the grocery store, or Justine Flannery at the post office." She shrugged, and the neckline of her peach knit top dipped, dragging Joe's attention away from witchcraft and onto creamy skin. "It's not a big secret or anything. The whole town knows, anyway."

"Black hat and broomstick sort of witch?"

Joe knew as well as anybody, better, in fact that there really *were* more things under the heavens than were dreamt of in *any* philosophy. He'd seen things during the course of his research that absolutely defied any rational explanation. He'd run from vampires in Rumania, fought mummies in Egypt, and those were just the tip of the iceberg. He'd spoken with the three-hundred year old descendant of an elf queen. He believed, totally, in the paranormal. It just seemed incongruous to him that the petite, feminine creature across from him could state such a thing so matter-of-factly.

"Not exactly." She licked a dab of sour cream off the corner of her lip, and a bolt of pure lust shot straight to Joe's groin. "I mean, I make potions and stuff, but I use herbs, not bat wings and eye of newt. And I practically never cackle." Her grin turned slightly lopsided, making it all the more engaging. "No flying about on cleaning equipment either, I'm afraid. More's the pity. I'd save a fortune on truck maintenance."

"You'd save an even bigger fortune if you'd invest in a vehicle that isn't older than you are," he returned dryly, not liking the thought of her old clunker letting her down on some dark and snowy night, far from help. Damn, this protective instinct was really getting to be a nuisance.

"So how did you get to be a witch?" He clung to the possibility that she was just a wanna-be. Television shows like *Charmed* and *Buffy the Vampire Slayer* had really popularized the occult lately. His own books hadn't hurt the phenomenon.

"I didn't exactly have much choice in the matter." She sighed. "It's a hereditary thing."

"Of course you have a choice," he disagreed. "Even if you inherited certain—abilities, you can always choose not to use them. We're ultimately responsible for our own actions if not for our DNA."

"Really? I suppose you're right. When I find a sick animal in the woods, I could choose not to help it. When a friend is hurting, I could simply walk away. I just don't think I could look at myself in the mirror afterward. I didn't ask to be a witch, but I am, and with power comes responsibility."

She stared at him unblinking, her mouth set in a straight line. Joe could tell she'd considered this subject at great length and was dead serious. A grudging sense of respect began to coexist with his lust and curiosity.

"I don't see that I have a real choice about whether or not to use my abilities; neither did my grandmother, or great-grandmother before her. My only choice is *how* I use them."

Joe couldn't argue with that. It matched the philosophy he'd spent much of his own life learning. He also noticed that she mentioned her grandmother and great-grandmother, but not her mother. He filed that away for future questioning.

"I told you I'm not a Wiccan, because I don't worship in a specific way, or practice a lot of their spiritual rituals. I do, however, hold fast to one of their primary tenets. 'And it harm none,' is sort of my personal golden rule."

"I can respect that. I'm a big believer in personal accountability myself, most vegetarians are. So, this witchcraft thing—it's passed down from mother to daughter, right? What about sons?"

"There haven't been any males in my family for over a hundred years, so I can't really say."

"That must have gone over well with the husbands in previous generations," he quipped, trying to lighten the sadness that had darkened her eyes. "Victorians were pretty big on the patriarchy thing."

Her flickering smile was tragic. "Yeah, well, the MacRae women haven't been real big on husbands either."

On that gloomy note, she lapsed into silence, and they concentrated on their meal while Joe let the information she'd given him roll around in his head. Her comments confirmed the information he'd gathered thus far. There had been MacRae witches living just outside of Sanctity for at least a century, and if they never married, that would explain the name staying the same.

"So what about your mother?"

"What?" Her spine straightened, her chin lifted, and the fork that had hovered halfway to her mouth thudded back to the table, food clearly forgotten. "What about my mother?"

"Well, you mentioned your grandmother and great-grandmother, but you didn't say anything about your mom."

"I'm sure the local grapevine has already told you all the juicy bits," she snapped. He'd clearly hit a sore spot, and an unfamiliar feeling, which he strongly suspected was guilt, roiled in his gut. "And if they haven't yet, I'm sure they'd be more than happy to."

"Hey." He held up both hands in a gesture of appeasement. He simply couldn't stand causing her pain. "I'm sorry. I didn't mean to pry. And, for the record, nobody I've met so far has said a word about your mother."

"Sorry," she echoed. "She died when I was three. She was real young when I was born and kind of wild. Add that to living in a small town, and being one of the MacRae witches, and you've got a great recipe for gossip."

"So why do you stay?" He certainly wouldn't have. "Surely you could sell your land and move somewhere else, where the locals aren't hostile toward your family."

"I didn't say they were hostile." She gave him just a hint of a smile. "At least not most of them, most of the time. Obviously you're not familiar with small towns. Gossip is part of the life force in areas like this. It doesn't mean this isn't where I belong."

Where I belong. It was an interesting choice of phrases. Joe had two homes of his own, a condo in New York and a cabin in Vermont, but he couldn't remember either of them, or anywhere else for that matter, was a place where he truly belonged.

"Well, well, well, I see you're showing your customers a *real* good time, eh, Melissa?" The voice was thick and oily, and Joe felt the hairs on the back of his neck stand on end as his primitive instincts responded to the intruder. Eyes narrowed, he looked up as an older man in an expensive suit approached their table.

"Mr. Talcott," Mel acknowledged coldly. "I wouldn't have expected to see you in Rosa's Diner. Did your chef burn the filet mignon, or are you just slumming?"

Talcott. Joe had done enough research on Sanctity to know the name. Byron Talcott's luxurious 'hunting' lodge sat on the other side of town from Mel's cabins, and catered to a far wealthier clientele.

The newcomer chuckled indulgently and offered Mel a patronizing pat on the shoulder, which had Joe suppressing a snarl. He absolutely didn't want this man putting his hands on Melissa, not in any fashion. Mel couldn't quite hide her instinctive recoil, and Joe stuck his hand between them, forcing a polite smile.

"Hi. I'm Joe Pierce, the tourist in question." He allowed his New York accent to thicken. "Ms. MacRae was kind enough to show me around a little, and to join me for dinner."

"Byron Talcott." The older man took Joe's extended hand and shook it with the firm grip of a professional politician or a used-car salesman. "Here for the fishing?"

Joe shook his head, and Talcott's grip on his hand tightened. "Nope." He squeezed back. Talcott might be twenty-five years older, and out of shape besides, but Joe had no intention of backing down from this little pissing match. "No fishing, just some quiet time away from the rat race."

"Well, if you get bored in your little cabin, we should still have spaces left at the lodge. Maybe next time you come to visit, Sanctity will have a real resort to offer you."

Joe raised one eyebrow, but didn't reply as he watched Mel bristle like a hissing kitten. Talcott released Joe's hand from his death-grip, and turned to Mel.

"Speaking of the Wilderness Resort, I hear my son paid you a little visit this afternoon."

"Did he? I'm afraid I was busy with plumbing and might have failed to notice any additional crap in the area."

Ouch! Talcott's fury was palpable, but he kept his menacing tone level. "Seems to me that a woman like you can't afford to go around calling people names. Now, Sean knows he's supposed to keep away from you, but you listen here, missy. You are the only thing standing between the people of Sanctity and a major resort with year-round employment for the townsfolk. I have no intention of letting some centuries-old superstition stop me from getting that land. If you really gave a damn about the people of this town, you'd save us all a lot of trouble and sell now."

Blue-green cat eyes narrowed and her nostrils flared. "No, you listen to me, Byron. MacRaes have lived on that piece of land and protected it for over a hundred years. It's survived loggers, miners, and trappers, and it will survive you too. My answer is no, and that isn't about to change, so you can just keep your greedy hands and your slimy offspring off my property!"

* * * *

It hadn't been the best of all possible dates. Mel's face flamed with embarrassment as she sat stiffly beside Jonas in his Jeep. They'd finished eating in stilted silence after Talcott senior had stalked away, and the awkwardness continued, even though they were halfway back to her cabin. So much for her plans! She stared out the window, and watched as fingers of plum and magenta began to streak the western skyline.

"You okay?" His voice was pitched low, and the deep soft tone wrapped around her like a hug, willing her tense muscles to relax.

"Fine," she lied. "I'm sorry about the scene in the restaurant. Sanctity's a great town, normally, but like every place else, we have our problems. I'm sure you can't have gotten a very good impression so far."

"Oh, I don't know. I've seen a few things I like," he rumbled.

Since she didn't know how to reply to that, she didn't.

"So that would be why people were grumbling about you at the hardware store," Joe offered a few minutes later. "Svenson must support Talcott's bid to put some sort of exclusive resort on your property."

"Rustic logs on the outside, full spa and conference facility on the inside. Four stories of luxury suites with indoor and outdoor pools, tennis courts, and an eighteen-hole golf course. I know the jobs would help Sanctity, but I just can't let them destroy the woods to do it. My little cabins sit within the wilderness, barely disrupting it, but with that—" She paused, groping for the right word. "Behemoth that Talcott envisions, there'd be nothing left of the forest except for his perfectly groomed riding trails."

"I see what you mean." Jonas's hand left the steering wheel briefly to gesture at the trees lining the road. "It would be a shame to see this destroyed. But one thing puzzles me. There's lots of undeveloped land in the area. Why does he need your property for his project? Surely there would be easier parcels to get hold of."

"Wetlands. Sanctity is surrounded by federally protected wetlands. My land is the only piece of high ground big enough for what he has in mind. And it abuts the Preserve."

There was more to it of course. Her land had a few other special features, but she didn't want to bring that into the conversation. The MacRaes had settled that particular parcel because it encompassed one of nature's truly mystical sites. If it had existed in Europe, it would have probably possessed a ring of standing stones. Local Native Americans had valued the spot long before Melissa's ancestors had arrived, and had deliberately relinquished the land to a MacRae, recognizing a kindred spirit, someone who would care for the land and guard its special properties. It had been a sacred trust of Mel's family ever since. As they approached her property, she noted each tree, every boulder, highlighted in gold by the waning sun. A great blue heron flew alongside the roadway, and Mel smiled. Her connection to this land and the living things on it went bone-deep, all the way to her soul.

"Well, I'm glad you're not selling. It would be a shame to lose all this prime habitat."

"It is prime habitat, for all kinds of wildlife. I even saw a wolf today." How nice to have someone to share her exiting experience, someone who might actually appreciate it. "He was huge, with a glossy black pelt and just one silver ear. I've never seen anything more beautiful."

His reaction surprised her a bit. She'd somehow expected him to share her awe and excitement. Instead, he stiffened up at first, before relaxing again beside her. "What's unusual about spotting a wolf? I thought they were relatively common in Upper Michigan."

"Not really." She shook her head and sighed. "They're rare, though they're making a comeback. I've heard them howling before, seen a few tracks, but today was the first time I've seen one up close."

"They're not hunted, are they?"

"No, at least not legally. I sure hope he has enough sense to stay away from town, though. And from bait piles come fall."

"Bait piles?"

"Apples, corn, carrots, and sugar beets that the hunters put out. The deer get used to having a handy food source, then come hunting season, the hunters can wait by the bait piles for the deer to show up."

"Doesn't sound very sporting."

"No, I don't think so either. It's become a pretty controversial practice, but unfortunately it's still common. I just hope my new friend stays away from the bait piles. Everybody knows that shooting a wolf is illegal, but some of the hunters really have it in for anything they think is competing for their game."

"Well, here's hoping your wolf is a smart one." He turned into her driveway, then shut off the engine.

"Thanks for dinner." Ignoring the hand she'd stuck out, he bounded gracefully out of the vehicle and around to her door before she could recover her wits enough to open it herself. Wow! She'd never had a man actually help her out of the car before. Each other time she'd ridden with Jonas, she'd just clambered out herself as usual, but this time he'd been too quick for her.

"You're welcome," he teased as he walked beside her toward her door. "It's early yet. Care to go for a walk? At least out in the woods, we probably wouldn't run into any annoying neighbors."

"I'd like that," she replied, her hopes for the evening briefly resurfacing. "But there are some chores I have to take care of first." Putting him to work twice in as many days should send him packing. Her grandmother had exhorted Mel at length about the inherent laziness of the male of the species.

"Can I help?"

Yikes! Gorgeous, well mannered, and helpful. This guy was down-right dangerous. Of course, she'd sensed that much from the moment she'd laid eyes on him.

"I guess." She eyed his shirt skeptically. "You might get dirty."

* * * *

"I'll wash." Joe had to laugh at the dubious frown on her face. Especially since she was the one in a skirt. She obviously still had him pegged as a do-nothing city slicker.

They walked to an old barn set back from the cabins. It was a log structure like the rest of the buildings, but had been updated at some point to feature an overhead garage door on one end, while a large set of old-fashioned double-doors remained on the other.

"No sudden movements," she warned, unlocking the double-doors. "And no loud noises, either."

This piqued his curiosity. What did the witch keep hidden in her barn? The old wooden doors swung open easily and silent, attesting to decades of careful maintenance. His keen sense of smell immediately informed him animals resided in the room. Blinking, Joe followed her inside, and watched as Mel pulled on an elbow-length, leather, welding glove. Not exactly the 'witchiest' of accessories, but as he scanned the room, understanding began to dawn.

Skylights on one side of the roof allowed most of the evening sunlight to penetrate the space, so his eyes adjusted quickly. Looking around, he spotted another presence in the room. While Joe watched intently, Mel moved slowly toward what had once been an old horse stall that had been enclosed all the way to the raftered ceiling with heavy wire mesh. Near the top, wired into place across the old stall walls lay a thick tree branch. A magnificent golden-brown bird perched proudly on the branch.

When Mel entered the enclosure, the eagle flew down and landed on her outstretched arm, the one protected by the heavy glove. The bird couldn't be very old, since it hadn't yet developed the distinctive white head that marked the American symbol. It had, however achieved its adult size all the same, and he marveled at the easy way she managed the heavy bird. The fierce beak and razor-sharp talons easily could have rent Mel's flesh from her bones. Instead, the eagle sat quietly on her forearm while she ran her other hand expertly across one powerful wing. While Joe watched in awed silence, she checked the bird, murmuring softly. Moments later, Mel said something in a quiet tone and raised her arm. The eagle tilted its head, made a soft squawk, and flew back up to the perch in a rustle of feathers. Joe waited until Mel had exited, latching the stall door behind her, to speak.

"I thought it was illegal to keep birds of prey as pets," he remarked.

Mel pulled a rabbit carcass from an old refrigerator, then tossed it through the cage door. The eagle flew down, and snagged the white bundle with long, deadly talons before it began ripping into it with that razor sharp beak. Joe looked away in distaste. Or fascination. He was never sure which. He knew that predators had to eat, too, that the eagle was only following Nature's edict to survive, but he still found it hard to watch. In the back of his mind, he always feared that if he stopped being horrified by the killing, he'd stop being human.

"She's not a pet." A soft, ungloved hand on his shoulder told him that Mel had finished her work. He turned to her, still avoiding the messy scene behind them. "And it's perfectly legal, I assure you. I have a permit from the DNR to rehabilitate injured wildlife."

"DNR?" That wasn't any witchcraft organization he'd run across in the course of his research.

"State of Michigan," she responded. "Department of Natural Resources. And another one from the U. S. Fish and Wildlife Service for the eagle."

"Of course." Duh! He looked away, determined not to show her how foolish he felt. Watching the eagle attack its meal, he found it hard to believe the bird had been injured. "Is she your only patient at the moment?" His senses told him otherwise.

"No." She opened the door to another stall, on the opposite side of the room from the eagle. "This is Bucky. Do you want to bottle-feed him, or rake out his dirty straw?"

The fawn was only a few weeks old, small and spotted. It hurried to Mel, butting enthusiastically at the oversized baby bottle she held in her hand. Joe reached for the rake that leaned on the outside wall of the stall. Somehow, feeding the fawn with a baby bottle seemed a little too much like playing house, and manual labor would be a lot less intimate. Besides, the fawn seemed to sense a threat from Joe and had instinctively backed away from him. He had no intention of forcing himself on the poor thing. Most animals knew a predator when they smelled one. "You feed."

He cleaned out the soiled straw, raking it into a compost heap outside the barn door, then spread a fresh layer on the floor from the half-bale that sat beside the stall. The manual labor didn't bother him in the slightest, but the sight of the beautiful young woman lovingly nurturing the orphaned deer unsettled him. He could picture her, all too easily, caring for a baby of her own, and felt a moment of longing to share that life with her. *Jesus!* He had to stop thinking like this, ASAP.

"How was he orphaned?" His question tuned out the sounds of the fawn's suckling.

"Car," Mel answered simply. "The mother didn't die right away, so there was time to save the fawn. He was only a couple days premature."

"Do you work with a vet?" She seemed remarkably knowledgeable, and he could almost picture her performing a C-section on a dying doe. While her affinity for the animals seemed practically magical, some of the instruments in her converted barn looked modern and professional.

"Sometimes." Her tone was cryptic, he couldn't figure her out. "And sometimes I use the gifts I was born with. Whichever works."

"Will you release them?"

"Of course." She laughed. "If I didn't we'd be overrun." She patted the deer as it finished the bottle of formula with a noisy slurp. "The eagle will be gone in just a week or so, the fawn in maybe a month."

"Is it hard to let them go?" She was so tenderhearted, he imagined she must suffer when she had to say goodbye.

"Not really. I know they're still nearby." She bustled around the little clinic, cleaning the bottle, putting things away. "And, regrettably, there's always something new to take their places. Man isn't usually kind to the creatures that share his planet."

That was a sentiment with which he could wholeheartedly concur. Taking her arm as she left the barn, he was a little surprised when she didn't pull away. Since it was her land, her home, Joe let her lead, guiding their walk as they moved away from the cabins and into the woods.

They walked past the small but tidy beach Joe had seen advertised in the Whispering Pines brochure. Three well-maintained canoes were stacked by the shore, and a discretely placed outbuilding offered restroom facilities for swimmers and boaters. The trail narrowed as it wound past the beach and deeper into the woods. Before long, they found themselves on the rocky shore of a smaller, hidden lake, which the deepening sunset had painted in glorious shades of red and purple. The tranquility of the place was powerful, and Joe allowed himself to be soothed.

He didn't know what to do next after he sat beside her on a fallen log. He'd never had any compunction about seducing a potential source, but had always made certain not to cause any harm. He enjoyed women, liked their company, liked sex, but what little conscience he had kept him honest. He'd never given any woman reason to expect a future with him.

He wanted Mel more than he could remember wanting any other woman. He'd convinced himself there would be no harm in a summer fling, but that had been before he'd gotten to know her. Now, less than forty-eight hours after making her acquaintance, he'd come to see Mel MacRae as a forever kind of woman. She'd make some lucky guy a great wife, and she deserved a houseful of kids. Home, commitment, and family. All these things practically radiated from Mel, and Joe just didn't have them to offer. He couldn't even lie to himself, pretend he was getting close her for research purposes. Mel made no secret of her beliefs, and would answer his questions anyway. No, he had no reason to seduce her. None, that is, except for the massive desire that twisted painfully in his gut. And lower.

He stared into the water while he wrestled his hormones into submission, then jumped when her slim, strong arm snaked around his waist. He'd watched her touch soothe the wild things in her care, but on him it had the opposite effect. Unable to resist, he wrapped his own arm about her shoulders, dragging her more firmly against him on the log.

She stiffened for just a moment before relaxing, melting into him as if she belonged there. Joe bit back a groan.

"You're playing with fire." His warning came out huskier than he'd planned. He buried his face in her hair and inhaled the clean, floral scent.

She didn't look up at him, just squeezed his waist. "I know. Is that a bad thing?"

"Not necessarily bad, just dangerous." But he wasn't sure who was at greater risk. He thought he was warning her to beware of him, but it had occurred to him that this witchy little woman might just be the most dangerous person he'd ever run across. Somehow the tables of seduction had turned, and he didn't think he was strong enough to resist.

"I can live with dangerous." She spoke quietly, but with such utter determination that Joe knew he was lost. He'd tried to be noble, wanted to be strong, but it simply wasn't in him to turn down what she was so freely offering. She felt too good, looked too good, smelled too good, and he wanted her too damned much. Using his free arm, he cupped her chin, tilting her head toward him, then lowered his head, claiming her lips with his.

* * * *

Mel had never imagined, never dreamed that any physical experience could be as intense, as consuming, as overwhelmingly beautiful as Jonas's kiss.

At first, his lips were soft. Gentle. Coaxing. His big, powerful hands held her firmly in place, but with such tenderness that it almost made her cry. Instinctively, she opened as his kiss changed, welcoming his questing tongue. Every fiber of her body surrendered, offering him total freedom, total dominance.

Her soft, mewling cry of submission must have pleased him, because Jonas's hands tightened and his tender exploration of her mouth intensified into possessive plundering. She loved it. Wrapping both arms around his neck, Mel clung, her fingers tangling in the silky, straight locks of his long hair. While her fingers dug into the solid muscles of his neck and shoulders, the rest of her body went boneless, so pliant that she would have collapsed without his support.

"Please tell me we're alone here." His murmur was rough, thick. He'd pulled away from her mouth to nibble his way along her jaw line, pausing to nuzzle and nip at her throat and earlobe. Thousands of nerve endings tingled in delight.

"Nobody…" She gasped, trying to draw enough breath to speak. "Nobody comes here. Ever." His tongue swirled into her ear, and she cried out as he shifted. Unsupported, she collapsed against him.

"Oh, I think we can fix that." With a wicked chuckle, he scooped her into his arms, then knelt, lying her down beside him on a soft bed of moss.

Mel couldn't help it, she giggled at his bold declaration of intent.

"I sure hope so." This was it! She was really going to make love with Jonas Pierce! Nothing had ever felt so good, so right.

His amber eyes glowed brightly, reflecting the last rays of sunlight as she looked up into his heated gaze. As his strong, calloused hands insinuated themselves beneath her top, he held her gaze with his.

"Last chance." It was barely a whisper on the breeze. "Tell me to stop. Now."

Part of her suddenly wanted to. She was way out of her depth, and a tiny little voice inside her brain was urging caution, warning her that whatever was happening right now was too perfect, too powerful, too out of control. Fortunately, over stimulated nerves and raging hormones completely squashed that annoying little voice.

"Don't stop." She wasn't sure she'd survive if he did. "Please."

Groaning gutturally, he lowered his body to hers, capturing her lips again. Her whole being delighted in the glorious feeling of his weight on her, pressing her into the mossy turf. His muscles were taut and corded beneath her wandering hands, and she could feel the thick ridge of his erection pushing against her thigh through her skirt and his jeans.

"Clothes," he muttered some moments later when he came up for a breath. "Too many clothes."

In total agreement, Mel let her hands fly to the buttons of his soft cotton shirt, but she was forced to let go as he dragged her top up over her head.

"Amazing!" His expression was awed, almost reverent as he leaned back on his knees to admire her breasts. She blushed, unaccustomed to such attention, but secretly thrilled that he found her attractive. Judging by the thick bulge in his jeans, he did.

She watched, fascinated, as one long, tanned finger reached out, gently circling first one aureole, then the other. Her breasts had swollen, grown heavier than normal, but his delicate touch helped soothe the unfamiliar ache, even as her nipples tightened and puckered.

When he bent and flicked his tongue across one taut peak, she nearly screamed, but the sound came out as a choked, shocked whimper, which seemed to please and amuse him.

"You like that, don't you?" His drawl was smug and teasing, then he lightly tasted the other breast. When she nodded helplessly, her head thrown back, he made an appreciative sound, deep in his throat, then promptly sucked the entire nipple deep into his mouth.

"Jonas!" This time she did scream, arching her back to thrust herself closer, deeper into his hot, magical mouth. She wanted nothing more than to be closer to him, close enough that their bodies merged into one. Her hands gripped his shoulders and head, clutching him to her breast. Moisture had begun pooling between her legs, and the core of her body actually ached. Her hips began to move without any conscious effort as he slowly slid his hands up under the hem of her skirt.

"You're not wearing panties." He gave an appreciative groan and splayed his hands across her buttocks.

Nothing had prepared her for this. Nothing had ever felt so good, so right. His strong, wonderful fingers cupped her mound, combed through her wet curls, and neither of them had any use for words.

Then her pager went off.

CHAPTER FOUR

At first he didn't register the beeping.

His fingers were combing through the tight curls between Mel's thighs, and she was reaching for the button fly of his jeans. That, the incredible taste of her succulent breasts, and the potent fragrance of her arousal were pretty much all his scattered thoughts were capable of focusing on. Eventually, though, his normally keen ears picked up the disruptive electronic sound. Pulling away from Mel's delectable body, he looked around. "What the hell…?"

"My pager," she whispered weakly, heaving herself into a sitting position. After unclipping a tiny gadget from her waistband, she studied the display, then ran a hand through her tumbled hair. "Damn!"

He restrained the urge to grab her pager and hurl it into the lake, picking up immediately where he'd just left off. Whoever heard of a witch with a pager anyway? He supposed it must have something to do with her cabins, though he was a tenant, and she certainly hadn't given him a pager number.

"I'm sorry, Jonas." She reached for her top, groping as though her eyes and hands weren't working together. He continued to watch while she adjusted her skirt. "I've got to go."

It took every ounce of honor and control he could muster, but he stood, reaching out a hand to help her to her feet. This wasn't a rejection, he knew that. He could still see signs of her arousal in the nipples that poked against the soft knit of her shirt, and the hot, musky scent that still clung to her skin and his hand. He plucked a leaf from her red-gold hair. "Where can I take you?"

"Just home." Her eyes were filled with apparent regret. She smoothed her clothes and brushed bits of moss off her skirt. "I've got to go see a friend. She has a—a problem that I've been helping her with. She wouldn't have called if it wasn't really important."

Though frustrated beyond belief, he couldn't be mad at her. Even in the darkening twilight, he could see she was begging for under-standing. Whatever this mysterious 'problem' was, it was obviously important to Mel. "Okay," he answered. "Let's get you home."

When they reached her cabin after a swift return hike, she didn't even turn to her cabin, just headed straight to her truck.

"Mel…"

She turned to him, eyes wary.

"You might want to go inside and brush your hair." He plucked another twig from one of her curls. "Maybe change, if you can take the time."

"Oh." She looked down at her mussed, moss-stained skirt. "I suppose you're right." Even in the dim light, he knew she was blushing, and he couldn't resist the urge to kiss her. He bent down and pressed his lips against hers in a light, brushing caress.

"Goodnight, Melissa."

"Goodnight, Jonas," she whispered from her doorway, where she'd fled after breaking their kiss. "Thank you for a lovely evening. I'm sorry about this, I really am."

"I know you are." He bounded up the steps and planted another soft kiss on her smooth cheek, ignoring the relentless throbbing ache in his jeans. The confusion, distress, and frustration in her eyes mirrored the emotions he was feeling himself.

"Drive carefully, okay?" Pulling a small card from his wallet, he handed it to her. "This is my satellite phone number. Call me if you need anything." He hopped down from the porch, before he gave into the urge to tackle her on her shiny kitchen floor. "Anything," he repeated as he turned away.

Standing beside his Jeep, he waited until he saw her climb into her truck and leave. He was going to find out what was going on, and not just because of his research. No, he was going to learn everything there was to know about Miss Melissa MacRae, starting with why a self-proclaimed witch was wearing a high-tech pager, he vowed as he watched her beat-up truck peel down the gravel drive. Then they were going to finish what they'd started by the lake tonight. Then, hopefully, after he'd satisfied his curiosity on both counts, he'd be able to get her out of his mind. And maybe, if he was lucky, get his mind out of his pants.

* * * *

Dawn was rapidly approaching by the time Mel returned home. Exhausted but edgy, she dragged herself up the steps to her back porch, flopped bonelessly into an Adirondack chair then stared blindly into the darkness of the forest. Last night had been one stressful situation after another, and the fact that she hadn't slept at all wasn't helping any. The jeans and sweatshirt she'd thrown on after a hurried shower last night protected her from the cool night air, and she gradually began to relax.

After a few moments, the fine hairs on the back of her neck prickled, warning her that she was being watched. She wasn't worried. Whoever or whatever was out there her wasn't a threat. She could sense that her observer had no intention of harming her. Studying the darkness, she smiled as a pair of familiar yellow eyes came into view.

"Hello, wolf," she called as a black shape began to emerge from the path to the barn. "What are you doing here, so close to civilization?" Her little cluster of cabins weren't exactly a town, but she was still surprised he'd ventured so close to any human habitation. His bright intelligent eyes gleamed, and the furry lip curled in what could have almost been a smile as he continued to approach. Mel couldn't help but smile back. "Well, I'm glad you're here, anyway."

Realizing she still held the bag of homemade peanut butter cookies her friend Karen had pressed into her hand as she was leaving, Mel opened it and tossed one to her visitor. There wasn't enough sugar in one cookie to upset the natural diet of a hundred pound animal, and Mel was in desperate need of this moment of quiet, undemanding companionship.

The wolf caught and swallowed the treat in one fluid motion, and Mel was reminded involuntarily of Jonas in the smooth graceful play of muscle and sinew. There was something else, a distant part of her mind noted. Another, deeper resemblance beside the white streak and amber eyes. Her reaction to Jonas had been bothering her since that first kiss. There was more to him than met the eye. He exuded an odd sense of preternatural power, sort of like her own, but different in some subtle way. Unique. She couldn't place it, and in the course of last night's events, had allowed it to slip from the forefront of her thoughts.

She looked down at her visitor, who now stood right at the base of the steps to her deck, his massive head tilted to one side in an almost quizzical fashion.

"Come on then," she called, breaking off a piece of another cookie and holding it out to him. Every instinct she possessed assured her that she would come to no harm from this majestic beast. With bated breath she watched him pad slowly up the steps. Using incredible delicacy, he lifted the treat from her fingers, his long, raspy tongue swiping gently along her skin. Mel shivered, again reminded of Jonas and the things he'd done to her body. Embarrassed, she watched as the wolf drew back a few inches, then sat, still eyeing her curiously.

"It's been a long night, my friend." She laughed ruefully, cautiously reaching out her hand. She sighed in pleasure as the animal permitted her to scratch his head right alongside his one white ear. "And there are parts of it you wouldn't believe—some parts so fantastic, even I don't quite believe they were real."

Heaving another sigh, she closed her eyes, still rubbing the large, furry head. "Then there was the rest of it. Running into Talcott, I can handle. That's a normal sort of nuisance, but I wish it hadn't happened in front of Jonas. It's kind of embarrassing to be hassled in front of the guy you're hoping to sleep with."

The wolf gave a low, rumbling sound deep in its throat. It didn't sound like a growl, it was almost a purr. Mel paused, but when the animal didn't move, she continued scratching and talking.

"Then getting paged, at the worst possible moment. If it had been anybody but Karen…" She broke off, fighting tears. The wolf seemed to sense her distress, leaning closer so that his sleek bulk rested against her knee. "She's dying, you know. I know it, her daughter knows it, even her grandchildren know it, and it's just not fair! I can fix a bullet hole in an eagle's wing, raise an orphaned fawn, heal a broken leg, but I can't save the people I care about most. It's just like when my grandmother died. None of my spells, none of my powers can do anything to stop the progress of the disease that's rampaging through every cell in her body." Tears streamed down her cheeks, but she didn't stop.

"She's only sixty, Wolf. That's not exactly a cub, in your terms, but it isn't a really long life, either. My best friend's mother is dying and there's nothing I can do to help."

"When I was a kid, Karen's house was the one place I felt normal. We played Barbies, and talked about movie stars and did each other's hair. Her mom, Gladys, was always there for me, you know? She never objected to her daughter hanging out with the witch kid, like other parents. She always treated me like I was her own. I owe her so much, but all I can do is make her more comfortable, ease the pain a little. And for Karen and the kids, I can't even do that. All I can do for them is watch them suffer."

The wolf whined in apparent sympathy, nuzzling her face with its damp, velvety nose. Accepting the comfort so freely offered, Mel wrapped her arms around the beast, burying her face in the thick soft fur of its neck. She cried then, great wracking sobs, and her new friend stayed close, licking the salty tears from her cheeks till she stopped.

"Thank you, friend," she whispered, still hoarse from weeping. "I'm so glad you came to see me."

With one last swipe of his tongue, he settled back on his haunches, assuming a vigilant pose by her feet. "I'm on guard," he seemed to be telling her. "You can rest now."

With one hand resting on the massive black head, Mel leaned back in her chair. She hadn't been sleeping well lately, between the difficulties with the Talcotts, Gladys's illness, and her own power fluctuations. It felt good to sit back for a change, and let somebody else watch over her, even if it was just a kindly wild animal. As the first rosy hues of dawn broke over the horizon, she closed her eyes and slept.

* * * *

The late-morning sun had warmed her east-facing deck when Mel awoke. It had warmed Mel, too, easing the aches she'd suffered due to her long, grueling night. She stirred, surprised that she'd rested so well out here on the deck, when she'd been sleeping so poorly even in the comfort of her bed. Then she looked around and remembered the wolf.

He'd moved while she slept. Instead of sitting at her feet, he lay in the shady spot just to the left of her chair. His golden eyes were alert, fixed on the steps and the path beyond.

"You've been waiting here guarding me, haven't you?" She kept her voice soft. She was sure somehow, that he could understand her.

He didn't deign to answer, however. He simply stood, stretching his sleek, muscular form. Remembering the dream she'd had just before waking, she flushed. She'd dreamed of him, her silent sentinel, standing guard while she rested. Then, somewhere during the course of the dream, the wolf had metamorphosed, his sleek black coat transforming into Jonas's glossy dark hair. Instead of protecting her, like his counterpart, Joe had become the predator, kissing her, touching her until her entire body had dissolved into a kaleidoscope of sensation.

"Hattie and Karen are right. I *do* need to get laid," she muttered, scratching idly at the shaggy head. She was glad it had been the wolf watching her while she slept. She'd probably moaned and writhed in her sleep, and it would have been utterly humiliating to wake up to the knowing gaze of the man who'd inspired the dream.

"Your life is so much simpler than mine." She gave a sigh as she heaved herself out of her chair.

He snorted, and if a canine face could be said to express disgust, his was it, with its raised eyebrows and curled upper lip. Mel couldn't help laughing. "Well, I suppose it doesn't seem that way to you."

Enough lounging around. There was work to be done. She turned toward the house. "Good-bye, my friend." She watched as the wolf slipped down the steps and toward the woods, then laughed at her fancies. She always talked to animals—it was part of the bond with the creatures who shared her land, but it was uncanny how much this one seemed to understand. As she opened her door, he let out a friendly yip, then disappeared into the underbrush.

* * * *

Joe had a problem. He padded around the kitchen area of his cabin, making coffee, scrambling eggs. It was after noon, but he was hungry, and hadn't eaten since dinner the night before. Not unless you counted a couple of cookies, that is. It had been a very long night.

Back to the problem. One word, one syllable. Mel. The lovely Melissa MacRae most definitely presented a problem. He'd never felt like this before, never been drawn to a woman so fiercely, on so many different levels. Oh, he'd lusted before. He was a healthy, thirty-nine year old male, and he liked sex. That part was easy, not much of an issue at all. He'd never had much difficulty getting laid when he needed or wanted to. It helped to be decent-looking, well off, and even a little bit famous

But before, sex had just been about physical gratification. The emotions he experienced around Mel had become different, more complex. He'd never wanted one specific woman to the point of making compromises, of giving up his plans like he considered doing now. He'd never been so fixated on a single goal that he'd lain awake the entire night, just thinking about her, wanting her so much it physically hurt. He'd most certainly never experienced the kind of jealous fury that had surged through him when he'd heard her pager go off.

During the course of his long, sleepless night, he'd come to a difficult decision. He could not use Mel as a research subject, at least not an unwitting one. He'd never met such a purely good person. Not perfect, she could be a little prickly, a little impetuous. Sure, she'd been the instigator last night, but her response to his lovemaking had been enthusiastic, not practiced. He knew she didn't make a regular habit out of sleeping with her summer tenants. Her innocence made what he'd been planning to do even worse.

No, it was time to be up front with the lady. He'd go to her, tell her the truth, who he was and why he was here. Then if she wanted to help him with his book, she could, and if she wanted to tell him to go to hell, she could do that too. The same went for sex. If, knowing the whole story—well almost the whole story, she still wanted a summer fling, he'd be happy to oblige. If she changed her mind, well, somehow he'd manage to keep it in his pants.

Finishing his strong black coffee, he closed his eyes and leaned back, letting the caffeine from the bitter brew infuse his tired body. He'd discovered a footpath through the woods last night, and he followed it now. The same one that led from her cabin to the lake also wound its way to his front door. Enjoying the quiet solitude of the forest, he walked, mentally rehearsing the things he had to say, trying to shut out the memory of Mel's luscious body gleaming in the rosy light of the setting sun.

He reached the mossy shoreline, where the memories hit him with the force of a two-ton truck. Unexpectedly, he sensed another presence, immediately becoming alert, poised for danger. Quiet, easy footsteps told him that the other person was as comfortable in the wilderness as he was, and Joe relaxed just a bit. Not too many people in the world could make that claim. Seconds later he caught a whiff of rosemary and lilacs, saw a flash of copper, and he knew.

"Hello, there."

She froze for a second, then caught her breath and looked over at him, smiling. "Hello yourself. I was just on my way to see you."

His eyes hungrily absorbed the sight of her as she moved slowly, inexorably toward him. The jeans she wore were ancient and faded; the soft cotton clung lovingly to her flared hips and narrow waist. A ragged gray sweatshirt with Lake State emblazoned across the front only hinted at the curves he knew lay beneath, and he longed to rip it off her. Preferably with his teeth.

"What a coincidence." He took one long stride to meet her half-way. He reached out to clasp both of her hands in his, then leaned down to drop a soft kiss on the tip of her nose. "I was just on my way to visit you."

Her musky, feminine scent surrounded him, her soft, liquid eyes looked up at him, and he simply couldn't resist. Using their linked hands, he tugged her closer, then bent down for a kiss.

It was everything he remembered and more. Mel returned the kiss with passionate enthusiasm, and Joe lost track of both place and time. She tugged her hands free to wrap them around his neck, and his went around her waist without any conscious effort on Joe's part. While her fingers tangled in his hair, his own explored up under the hem of her sweatshirt.

She wasn't wearing a bra today either. "Oh, God." He knew his moan had a hungry sound and he wanted, needed to fill his hands with her soft, warm flesh. Instantly, he forgot everything he had intended to tell her. The only thing in his universe was the beautiful, sensual woman he held in his arms.

* * * *

When Jonas's hands cupped her breasts, it took all Mel's concentration just to stand. She couldn't have spoken if her life depended on it. She knew she should call a halt to this; she'd been walking to his cabin to talk to him, to offer a much-deserved explanation about her desertion the night before. She hadn't intended to make love with him.

Oh, yeah? So why didn't you wear a bra then?

She didn't bother to justify her actions with a mental reply. She just gave up the fight, losing herself in Jonas's embrace.

Tension coiled through her even before he unsnapped her jeans and slid his hand inside. When he touched her intimately, she cried out, and her knees buckled completely. Joe's strong arm caught her as she fell, then he gently lowered them both to the soft, springy moss.

"I asked you last night, but now that it's daytime, is anyone likely to walk by here?" He punctuated his question with little nibbling kisses along her throat.

"No." She sighed at the beauty of the sensations he created, and, tilted her head to provide him better access. "Nobody."

"Good." The word came out as a fierce, guttural growl as he grabbed the hem of her sweatshirt with both hands and tugged it over her head. "Because I don't want any interruptions this time. Please tell me you didn't bring your pager."

She nodded. Gladys would sleep today after their marathon session last night and so would Karen. Nobody else had the number so she'd left it on her kitchen table.

"I've wanted to do this for days." His glowing golden eyes gazed at her, and Mel could feel her nipples pucker under his heated regard. He seemed to study every line and curve of her bare upper body. "Gorgeous."

She flushed then, feeling the heat on her face and breasts. Jonas smiled, and busily stripped off his own clothing while Mel watched in rapt fascination. A pelt of curly black hair covered his leanly muscled, rock-hard chest. A narrower band of dark curls trailed down to where… Mel's eyes bugged out. *That* was supposed to fit? Inside *her?*

Joe chuckled at her expression as he methodically peeled her own jeans and panties away. Then he lay down beside her and rested on one elbow. "It will work just fine."

"Are you reading my mind?" She strained upward for his kiss. "Or am I that transparent?"

He kissed her lightly, then more deeply, and spoke in a whisper. "It's those eyes. Aside from being gorgeous, they give away all your secrets."

She sure hoped not! But she refused to worry about that right now. As he kissed her again, thoroughly this time, she gave herself completely in response, all mundane thoughts driven from her mind. Her hands tangled in the length of his thick glossy hair, holding him close as his lips left her mouth, trailing his kisses further south.

"Jonas!" She cried out as he sucked one pebbled nipple into his mouth. She writhed at the pleasure, clutching his head to her breast. She didn't want him to stop what he was doing, but the ache growing in her lower body had her wishing he could be in two places at once.

And then he was. His big hand gently palmed her mound, and she rubbed against him, begging for his touch. Deft fingers slipped down. They parted her slick, swollen folds, before they finally, slowly, slid inside. Mel couldn't help it. The pleasure was so intense, she shrieked.

"Like that, do you?" He switched his mouth to her other breast, while his magical fingers stroked and gently stretched her.

She couldn't answer, lost in the ripples of pleasure that coursed through her body and coiled at her center. This was it! The passion she'd always dreamed of, but never really believed in. This was what started wars, toppled kingdoms, inspired fairy tales.

White-hot shards of elation filled her body, and she arched upward, legs open, waiting for him. She screamed his name as the pleasure erupted. While her body still pulsed, Jonas shifted, kissing her deeply, hungrily as he moved over her and positioned himself at her entrance.

"Please." She didn't care that she whimpered. Her arms wound around his shoulders, gripping him and pulling him closer. With a deep groan, Joe complied, sheathing himself fully inside her with one powerful stroke.

When he encountered the fragile barrier, he gave a hoarse cry. It didn't stop him, nor did her tiny squeal of pain. His strong thrust had carried him completely through. "Why didn't you…"

She strained upward, stopping his words with a wet, hungry kiss. She answered him moments later when they paused to breathe. "Because I wanted you. Here and now, I wanted you."

"Thank God!" He groaned, pulling himself most of the way out of her before plunging back in.

He kept the rhythm gentle, probably due to her untried state. Mel reveled in his restraint at first, savoring every slow, sure stroke. A salty-sweet layer of sweat coated his smooth skin, and he made tiny growling noises deep in his throat. She loved that she was giving him pleasure. Soon though, another climax began to build, all the more intense for the stretched fullness she felt where he joined with her. Her nails dug into the skin of his back, and she wrapped her legs around his hips, instinctively urging him on.

His restraint broke then, and he pounded into her like something wild, driving harder and faster with every thrust. Mel let the tears flow now, too lost in the passion to mind. This time she came with even more intensity than before, like something had captured her soul and hurled it out to the stars. She didn't know if the sparkling light she saw came from her imagination or a physical manifestation of her magic, but as long as Jonas didn't seem to object, she really didn't care. She vaguely heard Jonas call her name, felt his body tense. She did notice the warm, wet surge inside her, just as the world went dark.

CHAPTER FIVE

Joe couldn't move for several seconds. As a point of fact, he wasn't entirely sure that he'd ever be able to move again. When the blood finally began to return to his brain and other useful organs, he heaved himself to the side, took his weight off Melissa, and hoped like hell he hadn't hurt her. Her body was apparently as limp as his felt. She hadn't moved yet either.

"You okay?"

There was no reply, and his heart skipped a beat when he realized that her eyes weren't opening, and her breathing was light and shallow.

"Mel?" he rasped, concern giving him the strength to lever himself up on one arm and lean over her. He brushed her hair back from her face. "Melissa, are you okay?"

Her smile came first. A slow twitch of the lips that gradually widened into an ear-to-ear grin.

"Christ!" Heaving a sigh of relief, he collapsed next to her, his head on her breast. "Don't scare me like that!"

"Sorry." Her blue-green eyes finally fluttered open. He shifted his head to look at her more comfortably. "No wonder they call it *le petit mort.*" Her giggle sounded light, musical, and supremely self-satisfied.

"The little death," he translated smugly. "Then I don't need to ask if it was good for you, too?"

"You couldn't tell?" She sounded genuinely distressed, and he couldn't suppress a chuckle at her naiveté.

"Oh, I sort of figured it out, between the screams, the claw marks on my back, and the muscle spasms." He toyed with a lock of her auburn hair. His other arm wrapped tightly about her waist and secured her lithe body against him. He could still feel occasional aftershocks rippling through her, and combined with the heady scents of arousal and release, they were making him hard all over again. Damn, there really was something witchy about Mel. He hadn't recovered this quickly in years.

Propping himself up on an elbow, he ran an appreciative gaze down her gloriously naked form, from her tousled hair, past her beautiful face, down to her lush, swollen breasts. She was amazing, sweet and sexy, strong from years of hard work without being bulked like some women he'd known who spent too much time in the gym. Everything about Mel, from her rosy nipples, to her delicate toes, was pure femininity, even when she wrapped it all in denim and flannel.

When his gaze reached below her waist, it halted. A dark red smear marred the perfection of her thigh. Blood. He swallowed hard, reminded of the little surprise she'd given him earlier.

"Why, Mel?"

"Hmmm?" Her tone was languid and drowsy as her fingers absently toyed with the hair on his chest. "Why what?"

"Why me? For your first time, I mean. And why, for God's sake, didn't you tell me?"

"Because I was afraid you'd stop." She responded to his second question first. "And I really, really, didn't want you to."

He supposed that her answer made sense. If he'd known, would he have called a halt? He liked to think so, but he was probably deluding himself. Once he'd started making love to Mel, he doubted that any force on Earth could have stopped him. That bothered him more than any other aspect of this whole situation. Joe Pierce did not allow himself to lose control. Not ever. Not at all. Not until today.

"So why me?" He repeated his first question, the one she hadn't answered.

Mel shrugged against his chest. "Don't know," she replied sleepily. "Just felt right."

It was the second scariest thing she could have said. At least it wasn't the dreaded 1-word, but it was close enough to raise Joe's hackles.

"Right?" he asked harshly, pulling away from the temptation of her lush body and jackknifing into a seated position.

Mel must have realized that the romantic interlude had ended, because she sat up too, languidly, and reached for her sweatshirt. Moments later she'd tugged it over her head, and looked around wildly, till her eyes lit on her discarded jeans and panties.

"Just—right. I don't know what else to say. It seemed like a good idea at the time." She finger-combed her long tangled hair.

"Bullshit!" The curse exploded out of him before he could censor himself.

She stared at him, sitting there naked from the waist down, and her eyes narrowed. "I'm sorry if that offends your masculine sensibilities Jonas, but it really is that simple. I'm not trying to trap you into marriage, or looking for happily-ever-after. I quit believing in that along with Santa Claus and the Tooth Fairy.

"I'm thirty-four years old, Joe, and I'm sick of being the freaking vestal-virgin-witch. In case you hadn't noticed, this is a small town. I simply never had the urge to get it on with somebody I would have to face at the grocery store and the post office for the rest of my life. I was—hell, I *am* attracted to you, and I'm sorry if I misunderstood, but I got the impression that it was mutual!"

She wiggled into her jeans, then looked down at the blue silk panties she still held clutched in her hand, belatedly realizing she'd forgotten them. With an irritated shrug, she stuffed them into her back pocket, and gazed defiantly into his eyes.

"Oh, hell!" He'd been an idiot and made a mess of things. "Of course I'm attracted to you. This wouldn't have been possible if I wasn't." He gestured down at his persistent erection. "I've been hard for you since the moment we met, and there's nothing I'd like to do more right now than drag you back to my cabin and do it all over again, this time in a bed."

Her eyes had widened as she'd followed his gesture. He wasn't sure if her shocked expression was because he was hard again, or because of her blood smeared across his flesh.

"You do?" Her throat convulsed as she swallowed, then looked up at his face. "Really?"

"Really."

"Okay."

He couldn't have heard her right. "Okay, what?"

"Okay, let's go back to your place and do this all over again, only in a bed."

It took him less than five seconds to scramble into his jeans, gather up the rest of his clothes, and take her hand. Together, they fairly flew down the trail to his cabin.

* * * *

It was even better the second time. Lying back against the pillows in the oversized bed that had been hand-built by a distant ancestor, Mel faced facts. Sex with Jonas got better with repetition. Sure, she hadn't passed out this time, and, contrary to her expectations, it had still hurt a little, but this time, they'd gone slow. And slow, Mel had discovered, was good. Moreover, Jonas going slow, was very, very good.

"Sore?" He must have noticed the stiffness she'd hoped to hide, as she shifted positions.

"Some." She hated to admit it.

"It will get easier." He gently kneaded her lower back. "Your muscles will get used to it."

Mel hoped that meant he intended to make love to her again

"I'd suggest a hot bath," he teased. "But my landlady didn't provide me with a bathtub."

"Your landlady sounds like a real witch." She giggled, rolling toward the edge of the bed. Lying here with Jonas, laughing and caressing, evoked feelings of contentment to which she could all too easily become addicted, and she simply couldn't afford that.

Still, his answering chuckle was a treat for her ears. "She sure is. I don't think she'd object if you wanted to borrow the shower, though. Some hot water will help the aches."

He stood with his usual easy grace, holding out a hand to help her to her feet. She was too unsteady to refuse the help, but as soon as she was on her feet, she tugged her hand free, running it through her tangled mop of hair and looking around wildly for her clothes.

Seeming to sense her nervousness, Jonas backed off a little. He even dragged his jeans back on before escorting her down the ladder to the bathroom.

"I'm going to go make some coffee." He cupped her chin with one hand while he dropped a brief, hard kiss on her lips. "Come out whenever you're ready."

Standing in the shower while steaming pulses of water pummeled her aching body, Mel closed her eyes, leaned back against the tiled stall wall, and took stock. Wow, she'd finally done it. The big *it*. Her cherry was history, her virginity lost at last, and she'd finally, truly been initiated into the sisterhood of women. Moreover, the experience had been everything she'd ever fantasized about, and then some. Jonas had proved to be an excellent choice. He was thoughtful, considerate, skilled, and, by turns, both tender and voracious. He was very much the alpha male when it came to sex, she thought just a little smugly. He was incredibly generous about pleasing his partner. There was absolutely no mistaking the fact that Jonas liked being in charge.

Somewhat to Mel's surprise, she discovered that she liked it that way, too. While she would never be able to stand being bossed around in her everyday life, in bed she seemed to enjoy being mastered. Not that it mattered. The information she'd learned about herself probably wouldn't come into play again in her future. No, the memories she made this summer with Jonas were going to have to last her a lifetime. Luckily for her, every moment of sex with Jonas was definitely going to be worth remembering!

She washed slowly, savoring every ache and tingle of her well-used flesh. Her breasts still throbbed, heavy and tender from Jonas's ministrations, and even thinking about what he'd done to her had her getting wet again! Her hip and thigh muscles ached with fatigue; they'd certainly gotten an unexpected workout. As she scrubbed gently at the smears of dried blood on the inside of her thighs, she remembered the feel of his long, thick cock inside of her. She wanted him again even though her internal muscles, as well as the stretched, torn flesh around them, painfully objected.

Then she touched her abdomen. *Oh, shit!* How could she have forgotten birth control? Twice! She had always promised herself that she wouldn't pass her curse onto another generation of bastard MacRae women. When she'd decided to have sex with Jonas, she'd made sure she was prepared; she even had a condom tucked into the back pocket of her jeans, but as soon as he'd touched her, all her plans and precautions had flown right out of her head!

Even a witch couldn't tell this early whether or not she'd already conceived. It was definitely possible, though. The MacRae curse remained a powerful force, and it demanded one daughter from each generation. She'd never heard of a MacRae being anything less than fertile.

She closed her eyes, face turned up to the spray of the shower. Jonas hadn't stopped to think about it either, coming inside her twice without even mentioning birth control. She could understand his heedlessness if the attraction between them hit him anywhere near the way it did her, but she was a little disappointed, because she'd expected him to be more responsible than that. While part of her was flattered that he'd wanted her badly enough to take risks, another part was just the tiniest bit hurt that he hadn't even made a token effort to protect her.

Well, she told herself, stepping out of the shower and toweling off briskly. *No point getting upset about it today.*

She was either pregnant, or she wasn't. The smartest thing to do would be to stay away from him, to make sure things never had the chance to get out of hand again, but she didn't think she could do it. This summer might be the only chance she ever had to experience passion. She was very much afraid that she would have to take some serious precautionary measures, because judging by the way her body overpowered her brain whenever they got close to each other, until Jonas got tired of her, the man was going to have his very own love-slave.

* * * *

How did one broach the subject of birth control with a skittish ex-virgin? Having never slept with one before, Joe had no idea. He sipped a cup of leftover morning coffee, while a fresh pot brewed on the counter, and considered the possibilities. It wouldn't be fair to say nothing, he decided reluctantly. She was bound to think about it sooner or later, and then she'd worry. He supposed he should just straightforwardly lay out the facts. That way, neither of them would have to fret over the possible consequences. He'd wanted to wait till she'd showered and relaxed a little, though. It gave him time to think, and he knew Mel's body had to hurt, probably more than she wanted to admit. He'd never been with a virgin before, but he imagined she'd have been more comfortable with someone smaller. Joe didn't believe in false modesty. Small he was not.

It still floored him that Mel was—no, had been—untouched. He was ticked off at her, for not telling him, but he was also angry at himself for caring. The whole situation had his stomach in a twist. Why him, why now? Sure, on some level, he wanted to shout from the rooftops. Of all her tenants and all the summer tourists she'd met through her life, Melissa had chosen him, Jonas Pierce, to initiate her into womanhood. That was normal, wasn't it? Surely every male liked the idea of being the first, the only, and getting to teach his partner everything, just the way he liked it. He couldn't believe the moronic men of this town had known Mel her whole life, and apparently never recognized her for the gem she was. Their loss, Joe's gain. He might not be able to keep her for a lifetime, but right here, right now, the woman was *his* by right of possession.

"Coffee?" He managed to keep his tone light and impersonal as he looked over at Mel, who stood across the room, dressed once again in her rumpled jeans and sweatshirt. Her feet were bare, and he suppressed the urge to dash over, pick her up, and plop her on the heavy oak mantel so he could nibble on those delicate pink toes.

"No." She shook her head and walked over to him, curling her legs beneath her on one of the oversized dining chairs. She flashed him a shy grin. "Sorry, but I can't stand the stuff. Water would be nice."

Joe filled a glass with ice, then poured water from a bottle he kept in the fridge.

She widened her eyes and smiled. "The well water's a little rusty, but you can drink it." She took a drink anyway. "I usually do."

"It's an indulgence," he admitted, returning her smile. "When I travel for my research, I never know what the local water is going to be like. This way, at least the water tastes familiar anywhere I go."

The moment the words left his mouth, he realized his mistake. While he'd intended to confess his real occupation to Mel this afternoon, he'd gotten distracted and hadn't. Somehow, he really didn't think this was the appropriate time to admit to being a best-selling author of horror novels, and not the historian she believed him to be.

"You must do a lot of research." She didn't seem to see a contradiction. "That's nice. I bet most of your summers are spent in far more interesting places than Sanctity, Michigan."

Obviously, she still thought he was an academic. Even more than ever, he needed to explain things to her, but they'd have that discussion later. Right now, there were more important things to talk about.

"Mel…" He paused and took a seat across from her with a fresh mug of strong, black coffee. He'd been running on fumes since *before* he'd encountered her by the lake. Now he really needed the caffeine boost. "There are a couple of things we really need to talk about."

She sighed, eyes downcast. "I know. I guess you've probably figured out by now that I have no idea what I'm doing. I mean, what's the proper etiquette in situations like this? If I run into you at the post office, am I supposed to pretend we're strangers?"

He almost snorted coffee out his nose. "Somehow, I don't think that would work." Hell, the sparks between the two of them were practically tangible. Couldn't she tell? He wasn't a complete jackass. As long as she didn't get clingy, everything would be fine. Of course, maybe she had just used him to get rid of her virginity. Why did that idea bother him so much?

"You're right, of course," she was saying. "The whole town knows you're staying here, and they know you took me to dinner twice. They already warned you I was after your virtue anyway." She shrugged and flashed him an impish grin. "Guess it turns out they were right."

He chuckled. Humor was good. "I'm glad. I sort of hoped that was the case."

After a few moments of awkward silence, he brought up the subject he dreaded. "Given that you aren't exactly a regular at this sort of thing, I'm guessing you're not on the pill."

He imagined the flush darkening her cheeks went all the way down, and he ached to find out. Forcing himself to sip his coffee slowly, he managed not to lunge across the table at her.

"No." She shook her head, looking at the ground. Her voice was nothing but a whisper. "I'm not on the pill, but you don't need to worry…"

Her words trailed off. She probably meant that it was the wrong time of her cycle. He'd never trusted that kind of flexible protection, but fortunately, they didn't need to do so. He kept his tone as light and gentle as he could. "Neither do you. I'm disease-free, and I imagine you are too, but if it will make you more comfortable, I'll wear a condom in the future."

"That might be a good idea."

He was just about to explain why pregnancy wasn't an issue when he heard the sound of a car coming up the two-track. Mel had told him that nobody ever came here. Who the hell could it be? Joe reached over and laid a hand over hers. "There's more we need to talk about, but right now, somebody's coming."

"Coming?" she parroted, her train of thought clearly derailed. "Here? Who could possibly be coming up here?"

Grabbing the sweatshirt he'd left on a chair beside the door, he tugged it over his head, then slipped on a pair of sneakers. She cocked her head, then rose to follow him, fluffing her long damp hair. He couldn't resist a smile when she didn't even bother to look for her shoes, just padded after him onto the front porch barefoot.

They stood in the doorway on the wide wooden porch and waited, while a sleek silver sedan rounded the curve, pulling to a halt in front of the cabin. Mel must have recognized the car, because the minutes she spotted it, the tension drained from her posture.

"Hattie?" she murmured quizzically. "What's she doing here?" Then she clutched Joe's elbow and tensed again. "Something's wrong."

Since Joe wasn't the self-proclaimed psychic—she had mentioned visions the other day, hadn't she?—he didn't answer, just watched as a short, sturdy woman emerged from the car and strode toward them. Her close-cropped, silver hair was almost a perfect match for the car, and she wore a no-nonsense blue knit pantsuit. She didn't say a word till she'd climbed the two steps and stood in front of them.

"Harriette Sharp," she announced, extending her hand to Joe. "And you must be the famous Jonas Pierce."

Famous? Had someone in Sanctity found out who he was? Joe just returned her gaze, hoping he gave nothing away as he accepted her firm handshake.

"Joe Pierce." He kept his tone level and polite, and managed not to snarl. "What can I do for you, Ms. Sharp?"

"Oh, call me Hattie." She cast a knowing glance at Mel's damp hair and bare feet. "We're practically related."

"Hattie!" Mel let go of his arm and put her hands on her hips as she shrieked. Then she softened, hugging the older woman. "Be nice. What are you doing up here, anyway? Checking up on me?"

Hattie's features hardened. "There's been a little trouble back at your place, baby. I hoped you might be here, and I thought you might want to get there before the sheriff."

Sheriff? Joe wondered, stepping closer to Mel as if to shield her from any threat.

"Sheriff? What happened? Are the tenants okay?"

"Nobody's hurt." The older woman patted Mel's hand. She looked at Joe, whose arm had snaked around Mel's waist, and to his surprise, smiled with what looked like approval. He tried to return the smile, but he'd bet it looked more like baring his teeth. He wasn't sure what the older woman's claim on Mel was, but for the moment, he was damn sure his superseded it.

"Then what?" Mel made a move toward the steps, but stopped when she realized that Joe's arm had her trapped in place. "Hattie, tell me what's wrong!"

"Just a little property damage. Somebody decided you need a new truck. Your fishermen saw the mess, got a little upset, and called the sheriff."

"And you were listening on your police radio." Mel finished. "And decided you'd better come find me."

"Since you left your pager on your kitchen table, I thought I might find you up here," Hattie agreed. "Are you ready to go?"

"Get in the Jeep, Melissa." Still holding Mel tightly, Joe snaked his other arm in through the front door, snagging his car keys from the pocket of his leather jacket. Good thing the coat hooks were right next to the door. Pulling the inner door shut, he led her down off the porch to his vehicle. "Let's go."

Harriette raised one dark gray eyebrow, but climbed into her own car without comment, waiting to follow Joe and Mel down the trail.

* * * *

All four of her tenants stood nearby. The middle-aged couple from Milwaukee had discovered the vandalism upon returning from their morning fishing trip, and the honeymooners hadn't left their cabin today, until they'd been disturbed by the commotion of Mel's return. Now, all of them hovered in the drive in front of Mel's house, pointedly avoiding looking at the remains of Mel's beloved truck.

"I still don't see why anyone would do this." She hated that her voice came out as a weak, shaky whisper. Jonas and Hattie flanked her like a pair of ferocious guard dogs. Hatred and violence suffused the atmosphere around the desecration, and the pure psychic force of it was making her nauseous.

"I know Talcott has it in for you, but this doesn't seem like his style." Hattie's shrug showed confusion equal to Mel's own.

The sheriff's cruiser pulled into the drive with the red bubble-light on, but thankfully, no raucous siren blaring. Sheriff Warren Mott, a heavyset man in his early fifties, climbed out of the passenger seat.

"Well, now," he called, approaching with an easy stride that belied his girth. Mel knew that under the comfortable layer of padding, there was a toned body that Mott worked hard to keep fit. His lazy drawl and a shape that looked like he was under the influence of one too many donuts had fooled more than one tourist into thinking that Sanctity County was an easy place to get away with crime. They were wrong. All it took was one close look into Mott's sharp, dark gaze to realize the mind beneath was just as keen. "Melissa, Harriette, what seems to be the problem?"

Bill Harkness, Mott's chief deputy, came around from the driver's side to approach Mel and the others. She respected Mott, more or less, but Harkness she couldn't stand at all.

"Well, where's this so-called vandalism, Ms. MacRae?" Her name was said with a taunting sneer. Mott cast his assistant a sharp look, then held out his hand to Jonas.

"Are you the gent who called this in?"

"No, Sheriff, I'm Joe Pierce, another one of Mel's tenants," Jonas replied with ease, ignoring the fact that Harkness had whipped out a small notepad, and begun scribbling in it.

"Ah, you're the one renting Lonnie's old place." Jonas raised one eyebrow, casting a glance at Mel. She knew she'd have to explain that one as soon as the cops had left.

"Mr. Johnston over there is the one who called you." Jonas pointed out the couple. "I believe that he and his wife discovered the damage."

"And where were you this afternoon, Ms. MacRae?" Harkness interjected with a suspicious leer.

"With me." The look Jonas gave Harkness could have frozen lava. "Since about noon."

"Let's just see the damage, shall we, gentlemen, ladies?" Mott nodded at the well-to-do tourists. "You two want to show me what you found?" He looked pointedly at Harkness. "Then we can ask whatever questions need to be asked."

They all followed them down the winding drive, past Mel's cabin to where the road curved and opened into a small oval parking area that the six guest cabins clustered around. It was a short walk from Mel's house, but the bend in the road and the trees between gave her some privacy from her paying guests. It had also hidden the vandalism from anyone who might have just driven up to see Mel, though it had been prominently displayed for any tenants she might have.

Jezebel, Mel's grandmother's cherished yellow pickup truck, was history. Every pane of glass, from windshield to mirrors to tail lights, had been smashed. The same blunt object had dented and crushed every panel of metal on the vehicle: hood, fenders, doors, you name it. Then there was the spray paint.

Rhyming "witch" with "bitch" wasn't exactly creative. The phrase had been used to taunt Mel all her life. It was also the mildest of the insults displayed in hunter orange on the remains of her truck. Each surface offered a ruder and more graphic epithet than the last.

Harkness and Mott studied the damage, asked the requisite questions of the tenants, which drew a blushing admission from the newlyweds that a bomb could have gone off in the parking lot and they probably wouldn't have heard it. The older couple explained they had left before dawn for their fishing venture, returning just under an hour ago to find the truck, which had apparently been pushed down the drive to the center of the parking lot. Mel knew she'd left it right in front of her cabin, as usual, when she'd returned from Karen's house in the early hours of the morning.

"I sat up all night with Gladys Clark," she told the officers. "I got home about four, then slept for a few hours. Somewhere around noon, I took care of the animals, then went for a walk in the woods to clear my head. I ran into Mr. Pierce down by the lake, and he invited me back to his place for lunch."

Mott knew better of course. He shot a skeptical glance at Mel's bare feet, but he just nodded. "So this could have happened any time between six a.m. and three p.m.," he remarked with an understanding nod. "I'll see what I can find out, Melissa, but you know as well as I do that if it's kids pulling pranks, we'll never catch the culprit."

She returned a glum nod. This wasn't a prank. The hatred that pulsed around the truck was a palpable force. Nothing she could say would convince Mott, though, so she didn't even try. Instead, she finished up the interview, reassured her tenants that their vehicles would still be safe on her premises, and went inside the cabin to call her insurance company.

"I know it was more than a prank," she confessed to Jonas a half hour later. Hattie had taken Jonas's hint to leave, much to Mel's relief. She sat cross-legged on her living room sofa, watching Jonas pace around the big, cozy room. "But Warren doesn't like stirring up trouble, not if he can afford not to, and since nobody was hurt, he won't pursue the matter."

"Hmmph!" He gave a rude snort and resumed pacing with his clenched jaw and his hands fisted at his side. "The man should be horsewhipped! What's the matter, is he in Talcott's pocket, or something?"

Mel gave what she hoped was a philosophical shrug. Sure, the loss of her grandmother's truck was both a financial and an emotional blow, but even so, Jezebel was, after all, only a *thing*. Mel was just glad that whoever had set out to hurt her had taken out his anger on the truck, and not on Hattie, or Karen, or even one of the animals. "Well, county sheriff is an elected position, so it doesn't pay to upset the man with the most money to donate to campaign funds. Warren's fundamentally honest, though. He won't look the other way on purpose. If something turns up, he'll feel obligated to follow through."

Jonas was being overprotective, and she didn't need it, of course, but it was nice to have somebody other than Hattie or Karen looking out for her.

As he passed her in his pacing, she reached out a hand to stop him. "I'm all right, Jonas. Relax. My finances might get a little tight, but I'll be able to swing a new truck. The good news is, it doesn't look like whoever did this succeeded in scaring off my paying customers. That was obviously the intent, but it looks like they'll all be staying."

"They'd better." At least that's what she thought she heard him growl under his breath. At her insistent tug, he stopped pacing, and flopped down beside her on the cushy green-plaid couch. Then he kissed her. It started out soft and tender, and it was so sweet it almost broke Mel's heart. When she opened her mouth and sucked his lower lip in, he seemed to get the message. He pushed her back against the cushions, slid one hand up under her shirt, and she forgot all about her truck.

* * * *

The late afternoon sun slanted in through the living room window and right into Mel's eyes. She squirmed, too tired and sore and sated to move. Jonas groaned when she shifted, then seemed to sense the problem, since he rolled them off the couch, twisting his body so that she landed on top of him on her living room rug.

"What have you done to me, woman?" His rueful smile assured her that whatever she'd done, he didn't mind too much.

"I thought you knew. You're the experienced one, remember? Isn't this normal?" She kept her tone light and teasing. It would be a big mistake for either of them to take their passion seriously.

"Yeah," he snorted. "If you're sixteen." This time his smile was wide and genuine. "You're incredible, Melissa MacRae. Absolutely incredible."

Just then, his stomach growled loudly, and Mel couldn't suppress a giggle.

"You're not so bad yourself." She made an attempt to stand, but discovered a thousand sore muscles, and slumped back beside him. "Ow! I'll go make us something to eat, as soon as I can move."

"I'm sorry, sweetheart. I didn't mean to hurt you." Joe stood then lifted Mel gently to her feet. "Why don't you take that hot bath we talked about earlier? If you'll trust me in your kitchen, I'll rustle up something to eat."

"I'm beginning to think you have a cleanliness fetish," she taunted even though the idea of a hot bath sounded good. "But if you don't mind, I'll wait till I get my work done before I indulge in a long, hot soak. I'll just go wash up, then we can start on dinner."

"Sure," he agreed. Still magnificently naked, he picked up their discarded clothing, and followed her up the curved staircase. She was proud of her home, and enjoyed his open approval as he looked around.

Of course, she enjoyed his approval even more as he watched her dress. In deference to her abraded skin, she pulled on a pair of soft gray yoga pants and a zip-front sweatshirt, over a pair of plain cotton panties and a matching sports bra.

"I think my tennis shoes are still at your cabin," she told him. Her skin heated, and she knew she was blushing a little.

Clad once again in his jeans and a Mets sweatshirt, he chuckled. "They are. Maybe I'll hold them hostage."

"For what?" She brushed her long hair into a fresh ponytail, securing it at the nape of her neck with a gray scrunchie. Well, she decided after a glance in the mirror, if he still thought she was attractive dressed like this, their affair was definitely on the right track for the next several weeks.

"I don't know," he replied with a lazy, sexy grin. "I'm sure I'll come up with something."

Downstairs in the kitchen, they bustled around, working together in quiet harmony, tossing together a salad while the pasta boiled on the stove. Fortunately, she had a jar of homemade tomato sauce in the cupboard without any meat in it, and a fresh block of mozzarella cheese in the fridge.

Twenty minutes later they sat side by side on her back deck while they ate and gazed out at the wilderness. "You know, we never did finish our conversation."

"The one where you asked if I was on the pill?" The heat of another annoying blush burned her cheeks, and she really wished she could stop doing that.

"Yeah, that one." Setting down his fork, he reached out his hand, easily engulfing her smaller one. "I want you to know that I would never put you at risk."

She smiled at the warmth that swept through her at his touch, not paying too much attention to what he said. She had been a willing participant in the risky behavior, after all. All three times. Besides, after the mind-blowing pleasure he'd given her, she was inclined to be forgiving.

"I have plans for my life, Mel, and you may as well know that they don't include marriage, and they certainly don't include ever having children. Since I made that decision years ago, I chose to take total responsibility for it."

He had her full attention now. So he didn't want kids either? That was good, wasn't it? So why did it make her sort of sad?

"So I had the surgery," he was saying.

"What?"

"I can't get you pregnant, Mel. I've had a vasectomy."

Chapter Six

The hot bath water infused with cleansing and soothing herbs helped ease Mel's physical aches, but, unfortunately, it didn't do a thing for her emotional ones.

Vasectomy. It removed the only risk that might have stood in the way of a magical summer. It should have eased her mind, relieved her fears.

So why did she feel betrayed?

Part of her, a big part, didn't care about anything except the incredible pleasure she'd found in his arms. She knew she couldn't keep him in her life forever, but surely she was entitled to a little bit of time just for herself. Another, more responsible voice, kept insisting that she was risking something a lot more than pregnancy anyway; she was gambling with her heart. Then there was the whole issue of her powers. Sex didn't seem to have fixed them any. Just this afternoon, for instance, she'd tried reading Sheriff Mott's aura, and all she'd managed to see was a kaleidoscope of shifting colors. And she couldn't read Jonas's at all. It was like he was a completely alien species.

Her deepest fear was that if her magical abilities continued to wane, pretty soon she wasn't going to be able to heal. Mel's healing powers and the sense of responsibility that went with them made up the very core of her being. Without them, she wouldn't know who she was or what she was supposed to do with her life. Responsibility was important to Mel, and her failing magic was telling her that the time had come for her attend to the ultimate duty, that of providing another generation to care for the land and the living things that shared it.

Utterly depressed, Mel pulled on her ratty sweats and padded downstairs where she unearthed the rest of Karen's peanut butter cookies. She briefly considered the notion of taking them out on the back deck to share with her new friend the wolf if he returned for another visit, but it was a chilly night, and her hair was still wet from her bath. Instead, she plodded into the living room and flopped down on the couch, hoping to lose herself in an hour or so of mindless television.

Halfway through a rerun of *Bewitched*—and boy had the producers gotten just about everything wrong on that one—Mel heard the rev of an engine and the crunch of gravel in front of her cabin. She hoped it was one of the tenants, but the doorbell disabused her of that notion quickly enough. Please, please don't let it be Jonas, she thought. She just wasn't up to dealing with him tonight.

"Karen! What are you doing here?"

"I heard about your truck." Karen's grim expression brightened as she held up a clear plastic grocery sack. "I thought you might need ice cream."

Mel grinned as she held the door open. "Chocolate?"

"Better." Karen gave Mel a brief hug, and smiled back. "Mackinac Island Fudge."

"Ooh." Mel followed her friend to the kitchen. "Serious chocolate."

"I can only stay a couple of hours." A few minutes later the two women plopped down on opposite ends of the couch, each cradling a huge bowl of decadent fudge ice cream.

"Your kids with their dad?" Mel scooped up an enormous spoonful and popped it into her mouth.

"Yeah." Karen sighed. "They're in Marquette with Dave the dick." She stuck her tongue out at the mention of his name. Karen's accountant ex-husband had left Sanctity the moment after graduation and never looked back. They'd all gone to college together at Lake

Superior State, but then Karen and Dave had moved to the bigger city of Marquette. After she'd caught him screwing his twenty-one year-old intern, Karen had divorced him and moved back to Sanctity. When her mother had been diagnosed with terminal cancer, Karen and her kids had moved in with her folks.

"How are your parents?" Though mostly rhetorical, the question needed to be asked.

"Mom's having a pretty good day thanks to your work last night. Dad—isn't. This is so hard on him. If she were one of his patients, he'd have her stuck in a hospital, hooked up to dozens of tubes and wires, but as her husband, he understands the mercy of letting her go peacefully at home. It's so difficult for doctors to give up control."

"Isn't it for all of us?" Mel rolled her eyes. She sure hated the feelings she'd had lately—that her life was entirely beyond her control.

"I guess so." Karen nodded, and closed her eyes, presumably to better taste the ice cream. Then she shook her head and brightened, though Mel could tell it was forced. "Anyway, I desperately needed out of the house for a while, but we are not going to discuss my problems tonight. Tonight is all about Mel. I heard all sorts of juicy gossip from Justine Flannery by the way. Why didn't you tell me you had a date last night? Was he still with you when I paged you?"

Mel nodded, and knew she was blushing. Her pale Scottish complexion was a pain sometimes.

"Is he as hot as the grapevine says he is?"

"More," she admitted reluctantly.

"So why didn't you tell me about him last night?"

"You had other things on you mind," Mel answered. "I didn't want to worry you."

"Worry me?" There was laughter in Karen's tired voice, and Mel was delighted to hear it. "I've been worried about you for years because you *weren't* dating."

"Why should I date?" Mel shrugged. "It's not like I can actually find the perfect someone and settle down, so dating is pointless."

Waggling her spoon in reproach, Karen shook her head. "Moose puckey. Even if you're not looking for a husband, which I don't believe for a moment, mind you, dating isn't pointless. You need companionship, don't you? And trust me, there's nothing in the world more fun than great sex." Her sigh echoed with remorse. "I don't miss my sleaze-ball ex at all, but I sure do miss the sex."

Mel would have told her friend to follow her own advice and date, but she had to admit, Karen's excuse beat the heck out of hers. She'd been so busy teaching, raising her kids and nursing her mom, that no one could expect her to have much of a social life.

"Anyway," Karen refused to be deterred. Mel could see her friend was determined to keep the focus on Mel tonight. "As I've been telling you since high school, you need to get over your belief that you can never get married. We both know a woman doesn't need a man to be happy, but you shouldn't deny yourself based on a stupid family tradition."

"It's not a tradition." Mel rehashed the well-worn argument for maybe the thousandth time. "It's called a curse."

"Curse, schmurshe. It's called a cop-out."

"Since when don't you believe in witchcraft?"

"I don't, in general."

That was a surprise. Mel just stared, a spoonful of ice cream half-way to her mouth. "Huh?" she finally managed.

"In general," Karen repeated. "I didn't say I don't believe in you. Hell, I rely on your powers and you know it. What I don't believe is that one selfish woman could curse an entire family from beyond the grave. It's been a hundred years, for heaven's sake. Quit buying the bullshit, and get on with your life."

"But the history says otherwise." Mel would give anything to believe her friend. If only she could overlook what had happened anytime one of her female ancestors had ignored the curse and tried for matrimonial bliss. She quoted the lines that had haunted every member of her family for the last century and a half. "*None of your blood shall bear a son, nor have a man to keep. One daughter to bear this curse shall each generation reap.*"

She sighed, dropping her spoon with a clatter into the empty bowl. "Look at my great-grandmother, or my mother for that matter. MacRaes and marriage just don't mix."

"So your great-grandfather died young. So what? That wasn't exactly unusual around here during the Depression. Your mother was an out-of-control teenager in the seventies. She got pregnant, got into drugs and OD'd. Again, not too unusual, although it sucked for you."

"But don't you think that it strains the bounds of coincidence that every generation has consisted of a single or widowed woman with exactly one daughter? No successful marriages, no sons, no second daughters. Doesn't that prove the existence of the curse?" She'd had the same discussion with Hattie not too long ago, and it was beginning to wear Mel down. What if the curse she'd grown up believing in was just so much coincidence and self-fulfilling prophecy like Hattie and Karen claimed?

"It doesn't prove a thing except for a genetic predisposition toward female offspring, and a strongly suggestion-influenced subconscious," Karen asserted firmly. "You've gotta live your life Mel. Face it, since old Miss Garrison died, you're probably Sanctity's oldest living virgin."

"Not anymore," she muttered. There went that blush again. Her face flamed with heat, and even her hands turned beet red.

"What? When? You didn't?" Karen didn't even pause for Mel to answer the shrieked questions. "Oh my God! With your new tenant? What's he like? Was it good?"

"Phenomenal!" Mel answered the last query first. "Oh, Kare, it was everything I ever imagined and more." She squirmed a little on the sofa as her well-used muscles tingled in reminiscence of the pleasures she'd experienced that afternoon. "Jonas is—he's incredible Karen. Really amazing."

"So when do I get to meet him?" Karen demanded. "You're not even thinking about keeping him locked up back in Lonnie's cabin, are you?"

"Part of me would like nothing better than to keep him back there chained to the bed."

"So what's wrong, then?" Karen set her own bowl on the coffee table and crossed her arms over her chest. She studied Mel's face with a look of concern in her big blue eyes. "Did he say something wrong, or get all goofy afterward?"

Mel just shrugged and twisted her hands in her lap.

"Oh, come on. Tell Auntie Karen all about it. Is it just that you're falling in love with him? Because I keep telling you, sweetie, that doesn't have to be a bad thing."

Mel sighed and looked down at her hands. Karen knew her too well for Mel to be able to keep secrets. "I'm not in love with him." Not yet, anyway. She was *not* going to let herself be that stupid.

"Then if you don't want to keep him, what has you so upset?"

"It's not that I might not want to keep him, it's that I can't," Mel cried. "Even if I discounted the curse, and I'm really not sure I ever could, Jonas has already made it perfectly clear that this is just a fling."

"How's that? He isn't married, is he?"

"No," Mel assured her friend with just a flicker of humor at the thought. "Far from it. He was very up-front, though, about the fact that he's not interested in marriage or children. Ever. In fact, he told me that he's had a vasectomy, just to make sure he doesn't ever accidentally end up a father."

"Sounds like a really responsible guy," Karen noted wisely. "But since you've got the same plans, I don't see why you look so bummed out by the idea."

"I don't know. I'm happy that there's no risk, of course, but…"

"But you don't like the idea that he's starting something that has a finite end date in mind."

Embarrassed by her friend's intuition, Mel stared downward, picking up her ice cream bowl for something to fidget with.

"Oh, Mel, honey, you can't start a relationship worrying about how it's going to end. Enjoy your fling if that's all it's destined to be. God knows, you deserve a little fun in your life. If it's meant to be more, let it happen. Remember, sometimes people change their minds. Maybe if you're still together in a year or two, you'll both decide you really do want kids. They can reverse vasectomies these days, you know."

"It doesn't matter, anyway," Mel replied sadly. "I can't take the chance of a long-term relationship or a child. Every man who ever tried to settle down with a MacRae witch has met a horrible end. How could I ask someone I cared about to take that risk?"

"Life is risk," Karen reminded her. "Look at me. I didn't start out with a curse, and yet, things aren't exactly going well. My husband dumped me for his bimbo intern, my son's talking about living with them, and both of my kids are watching their grandmother waste away before their eyes."

"Oh, God, Kare, I'm sorry," Mel sighed. "I know that bad things can happen to anybody, but that's just my point. They seem to happen with greater frequency to anybody who gets too close to me or my family. I'd never forgive myself if I thought that any of your troubles were an indirect result of the MacRae curse."

That was Mel's deepest fear, and Karen probably knew it. Mel had always believed that she was doomed to a solitary existence, at least romantically, but it terrified her to think that by her very existence she allowed the curse to contaminate those dear to her.

"That's the biggest load of crap I've ever heard!" Karen re-crossed her legs in front of her on the sofa and reached for Mel's hand before gentling her voice. "Look at Hattie. She was your grandmother's er—friend for what sixty years? And she's still doing great."

"But Hattie never married," Mel pointed out. "Or had kids of her own. She was just another old single woman."

Karen laughed, and the sound of it cheered Mel in spite of herself. After all Karen had been through, all she still faced, it was good to know there was still joy in her soul.

"Mel, you are priceless. I can't believe you never figured it out. Hattie never married for the same reason your grandmother didn't. They were a couple, Mel. Sure, they kept it in the closet, because that's how you were supposed to behave in their generation. I know you don't want to believe it, but your grandmother was effectively married for, like, forty-five years!"

* * * *

Just how many nights could he go without any sleep, Joe wondered. He'd gotten virtually none since his arrival in Sanctity, all because of Mel. Why did the red-haired witch get to him so much? Maybe because due to her own heritage, she could calmly accept the paranormal? That could be a big part of it. But it didn't account for the whole thing. In the course of his research, he'd met plenty of other not-quite-humans, and not one of them had ever appealed to him like Melissa MacRae.

Her boundless, selfless compassion was a big part of his fascination for her. She truly walked as one with all living things, and he hadn't met anyone like that in a long, long time. Still, even that couldn't explain the enormity of the magnetic pull that existed between them. He'd expected sex would sate the hunger he felt whenever he thought of her, but instead, he wanted her more, even after making love to her three times in one afternoon.

Three times. And less than twelve hours ago, she'd been a virgin. That's why he'd left after dinner, though he'd stayed to help her with her evening animal chores. He was afraid that if he'd followed her back inside her cabin, he'd have ended up back in bed with her yet again. He was already feeling a little guilty. After the third time, she had to be unbelievably sore.

Restless, he paced trying to ignore the tingling frustration in his body, until he sensed it meld with another, equally visceral need. Damn, he shouldn't be feeling like this, not so soon! He could only figure it was a side effect of the sexual tension. It had been less than twenty-four hours since he'd had a run through the woods, and usually, a session like that left him good for at least a week. Joe had spent years coming to grips with his unusual heritage. He'd learned through careful trial and error experimentation just how to cope with both the positive and negative aspects of his unique genetic characteristics, and he'd thought he had everything under control. He'd believed he knew himself as well, if not better than any other man alive; that his own body held no more surprises for him. Tonight proved him wrong.

He glanced up at the brilliant half-moon shining through his open window. It was a nice night, he decided ruefully, and it wasn't like he had anything better to do. Besides, whether he liked it or not, there was only one way to silence the itchy tingling that pervaded his bones. He stood and stretched as he toed off his sneakers and socks, then stripped his sweatshirt and jeans, leaving them carefully on a kitchen chair that stood just inside the back door.

He turned off the kitchen light, and checked out the window to be sure that no one was near, then stepped out onto the porch, and waited, allowing his senses to become one with the night. Good. There was no one around. He turned his face up to the sky and closed his eyes, relaxing every muscle in his body. His consciousness altered; sounds, scents sharpened, and mass shifted as Joe willed himself to *change*.

He wandered the woods, not surprised when he found himself outside of Mel's cabin. There was an unfamiliar car in the driveway, which made his hackles rise. He found a spot on a slight rise where his better-than-human vision could see through the crack in her living room drapes, and spotted her sitting on the sofa, laughing and eating ice cream with a blonde. Ah. Girl talk. The strange surge of jealousy subsided, and with it the restlessness he'd experienced at the sight of the car. It started to come back when he moved toward the path that led to his cabin, so he returned to Mel's front yard. It seemed his wolf instincts wanted him to be here. Fine. He found a soft patch of thick grass under a tree where he could watch her front door and curled up with his chin on his paws.

He continued to watch as Mel's friend left in a flutter of feminine giggles and hugs. Joe's furry upper lip curled in what might have passed for a canine smile. He'd never seen Mel like this, so lighthearted and silly, but he could still sense the sadness that hung around the pair like a shroud. This must be Karen, the woman whose mother was dying, and who had such problems with her ex-husband. Tonight, though, it looked like she'd put her own troubles aside to come comfort Mel. Good. Mel deserved friends who cared about her, strong women like Hattie and Karen who could appreciate the strength and goodness in Melissa.

He stood and stretched, then crisscrossed the area around Mel's cabin, tracking what scent trails he could isolate. Between the cops, Mel's tenants, and a handful of curious townspeople, there were so many men who had traipsed over her parking lot today that he couldn't pick out one individual who didn't belong. He absorbed the traces and made a mental note of each individual scent then filed it away in his brain. He hoped he could sort the vandal or vandals from the others at some point.

A quick circuit around the compound assured him that all was well in the various buildings. All of Mel's tenants and animal patients were secure and accounted for. He watched the house until all the lights had been extinguished, just to be sure she didn't decide to do something stupid, like go for a solitary moonlit walk. Finally, when his heightened senses could no longer detect any movement from inside the cabin, he padded silently up the steps. Once on the wide front porch, he circled twice, then curled up on the doormat and allowed himself to sleep.

Chapter Seven

Sanctity's small library was only open three days a week. Feeling unexpectedly rested after sleeping outside last night, Joe decided that today was the day to begin his research.

"What, exactly, are you looking for?"

Barbara Halloran, the township clerk, doubled as the librarian, according to the plastic nametag pinned to her lapel. The woman had to have come with the building, as the township hall/library complex sat on a plot of land labeled "Halloran Park." Her snow-white hair and parchment-like skin perfectly matched the sober, dignified atmosphere of the small, tidy building. Her smile was polite and vaguely welcoming as she peered at Joe through half-glasses perched on the tip of her patrician nose.

"Just a little local history," he answered easily. "This area was originally settled by French fur traders, right?"

"History section." Her regal nod conveyed acceptance of his request, if not approval. "South wall of the back room."

The public part of the library consisted of two large chambers, separated by a small tidy office, the circulation desk, and a scrupulously clean rest room. Fiction and children's books in the front, while all the nonfiction was in the rear. Joe followed the librarian's directions and discovered a display shelf labeled Michigan History, which contained a small collection of local memorabilia along with books on logging and mining in the region. He selected several volumes, and then checked the catalog, which was on a surprisingly up-to-date computer program, for anything on the occult.

Bingo. *Midwestern Witchcraft*, by an author Joe had never heard of from Chicago, claimed to list all the "known" incidences of the paranormal in the region up until the time of its publication in the 1920's. Surely, there'd be something in here about Mel's ancestors. Otherwise, why would a copy be here, in Sanctity? He found the slim, leather-bound volume, and tucked it in amidst the others, before returning to the circulation desk, where he tried to convince the eagle-eyed Mrs. Halloran to let him check them out.

"Sorry, sir. Not unless you have a permanent address within the county," he was told sharply. "You're welcome to read them here in the library."

"Put them on my card, Barb," another voice cut in. "I'll make sure he gets them back to you in one piece."

Hattie Sharp passed a small, plastic card to the other woman, who accepted it with a moue of disapproval.

"Hattie!" He must be tired. He'd completely missed hearing her come up behind him. "Thanks." Ignoring the librarian's scowl, he accepted the books, then turned back to Harriette. "Can I buy you lunch?"

"Sounds good." The silver-haired lady gave a crisp nod, her expression giving nothing away.

After dropping the books into the passenger seat of his Jeep, he walked with her down two blocks to Main Street and Rosa's, where he was already welcomed as a regular. The little diner was crowded with the beginnings of the lunch-time rush. Joe followed Harriette to a back corner booth, as far as possible from the bulk of the crowd. Her eyebrows drew together and she drummed her fingers on the table. This time he ordered the vegetarian lasagna, while Hattie ordered a bacon-cheeseburger and fries.

"So you're not a missionary vegetarian," Hattie observed, after the waitress had taken their order and left. "You don't mind if I eat meat."

"Nope. And I hope you don't mind if I don't. People should eat what they want to eat."

"Damn straight." Hattie bobbed her head sharply. "I hate people telling me what to do."

He raised one eyebrow and suppressed a grin. "I don't imagine there are many people brave enough to try."

That earned him a chuckle. "You'd be surprised." There was humor and exasperation in her wry tone. "After all, us old folks need looking out for, don't you know."

Joe snorted a laugh. "Right. And I'm the Easter Bunny."

"Good boy." Hattie laughed out loud, drawing a look or two from the crowd. "Knew I liked you." Then her tone and expression turned serious, and her voice dropped to a near whisper. "Now. Tell me about your intentions toward my granddaughter."

The eyebrow went up again, but he kept the rest of his features deliberately blank. "I thought her grandmother was dead."

"Okay, quasi-adopted granddaughter then. Same difference, really. We're not blood relatives, but I helped Mart raise the girl. None of which changes the question, young man. What are you up to with Mel?"

"As of this morning, not a damned thing." The disappointment he heard in his own voice appalled him. He'd stopped by Mel's cabin on his way into town, eager to see her again. Instead of welcoming him with the proverbial open arms, she'd turned the cold shoulder, making it clear she wanted nothing to do with him on the morning after. Even a couple hours later, her rejection still smarted.

Hattie absorbed his response, and its implications, without a blink. "Blew you off today, did she? Well, that's not really much of a surprise. Don't let her get away with it, though."

"What?" Whatever he'd expected Hattie to do, it hadn't been this. She was supposed to warn him off, tell him to leave her darling alone. "Listen, Ms. Sharp, where I come from, no means no. If the lady isn't interested, then that's the end of it." He'd been reminding himself of that ever since he'd left Mel's cabin. He only wished he meant it.

"Oh, she's interested, all right. She's just running scared." Their food arrived, and Hattie paused while the pretty young waitress delivered their orders, then moved back to the counter. With silence at their table, Joe took time to note the other sounds that filled the air. Patrons came and left, dishes clinked, and only the occasional laugh or cough rose above the general buzz of conversation. Hattie looked down at her plate and picked up a French fry. Joe didn't know what she wanted from him, but he knew he wanted information from her, so he continued to play things her way.

The garlicky aroma of the pasta filled his nostrils, blotting out the scents of so many people. His sense of smell was better in wolf form, but even as a man, he could pick up more than most people. He paused long enough to take a bite. The lasagna was warm and gooey with a rich blend of cheeses. The flavors of and basil and oregano harmonized perfectly with the spinach and zucchini, he thought as he chewed, then swallowed.

"Why?"

Hattie's eyes flew up to meet his, and she paused in her chewing for a moment. Good, he'd taken her off-guard. It took a few seconds for her to respond. "Why what?"

"Why is she running scared?"

Hattie took another bite, and Joe could practically hear the mental gears turning as she debated about what to tell him.

"You want me to try again, I'm going to need more information."

She tilted her head back and forth, as if weighing her options. Finally she pinned her piercing blue gaze on him and nodded. "All right. How much has Mel told you about her family?"

"Well, I know she's a witch if that's where you're going. Her family have all been witches, and lived in the same spot for a century and a half." He thought for a second, trying to remember what else he'd learned. "Oh, yeah, she also mentioned something about the family not being big on husbands. I gather she never knew her father."

"No." Hattie must be a hell of a poker player, because she continued to eat calmly, her lined but still elegant features betraying absolutely no trace of emotion.

"Why not?"

Now Hattie's lips hardened a little as she swallowed. She took a sip of water then a deep breath before she continued, her eyes slightly narrowed. "Slimy bastard never even acknowledged being involved with Marilyn—Mel's mama—let alone being the father of the baby. Of course, it wouldn't have worked out anyway, even if he hadn't been already married. Marilyn was pretty much into drugs and booze even then. She couldn't have managed a relationship. She died of an overdose when Melissa was only three."

"That's rough." His own childhood had been far from perfect, but at least he'd known both his parents for a while. Mel probably couldn't remember having one, let alone two.

"Yeah," Hattie agreed with a tight nod. "Marty, Mel's grandma, raised her with a little help from yours truly. Since Mart never married either, Mel never had what you might consider a father-figure in her life."

"Another married lover?"

Hattie's features hardened completely, her voice turned cold and crisp. "No. Mart never had much interest in men, never intended to marry or have a child. Some drunk backwoodsman attacked her behind the barn one night. They never caught the bastard, but then, I don't suppose they ever tried. That's how I met her, incidentally. I was the social worker assigned to her by the court system when she tried to file charges."

Wow, the MacRae history was even more sordid than Joe had imagined. No wonder Mel didn't believe in happily ever after. There was something, though, in the way Hattie spoke of Mel's grandmother that made him wonder. Maybe Mel had, in fact, witnessed a long-term relationship, just not a traditional one.

"Marty was never very fond of men." Hattie stared at her food and avoided eye contact. She nibbled at the big messy cheeseburger with tiny ladylike bites, then spoke in between. "And especially not after that. I'm afraid she may have passed a little too much of her own bitterness onto her daughter and granddaughter. Marilyn couldn't think of anything but getting out of Sanctity, and men were just tools, a means to that end. Mel went the other way, closed herself off. She's never let herself get close enough to a man to know if she could trust him—except for Lonnie of course, and he wasn't exactly normal."

Lonnie. He'd heard that name before. It was the one attached to the cabin he was renting. "Who's Lonnie?"

"Mel's great-uncle, more or less. Marty's stepbrother. These days, I suppose he'd be called developmentally disabled, but back then he was just, slow, simple Lonnie."

"So there have been men in the MacRae family?" Stepbrother implied marriage, so there must have been a husband at one point in time.

"Briefly. Marty's mother didn't believe in the curse, and she decided to get married to a widower with a young son. Her husband died a couple of years later, and left her with Marty and his boy to raise. She changed her mind about the curse, changed her name back to MacRae, and convinced Marty to stay away from men. I never bought into the idea that the curse killed Marty's dad. After all, hunting accidents are pretty common up here even now. They were sure nothing out of the ordinary in 1932."

All the hustle and bustle of the busy restaurant disappeared as Joe's attention narrowed, focusing exclusively on the woman across from him. One word stuck out in Joe's head out of everything she'd just told him. One word that probably lay at the crux of the whole matter, maybe at the crux of Melissa herself. He turned his own stare on Hattie, the hard one he'd practiced to keep people at bay, the one that had once made an editor cry. He watched, gauging the movement of every telltale facial muscle, every hint of expression. He tried not to growl, forced his voice to stay low as he repeated the word, turning it into a question. His voice sounded rusty, even to him, since all the saliva had drained from his mouth.

"Curse?"

* * * *

Insurance agents had to rank somewhere just below banana slugs on the evolutionary ladder. Surely the only life-form lower was whoever had trashed her grandmother's beloved truck. After a long morning of cutting through red tape, Mel finally had the claims adjuster on the premises, and he circled the remains of Jezebel like he was examining a leper colony.

"Your policy doesn't cover body work," the man announced, waggling his clipboard in Mel's face.

"I know," she sighed. "But it should cover totaling the truck, so I can move on and get a new one."

Apparently, the adjuster didn't agree.

"One could argue that you've brought this on yourself, you know."

She gazed at the pompous little man in the plaid polyester suit through narrowed eyes. "What?"

"All your satanic activities make you a natural target for the God-fearing people of this town. This is certainly someone's attempt to convince you of the errors of your ways."

"So God condones vandalism?" Mel had heard it all before, but something in the man's earnest yet nasty tone really pushed her buttons today.

"No, but he does enjoin his followers to cast out the sinners among them."

"Well, strangely enough, the police report says this was the act of a criminal, not an act of any god, yours or otherwise. And my policy covers that."

He postured and argued, but when he finally left, Mel had a check in her hand. For a whopping five-hundred bucks.

She went inside to call the towing company, letting them know they could now come claim the wreckage, and haul Jezebel away, never to be seen again. Blinking back tears, she hung up the phone, forcing herself to get on with what she needed to do. Slowly, methodically, she went through the vehicle, searching under and behind the seats for stray personal possessions.

She removed maps and pens from the glove box, sniffling as she sorted out twenty years worth of registration and insurance cards. There was a birthday card from her to her grandmother, that Gran must have stuck in the glove box and forgotten, long expired coupons and a couple of hair ties. No surprise there; Mel tended to leave those lying about everywhere.

She lifted out the floor mats, which were mostly free of the spray paint, thinking she could find a use for them in the barn, or perhaps the tool shed. She shook out the gravel and road dust, then tossed them onto the small pile of salvageable goods. There were a couple of quarters on the now-bared floor, so she scooped those up. Money was money. A dried up pen, and a movie ticket stub, she left behind. Let the junkyard worry about the trash.

As she was climbing out, she noticed a small strip of fabric had been snagged on the rusted metal of the doorframe. She picked it off, then immediately fell back away from the vehicle, landing hard on her backside on the cool grassy ground, dropping the scrap. The oily sense of hatred and violence that clung to the bit of material was more than enough to convince her that it had been worn by the vandal. Forcing her roiling stomach into submission, she reached for the shred, trying to get a picture of the owner. Nothing. All she could see was the swirling aura of fury and loathing.

She stood slowly, giving her now-shaky legs time to recover, and made her way to the office, where she dropped the scrap into an envelope. She knew the sheriff wouldn't consider it evidence, though she'd recognized the bright blue cotton knit. There was no practical way of linking it to Sean, or for that matter, to anyone else. Practically everyone in town owned one of those shirts. Not only did the entire staff wear the resort-logo polo shirts, Talcott made a big profit selling them at the restaurant and lodge. Mel shivered. Whoever it had been, he'd managed to scare her. Mel had been an outsider all her life, but based on the vibes she'd gotten from that cloth, this time, she had a genuine enemy.

* * * *

"Curse," Hattie affirmed. "You'll find it mentioned in that book you checked out. Most of it is pretty common knowledge around Sanctity."

"Then you shouldn't mind telling me about it." He forced himself to breathe, to take in his surroundings, and immediately the clatter and chatter of the restaurant pounded in his ears.

"You sure you want to hear about it?"

He dipped his chin slowly. "Go on."

She shook her head. "Not here." She paused as a mother and young child ducked past their booth toward the restroom. "Finish your lunch, then we can take a walk. It's a long story, and not a very pretty one."

He downed the rest of his lasagna in record time, sending a silent apology to the chef. Her masterpiece had deserved savoring, but he'd have to do it another time. He paid the check without a word, and waited silently while Hattie had the waitress box up the remaining half of her burger.

She kept her poker face and poker-straight posture, all the way down the street to her car. He gritted his teeth while she opened the trunk, and placed her purse and her take-out box inside. Then she gestured for Joe to follow her across the street to where a small park sat rimmed by pine trees along the bank of a meandering stream. The apparent tranquility of the place was at odds with Joe's impatience for knowledge, but he bit his lip and loped alongside her, her pace brisk for such a tiny older woman, but still too slow for Joe's long legs.

Finally, Hattie settled on a bench beside the stream, several hundred yards past the few mothers and children who dotted the small playground. Hattie dusted off a section of bench with her hand, then took a seat, crossing her ankles and folding her hands primly in her lap. Too restless to sit, Joe leaned against a nearby boulder.

"Continue." It wasn't quite a snarl, but it probably didn't sound too polite, either. "Please."

She gave him a brisk nod. "Right. The MacRae family curse. Well, the story goes that the first MacRae who came over here from Scotland emigrated because his wife had run into trouble for being the village witch back home. People never change, do they?" Her voice wavered for a moment, and she shook her head before continuing. "A couple of years of crop failure, and suddenly everybody starts pointing fingers at the woman who has birthed all their children and tended their dying parents. So the MacRaes left Scotland and started a trading post here. They got along well with both the French traders and the Native Americans, and for a couple of generations, all was well. In each generation, one daughter typically followed in her mother's footsteps as the local healer. Then in the mid-eighteen hundreds, there were two daughters, both of whom had unusual gifts. The younger one, Millicent, was the healer. According to the legend, she was pretty enough but nothing spectacular. Still, she was sweet and unselfish." Here, Hattie paused and sent Joe a sharp glance. Did she want to make sure he was listening?

"Much like Mel, is what you're trying to say. I get it, though I might argue the 'nothing spectacular'."

"Anyway, the story is that Millicent couldn't hold a candle to her older sister Miranda. Miranda was different in other ways too. Her abilities didn't run to healing, and they weren't as visible as her baby sister's. Miranda had the power to manipulate people, to sway their minds. I suppose it was some sort of combination of magic and natural charisma. On top of being beautiful, she was also the oldest in line to inherit the property, and the apple of her father's eye."

"In other words, a spoiled, rotten brat." He looked away from Hattie and watched a mother duck lead her ducklings into the rippling water of the stream.

"Exactly." There was a hint of warmth in her voice as she agreed, the first sign of emotion since she'd started. The softness faded as soon as she continued the tale. "Anything Miranda wanted, Miranda got. And she particularly wanted anything that belonged to her little sister. Including the sister's boyfriend."

A child shrieked and Hattie paused as they both turned to watch the laughing child being pushed on a swing by an older boy. The scene was so damn domestic it made Joe's chest hurt. He turned his gaze back to Hattie and made a small move with his head to get her to keep going.

"Millicent was engaged to a boy named Brandon, the oldest son of a local lumber baron named Morgan Talcott…"

"Talcott? As in Byron Talcott and the proposed Talcott Wilderness Resort?"

"An ancestor." Her stern look chastised him for the interruption. "Apparently the son was a different breed from the father—and the current generations. He was, the story says, genuinely in love with Millicent, at least until Miranda interfered. First she got the father to put pressure on the boy to marry the prettier, richer sister, who didn't have the reputation for being a witch. Then she cast some sort of spell on the son, forcing him to shift his affections. Her spell worked, and the wedding was scheduled just a few weeks later."

"Doesn't sound like much of a loss." Joe shook his head in disgust. "Any man who can be swayed that easily isn't worth the name."

"Interesting perspective." Hattie pursed her lips and tilted her head as if considering his point. "I tend to agree with you. But the MacRae tradition has always excused the boy and blamed Miranda exclusively. Anyhow, he did redeem himself at the last minute. On the morning of the wedding, Millicent confronted the two of them in the back room of the village church. Apparently the shock of hearing that she was pregnant was enough to snap Brandon out of his spell and remember that it was Millicent he loved.

"When he told Miranda that the wedding was off, she blew a gasket. She called down a stroke of lightning on the spot. Brandon was killed instantly, but Millicent was flung clear of the building, unconscious, but unhurt. In the fire that followed, Miranda was horribly burned, though she didn't die right away. Unfortunately, she managed to hang on for a few days."

"Her sister couldn't heal her?"

"Millicent's powers were limited, just like Mel's. She did what she could, but her sister was too far gone. Miranda didn't believe that she was trying. Right up to the end, she insisted that everything was all Millicent's fault."

"Which brings us to the curse?"

"She knew she was dying." Hattie took a deep breath, and Joe could see her chin quiver slightly. Deep lines of stress bracketed her mouth and furrowed her forehead. Her flat delivery and stoic tone had been a sham. She'd obviously heard the story many times, and had a deep emotional reaction to the tale. "She also knew she'd lost everything even if she lived. She'd lost her looks, her man, her reputation, even her father's respect, and she was predictably bitter. With her dying breath, she cursed her sister, and all her sister's descendants. She vowed that no woman of Millicent's line would ever bear a son or ever have a happy marriage."

Joe couldn't stop the small snort of laughter that escaped. "This sounds more and more like a bad soap opera."

"No comments from the peanut gallery!" Hattie glared at him, eyes narrowed. "Not if you want to hear the ending."

His lips twitched, but he repressed the smile. "My lips are sealed." He, moved his finger in an x across his chest. "Please, go on."

"I have to admit, it is pretty melodramatic." She relaxed her shoulders and rolled her eyes. "*None of your blood shall bear a son, nor have a man to keep. One daughter to bear this curse shall each generation reap.* Doesn't sound like much, does it?"

"Actually, I think it sounds like a load of horse shit."

Hattie laughed and scrubbed her hand through her short gray hair. She patted the bench beside her with a shake of her head and a weary smile. Joe left his rock and took the seat, then she took one of his hands and squeezed. "You and me both, boy. I've been trying to convince Mel of that for years. And her grandmother before her."

He shot her a conspiratorial grin. "So you don't believe in curses?"

She sobered instantly and released his hand to cross her arms over her chest. "Didn't say that. If you can't bring yourself to believe in magic, boy, then you might just as well head back east."

"Let's just say I have an open mind." In fact, he believed in far more of the paranormal than he could ever tell another living soul, but he always met each new tale with reserved judgment. The mother duck led her children back into the underbrush and out of view as he thought out his next words. "I've seen Mel with her animals, and I'm sure prepared to believe there's something magical about the woman."

"Fair enough," Hattie allowed. "Though I'll warn you. After fifty years of knowing the MacRaes, I'm ready to believe almost anything. I once watched Marty fix a boy's leg when I knew for a fact it was broken. That eagle Mel's got in her barn was shot. Twice. Thing should have been dead. Instead, she'll be setting it free in a week or two. I may not believe in the curse, but I believe in Melissa beyond a shadow of a doubt."

When Joe nodded in understanding, she went on. "What I do not believe in, however, is that one spoiled child had enough malignant power to ruin lives for over a hundred and fifty years. I don't believe she had enough power to focus a concentrated force of evil that could counteract the decades of selfless good done by Millicent's descendants."

"So why do they still believe it?"

"Because life out here in the backwoods has never been easy." She gestured at the trees and stream, a finger of the surrounding wilderness even though they were in the heart of the town. "Besides, I do believe in the psychological concept of the self-fulfilling prophecy."

"So if they think they can't have happily ever after, they'll subconsciously make sure they don't?"

"Something like that. Toss in a few coincidental accidents, and a genetic predisposition to bearing daughters, and you've got yourself a curse that seems substantiated."

"Interesting theory." Joe watched the play of dappled sunlight on the water. "So the upshot is, real or not, Mel still believes in the curse."

"With all her heart. It's the one thing Marty and I disagreed about on a regular basis. I tried to keep her from poisoning the girl's mind, but it didn't work, at least not entirely. I may have softened the impact a little. Marty really, truly hated all men. I think Mel's just afraid of them."

That fit with what Joe had observed. She wanted him, and her body had responded like wildfire, but as soon as they got physically close, she'd backed away. She'd been shocked, he'd suspected, by her own sensual nature, and her uninhibited response to his lovemaking. Surely, after discovering the joys of passion, she'd eventually be back for more. He could be patient and wait till she was ready to renew their physical relationship.

Who was he kidding? Patience wasn't exactly his strong suit. Determination, however, was. Mel would be his again, he vowed. He'd never wanted one particular woman badly enough to focus on her, but this time he did. She would be back in his bed. Soon. Then, maybe, this bizarre attraction would have the chance to burn itself out.

"Thanks for the lunch." Hattie stood, and held out her hand to Joe. "You think about what I told you, and if you have any more questions, you call me and ask."

Rising to shake her hand, he smiled. "I will. And lunch was my pleasure, Hattie. I can honestly say I'm glad to know you."

"Good. You just be sure you don't hurt my girl," the woman warned in all seriousness. "You break her heart, and I swear you'll wish you never laid eyes on me."

He believed her. He wouldn't want to get on the wrong side of this harmless looking woman. He had to resist the urge to cover his balls with his hands as he saw the glint in her eyes. He managed to give her a crisp salute instead. "Yes, ma'am. Message received."

* * * *

The tears she'd kept at bay since the previous evening finally broke as Mel watched Jezebel being towed down the tree-lined dirt road, the late afternoon sun reflecting off the few unmarked areas on the bumper. It was stupid to be so attached to a hunk of metal and rubber, but Mel's grandmother had been so fond of the crotchety vehicle that Mel had held onto it as a sort of last link to the woman who had raised her. As she cried, she knew that part of her tears were for her grandmother, even though it had been four years since Martha's death. A small voice in Mel's head said that she was probably crying about her relationship with Jonas too, but she refused to admit to that even to herself.

The deepest pain was caused by the fact that someone had gone to so much trouble for the specific purpose of hurting Mel. She'd never been popular, but she wasn't used to being outright hated either. The sheer malevolence of the act simply overwhelmed her. Who would want to do this? And why? Scariest of all was the question, what came next?

A short while later she realized she was sitting on her front steps, trying hard to breathe. Her throat hurt as did her chest and shoulders, and the collar of her shirt was soaked. She'd evidently been crying for several minutes. She mopped her face with a sweatshirt she'd found in the truck, too wiped out to care that it wasn't particularly clean.

At least she'd been alone when the storm broke, Mel thought, trying hard to find any sort of silver lining. She hadn't completely undermined her dignity by blubbering all over the tow-truck driver, whom she'd known since kindergarten. Her tenants, fortunately, were off doing their separate things. The honeymooners had driven to one of the Native-American owned casinos that dotted the region, and the Milwaukee couple was, predictably, out killing fish. More tourists would be arriving tomorrow to start the holiday weekend, but for the moment at least, Mel was blessedly alone.

She stepped inside, dumped the sweatshirt and her cotton sweater in the laundry bin and padded upstairs in her bra and jeans. After washing her face and hands, she tossed on a favorite flannel shirt that had once belonged to her grandmother, comforted by the memories infusing the soft cotton fabric. She'd had her time to wallow in misery, but moping was a luxury she simply didn't have time for. There was work to be done, she chided herself. Her patients weren't going to care if her eyes were puffy or her nose was still red. Priding herself on her sense of duty under fire, Mel squared her shoulders and marched down to the barn.

"It won't be long, now, baby," she cooed to the fawn. There was no unsteadiness in the leggy little creature's gait, and he was already eating fodder to supplement the bottled formula. She gave his velvety nose a final pat before stepping out of his stall and carefully latching the door behind her.

"Talking to your dumb animals again?" The soft sibilant voice startled Mel, causing her to shriek, and spin around. "I've got better things for you to do with that mouth, sugar." Mel knew that voice, which came from just outside the barn door. She had known it all her life.

"Sean." Her tone was as flat and unemotional as she could make it. It never paid to show fear. "What do you want?"

Well that probably wasn't the most intelligent question she'd ever asked.

"Why you, of course. And your land."

Same old song. He wanted to be the one who got her to sign the sale papers. Not only would he consider it a victory over her, a woman, but it would boost him in his father's esteem. The other part, inestimably more creepy, was also more confusing. She wasn't a raving beauty. Why would a rich, handsome man like Sean Talcott be so determined to get her into bed? Probably just because she'd always been the one girl in town who wasn't interested in him.

"You know you're not supposed to be here." Crossing her arms in front of her, Mel looked around for the hay rake. Unfortunately, it was leaning right next to the door that Sean had just stepped inside. "Your father isn't going to like this."

"He won't mind at all once you sign the purchase agreement."

Asking him to leave was pointless. So was screaming; there was no one around to hear her. She suddenly wished she hadn't chased Jonas off this morning or that the Johnstons would return to their cabin. Heck, at this point, she'd even welcome the insurance agent.

"What do you think is going to happen, Sean? That I'm going to fall in your arms and beg you to steal my land? Go away, Junior, before I do put a curse on your dick."

"Try it, bitch." The chiseled perfection of his face hardened into something ugly as he snarled. Instinctively, Mel stepped back.

"Did you know that Michigan still has laws prohibiting the practice of witchcraft?" He stepped forward, exuding menace. "They might be archaic, but they're still on the books. How does prison sound?"

A powerful screech split the air as the eagle must have sensed the disturbance in the air around it. Startled, but not deterred, Sean stepped forward again, this time closing the gap between them and grabbing Mel by the shoulders.

"Quit fighting it. You and this property are both going to be mine." He shook her shoulders to punctuate his words, throwing Mel off balance and halting her struggles to free herself from his grip.

"Let go, Sean." She glared up at him defiantly, refusing to be cowed. She tried to bring her knee up into his groin, but he twisted his body just enough that his lean, muscled thigh held her leg in place.

"Oh, I don't think so, sugar. First, I think you need a taste of what you're missing." His head lowered toward hers as Mel twisted and jabbed with her elbows, fighting to escape.

"I believe the lady said no." A deep, harsh voice interrupted from the doorway just behind Sean. "Now let her go."

Jonas! Mel's whole body sagged with relief. Never for a moment did it occur to her that he couldn't or wouldn't rescue her from Sean.

"Who the hell are you?" Her captor spun, releasing his hold on Mel so fast she stumbled, then caught herself with one hand on the stall door.

"A friend of Melissa's." Jonas's voice was calm, but there was a dangerous glint in his amber eyes. He took one step toward Sean. "And the man who is going to make sure that what you do next is get into your car and get the hell out of here as fast as it can take you."

"Oh, yeah? You obviously don't know who you're talking to, buddy. You don't want to mess with me."

"I know who your daddy is," Jonas replied. Mel was surprised at his perception, but then, there was a strong resemblance between father and son. "And I'm still going to wipe the floor with you in about two seconds."

Sean sneered. He was the taller of the two, but he had nowhere near Jonas's muscle mass. It could only be pure ego that made him think he could stand up to the out-of-towner.

Jonas moved then, so swiftly and gracefully it was just a blur. In a heartbeat, he had Sean's arm twisted behind him at an awkward and uncomfortable-looking angle.

"Do you want to press charges for assault." Jonas looked over his shoulder at Mel as he propelled a sputtering Sean to his SUV.

"No." She sighed. "He didn't actually hurt me, and his father's lawyers would have it all swept under the rug by dinnertime."

Jonas bared his teeth in a feral grin.

"Well, pal, Daddy's lawyers aren't going to save you if you come sniffing around Melissa again." Snarling, he shoved Sean roughly toward his luxury truck. "Because they won't be able to find enough pieces of you to make a case."

"Oh, you'll be hearing from my lawyers, you asshole." Sean climbed into the Escalade and turned the key, still sneering at Jonas. "You just assaulted me, remember?"

"Prove it." Jonas's retort was soft, almost pleasant, but his narrowed eyes and tight smile sent chills down Mel's spine. She was sure glad he was on her side.

Cowed, at least for the time being, Sean opted for retreat. Gunning the Caddy's engine, he sent gravel flying up at Mel and Jonas as he spun out of the drive.

Chapter Eight

"Thanks," Mel whispered. Now that Sean was gone, reaction was starting to set in. Jonas swore as he studied her face and must have noted her trembling.

"Are you hurt?" His big hands were amazingly gentle as they skimmed over her arms and ribcage, checking for injuries.

"N-no." She wasn't, not physically anyway. But she'd been scared out of her wits. "I'm fine."

"Yeah, I can see that." So quickly she didn't see it coming, he wrapped her in his arms, lifting her off her feet. Swift, sure strides took them into her cabin, where he deposited her carefully in one of her kitchen chairs. "Don't move." Before she could even think about arguing, he had stepped over to the counter and had her teakettle heating on the stove. Neither one spoke.

"Do you own a gun?" A few minutes later, he thrust a cup of steaming tea, heavily laced with fresh clover honey into her trembling hands.

"No," she whispered, obediently sipping as his hands steadied hers and guided the cup to her lips.

"Get one."

She shook her head.

"Then get a dog."

"A dog would frighten the animals I take care of," she demurred. "And, unfortunately, I don't think I could use a gun, not even in self-defense."

She could use one to defend a child, though. When Sean had been holding her, one thought that had been running through her brain was that she shouldn't fight him too hard in case she was pregnant. Of course, she couldn't be, so she'd dismissed the thought immediately. Still the fact that it had entered her mind at all left her more confused and depressed than ever.

"So can we safely assume that he's also your vandal?"

"Probably," Mel shrugged. "The hatred that he was radiating felt the same as the residual emotion I sensed around my truck. But without any evidence to prove it, the sheriff won't be able to do anything."

He growled in frustration as he paced back and forth across the kitchen. She'd intended to avoid him for a couple days, till she sorted out her feelings, but right now, Mel didn't think she could stand it if he left. She needed to feel safe and cared for even if it was only an illusion.

"Jonas," she whispered, hoping he wouldn't refuse her. Standing, she halted his pacing with a hand against his chest. "Take me to bed now. Please."

A stunned expression crossed his face, and under other circumstances she might have laughed. Right now her need was too great, too urgent. Then he growled deep in his throat, and dragged her unresisting body into his arms.

His kiss was hot, fierce, possessive, and she reveled in it, using the pleasure to drive thoughts of her near miss out of her mind. She knew Jonas had to be feeling something similar by the way his lips claimed hers, branding her as his as he carried her up the stairs to her bedroom. He stood her on her feet between her dresser and her bed then bent down to take her lips in another deep, hungry kiss. When she could barely still breathe, he pulled away and ruthlessly stripped them both of their clothes.

Mel strained against him, pleading for him to take her. He paused, holding her at arm's length, while he examined every inch of her skin, growling again when he found the faint purple finger marks that had started to show over her collarbone.

"Shit!" He closed his eyes and breathed deep, as if trying to keep control. "If I hadn't stopped by on my way home, hoping to change your mind…"

"But you did." The anguish and guilt in his voice helped her put her own distress aside for a moment. "And I'd have managed to stop him somehow, Jonas. Frankly, I'm not sure he had the guts to follow through anyway. But," she finished with a smile. "I'm glad you came."

Growling one more time, he stopped her with a kiss that seared her to her toes. She raised herself up to meet him halfway, locking her arms around his shoulders to hold him tight. He lifted her up to the top of her dresser, and she instinctively wrapped her legs around his waist.

He entered her then, swift and deep, without further preliminaries. She tilted her hips forward, welcoming his invasion. She'd forgotten about her soreness, about all the reasons why she wasn't going to do this again. All that mattered now was Jonas, his arms wrapped tightly around her, his tongue thrusting into her mouth in the same rhythm as his rock-hard erection was possessing her below. Her short nails scored his back, and her breath came in shallow gasps, punctuated by mewling cries.

"Jonas!" She shrieked as her climax exploded. When her inner muscles spasmed around him, he stiffened, calling out her name as he flooded her body with liquid heat. Then he collapsed against her, pressing her back to the mirror. A glass perfume bottle poked into her ribs, but right now, she was too replete to care.

When their breathing had almost returned to normal a few seconds later, he braced his hands on either side of her thighs and straightened, visibly unsteady. Mel slipped down from the dresser, holding his hand as they staggered toward the bed, and collapsed into a heap on top of the comforter in each other's arms.

"Thank you," she murmured, her head tucked into the curve of his throat. He smelled better than anything she'd ever known, all warm and musky and salty. She burrowed her nose against his skin to better enjoy the sensation.

He rewarded her words and actions with a soft chuckle. "If we keep this up, you're not going to be able to walk."

"It's worth it." Wincing a little, she stretched her legs, rubbing them slowly against his. "I'm sorry I clawed your back."

"You didn't."

Puzzled, she looked at the fingers of her left hand. "There's blood under my nails, doofus. Let me see your back." She couldn't believe she'd just called him that, but he didn't seem to care.

"I didn't feel anything." He nuzzled her neck. "And I don't want to move." Then a thought seemed to occur to him and he shifted, his eyes traveling down her body, and his hand combing through the wet, sticky curls between her legs.

"Are you sure the blood isn't from you? You're still new at this, and I haven't been exactly gentle." He checked his fingers. "Nope, no blood."

"Quit stalling and roll over." He was right about the tender flesh, but she knew she hadn't been bleeding again.

Heaving a huge sigh, he obliged. "Women!" Apparently his disgust had been justified, she discovered. There wasn't a mark on his back, except for a small brown smear on his right shoulder.

"Maybe you fixed it." He tugged her back into his arms as she expressed her confusion. "You have a natural healing ability, right? Maybe you nicked me, then just instinctively healed it."

"I suppose that's possible." But she didn't really believe it.

"Well, neither of us seems to be bleeding to death, so stop worrying about it."

He had a point. She was too comfortable and content to worry about anything, right now. Sure, she had plenty of concerns, but they would all wait. Burrowing her face into his chest, Mel gave herself up to the security and warmth of the strong arms that were holding her close. Then she slept.

* * * *

That had been close. Way too close. In more ways than one. Joe shuddered, as he considered the several close calls he'd had today. What would it be like to be able to completely relax with a woman, and not have to worry about guarding monumental secrets, even during moments of intimacy? He rubbed the spot on his shoulders where her nails had bitten into his flesh. Only his last-minute memory of her supposed healing abilities, and he'd had to take Hattie's word that they existed, had saved him from a long, awkward discussion. He sighed, wishing, for the first time in many years, that he was something other than himself. In Mel's arms, he really wanted to be just an ordinary Joe.

The worst of the close calls hadn't been here in the bedroom. Joe was still faintly surprised that he'd managed not to rip out Talcott's throat. It had been years since he'd felt anything on the scale of the fury that had flooded his bloodstream when he'd caught the bastard with his slimy hands on Mel, and seen the fear in her turquoise eyes. Joe had hesitated a moment out of sheer necessity, actually needed to pause and tame his reaction, to keep himself from literally killing the other man.

At the time he hadn't questioned his reaction, hadn't taken any note of the fierce surge of protectiveness and possession that the attack had aroused. While he'd been feeling a little proud of himself for his restraint, now horror slammed into him with nauseating force. Holding her while she slept in the aftermath of their lovemaking, he was forced to face the facts. Every instinct inside him had been claiming Mel as his. That's why the sex had been different this time, more intense than anything he'd ever felt before. For Joe, sex had always been just fun, an enjoyable physical release. That was all he could ever allow it to be. But today, he hadn't been just screwing around, pun intended. This time, with Melissa MacRae, he'd been *mating*!

Shit! He sagged back against the pillows, aghast, and shoved his hair back out of his face. He needed to leave, and soon. There was simply no other way around it. The only way he would be able to back off from Mel was to quit cold-turkey, because as long as he stayed anywhere near her, he wouldn't be able to resist her. The whole thing burned in his gut, scared him absolutely shitless. He'd come to Michigan to get away from it all, and instead he'd found the one thing he couldn't let himself have. A woman he could love.

He had to get out of here, but how? Oh, the answer was simple from a logistical point of view. He could just pack up his Jeep and hit the road. Sure, he'd originally come here to hide out, because a tabloid reporter had uncovered his real identity, and was stalking him, staking out his lake house in Vermont. His flat in Manhattan was probably still under surveillance as well, but that was all incidental. Joe had lots of money and a valid passport. He didn't need to stay in Sanctity, he could go anywhere in the world he pleased. So what was holding him back?

The answer snored softly in his arms. Mel. He knew he had to go, but he couldn't. Not yet. Not until something had been done about

Talcott. Joe absolutely could not leave until he was sure that Mel would be safe.

A loud gurgle intruded on his thoughts. Startled to realize it was his own stomach, Joe glanced at the clock radio beside the bed. Dinnertime had come and gone. Moving carefully, he disentangled himself from Mel and slid from the bed, then leaned back down to tuck the covers snugly around her sleeping form.

Dressed only in his jeans, his pulled his hair back into a ponytail, then rooted around in her kitchen, helping himself to salad and omelet ingredients. It pleased him, though he knew it shouldn't matter, that she didn't have a lot of meat in her fridge, just one half-empty bag of frozen chicken breasts. It wasn't that Joe had any moral objection to eating meat. Hell, humans were omnivores and a natural part of the global food chain. Joe's problem with meat was personal, not philosophical. He didn't like the way it affected his system. There'd been enough things arousing the more primitive, visceral side of his nature lately. He didn't need to compound things with the taste of animal flesh.

While the eggs were cooking, he made a couple of quick calls on his satellite phone. His agent in New York had to be contacted on a semi-regular basis or he got cranky. Same with his editor. In this instance, both of them had to be lied to concerning the amount of work Joe had gotten done so far this week. Crap! He really did need to make time for his writing. This wasn't a vacation; he was supposed to be working. And he would, as soon as Mel's safety was assured.

With that in mind, he placed another call, chatting while he cooked. Money might not be able to buy happiness, but it could sure do wonders for peace of mind. He smiled when the operator at the other end assured him of next-day-delivery. Then he checked in with his friend Kent, listened to the man's stories about his wife and kids, and fought down the pangs of jealousy, which weren't new, but had taken on a whole new level of intensity. Finally, he dialed the graduate student who periodically handled research for him and assigned a few tasks. If he wasn't going to write a book about witches, he needed another topic.

When his culinary masterpiece was finished, he plated it up and placed it on a tray along with the salad, some homemade bread he'd found, and a pot of green tea. Though he'd never delivered a meal to anyone in bed before in his life, he didn't feel strange about it.

Mel had had an exceptionally difficult day; she deserved a little pampering.

"How are you feeling?" he asked, as he watched her sit up against the headboard, and tuck the sheet snugly over her breasts and under her arms.

"Fine," she answered shyly. "I'm not sick or anything, you know. You didn't need to feed me in bed."

He could tell she wasn't used to any kind of special treatment, and it pleased him to be the one to provide it. "I wanted to," he answered, sitting cross-legged on the bed beside her and helping himself to his own plate. "And I know you're not sick. Believe me, I'm very aware of that fact." He waggled his eyebrows in an exaggerated leer, then turned serious again. "But you have had a rough couple of days."

Her smile vanished in a heartbeat, making him wish he hadn't reminded her.

"You know," she began. "Earlier today when you stopped by, I was trying to break things off with you."

"I got that impression." He chewed slowly as he watched her, waiting to see where she was going with this.

"I'm sorry. You know I don't have much experience with this sort of thing. I meant to tell you that it had been fun, but since we both knew it wasn't going anywhere, we shouldn't see each other again."

"Go on."

"But that isn't what I really want. I don't know the etiquette, how things are supposed to work, so please don't get offended if I say this wrong."

She paused, shooting him a look that he couldn't interpret. All he could do was nod, and hope she'd continue. She did, but stared down at her plate instead of looking at him. "We both know this isn't forever. You're only here for the summer, and that's okay." She flushed, and this time she did look up at him, a world of vulnerability in her wide-open eyes. "Would it be wrong of me to say that I'd like to sleep with you again? To have an—an affair for the rest of the summer? Or at least until one of us gets tired of it?"

It wasn't what he had expected to hear. She hadn't told him to get lost, and a huge wave of relief that he didn't want to feel crashed through him, roaring in his ears. The only thought that registered was that he didn't have to give her up. Not just yet.

"Let me get this straight," he growled. "You want to know if I'd mind a short term, no-strings-attached fling with the woman who's given me the hottest sex I've ever had. Right? Geez, woman, do you think I'm nuts? In case you hadn't noticed, Mel, I'm a guy. No red-blooded male in the world could refuse that offer!" Not that she'd better make it to any other guy!

"Of course I noticed you were a guy." Her lopsided smile made something in his stomach twist. "I wouldn't be interested otherwise."

Her skin turned pink as she teased him, and he took the plates and cups, then set them in a haphazard pile on the floor beside the bed. He loved the fact that she could blush even while sitting stark naked in bed with the guy who had just made love to her. The guy who was about to make love with her all over again.

* * * *

Jonas didn't come to her cabin every day. Sometimes it seemed like weeks between their 'dates', but in reality, only ten days had passed since they'd first made love. Which meant, she thought with only a little bit of shame, it had been less than two weeks since they'd met.

"So your powers have stabilized?"

Hattie sat with Mel at her kitchen table, sipping tea and staring out the window at the rainy afternoon.

"So far," Mel agreed, looking down at her teacup to hide her flush. "I haven't had any problems in the past few days."

"And you've tried?"

"Sure." She shrugged. "I do little stuff around the house all the time, taking care of my plants, the animals, whatever. And those are the abilities that had really been failing."

She'd added a new patient in the last few days, a raccoon who had lost one foot to a trap. Though it was beyond the scope of her ability to regenerate a missing limb, she'd cleaned out the infection, and easily closed the gaping wound. Right now the fat little guy was eating his head off, and learning to get around with his stump. If it was nice out tomorrow, she'd probably be letting him go.

"Well, your usual green thumb seems to be back in evidence." Hattie inspected the kitchen, smiling in approbation at Mel's potted herbs, which had regained their normal lushness. A week ago they had been drooping and bedraggled. "How's Gladys?"

"Dying." All Mel's grief and helpless frustration were summed up in the single tense word. "But you know that. What you're asking is if my powers still work to help her. The answer is yes. Thankfully, that's the one area where they've never wavered."

"How about auras? Are you back to normal with those?"

Mel had never kept secrets from Hattie, not even as a teenager. It was such a relief to have one person in the world who knew everything about her and still didn't treat her like a freak. Hattie accepted Mel's unusual abilities as basic traits just like her red hair and blue-green eyes.

"Mostly. I still can't make heads or tails out of Jonas's. It swirls like a kaleidoscope. There's something out of the ordinary about him, Hat." She chewed on her lower lip in consternation. "Something—different. Maybe even—like me."

"You think he might be a witch?"

"No, not a witch," Mel assured her friend. "Not a warlock either. But there's something odd about him, something I can't pin down." She swirled her teacup as she thought about it. It definitely had to do with his eyes, though. Somehow, those penetrating amber eyes were the key.

"Well, let me know if you figure it out," Hattie replied, dry amusement crackling in her voice. "Now get back to the juicy parts. Have you had sex with him more than the one time?"

"Harriette!"

"Judging by that blush, I'd guess you have. He's good then? You're enjoying it?"

Okay, she'd never kept secrets from Hattie, but this was way more detail than she wanted to get into with a woman she thought of as a parent. After a few moments, she sighed. Hattie wasn't going to let her off the hook, so she might as well confess. "He's incredible!" More than that, he was addictive. Each time he'd come to her cabin in the last few days, she'd welcomed him with open arms. And legs.

"So I was right. Your power fluctuations were simply your mind and body letting you know that you've neglected an important aspect of your life."

"Sex isn't important Hattie," Mel contradicted. "Love maybe, but we both know I can't have that."

"That's horse shit, little girl, on all counts!" The crude language might have seemed incongruous coming out of such a refined-looking, silver-haired lady, but Mel was accustomed to Hattie's plain speaking.

"First of all, sexuality *is* an important part of life, including your life. It's also a part of your nature that you've completely denied for the past twenty years or so. That simply isn't healthy.

"Secondly, never forget that love comes in many different forms. You may never have had a lover before, but you have always been loved, Melissa."

"Oh, Hattie, I know that! You and Gran were the best parents I could have asked for. But that isn't what I meant, and you know it."

"No, we weren't the best possible parents, but that's another conversation. I do know exactly what you meant, and you're wrong about that, too. What you have going with Jonas Pierce is more than just sex. I know you far too well to believe you could be involved with a man you didn't care for."

Mel opened her mouth to interrupt, but Hattie held up one slender hand. "Shush! I'm not finished. What you feel for Jonas may not be, probably isn't, a forever-and-ever kind of love. You haven't really known him long enough for that. Since you both went into this affair with the agreement that it wasn't going to be permanent, that's fine. Still, that doesn't mean you don't love him, in some sense of the word, or he you. I strongly suspect that long after this affair is over, he'll still hold a special place in your heart. Right?"

"Right." Drat, she hated it when Hattie knew her better than she did herself!

"That's okay, darling. Enjoy it. Love him for the summer, then move on with your life. You've needed this for a long time, needed to wake up and admit that you're a flesh-and-blood woman. Too much abstinence simply isn't healthy."

"But you never have sex. Neither did Gran!" Her face reddened again as she regretted the words that had tumbled out before she could stop them.

"Do you really believe that?" Hattie leveled her piercing, ice-blue eyes at Mel. "Do you?"

Abruptly reminded of her earlier conversation with Karen, Mel considered the two women who had raised her in a whole new light. "I don't know," she replied choosing her words with care. She paused and licked her lips. "Why don't you tell me?"

The older woman tensed her shoulders, and gripped her teacup so tightly that the porcelain nearly cracked. The she stared out the window into the murky rain. "There was one other issue, along with the so-called MacRae curse, about which your grandmother and I disagreed. I thought you and your mother before you had a right to know. Marty insisted on remaining firmly in the closet. In her defense, Sanctity is a very small town. I would have almost certainly lost my job in the early years if we'd gone public. Being a lesbian was a far, far bigger taboo for our generation than it is for yours."

"I see." But she didn't really. Her mind was whirling. How could she not have known? Karen had obviously guessed, but Mel had remained in blissful, or maybe willful, ignorance.

"I loved Martha," Hattie stated with firm conviction. "She was my friend, my lover, my soul mate, my other half. We were together for forty-six years, and my only regret is that it wasn't longer. And yes," she looked Mel in the eyes now and nodded calmly. "To answer your next question, we enjoyed a very healthy and satisfying sex life right up until the end."

"I see." She sounded like a parrot, but right now she was too muddled to care. "So Karen was right. The curse only applies to marriage. Long-term relationships are apparently okay. Or maybe it's just men. Being gay could have been the perfect loophole."

"Young lady, my relationship with your grandmother was not a loophole!" Icy blue eyes narrowed. "And even though I disagreed with her on certain issues, you will notice that I respected her wishes. I expect you to respect them as well, understand?"

"Oh, don't worry Hattie. I'm not going to spill the beans. And I'm not being flip either." She stood, and moved quickly around the table to wrap Hattie in a fierce embrace. "I'm glad, really. I'm delighted that both of you found that kind of happiness in life. A little envious, maybe, but glad all the same."

"Don't be jealous. You are a smart, sweet, loving young woman, and I've never believed that you were destined to spend your life alone. You can find your own happiness, Melissa. I'm so relieved that you're finally opening yourself up to those possibilities."

This wasn't a direction Mel wanted to follow, so she perched on the edge of the table and vented her own curiosity instead. "Did you always know that you were…?"

"A lesbian?" Hattie offered bluntly. "Pretty much. I knew I wasn't cut out for a husband and children. I'd dated a little, but it was never very appealing. Then in college, another girl approached me, and suddenly, there it was—the magic I'd been missing. Of course, back then, it was even less socially acceptable than it is now, so it wasn't something you talked about. Not even to your grandchildren."

"Gran never lived anyplace but here," Mel stated, her curiosity piqued. "How did you and she…"

"Get together? You know that part Mel. I was the social worker assigned to her after the rape. I didn't want to take advantage of her, though. We didn't become lovers for several years, and then only after she let me know in no uncertain terms that it was her idea."

"Was it because of the rape?"

"That we met? Yes. I was working out of Escanaba, and Martha rarely left Sanctity."

"No, I mean…" Mel couldn't come up with a graceful way to ask the question, but Hattie knew her too well. The older woman shot her a disgusted look, and laughed.

"Heavens no, Mel. Martha was born a lesbian, just like I was. It isn't something you become, sweetie, it's something you are. The rape did have an impact in so many other ways. It took her innate distrust of men and magnified it into a phobia. Your mother rebelled against that by looking for male approval in any form she could get it. You simply grew into a woman who is too staunchly independent for her own good."

To change the subject, and because she couldn't resist lightening the mood a little by teasing, Mel grinned. "So there's no chance I could convert, huh? It could make my life a whole lot easier."

"Sorry, kid. You are definitely one hundred percent straight—to your Gran's eternal disappointment. It killed her to think you'd have a man in your life one day. Almost as much as it killed her to watch your mother throw her life away on drugs and men in general. That was the one thing that relieved her—the fact that though you weren't like her, you also weren't anything like Marilyn."

"It's like she never existed, isn't it? I can't remember her at all, and I'm nothing like her."

"No, you're stronger, smarter than she was. Your mother was so very needy, so insecure, that she took any route she could find to feel wanted or happy. You, thank heavens, know that happiness comes from the inside."

Mel's mother Marilyn had been real to Hattie. Mel realized for the first time that Hattie had helped raise Marilyn too, and that when she'd died, Hattie had in effect lost a daughter. Mel wished she could remember the young woman who had died of an overdose when Mel was a toddler. She'd only been nineteen, over a decade younger than Mel was now.

"None of us MacRaes have a lot in common, do we? Gran, Mom, and me, we're all such different people."

"Oh, not entirely," Hattie countered fondly. "I like to think a little of Mart lives on in you. You and Marilyn both got Mart's smile, and you certainly have her stubbornness and strength of purpose. I like to think there's a little of me in you too, though not in your genes. I tried to teach you a little bit about thinking for yourself and questioning society's expectations."

"You did." It was true, and Mel could only be grateful.

"Well, that includes your grandmother's expectations, and beliefs, Mel. Don't accept that a hundred-year-old story has the power to rule your life. Your life is what you make of it, baby. Promise me you'll remember that."

"I will," she vowed, then stood and leaned over for another hug. "I love you, Hattie. Thanks for being part of my family."

Hattie's eyes misted. "I love you too, sweetheart. And I'm very proud of the woman you've become."

"I wish I could risk having kids," Mel sighed. "That someday I could be as good a mother as you and Gran were to me."

"You'll be better," Hattie insisted. "And I still think it will happen for you, one day, if you let it. But there's no rush. Enjoy your summer fling. Even *I* can tell he's a hot one. Make the most of it."

"I intend to." Mel grinned widely. "Every minute of it."

* * * *

"You're sure you don't mind?" Mel cast Hattie a worried glance. It had been two days since their heart-to-heart chat at Mel's kitchen table. After several days of wind and rain, the weather had finally cleared. The warm sunny afternoon was ideal for truck-shopping, but she hated to impose further on Hattie. "The couple from Saginaw said they'd be here by about two, and I have no idea when the three college boys will arrive."

"I've done this before, you know." Hattie shook her head and grinned. "I think I can handle a couple of check-ins."

The upcoming holiday weekend was the official start of Mel's busy season, and she really needed a new truck before the summer got underway. So why was she standing here on her porch dithering? "I've got the new satellite phone just in case."

She saw Hattie and Jonas exchange knowing looks, but she decided to ignore it. She'd reluctantly accepted his gift. If the phone gave the pair of them some peace of mind, she could live with that. She hated to admit it, but it was comforting to know she could reach him if she ran into any trouble. She'd insisted on paying for the monthly service herself, though. She wasn't going to give up all her independence.

"If you don't hit the road, it'll be dark before you get to Marquette," Hattie pointed out. "Go on. I'll be fine." Mel gave Hattie a hug, then climbed into Jonas's Jeep.

"Why Marquette?" Jonas waved goodbye to Hattie as he maneuvered the Jeep down the gravel drive. "Aren't Escanaba and St. Ignace both closer?"

"Marquette's bigger. And I thought maybe we could stop at the mall while we're there."

"Aha! Your secret is out. This is really a glorified shopping trip."

"Well, maybe in part." She saw the little crinkles around his eyes and relaxed. She wasn't used to being teased by anyone but Karen, but with Jonas, it felt right. "I don't get a chance to go to the mall very often."

"Well, your chauffeur also carries packages, so you're in luck." He shot her a lascivious grin, and waggled his eyebrows. "Of course, I'll be expecting a bigger tip."

She rolled her eyes, though he was watching the road and probably couldn't see her. "You already got your tip this morning." And it had been wonderful. He'd arrived early to pick her up, and introduced Mel to the joys of making love in the shower.

"No, that was incentive, and a very good one. Tonight is payback."

"Yum. What kind of payback?" Her voice trembled as she pondered the possibilities, and he uttered a low growl she took for approval. Apparently he liked knowing that she wanted him.

"Tonight," he decreed, satisfaction fairly dripping from his voice. "Tonight, I get to spend the night."

Mel went still, but she didn't argue. She could understand that he was getting tired of sneaking home every night like a teenager, and she had to admit, the idea of waking up beside him in the morning held tremendous appeal. She gave a contented sigh, and laid her hand on his thigh. "Okay. I'd like that."

Gripping the wheel so tightly it looked like he was having trouble staying on the road, Jonas groaned. "Maybe I should pull over. We haven't done it in the Jeep. Yet."

A nervous giggle escaped her throat. He wasn't serious, was he? Since he wasn't slowing down, she assumed he wasn't. "Maybe later."

Bleep. Bleep.

Jumping at the electronic interruption, Mel sighed. This couldn't be good. She pulled out her pager and took a quick glance.

"It's Karen." During the past week or so she'd told him a little about Karen and Gladys. "I have to go."

"Of course you do." His matter-of-fact tone made her heart swell. It was so good of him to understand her need to help. He stopped the Jeep at the next intersection. "Which way?"

She gave him directions to the little residential area south of town. When they pulled to a stop in front of the Clark's sprawling Victorian house, Mel leaned over to kiss him, only to be confounded when he climbed out of the car and opened her door before she could even react.

"You don't have to come in." She shook her head as he handed her out of the car. "I'm going to be a while."

"I know," he acknowledged. "But you'll need a ride home, and I want to meet your friends."

There was no use fighting him once he'd decided on a course of action; Mel had learned that much over the last several days. Shrugging, she let him follow her to the door.

Karen poked her head out the front door, and blinked when she saw Jonas. She immediately hid her surprise and held the screen door wide. "You must be Jonas. Thanks for bringing Mel. Come in."

Mel knew she should introduce Jonas to Karen, but she had no idea what to say, so she ignored him and focused on her friend. "Anything different?"

"Have a seat, Jonas. Mel will be a while." As usual, Karen didn't seem at all flustered, even though Mel had never brought a man with her in her life. They all stepped into the cozy living room, and Karen gestured to a chair before responding to Mel. "Nothing new, just more of the same. Dad's at work."

She looked so tired, Mel thought. Who knew, maybe having a handsome visitor to talk to while Mel was with Gladys would be a helpful distraction for her friend. She dropped a quick kiss on Karen's cheek and waved her into a seat while she continued through the living room and up the stairs. Poking her head into the sunny yellow room filled with pictures of Karen and her children, and even a couple of herself as a child, she steeled her emotions.

"Hey, you awake?"

The emaciated figure on the bed opened wide brown eyes and offered a fleeting smile. "Hi, Melissa." Her voice was a husky croak. "Was that your new boyfriend I heard come in with you?"

"Umm—I guess so." Yikes, had everyone in town heard about Jonas? How much had Karen told her mother?

"The ladies from church stop by, and they try to keep me up on all the news," Gladys whispered as though she'd heard Mel's thoughts. "Rosa says he's a hunk."

"He is." Mel couldn't argue that one. "He's a historian from New York City."

"Can I meet him?" Gladys closed her eyes again. She'd lost weight in the past few days, Mel noted with a profound sense of sadness, and she'd gone completely bald from her last attempt at chemo.

"If you want." Mel couldn't deny the woman anything. She just hoped Jonas wouldn't mind. "Let's get you fixed up a little bit first."

"Okay."

Mel sat on the side of the bed, and clasped both of the older woman's hands in hers. The skeletal fingers were cold to the touch, forcing Mel to swallow the lump in her throat before she could focus. Finally, she pulled herself together and closed her eyes, willing her consciousness to expand and brush against Gladys's.

The waves of pain swamped her at first, making her wonder how Gladys had even managed to open her eyes, let alone smile. Mel's body swayed, but her mind remained firm as she allowed her own life force to absorb some of the pain, whisking it away from her friend. She couldn't explain how this worked, doubted there was a scientific explanation, but right now she didn't care. All that mattered was that Mel had the power to provide some relief. The pain was massive today, wracking every cell of Gladys's frail body. Mel's own breath grew labored, while she absorbed as much of the pain as she could. Then she paused, leaning back against the headboard alongside her patient.

"Thanks, sweetie." Gladys spoke in a stronger voice a few minutes later, once Mel had gotten her breathing back under control. "Could I have a drink now?"

"Sure thing." Forcing herself to ignore the pain and fatigue she had absorbed, Mel dragged herself to her feet. The discomfort would pass, as it always did. Taking the glass of Gatorade from the nightstand, she held the straw to Gladys's pale lips.

"Thanks."

"Hungry?" This short session had provided a brief respite from the worst of her symptoms, but it wouldn't last too long. After a while, when Mel had recovered her stamina, they'd do it again, but that time Mel would end the session with a strong suggestion to sleep. Then Gladys would have several hours of peaceful rest, which was becoming increasingly rare as the disease progressed. "Want something to eat?"

"Sure." Gladys smiled. "I hear my daughter bought Twinkies today."

At this stage, the patient got anything she could or would eat. Long-term nutrition had ceased to matter.

"Sounds good. Maybe I'll swipe one on my way out."

Still dragging, she made her way back to the living room, finding Jonas and Karen in deep conversation. Karen sat cross-legged on the sofa, and the lines of stress and fatigue on her face had eased. Apparently Mel wasn't the only one who found Jonas's company therapeutic. Jonas sprawled in a leather recliner, looking relaxed and at home.

"Your mom's hungry," Mel announced, interrupting their chat. She wasn't jealous, was she? Absolutely not. "She mentioned something about Twinkies. And she wants to meet Jonas. It seems somebody told her I had a new boyfriend." She used her fingers to symbolize quotation marks, hoping Jonas would realize that the label wasn't from her. She shot him an anxious glance. "You don't mind, do your?"

"Not at all." He nodded to Karen, then with few quick strides, he joined Mel at the stairway, and wrapped one arm snugly about her waist, as if sensing her need for support. She guided him up the stairs and down the hallway. Then she slumped against the doorjamb, and watched in awe as he sat in a chair beside the bed, and chatted with Gladys as if he'd known her forever. The man was simply a chick magnet. Women of all ages couldn't help falling under his spell. As annoying as it was to feel like one of a crowd, she couldn't help a sense of pride as well. Nobody liked being in a sickroom, so it meant a lot to her that Jonas would do this.

Later, while Karen took Gladys her lunch, Mel and Jonas sat in Karen's small but cheerful kitchen, helping themselves to sandwich fixings. As her depleted strength returned, she managed to finish half a turkey and cheese sandwich, while Jonas polished off an entire bowl of egg salad. They sat kitty-corner at the small Formica table where Mel and Karen had shared girl talk as teenagers. It was both weird and exciting to see him in the places that made up her life.

"So what were you and Karen discussing so intently?" So what if she sounded a little bitchy even to her own ears. He was *her* hunky new boyfriend right? And Karen was her best friend.

"Hockey, mostly." His grin suggested he understood her idiotic jealously, and fortunately, he didn't seem to mind. The answer rang true as well. Karen was a rabid Red Wings fan, and Jonas had admitted a fondness for the Islanders. Then he chuckled wickedly. "And you."

"Me?" Could that high-pitched squeak have possibly been her voice?

"Yes, you. She filled me in on what you've been doing for her and Gladys. She wanted to make sure I know just how special you are." Leaning across the corner of the table, he kissed the tip of her nose. "When will you be ready to leave?"

"Probably an hour or so." Glancing up at the clock on the wall, she sighed. "We'll still have enough time to go truck-shopping, but I guess the mall will have to wait."

"We could have dinner in Marquette," he offered. "Then go to the mall after we eat. I'm sure Hattie wouldn't mind holding the fort for a few extra hours."

It was so tempting. How wonderful it would be to spend the afternoon and evening on the town with Jonas, away from Sanctity and all its problems. It would be almost like they were a real couple. She hesitated, still reluctant to ask Hattie for yet another favor.

He must have sensed her struggle, because he squeezed her hand.

"Or, we could just play it by ear." His simple words lifted the pressure she hadn't even realized she felt.

They joined Karen and Gladys in the sickroom where they all visited for half an hour. When Gladys's strength began to fade again, Mel shooed Karen and Jonas from the room.

"So what do you think? Is he as hunky as your sources told you?" She squeezed Gladys's fragile hand as she sat down beside her on the bed.

"Oh absolutely!" Gladys sighed dramatically. "Karen was right—he's definitely a keeper. You should marry him!"

CHAPTER NINE

Patience was seriously overrated.

It wasn't that he didn't like Mel's friend Karen, but how long was he going to have to sit here making conversation when both of them knew that the other's thoughts were up the stairs in the sunny yellow bedroom?

It had been twenty minutes since Mel had kicked them out of Gladys's room, and they had already exhausted the topics of hockey, Sanctity, and Joe's supposed book on the American Revolution. He had to suppress an unfamiliar pang of guilt every time that subject came up. He'd meant to tell Mel the truth about what he did for a living, but somehow the subject had just never come up. Who was he kidding? He was just chicken. He was wallowing in the ability to be with a woman who only knew him as Jonas Pierce, not J. P. Wolfe, famous author. It was such a relief not to have to wonder whether she liked him for himself, for his wallet, or for his connections.

Besides, he'd hesitated so long that telling her the truth now would be risky. He should have come clean before he'd slept with her, or at the very least after the first time. She'd be hurt at his lack of trust, and knowing Mel, probably pissed off too. And he simply wasn't ready to lose her yet. Now he sat here, his gut twisting every time he told the familiar lies. This guilt thing was new to him, and he didn't like it a bit.

"Don't hurt her," Karen warned, and Joe was dragged back into the conversation at hand. "She's had so much of that, and she doesn't deserve it."

"Anyone who tries to hurt her is going to have to go through me to do it," he answered gruffly, amazed and horrified to discover that he meant it.

"Good." Karen tapped her fingers on the arm of her chair, turning her head toward the stairs. "It shouldn't be much longer."

A door closed above them, so Joe followed her gaze. Mel staggered into view, leaning heavily on the stair rail. He stood instinctively, needing to go to her. Her pallor was terrifying. She'd said that healing took a lot out of her, but this was ridiculous. Her normally pink cheeks were chalk-white, and her breathing was ragged.

"She's asleep." Even her voice was weak. Joe moved swiftly toward the steps.

"Thanks." Joe heard the concern in Karen's voice, but it didn't really register until she continued. "Mel, are you all right?"

She wasn't. She was halfway down the flight of stairs when she fell, and he only just managed to catch her before she hit the floor.

"Does this happen every time?" He cradled Mel in his arms and followed Karen up the stairs.

"No. Not like this." Karen sounded nearly as worried as he was. Not good.

He laid Mel on an antique-looking patchwork quilt in what was obviously Karen's own bedroom, then covered her with another quilt from a bench at the foot of the bed.

"Should we call a doctor?"

"I don't know," Karen confessed anxiously. "If she doesn't come out of it in a few minutes, I'll call my dad."

She must have caught his curious look, because she explained. "He's a doctor, but he understands Mel. Her physiology isn't always, well, normal. She doesn't usually get along very well with most of the traditional medical community."

"Right." Well, that was something they had in common.

"Her pulse is okay, and her breathing is shallow, but steady," Karen announced. She'd apparently picked up some basics from her physician father. "I'm going to go check on Mom. This isn't normal. Something must be very wrong."

"I'll wait here, keep an eye on Mel." Since he was sitting beside her on the bed, holding her hand, his statement was probably redundant. Karen slipped out of the room. Silently, Joe watched Mel's pale face for signs of returning consciousness. She hadn't stirred by the time Karen returned a few minutes later.

"Sleeping." Sinking onto the padded oak bench, Karen cast him a helpless look. Joe didn't consider himself particularly empathetic, but he couldn't help feeling her grief and wishing he could help. "This will have to be the last time, then. I won't let Mel risk herself like this. It's time for drugs."

From what Joe had been told and deduced, it was only a matter of weeks, maybe days, for Gladys. Any other patient at this stage would be strapped to a hospital bed with an arm full of IV's. Mel had taken the place of heavy narcotics for her friend's mother, so the woman's precious last days could be spent at home, and lucid, rather than in a drug-induced stupor. Mel might wish she could do more, but what she was doing was probably the greatest gift anyone could give to Gladys and her family. Time.

Here was another reason he couldn't leave yet. Mel was going to be devastated when Gladys died, and she'd need some emotional support. Besides, he had an idea. Maybe he could do something else to help.

"Can she draw on someone else, do you think?" he wondered out loud. "Tap into another person to share the energy cost?"

"I don't know," Karen answered slowly. "What a good idea. Maybe I can help."

"You've got your hands full already," he demurred. "I don't think you have much strength to spare. No, I was thinking of me."

Dark eyebrows lifted, but Karen didn't say a word. They both watched Mel's inert form intently, their joint concern growing by the minute.

"I should call my dad," Karen sighed finally, hauling herself to her feet.

"Don't."

"Mel?" Joe and Karen cried out in unison.

"I'm all right," murmured the slurred voice from the pillows. Her eyes fluttered open, and it was one of the most beautiful sights he'd ever seen. "Just give me a minute."

"We've already given you ten," he barked. This was why he avoided intimate relationships, damn it. You had to share other people's pain, feel things you didn't want to feel. Why couldn't this thing with Mel have continued to be just about sex, the way he'd intended?

"I'm fine," Mel insisted, struggling to sit up. "I was overtired, that's all." She brushed her hair back behind her ears and glanced up at Karen in concern. "Gladys is okay, isn't she?"

"Sleeping." Karen and Joe chorused.

"Good." Leaning heavily on Joe, she managed to stand, swaying noticeably. "So much for truck shopping. Jonas, please take me home."

He let her walk to the car mostly under her own steam, but once they were back at her place, under the concerned eye of Hattie, he had no qualms about asserting his own authority.

"Bed." His hand on her waist both propelled her toward the stairs and supported most of her weight.

"I don't need to…"

"Well, I damned well do!" he yelled in response to her protest. Then he groaned. The last thing she needed right now was him going nuts on her. He kissed the top of her head in silent apology. "I'm sorry, sweetheart. But you're about as steady as a half-drowned kitten, and you scared ten years off my life." He'd never forget the sheer terror he'd felt when he saw her pitch down that staircase, and he wanted to wrap her in cotton to keep her safe. He forced his voice to gentle, and his fists to unclench. "Go lay down for an hour or so. Please."

She sagged against his arm as the fight leeched out of her. "Okay, but you'd better tell Hattie I'm fine before she takes your head off."

Hattie did bear a distinct resemblance to a lioness guarding her only cub, but Jonas wasn't worried about that. Joe could handle anything the older woman dished out, as long as Mel was okay. "You're not fine!" Again, he forced his voice to gentle. "At the very least you're overextended and exhausted." Then he flashed Hattie what he hoped was a reassuring grin. "But as far as I can tell, that's all that's wrong with her. She passed out at Gladys's."

"Gladys's?" Hattie's silver head tilted inquisitively. "So you never made it to Marquette?"

"Nope." He scooped Mel into his arms before she could fall down again, and started up the stairs. "I'll explain in a minute," he called back over his shoulder.

He did over coffee, seated in a wooden rocking chair on Mel's wide front porch.

"Thanks for bringing her home," Hattie offered after Joe finished the story. "She can be prickly as a porcupine when anybody tries to take care of her."

"Yeah, fortunately I have a very thick skin." He suppressed a grin at the ironic truth behind that seemingly innocuous statement.

"You've been here a lot these last few days."

"Yeah." Oh great, where was she going with this?

"Any more trouble she hasn't told me about?"

Ah. This wasn't about his intentions, then, but checking up on Mel's safety. He could deal with that issue. "Not much. Somebody flattened her mailbox, which *could* have been an accident, and there have been a couple of hang-ups on her phone. She's getting caller I. D. installed next week." Only after a long argument, but he'd eventually won her agreement. He didn't tell Hattie about that part.

A short while later, Hattie left, after having taught Joe how to handle checking in a new tenant, or in this case, tenants. The three fraternity boys went to their cabin with the idea that there would be no partying on the premises, and the understanding that any trouble they tried to cause would be dealt with by Joe. They seemed harmless enough, but Mel certainly didn't need any additional hassles at the moment.

Feeling like the walls were closing in on him, he prowled uselessly around the cabin, wishing he had his laptop with him. He desperately needed to get some work done, but he wasn't going to leave Mel alone while he went to get it. His skin tingled and his muscles twitched. It must be closer to the full moon than he'd realized. This was odd. He'd changed several times in the last couple weeks, and usually once or twice was enough to hold him for a month, especially if he was getting laid on a regular basis.

Weird or not, the urge was simply too powerful to fight. As much as this unexplained loss of control over himself worried him, he wasn't going to be able to think rationally or do anything about it till he'd dealt with his body's demand. He walked out the back door and into the bushes, then after making sure there was no one around to see, he stripped off his clothes, stacking them neatly beneath a bush.

Closing his eyes, he allowed the power to infuse his body, to take it over. Moments later he stood on all fours, stretching his long, furry body. Then he began a slow, loping circuit of the area.

Keeping the house in sight and earshot was no problem; his senses, even in wolf form, were uncannily attuned to Mel. He'd know when she woke. He monitored the other cabins, noting nothing out of the ordinary. The couple who had arrived while he and Mel were at Karen's was still unpacking their station wagon, so he steered clear of that unit. He didn't want to cause a panic among the guests. Most people were afraid to encounter a wolf up close and personal.

But not Mel. She'd been as warm and welcoming of him in wolf form as she had of the man. Actually, he corrected himself, she'd been even less wary of the wolf. Animals didn't seem to scare her nearly as much as sexual attraction. Fortunately for him, she seemed to be getting over that. It was fun to help her discover her own sensuality. She might not be very experienced, but once she'd gotten past her initial reticence, she'd become a creative and enthusiastic partner. These last few days had been filled with the most intensely erotic sex that Joe had ever known.

Sticking to the verge of the woods, Joe ran, stretching and working the taut, ropy muscles of his canine body. The bright mid-afternoon sun filtered through the evergreen boughs, creating vividly striped shadows that challenged his keen sense of sight. He heard and smelled small animals scurrying through the underbrush away from him. They were safe, though his lupine instincts urged him to hunt, and his sharp-fanged mouth watered for the taste of flesh. He would not, could not, act the predator, as either wolf or man. He might not be able to control his body's need to change now and then, but he could and would control his actions in both forms. It had taken years of discipline and determination, but he was no longer a creature of his instincts. The taste of blood and flesh only increased the pull of his animal nature, and he'd learned that refusing to indulge helped him maintain his control. So, at this moment, Jonas Pierce was very likely the world's only vegetarian wolf.

There were no intruders on the property during the hour or so he watched. Tenants came and went, including a boisterous young family. Watching the children laugh and run caused him a pang of envy. Years ago he had come to the decision that it would be unfair of him to pass his tainted genes onto another generation. The curse would end with him; hence the vasectomy. He still believed he'd made the right decision, but that didn't mean he didn't occasionally wish things could be different.

It was late afternoon when his pointed ears detected sounds of movement from the house. Not wanting Mel to find herself alone upon waking, he hurried back to his clothes, changed, and dressed. He was waiting in the kitchen when Mel descended the stairs.

"I thought you'd gone." She smiled as she walked toward him.

"No." Meeting her halfway, he pulled her into his arms, and dropped a kiss onto her nose. "I just went for a walk around the cabins."

It must have been a good enough answer, because she stood on her tiptoes to plant a brief but sexy kiss on his lips.

"I take it you're feeling better?"

"Much."

"So that's how your healing ability works. You don't just make the pain disappear, you absorb it into yourself."

"Umm-hmm." She averted her eyes.

"And it knocks you on your ass." He tried unsuccessfully to keep the anger out of his voice. He did manage to keeps his hands from clenching around her slender shoulders.

"Only for a little while. I sort of absorb it, then it dissipates. It's never been that bad before, though."

"Has it ever occurred to you that you can't single-handedly save the entire world?"

"Now and again." She reached up and touched his cheek. "I do know that, Jonas, believe me. I couldn't save my mom, or my grand-mother, and I can't save Gladys. I only wish I could."

"That isn't what I meant."

"I know, you're thinking about me, and that's sweet, but you don't need to worry. The pain I absorb passes quickly. All I need is some sleep, and it just fades away. For Gladys, it's a constant companion. If I can take it away for a few hours, it's worth the cost."

"I suppose. I still don't like it, but I guess I understand." Her wistful smile tugged at emotions he would have sworn a week ago he didn't possess. "I know what you need."

"What?" This time her smile was perkier, lit with curiosity and sensuality.

"A night on the town. Let's pretend, just for a little while, that we're normal people. We can get dressed up, drive to the nearest big city, have a nice dinner and go to a movie. What do you think?"

"I think that underneath your crusty academic exterior, you're really a big softie," she returned. "It's a great idea."

"Then go put on your dancing shoes, woman."

* * * *

They ended up in Escanaba, which she supposed was a pretty small town by any standards other than those of Upper Michigan. It did, however, boast a theater and a selection of restaurants. They settled on Chinese stir-fried vegetables, and the latest spy thriller. Mel had chosen the movie over Jonas's protests, aware that anything romantic or touching was bound to make her cry. Her emotions were riding so close to the surface these days.

"Would you like to go dancing?" Jonas tugged her body close to his as they left the theater hand in hand. She leaned into him, enjoying the feel of his heat up against her. The tingle she felt whenever he touched her hadn't faded with familiarity like she'd expected. Now it went clear through to her heart as well. "I spotted a nightclub just down the street."

She let out a contented giggle. "It's not a nightclub, Jonas, it's a bar. Nightclubs are definitely big-city things. And I'd love to go dancing with you sometime, but Hattie's been at the cabins almost all day. We can't ask her to stay all night, too." Hattie had cheerfully returned to cover the office while Mel and Joe went out on the town.

"And you're beat." Damn, the man was way too perceptive.

"Yeah, I'm still a little wiped out." More than a little, but he didn't need to know that.

"Then I'd better get you home." He handed her into the passenger seat of the Jeep. His solicitous attention made her feel like a princess, but the heat that blazed in those amber eyes when he gazed at her made her feel like a woman.

"I wish this summer hadn't started out so badly." Mel snuggled close to Jonas's side as he drove across the wide flat terrain of the central U. P., into the red-gold glory of the setting sun.

"What?" He sounded startled, maybe even offended. "What do you mean, badly?"

She looked over, then chuckled at his chagrined expression. "I didn't mean you, dummy. Believe me, I'm very much enjoying our…" She just couldn't bring herself to use the word 'affair', but she didn't know what else to call it.

"Relationship," he supplied through clenched teeth. "Glad to hear it."

"Don't get snarky, it doesn't suit you." She punched him lightly in the shoulder, though it probably came across as more of a caress. "What I meant was that I wish I'd met you when the rest of my life wasn't so messed up. I hate the fact that you're always around when I'm depressed or exhausted. I'm usually a pretty happy, energetic person."

"I know."

"How's that?"

"Every time I've seen something go wrong for you, you've rebounded in nothing flat. You're holding up remarkably under circumstances that would have flattened a weaker person. Trust me, your positive attitude shines through. No one could ever mistake you for a victim."

"Thanks." His approval meant a lot to her; too much really, but she was just too tired to care about keeping her emotional distance right now.

The Jeep pulled up in front of her cabin, and Hattie waved at them from the rocker on the front porch. "Will you stay tonight?" She really didn't want to be alone. Tired or not, she wanted him, and then she wanted him to sleep beside her. The world was just a better place when Jonas held her in his arms.

"Sure." The sizzling look he gave her left no doubt about his opinion. Oh, yeah, he wanted to stay. The thought sent a warm rush of anticipation up and down her spine.

They saw Hattie off, checked on the animals, and walked the perimeter of the grounds. It felt good to walk beside him, quietly holding hands in the light of the bright gibbous moon.

"So all the units are full now?"

"All but number one. I've got a family arriving Sunday for that."

"And you don't hire any outside help?"

She squeezed his hand, understanding that what sounded like censure was a mark of concern. "That's not entirely true. I have a grounds crew that comes in once a week, and a part-time assistant who starts this Tuesday. With Hattie helping out, it's enough."

"Local people?" he asked cautiously. "Are you sure that your friend Talcott hasn't scared them away?"

"No, the landscaper is an old friend of Gran's and his crew is made up of his kids, grandkids, nieces and nephews. I've helped all of them from time to time with various bumps and bruises. They're good, loyal friends. My assistant is Karen's cousin Sheila. She's a college student, who's worked for me since she was in high school. This will probably be her last year, though. She graduates next spring."

"That's the beauty of small town life. Everybody's related to somebody."

"That's for sure." Laughter bubbled in her throat at his light-hearted teasing. "Usually in more interconnected ways than you'd really like to think about."

He laughed, throwing his arm around her waist to squeeze her tight. She leaned into him as they walked down the wooded trail, savoring the warmth of his body alongside hers.

"You seem to know a lot about small towns," she observed. "Did you always live in New York?" In the short time they'd known each other; he'd disclosed almost nothing about his life. Every time it came up, he changed the subject.

"I grew up in a bunch of different places," he hedged. "Some of them were even smaller than Sanctity."

"Your parents moved around a lot?"

"Both of them." He stopped walking and pulled his arm away from her, then shoved both hands in the front pockets of his jeans. "They split when I was pretty young. Every so often, they'd get back together for a few months, then they'd take off again. Neither of them was big on staying in one place very long, and I got bounced around between them."

"Sounds rough."

"I guess." His voice was taut, his lips were a thin white line, and he looked out into the woods rather than at her. His childhood was clearly not his favorite topic of conversation

"Are your parents still living?"

"My mother died when I was fifteen." She heard a small break in his voice then, before it hardened. "I have no idea about my father. He's probably out there somewhere, unless somebody's managed to kill him by now."

Ouch! She winced at the pain she could sense radiating off of him. For just a second there, he'd sounded almost violent. She laid a hand on his arm, the muscle tensed beneath his shirt.

"Any brothers or sisters?"

"No." He barked out a short, sharp laugh. "I guess I'm just a lone wolf."

Okay, time to change the subject. She wanted to know more, but not at the cost of causing him pain. She took his hand and tugged him further down the well-worn path. It was dark, but she knew the path by heart, often walked this way when she needed to connect with nature and have time to think. "So what university do you work for?"

"None, actually. I'm strictly free-lance." There was a note in his tone she couldn't identify. He was holding something back, but she couldn't tell what. Her extra senses still didn't work with Jonas, and it was frustrating her no end.

"But you live in New York City?"

"Most of the time. I also have a house up in the mountains of Vermont."

"You do? Then what are you doing here?" The question popped out before she could stop it.

"They're building a subdivision down the road. The noise was driving me crazy." Again she sensed that he was telling her only a partial truth.

"You must do pretty well as a free-lance writer to be able to afford two homes and still rent a third for the summer." Great! Now she was asking him about his financial status. Next thing you knew she'd be asking him if he'd ever been married. She had to end this before she got herself in even deeper.

"I get by."

They'd arrived at the lake, though she hadn't realized they'd gone so far. The moonlight glimmered off the placid surface of the water, and the crickets and spring peepers sang a refrain in the background.

"It's okay, Mel," he whispered, apparently sensing her embarrassment. "You have a right to know about the guy you're sleeping with." Stretching his long legs, he sat down on the log and looked out over the water, then tugged her down beside him.

"For the record, my full name is Jonas Robert Pierce, but my friends call me Joe. I was born in Buffalo, New York, on January fourth, thirty-nine and a half years ago. I graduated from Columbia with a degree in history, and I make a damn good living writing books." He seemed like he was about to say more, but she stopped him with a kiss.

When they came up for air, he gave a ragged sigh and pulled her onto his lap.

"I've never been married, never intend to. You knew that, right?"

"Right," she answered breezily, ignoring the stab of hurt his words had caused. "No wedding, no babies. Don't worry, Jonas, I'm not expecting a ring, and I'm not going to get clingy."

"I've got no communicable diseases; you should know I'd never put you at that kind of risk. I don't even get colds."

"How'd you get this?" She brushed her finger along the thin white scar high on his left cheekbone. Even in the moonlight, it stood out, a pale slash against his dark, tan skin. "Rugby? College football?"

"No. I've never played organized sports." He'd stiffened noticeably and his voice thickened. Something about that scar reached deep into his soul. "It was a—disagreement."

He clearly didn't want to talk about it, so she filed that topic away for another time. "So what do you do besides writing? I mean for fun. You must have some free time."

"Well, you might have noticed that I'm partial to long walks in the woods."

"And when you're in New York?"

"Long walks are still an option. I've memorized just about every inch of Central Park. The walks are nicer, though when you have good company to share them."

"Thank you." They both stood, seeming to understand without saying the words that it was time to move on, to return to her cabin. Still arm-in-arm, they headed back up the trail at a leisurely pace.

"I also watch hockey and baseball, listen to music, and read." She heard the wry amusement in his voice, knew he was humoring her and trying to lighten the mood. "I dabbled at playing guitar for a while, but it didn't last very long. Neither did singing. Turns out I have no musical talent whatsoever. Can't paint worth a damn, either."

"Well," she laughed, relieved to hear him admit to even such slight imperfections. "We have that in common, then. I love to sing, but in college, I was politely asked to quit the glee club. I can't seem to stick to one key at a time."

* * * *

It was strange to be having this conversation, Joe thought, stranger still that he hadn't whisked her up to her bedroom the moment they'd returned to her cabin. Instead they'd sprawled on the sofa in her living room, laughing, talking and holding hands. Anecdotes about the pranks he and Kent had pulled in college had her laughing uproariously. They'd discussed television, books, and all kinds of music, then drifted off into companionable silence. A quick glance at Mel's face confirmed his suspicions. She'd fallen asleep on him. Her head was tilted back against the sofa cushion, and a delicate snore escaped her slightly parted lips.

"Poor baby," he murmured, tracing the hollow of her cheekbone with one fingertip. His hand was so dark and coarse against her porcelain skin. Between all the stress she'd been under and their unexpectedly passionate lovemaking, she hadn't been getting much sleep in the last couple weeks. His stomach lurched as he remembered her fainting spell that afternoon. He hadn't been that scared in years. He hoped she was right when she said sleep was all she needed to recover her strength.

Her invitation to spend the night had delighted him; he intended to stay even if she wasn't awake to enjoy it. Just being with her was nice. For the first time in days he felt comfortable in his skin, like he was exactly where he needed to be. There'd be no midnight excursions for him tonight; he had no urge at all to change and prowl. What a relief!

The yawn that split his jaws caught him by surprise. Come to think of it, he hadn't been sleeping much lately either. He would tonight, though, all warm and snug in Mel's bed. It was a luxury he couldn't afford to get used to, but tonight he was going to enjoy it.

She showed no signs of waking when he bent to pick her up, but she snuggled against his chest as he carried her up the stairs, burying her face in the hollow of his throat. She didn't even open her eyes when he laid her on the bed and stripped off her clothes, though she did cooperate, limply lifting her arms or feet as directed. When he'd peeled off his own garments, Joe crawled into the bed beside her, drawing the covers up over them both. With a contented sigh, she cuddled back against him, instantly falling back into her deep slumber.

This was a first for Joe. He'd never before spent the night with a woman without having sex. He pulled Mel closer, so that her enticing little butt was pressed tight to his groin. His sex stirred, but the reaction was controllable. The sweet floral scent of her hair was the last sensation that registered before sleep overtook him as well.

* * * *

Sunday Mel slept late. Waking in Jonas's strong arms, she felt more rested than she had in days, and the feel of his rock-hard erection pressed against her backside definitely put a smile on her face. She turned in his arms, kissing him good morning, loving the sensation of his chest hair rasping against her already sensitized nipples. It was another hour before either of them made it out of the bed.

He still had new things to teach her, Mel thought later. There was a smile on her face as she drove Jonas's Jeep into town. It took her a while to find a parking space. The town was packed, or at least as close to it as Sanctity ever came. The holiday weekend was the kick-off of the summer season, and Sanctity held a big festival to celebrate. There were concerts in the city park, and all the shops in the downtown area offered sidewalk sales and activities for kids. Mel waved at one of her renters, pleased to see that many of them were taking part in the festivities.

Mel didn't mind the crowd. Tourists were her livelihood, after all. She was actually humming when she walked into the grocery store, and even a nasty glare from one of Talcott's secretaries couldn't dim her mood. She smiled sweetly back at the sour old bat, knowing it would irritate her no end. She filled her cart with odds and ends, stopped to chat with an old schoolmate, then moved over to the customer service counter to pick up her standing order of paper products and other supplies for the cabins.

She forced a polite smile as she asked to have her order brought around. It would be tricky getting the pallets of paper towels and toilet paper all into Jonas's Jeep, but she'd manage.

Phil Mercer gave her a tight smile that didn't reach his beady dark eyes. "Sorry Melissa. Must have forgot. Order didn't get placed this week."

"What do you mean you forgot?" This was the start of her busiest season. She needed those supplies, especially since she'd run out of laundry detergent the day before and there were still sheets to be washed for incoming guests.

Mercer gave her a careless shrug. "I mean, the order didn't get placed. Guess you'll have to go somewhere else."

"There is nowhere else. This is the only store in town!"

This time his smile was nastier than an outright sneer would have been. "That's your problem, not mine."

He turned his face back to his computer screen, patently ignoring her.

"Will it be in anytime soon?" She modulated her tone carefully, though she wanted to scream.

"Doubt it." This time, he didn't even look up at her.

"Fine." She wheeled her cart around and went back into the aisles. She could deal with standard sized supplies for the short term, even though they were less cost-effective than the commercial products she normally ordered. She grabbed three jumbo packages of paper towels, two of toilet paper, and the biggest box of detergent she could find. By the time she wheeled it up to the checkout counter, the cart was piled so high she couldn't see over it.

And, just to make her day complete, Phil's wife Edna was working the checkout counter.

"Sorry, the credit-card machine isn't working today." She didn't look sorry, she looked as pleased as a cat playing with a tasty mouse after ringing up Mel's purchases. "It will have to be cash."

"Edna, you know I don't carry that kind of cash. I'll have to write a check."

"Sorry. Can't take a check for over a hundred."

"Since when?" They'd always taken business checks before. The Mercers knew darn well that Whispering Pines had never bounced a check.

Edna shrugged. "New policy. If you don't like it, shop somewhere else."

Customers in line behind Mel were beginning to stir restlessly, and she hated to cause a scene. She gritted her teeth and squared her shoulders. "Fine. Can you hold this stuff here while I run to the bank for cash?"

"No, sorry."

"And if I do come back, will I find that all the stuff I need is mysteriously sold out?"

The other woman bared her teeth in a feral grin. "Could be."

"Fine!" Mel shoved her wallet back into her purse and stalked out, refusing to so much as blink until she was back in Jonas's Jeep. Then she gave into the tears for all of a minute before starting the engine and driving off.

If Talcott had been at it again, then she wouldn't have any better luck at the hardware store, which was the only other place she could think of in town to buy laundry soap. Maybe she could borrow some detergent from Hattie or Karen till she could get to a bigger town for supplies. No, that wasn't going to work. The last thing she wanted to do was involve her friends any deeper in this mess.

For the first time, Mel seriously contemplated giving up—she debated it with herself the whole way back to Whispering Pines, and even back in her cabin. It was possible; she could release her animals, sell the land and the cabins, then start over again somewhere else. Her heart and soul were in this place—the land and the wildlife, but maybe it was time. She had her degree in botany, maybe she could go back to graduate school. Then again, maybe she could get a job somewhere in the hotel industry, at least she was pretty sure she could. Years of running her own place should count for something! Who knew, it could be the smartest thing she ever did. If she broke the bonds that had tied her family to the land for generations, might she also break the curse? Maybe away from Sanctity and the legacy of the MacRae witches, she could change her destiny and actually lead a normal life.

On that note, she hefted a bucket of cleaning supplies and walked toward cabin one. Her newest visitors would be arriving tomorrow for a weeklong stay, and Mel wanted the place spotless.

She was on the porch when she noticed that something was wrong. It was her intuition, her "witchy" senses going off, even though nothing looked out of place. The twin Adirondack chairs still flanked the green-painted door, and the simple plaid curtains blocked off any view of the inside. Something, however, was definitely triggering her internal warning system. Setting down the bucket, she listened intently at the door. Nothing.

The phone clipped to her sturdy leather belt chirped loudly, and Mel shrieked. She still wasn't used to the satellite phone Jonas had given her, and the timing was impeccable. "Hello?"

"Don't sound so terrified, it's only me." His voice was low, sexy and soothing. "Are you all right?"

"Fine," she managed. "Why are you calling?" And why right now?

"Just checking in," he replied. "And missing you."

"That's too bad." Her voice was firm, but she was softening inside. "Aren't you writers supposed to be solitary types?"

"I am," he insisted. "Or at least I was till two weeks ago. Now, every time I try to write, I end up thinking about a certain red-headed witch."

"I'm flattered." Flattered, hell, he was turning her on, damn it!

"Good. Now stop fibbing and tell me what's wrong. I can hear it in your voice."

"Nothing really, just some minor hassles in town." Sure, total lack of groceries was minor. She'd have to spend the whole day tomorrow driving to Escanaba, and she still didn't have a car, but she didn't want to tell him the whole story and have him come rushing to her rescue.

"What else?"

Cripes, was the man psychic or what? "Well, I'm back at Whispering Pines, and I got this strange feeling…"

"Strange how?"

"Creepy strange. I'm standing in front of cabin one, you know, the big vacant one, and it's like there's a voice telling me not to go inside."

"So don't." His command was harsh and emphatic. "I'll be there in ten minutes. Meet me on your back porch."

"You're supposed to be working," she reminded him weakly. The truth was, she wanted his strong, dependable support when she opened that door. When had she turned into such a wimp?

After agreeing to wait, she shook her head and broke the connection. Leaving her bucket on the porch of cabin one, she walked slowly back to her home to wait for Jonas.

He must have jogged, because it was less than five minutes later when he came trotting up her back steps. His breathing was easy, but the hair at his temples was just slightly damp from the exertion, and Mel had to tamp down the urge to smooth it back from his face. She also had to fight the urge to fling herself into his arms, and take him right here on the porch. The man was delicious! She'd like nothing better than to peel him out of his snug jeans and striped rugby shirt.

"Hello to you too," he purred, wrapping her in his arms for one hard but regrettably brief kiss. "But I thought I was here to check out a cabin?"

"So now you can read minds?" she blustered. "I didn't say a word!"

"Sweetheart, you don't have to." He laughed. "It's all right there in those gorgeous aqua eyes." He bent to drop a feather light kiss on each eyelid.

"Sorry."

"Don't be. It obviously offends me." Pulling away a little, he gestured to the insistent bulge in his jeans. "But unless you want to find out right now just how sturdy your kitchen table is, we'd better go check on cabin one."

"You're right," she sighed as they moved side-by-side down the driveway. "Do you really think the table would work?"

"Ask me that again tonight," he muttered thickly. "And I'll prove it to you."

The doorknob of the cabin turned easily to his testing. "Did you unlock this?"

"No. I never leave them open."

"I didn't think so. Still got that spooky feeling?"

Her stomach churned in response. "More than ever."

"Wait here." He reached down and unclipped the phone from her belt, punched 9-1-1, and handed it back to her. "Be ready to hit send," he instructed, then stepped inside, partially closing the door behind him.

After a few moments, he returned, his face set in a grim mask. Pulling the phone from her hand, he pressed the 'send' key.

"Yeah, this is Joe Pierce, up at Whispering Pines. Get somebody up here, there's been more vandalism."

"How bad," Mel asked as soon as he'd hung up. She could tell it was awful by the way he was avoiding her gaze. Unable to stand there and wait, she pushed past him to see for herself.

It was bad. Jagged holes had been bashed into the drywall, and every surface sported hunter-orange obscenities. Stuffing from the sofa, chairs, and mattresses was strewn everywhere. Every single dish or mirror in the place had been reduced to shards.

"It will take the whole summer to get this repaired," she breathed, her voice breaking. "That's if I can get contractors willing to buck

Talcott and work for me. Which is going to be tough, since I can't even buy groceries in this stupid town."

"You could sell," he suggested, taking her elbow to guide her back out to the porch. "Or I could take you to Paris for a few weeks till you figure out what you want to do next."

"Paris?" He was looking at her so earnestly. He probably didn't even realize how over the top he sounded. "Gee, why not Rome or Hong Kong?"

"Fine. Wherever you want to go."

Oops. She guessed he hadn't realized she was teasing. Fury and concern were pouring off of him in waves, and distraught as she was over the destruction, she couldn't help being touched and a little amused at the intensity of his response.

"I'm not selling, Jonas," she corrected him gently. She wasn't sure what she was going to do, but running wasn't, couldn't possibly be the answer. Her insurance would cover the cost of the repairs, but she'd be losing a big chunk of this summer's income. Probably more if this scared away any of her other tenants. It wouldn't be enough to bankrupt her, but, combined with the unavoidable damage to her reputation, it would certainly hurt.

"I'd better go call the Hansens, tell them the cabin is unavailable," she sighed. "I guess I'll have to send them over to Talcott's." That was the ultimate indignity of all, that Talcott would benefit from her misfortune.

"Would they object to my cabin?" Jonas's voice had gone distant and speculative. His eyes were focused somewhere in the distant woods.

She shot him a funny look. What was going on in his head? "It's kind of small for a family of four, and with kids they'll probably want a television."

"Or could you shift another tenant up there to free up one of the two-bedroom units?"

"Probably." Jonas was leaving? Why now? And why did it have to hurt so much? "The surgeons are leaving Monday anyway. They won't mind being shifted for one night, and their cabin has two bedrooms. A single fisherman was taking their unit. If I give him a hefty discount, I don't think he'll object to cabin seven." Even as she processed his question, she wanted to wail at him for deserting her, but that was something she'd promised she wouldn't do. "You're leaving then?"

"Don't be silly." His lips were set in a thin straight line. "I'm moving in with you."

Chapter Ten

What the hell had he just done?

The question kept echoing inside Joe's head over the next hour as he stood beside Mel and dealt with the bucolic sheriff and his sycophant deputy. Had he really just suggested moving in with Mel?

No. He hadn't suggested it. He'd announced it. It was slight consolation that Mel had looked just as stunned as Joe felt.

The hell of it was that as much as the idea disconcerted him, he'd meant exactly what he'd said, and he had no intention whatsoever of changing his mind. The thought of her sleeping alone while some lunatic stalked her sent cold shivers down his spine. This vandalism was escalating, and the next move could easily be arson or assault. He'd meant his offer to take her away from here, but he knew she wasn't going to budge. No, until the bastard was caught, Joe had only two options that his conscience could consider. He could spend every night curled up in four-legged form on her front doormat, or he could sleep in his own shape in her nice warm bed. It was easy to see which option held more appeal, even if it meant cohabitating with another individual for the first time since his junior year of college.

"Well, if you spot anybody sneaking around the place, give us a call," Mott sighed, climbing back into the passenger seat of his cruiser. He hadn't been particularly helpful, but at least he wasn't openly disparaging, like his deputy. Joe stood in the gravel driveway with Mel, his arm wrapped around her waist and her head leaning against his shoulder like it belonged there.

"It's probably just kids," Harkness sneered. "Nothing for it but to catch 'em red-handed."

"Kids, huh?" Joe bared his teeth and was amused to note that the weasel had enough presence of mind to scurry around the car and hustle his skinny little ass into the driver's seat. Moments later there was nothing but a dust plume down the road to indicate the presence of the county's finest.

"Idiot!" He kicked a rock, sent it sailing into the underbrush. "Absolute freaking morons!"

"No." Mel slipped out from his grasp and trudged back toward her cabin. He followed, loathe to let her out of his sight. "Warren isn't an idiot, he's a pragmatist. Without solid evidence, you can't just accuse a pillar of the community of senseless vandalism. Harkness isn't an idiot either, but he is a weasel, and he's firmly in Talcott's pocket. Furthermore, he goes to one of those ultra-right-wing charismatic churches. That congregation considers my very existence an abomination that needs to be 'cleansed'. He'd be thrilled if somebody actually managed to chase me away from Sanctity."

"Any chance that church, or somebody from it, is behind these incidents?"

He watched her eyebrows knit as she pondered the question. "I don't think so." She chewed on her lower lip, then shook her head. "It just doesn't feel right. They're not violent, or haven't been so far, and most of them live away from here, in the next county over. While I think they'd be happy to see me go, I don't see any of them having enough animosity or even the guts to try to make me."

Once they were back inside, she sat down at the broad pine kitchen table and placed another call to her insurance agent, while Joe paced and watched her. He could see her teeth clench as she agreed to leave the mess undisturbed until they came out to assess the damage. She switched off the phone and tossed it onto a woven mat in the center of the table.

"The agent won't be able to do anything till Tuesday," Mel grumbled. She slumped forward over the table, chin propped up on her hands. "At least."

"Assholes." Joe stopped pacing, wishing there was somebody he could slug to make things better for her. The violence he felt scared the hell out of him. He needed something to do. Now. "Let's go clean out my place," he suggested. "Then you can move your fishermen whenever they're ready."

"You're sure about this?"

"Yes."

* * * *

"You're sure you want to do this?" She'd repeated the question in various phrasing at least half a dozen times in the last forty minutes. Joe switched off the vacuum cleaner and strode across the main room of his erstwhile cabin. As small as it was, and as little time as he'd been spending there, it hadn't taken them long to clean. He relieved her of the dust rag and furniture polish she clutched so he could take her hands.

"Stop worrying about it. I'm sure."

"It's just that it seems so… I don't know, it feels kind of…" She trailed off again, and he couldn't help wondering what she was trying to say.

Intimate? Permanent? Committed? He wasn't comfortable with any of the possible ways to end her sentence, and judging by the way she was gnawing at her lower lip, neither was she. Still, it came down to a single issue, and since that was her safety, he wasn't going to budge.

"I'm not letting you stay there by yourself." He didn't know what he'd do if she refused, but he'd figure something out. "Either I move in for the duration, or you move out."

"We've been through this, Jonas, I can't just leave. I've got responsibilities and a business to run."

"Then I guess you're stuck with me till this mess gets sorted out." He let go of her hand to brush his thumb along her cheek. "I'll sleep in the spare bedroom if you want me to."

Her eyes brightened and color suffused her cheeks. "Don't be stupid. We'd have probably ended up spending most of our nights together anyway. I guess I'm just nervous. I haven't shared a house since Gran died. You can use the spare bedroom for your writing."

They gathered up his suitcases and boxes of research and together carried them out to his Jeep. "Neither one of us believes for a minutes that you'd end up staying in the spare room. If we're going to play house, we may as well at least be honest about it with each other—and ourselves."

She had a point, but right now he wasn't sure he wanted to be honest with himself. Thick silence filled the air between them as they drove back to her cabin. "I've never done this before either, you know." He finally couldn't stand the quiet for another moment. "It's uncharted territory for me, too."

"You never shacked up with a woman before?"

"Ouch. When you say honest, you mean it, don't you? And, no, not for more than a weekend. I told you before, I don't do long-term commitments."

Her lips twisted, but she didn't say anything. Women? What did they want? Lies didn't please them, but neither, apparently did honesty. The female human was more confusing than all the vampires, ghosts, and monsters he'd ever encountered. Put together.

"So why change now?"

"Because I do have enough of a conscience to not want to see you hurt! Haven't we already had this conversation?" He wasn't about to tell her that the thought of someone hurting her made his stomach clench, or that he was secretly thrilled by the idea of waking up with her every morning, at least for as long as she'd put up with him.

"So far there hasn't been anything but property damage."

"Don't forget the attempted assault in your barn," he fired back. "Which I noticed, by the way, that you did not report to the cops."

"I told you, it wouldn't have done any good. It would have been my word against his."

"Even with my statement to back you up?"

She chuckled then, and the genuine amusement in the sound made his insides go mushy. Damn, he loved it when she laughed.

"No offense, Jonas, but the whole town knows you're sleeping with me. You have no local credibility anymore. Who's going to believe a wacko tourist who's bonking the local witch?"

They carried his belongings inside her cabin, and Mel obligingly made space in her closet for his shirts and pants, and cleared a dresser drawer for his socks and underwear. She'd been right earlier. This felt way more—something—than sharing a hotel room for a weekend.

When he joined her in the kitchen, she looked up from the refrigerator where she'd been adding his supplies to hers. "We need groceries. You were getting low, and Phil Mercer wouldn't sell me anything today."

"What?" She'd mentioned something about minor hassles in town, but not anything about outright harassment.

"Mercer's mother was a Talcott," Mel informed him. "So Phil tends to follow where his richer, smarter cousin leads. He'll get over it, especially once Byron's lawyers get into the act. But for a week or so, I'll have to drive into Escanaba for supplies, which is tricky, since I still don't have a car."

Ah, yes, the aborted truck-shopping trip. "As soon as you get your fishermen resettled, we can go." She'd stuck a note on the door of their cabin, asking them to check in with her when they returned from their day on the lake. "We can look for a truck and go shopping in one trip."

"Nope. Then we have to clean their unit and prep it for the family that was going to be in cabin one. Meanwhile, we have to take care of the animals. We can go tomorrow after the new guests check in."

He didn't like the resignation in her voice, or the dark circles under her eyes. Rage at whomever was stalking her rose up in his throat, and he fought the desire to change and to deal with the perpetrator in the most savage, visceral manner possible. With his teeth. He could almost feel his fingers lengthening into claws. This kind of rage was why he avoided commitments, damn it! He'd worked too hard at perfecting his control to lose it because he'd allowed himself to get emotionally involved. Involuntarily, he took a step backward.

"Animals. Right." He nodded, then followed her out of the house and down the path to the barn. The simple manual labor would give him time to regain his control. And his perspective.

It seemed to work for her, too. After a few minutes in the warm, sunlit barn, the tension visibly ebbed from her shoulders, and her smile was genuine when the fawn butted her hand affectionately. Joe reached for the rake automatically, having helped out often enough to know what needed to be done.

"I see you've got a new patient." His nose worked overtime here in the barn, and he smelled the raccoon before he saw it, even over the scents of the eagle, the fawn, and the bales of fresh straw. It looked fat and happy, despite its missing foot. If fact, Joe would swear that the rotund little critter wore a downright smug expression.

"He's malingering, the little pig." Mel reached through the wire fencing to scratch its furry head. "I'd intended to let him go by now, but he doesn't seem to want to leave."

"Understandable." Joe laughed. "A warm place to sleep, plenty of free food." Mel to tuck him in at night. "He knows when he's got a good deal going." What more could any intelligent mammal want, after all? Then Mel twisted and bent to get something from the lower level of the fridge, flashing Joe a generous view of her backside. Yeah, well there was that. He felt a pang of sympathy for the raccoon, isolated from his own kind. Just like Joe had been before meeting Mel.

A knock on the barn door put a stop to his thoughts of taking her right here on one of the hay bales. Her two loyal fishermen tenants stood outside, and after only a brief discussion proved more than willing to relocate for the duration of their stay. Joe watched them closely, relieved to note that both of the pleasant-looking middle-aged men sported wedding bands, and that neither of them seemed interested in Mel in a sexual manner. Good. He didn't need either of them panting after his woman.

His woman? Where the hell had that come from? He swallowed hard as he shook hands with the two physicians, acknowledging Mel's introductions.

"Nice to meet you." Dr. LaBreque, the more outgoing of the pair, was probably about fifty, with gray-streaked dark hair and a generous middle-aged spread. He eyed Joe speculatively, then gave him a smile and a nod. "Glad to know that somebody will be keeping an eye on Melissa. We've been coming up here every year since she was a little kid, and nothing like this has ever happened before. Hell, I thought the whole town loved her."

"Me too," echoed his friend Dr. Martin, a slender man of similar age, with thinning blond hair. "None of this makes any sense. Who would have it in for a sweet kid like Mel?"

Joe shrugged. "I don't know, but I'd sure like to find out. You two seen or heard anything?"

They shook their heads. "If we do, you can be sure we'll let you know." Promising to have their gear ready to move within the hour, they headed back up the path to their cabin.

Mel stood watching them go with a fond smile on her face.

"I wish all my guests were like them."

"Have they really been coming here for thirty years?"

"Umm-hmm. Almost since Gran started the business. Steve LaBreque used to come with his dad when I was just a baby. Then he hooked up with Glenn in medical school, and the two of them have been fishing buddies ever since."

"No wives?"

"They tried bringing them one year, but the women both hate the woods, so they made a deal. Two weeks a year the boys come up here fishing, and their wives go away to some luxury spa for facials and body-wraps."

"Whatever works, I guess."

"I guess." Mel laughed. "I can't imagine wanting to take separate vacations from a spouse, but since I've never had one, what do I know? It seems to work for them."

"Feel like going into Rosa's for dinner, or do we have enough supplies left to scrounge something here?"

"It's still the festival in town, you know," she reminded him. "Let's try the scrounging thing. I don't feel like facing down any more angry villagers."

That was probably a good idea. That way he wouldn't have to hurt anybody for bothering her. A quiet night at home it was. Home. The word sent a chill down Joe's spine. He had to quit thinking like this. And he would, he promised himself. But not till after dinner.

* * * *

He could tell Mel fretted throughout the impromptu meal of grilled cheese sandwiches and canned tomato soup. She stared out the window into the gathering darkness and toyed with her hair almost as much as she toyed with her spoon. Jonas knew the time had come when he had to quit making excuses and tell her the truth.

"There's something I need to tell you about." His face was taut, his jaw locked.

She set down her spoon and leaned her chin on her hands. "Go ahead."

"It's about my job." He fidgeted with his sandwich before shoving his plate aside.

"O-o-okay. If you're really unemployed and broke, you can just tell me. At least you won't have to worry about rent for a while. I certainly can't charge you for staying with me."

"No." He couldn't help a chuckle. She was a hundred and eighty degrees off the truth. "I'm not exactly who I said I was."

"You mean Jonas Pierce isn't your real name? I don't believe that. You showed me your driver's license and credit card when you checked in."

"It is. It's just not the name most people know me by."

"Huh?" She tilted her head and pursed her lips.

"I told you I'm a writer, and that part is the truth."

She rolled her eyes and gave him a wry grin. "Duh! Jonas, I've seen you write. You totally lose touch with reality." He nodded, still embarrassed about the afternoon when she'd shown up at his cabin and watched him for almost a half an hour before he'd even noticed she was there. He should have told her the truth then, but he'd gotten distracted by the fact that she'd stripped while she was watching him.

"You're right, I really am a writer. I'm just not a historian."

"Let me guess. You travel around the world researching the paranormal, and then you write about it." Her incredible intuition never failed to impress him.

"That's right." He was glad she seemed to be taking it so well. Just as he opened his mouth to tell her so, though, the smile faded from her face and her eyes narrowed.

"That's why you came here, isn't it? You're researching me?" Her voice cracked and tears welled in her beautiful eyes. "Gee, do you always sleep with your research subjects? You could have just asked."

"No. I mean yes. Oh, hell I have no idea what I mean." He threw his napkin to the floor, reached across the table and snatched her hand. "Yes, I'd heard that you were a witch, and that did figure into my decision to come to Whispering Pines, but it wasn't the reason I needed to get away in the first place. I really did come here to finish another book, one I already have all the research for." Why was his gift for words failing him now? He was tripping over his tongue like a schoolboy on his first date.

She tugged at her hand and he eased the grip suddenly afraid that he'd hurt her. Well, physically. He knew he'd already hurt her emotionally.

"Straight out, Jonas. Did you seduce me to get information for your work?"

"Hell, no." His own voice came perilously close to cracking. It was hard to talk around the massive lump in his throat. "That might be why I asked you to dinner that very first night, but after that, I swear, it was all personal." He released her hand, ran both of his through his hair, which yanked. "Damn, woman, I get hard just being in the same room with you. Do you think I can fake that just for research purposes?"

"You could just be combining your work with a convenient outlet for sex. Or maybe you're just not picky, and would sleep with whoever was available."

"Bullshit." That one stung. "I'll have you know I'm *extremely* picky!"

"Okay, so I'm just irresistible." She rolled her eyes again, still not believing him, and it drove him crazy. "And Sanctity was simply the best place for some quiet work. Does that about sum it up?"

"Well…" Another thought had occurred to him, and he didn't figure he had anything to lose by sharing it with her. "It's just remotely possible that Kent had ulterior motives when he recommended this place so highly."

"Ulterior motives?" She was still skeptical and he couldn't blame her.

"Matchmaking," Joe stated. "I think he might have guessed that with our common backgrounds we might find each other attractive."

He could tell that that made her think. After gnawing on her lower lip for a while, Mel nodded at him. "Maybe. It sounds like something Karen would have done."

"I promise you, Mel, what happened between us had nothing to do with my work. I've already told my agent that there won't be a book coming from this summer. I wouldn't take advantage of you like that." In fact, being with her had been the closest feeling to coming home he could ever remember. He could almost let himself believe that they had future together. Almost.

Something in his demeanor must have convinced her—at least a little. She nodded slowly. "Okay." Her smile was tentative, but it was there, and a huge weight lifted off his chest.

"There's more. My books aren't academic at all. They're based on paranormal fact and legends, but what I write is fiction."

"And…" Her eyes were wary. It was time for the other shoe to drop.

"I write them under a pseudonym. It's kind of well known. In fact, it's sort of, well, famous." He'd been compared to Stephen King and

Dean Koontz, though he didn't consider himself anywhere near that league.

Her brows knit together. "Go on."

"Ever heard of J. P. Wolfe?"

Her jaw dropped and her eyes went wide. She blinked twice, then he saw her throat clench as she swallowed hard. "Wow. So explain to me again how you wound up in my little cabin in Sanctity, Michigan? If you wanted a quiet place to work on your next blockbuster, why didn't you just buy an island somewhere or something?"

"Actually my place in Vermont is usually pretty quiet. Right now, though, there's construction going on nearby, and the noise was driving me crazy. There's one more reason, too."

"Fresh out of private planes?" Her sarcasm stung, but at least she wasn't lunging across the table to strangle him. He supposed that was good.

"I'm hiding," he admitted, answering her first question. His bluntness seemed to stop her cold, so he continued. "There's a reporter from *Personalities Weekly* who's been essentially stalking me. He's discovered my real name and he's been staking out my apartment and my house in Vermont."

She nodded and picked up her sandwich. She took a bite and chewed methodically, her eyes still glazed. "Of course. It makes as much sense as anything else has this summer."

* * * *

She spent the rest of the evening ignoring Jonas and trying to come to grips with his big confession. It wasn't working. All she had to show for all her effort was a whopping headache! She was also exhausted. All this stress must be getting to her; she was always tired lately. She looked over at Jonas, who had set his laptop up in a corner of the living room and had been diligently typing for the last hour or so. No, there was no doubt he was a writer. It was just the rich and famous part that took some getting used to.

But he'd looked so lost when he'd told her, so sad. He'd apologized over and over, and admitted he'd been afraid to tell her after things between them had gone so far. She just couldn't stay mad at him, so she might as well forgive him.

"I'm going up to bed," she announced around a yawn. "Come on up whenever you're ready; the lights and stuff won't bother me at all." The domesticity of what she'd just said made her stomach do a skittery little flip.

"I'll be up in a bit," he responded absently.

She smiled. If she'd felt better, she'd start peeling her clothes off right here in the living room, and see if that caught his attention. She stood there with a smile hovering on her lips as she considered the idea, till another massive yawn split her jaws. Ouch! So much for seduction. Her body definitely had other plans.

Once she was in bed, however, sleep proved elusive. Any moment now, she'd hear Jonas's footsteps on the stairs, and know he was headed here to her bed. Sure, he'd been here before, but those times had started with sex, not with him joining her when she was presumably asleep.

Would he expect to have sex? Part of her hoped so. They hadn't anywhere near reached the stage where she could take his lovemaking for granted. The thought of his powerful hands, his clever lips and his…well, everything about Jonas was talented, and just thinking about it made her wet and achy, even though her brain acknowledged that she was too wiped out to do anything about it.

It had been an hour, she realized when she glanced over at her bedside clock. He was probably so caught up in his story that he forgot to come to bed. He was cute when he worked, all intense and brooding. Unable to fight her weariness any longer, she snuggled up to the pillow he'd used the night before, and drifted off to sleep.

* * * *

She was out cold. Joe turned out the bedroom light and shucked his jeans and shirt, laying them across the chair beside Mel's dresser. A slim shaft of moonlight illuminated her face, soft and peaceful in her slumber, and Joe smiled ruefully. He hadn't meant to work till two a.m., but it wasn't unusual for him to type till his eyes burned and his fingers cramped. Once he got started, he generally just kept on going till the words stopped wanting to come. Usually though, he didn't have such a tempting incentive to quit and come to bed. Nonetheless, he'd resisted since he was way behind schedule, and tonight was the first time he'd gotten any significant writing done in days. There was something about Mel's peaceful, undemanding presence that had put him more at ease than he'd been ever even when he was alone. He hadn't felt the urge to change tonight either, which was a relief, especially given that it was almost the full moon.

He climbed between the sheets, moving slowly so he wouldn't disturb her rest. Mel snuggled back against him in her sleep, and his arms went around her automatically. He was tired and at peace, and there was nowhere else he'd rather be than right here holding Mel in his arms. Well, that wasn't entirely true, he thought, shifting slightly to avoid stabbing her when she rubbed her delectable little ass up against his groin. Being beside her was great. Being buried inside her would be even better.

As if she sensed his thoughts, Mel moaned softly in her sleep, rubbing up against him again. Damn, she was hard to resist, and he was just plain hard. Gritting his teeth, he debated the wisdom of staying here. Writing had left him too wired to sleep, especially in the face of this much temptation.

She wiggled again and he groaned, then tossed the blankets back as he prepared to leave.

A soft, feminine giggle replied to his groan.

"You're awake, aren't you, witch?"

"Umm-hmm." Her giggle turned to a gasp as his hand slid up her smooth stomach to palm one plump breast. "Your cold feet woke me up."

"I'm sorry." He wasn't.

"I'm not."

The lovemaking was slower this time, more leisurely than they'd managed in the past. He kissed her cheeks and her forehead as he rolled her to her back then slowly slid home. Her soft, wet pussy gripped him snugly, enveloping him in heat. He propped himself up on his elbows, keen night vision allowed him to discern her features in the pale moonlight.

"You're beautiful," he whispered, despising himself for the catch in his voice.

"Easy to say in the dark, doofus." She giggled again, and her internal muscles clenched, milking his cock.

"Do that again," he growled.

"Do what?" she asked, still chuckling. Her arms were looped around his shoulders, and her sigh sounded like unfettered happiness.

"Laugh." He couldn't help but grin back at her, even though she probably couldn't see. It was so rare to actually have the chance to *play* with a woman in bed. You didn't get a lot of laughter out of one-night stands.

"Why?" Her eyes went wide with confusion and interest.

"It feels good."

"Oh." He couldn't see her blush, but he could feel the sudden warming of her skin. God, she was such an innocent! She tried a tiny, fake giggle, but was clearly embarrassed. So he forced the issue, tickling her under the arms.

"Oooh!" she shrieked, then laughed gloriously, her arms tightening around his back. He let out a chuckle of his own, feeling oddly proud that he'd made her laugh.

"I see what you mean," she breathed. "When you laugh, you sort of…pulse."

Apparently now that she was fully awake, Mel was feeling adventurous. That boded well. She tried out a variety of sounds and movements, pausing between as if to gauge his response. He tried not to disappoint, letting her play with him all she wanted, then kissing her between experiments. Everything she did felt incredible, and after their conversation tonight, he hadn't even expected her to let him in her bed. Just being with her was a gift. Finally, she rolled him to his back, coming to rest astride him, her internal muscles still clutching him tight. It felt so damn good he could almost believe in heaven.

"This is nice too." She whimpered, rocking back and forth to sample different depths and angles. "Is it good for you?"

"Nah," he teased, flexing his hips to impale her more deeply. "Doesn't do a thing for me." Couldn't she hear his pulse pounding, feel the sweat that slicked his skin? His hands plucked rhythmically at her puckered nipples, then he leaned up to take one succulent peak into his mouth.

"Liar." She giggled, her head flung back as she leaned into him. His mouth was full, so he just grunted his agreement, suckling her deeper and harder. Her hips began pumping faster, tormenting him, so he reached down to clasp them with his hands, guiding her movements.

Melissa was a screamer, he thought with delight. He'd discovered that fact days ago, but it still turned him on to hear her cry out when he gave her pleasure. He'd always been the silent type in bed, but not apparently with her. When her body tensed and shattered, with her shriek of fulfillment, he found his own completion, shouting her name while he poured himself into her.

She remained poised above him, her body still twitching convulsively for a moment before collapsing into a musky-scented heap on his chest. He gathered her into his arms, lying back against the pillows with her snuggled on top of him, her head tucked into the hollow of his neck. He buried his face in her hair and breathed deeply, inhaling her scent and soaking up the softness of her skin, the slippery sweat of their bodies. Finally, he spoke.

"You gonna stay there all night?"

A soft snore was her only response. Damn it, he'd worn her out again. His arms still tight around her, he eased her to the side and tucked a pillow under her head. Then he tugged the duvet up around them both, and drifted into slumber, an unaccustomed smile still on his lips.

* * * *

Jonas had gone off on one of his solitary walks, but only after a lengthy argument. These last few days he seemed reluctant to let her out of his sight, and as pleasant as the sight of him was, sometimes a girl just needed some time to herself. Two days had gone by since he moved in, and the only time she'd spent alone so far had been in the bathroom.

That had to be the explanation for her rotten mood, she thought. She slammed the dishwasher shut and turned it on, looking around the kitchen for something else to do. She'd promised Jonas she wouldn't leave the house, so her options were limited. Having stayed close to home for the last two days, she was caught up on all her housework.

Fine. Maybe a short meditation session would help her mood. And the ache in her lower back, though that was probably just a harbinger of her period, which was due any day now. Come to think of it, that probably accounted for the crabbiness as well. A snicker escaped her lips as she climbed the stairs. "I wonder how Jonas is going to enjoy that little bit of domestic bliss."

Settling onto the mat in front of her makeshift altar, Mel lit a fat beeswax candle she'd made herself. The gentle flame scented the room with the oils of herbs from her own garden, and the calming fragrance helped her center herself. Closing her eyes, she uttered an incantation for peace and relaxation, sure that stress was at least partially responsible for her discomfort, including the fatigue she just couldn't seem to shake and her mildly queasy stomach.

She needed to recharge, so she added another candle and another spell, this time seeking renewal of both spirit and body. She'd had another session with Gladys the day before, and even with Jonas's generous help, it hadn't been easy. Finally she lit a third candle, and this time the spell was for personal insight. Sorting out her tangled emotions couldn't hurt the situation.

Once the candles were lit and the incantations complete, she straightened her posture into a perfect lotus position and closed her eyes. Inhale. Pause. Exhale—slowly. The ritual was calming in its simplicity and familiarity, and Mel could feel her muscles relaxing and her senses mellowing toward external influences, gradually focusing inward instead.

Jonas. His name echoed in her consciousness. What had he become in her life? Friend, protector, lover. A brief thrill ran through her at the thought, then she drifted back into her trance. In this state all the nasty little voices that had been warning her away from him were silent, and the respite from that internal battle was welcome. Apparently her subconscious was all in favor of her relationship. That was good. She'd learned a long time ago that her subconscious mind was smarter than her conscious one.

Now her other issues swam to the forefront of her thoughts. Talcotts, Junior and Senior, the townsfolk, and the horrific vandalism. She could feel the hatred, the anger of the vandal, and she was more sure than ever that it was Sean, but she faced the fact that right now, the only things she could do was to protect herself with Jonas's help, and to watch. Eventually, she realized, he'd make a mistake, and then he'd end up caught in his own web of destruction.

At peace with some of her more pressing worries, she let her thoughts and her healing ability turn toward the physical, focusing on her fatigue, backache, and persistent headache. While she couldn't actually cure menstrual cramps, they were too much a part of the natural process, she could usually convince the muscles to relax a bit, and alleviate most of the pain.

But—something was different this time. A wave of panic swelled and rolled, threatening to bring up Mel's breakfast with it. Not cramps then. It must be the flu, she thought wildly. Settle down, Mel, focus. Breathe.

"No!" She cried out loud, nearly breaking the trance. It wasn't the flu. Her diagnostic senses weren't going to let herself hide from the truth. "It isn't possible!"

It wasn't her period, and she wasn't sick. Unless her powers were still off-kilter, way more than they'd ever been, Mel was at a loss to explain her findings. She came out of her trance with tears pouring down her face, and her hands clasped reverently over her tummy.

"Oh my!" She stared into the candle flame still woozy and a little nauseous. "I'm going to have a baby!"

Chapter Eleven

Listlessly tapping her fingers and staring out the passenger window, Mel sat beside Hattie in the silver Mercedes. The older woman had errands to run in Escanaba, so Mel had chosen to ride with her rather than accept Jonas's offer to act as chauffeur on another truck-shopping trip. She'd spent the morning with Gladys, so there was a good chance that this time she'd actually manage to purchase a new vehicle, or at least make it to the dealership.

"You going to tell me what's wrong, or just keep beating up my window?" Hattie asked after they'd traveled a few miles.

"You know what's wrong," Mel snapped. "Gladys. My truck. Cabin one!"

"Umm-hmm. Now tell me the rest of it. Three days ago when I had dinner at your place, you and Jonas were looking as cozy as two foxes in a den. You couldn't keep your hands or your eyes to yourselves, either one of you. Today, on the other hand, you couldn't ditch him quickly enough. So spill it, kiddo. I know something happened."

"It's complicated," Mel hedged. "I don't even want to think about it, let alone talk about it yet." She managed to keep her hand away from her stomach, an urge she'd had to resist a lot in the last few days. That and the urge to tie Jonas down and demand an explanation for his lies. Vasectomy. Yeah, right!

"Want to doesn't matter. I've known you too long, baby, and I can tell you need to discuss it, whatever it is."

"I'm pregnant!" This time her hand flew to her mouth. The words had popped out totally without her permission. She hadn't meant to tell anybody, not even Hattie. Not yet.

The Mercedes swerved and Hattie swore viciously as she applied her full attention to getting the big car back under control. Moments later she pulled onto a narrow, dirt, side road, and switched off the engine.

"Congratulations." Her voice was shaky and her bright blue eyes blinked rapidly. "I think."

Mel gave her a half-hearted smile and swallowed hard. Once she'd figured out the reason for her nausea, she'd been able to control it, but in moments of stress, a faint queasiness managed to resurface.

"Are you feeling okay? Are you happy about this?"

"I'm feeling fine. Mostly, anyway. And while I'm not exactly thrilled about this, part of me is over the moon. I'm still a little shell-shocked." She twisted a strand of hair around her finger, staring at that to avoid looking at her friend.

"What about Jonas? How does he feel about it?" Now Hattie was the one tapping, her manicured nails drumming lightly on the leather steering wheel cover.

"I haven't told him yet." Mel looked up and faced Hattie's gaze. No condemnation there, only concern. Her tense shoulders relaxed just a little. "He's made no secret of the fact that he doesn't want kids, ever."

Hattie shrugged, her eyes narrowing as she studied Mel's face. "Maybe he doesn't, but he still deserves to know."

"He claims he had a vasectomy."

"And?"

"And what?" Hattie wasn't going to let Mel get away with an inch, was she?

"And he obviously lied!"

"Or maybe his vasectomy failed." Hattie reached out and tucked a loose curl back behind Mel's ear. The maternal gesture brought tears, never far from the surface in the last few days, to Mel's eyes. She turned back toward the window and blinked. "It does happen, you know. Medical science isn't one hundred percent efficient. Nature has a remarkable ability to confound our best intentions, especially when it comes to the continuation of the species."

"True." Mel sighed and laid her forehead against the glass. "And curses find a way to keep going, even if it means defeating medical science." This was her worst fear. That she had betrayed Jonas by inflicting the curse on him and his seed. "I do want the baby, Hattie, but I hate deceiving Jonas. And it's going to be hard now that he's moved himself in for the summer. What if he's still here in August, and I start showing by then?"

"So tell him. It's his responsibility, too." Mel felt a comforting hand grip her shoulder.

"I know. It's just that I can't help but feel that I've betrayed his trust."

"By getting pregnant, or by not telling him?"

"Both."

"Then tell him," Hattie's gentle hand rubbed small circles on Mel's tight shoulders. "He has a right to know, as well as the responsibility. It is his baby too."

"But he doesn't want children, Hat. If I did tell him, he'd be furious. What if he demanded that I have an abortion?"

Hattie's fingers clenched then opened again on Mel's back. "He might be angry, but I doubt he'd go that far. Seems to me you could give the man a chance."

"Then there's the other end of the spectrum. What if he demands that I marry him?" Mel turned her tear-damp face to look at Hattie, and was rewarded with a warm, loving smile.

"Then you follow your heart, like every other woman under the sun."

Mel shook her head and swiped at her cheeks with the back of her hand. "It would never work. He'd hate me, Hattie, and resent the baby." Hattie had always been a bastion of practicality and sense in Mel's sometimes-surreal existence. It was beyond frustrating that now, when Mel really needed some sound advice, Hattie seemed fixed on a course that simply wasn't possible. "Have you forgotten everything you've ever known about the MacRae family? How could I ever expect him to be a permanent part of my life? It's a death sentence."

If getting pregnant had done one thing for Mel, it was to convince her of the validity of the curse. By her calculations she'd gotten pregnant that first night, and right after that her powers had started to come back. The curse was finding its way.

Hattie reached into her purse and pulled out a tissue, which she used to wipe Mel's tears, just like she'd done when Mel was little. "We all die, baby girl. Life is a terminal condition. Besides, if you told him the whole story, he might just decide it's worth the risk."

"I can't take that chance. Letting him go will be hard enough. Watching, waiting for the curse to strike, knowing I could lose him at any time, and that it would be all my fault… It just isn't possible." She took the tissue from Hattie and blew her nose, then stuffed it in the pocket of her jeans.

Hattie's lips twisted into a rueful smile, and she tapped Mel lightly on the nose with the tip of one finger. "Because you love him."

Mel gasped. She tried to frame a denial, but the words wouldn't come, so she sat there, gaping like a fish.

Damn! She did. She loved him! When had that happened? "Oh, great. There's another whopping huge secret I have to keep from Jonas." As if the strain of keeping quiet about her pregnancy wasn't already driving her crazy. They'd hardly talked in the last couple days since she'd made her discovery, let alone made love. He'd noticed her withdrawal when he'd returned from his walk that day, and though he'd seemed to accept it at first, today he'd begun showing signs of impatience and frustration. When she'd announced her intention to ride into Escanaba with Hattie, he'd been ticked, and though he hadn't said a word, she'd thought he was maybe even a little bit hurt.

Hurting someone you loved really sucked. It stunk to cause them pain, and she knew she was going to hurt Jonas, one way or another. Still, it was a whole lot better to cause hurt than to cause them to be dead. She stared out the window in silence for the rest of the trip.

"But you're going to keep the baby?" Hattie's tone was completely nonjudgmental.

"Of course." Mel nodded and sniffled. Hattie handed her another tissue.

"Because despite all your bluster about not passing on your so-called curse, deep down inside, you've always longed to have children of your own." Hattie leaned across the console and wrapped Mel in a warm, motherly hug. Mel returned the embrace, her arms wrapping tightly around Hattie's slim shoulders.

"Yeah, well *wanting* a baby is an abstract kind of thing." As she straightened, Mel bit her lip and tried to smile. Then she took a deep breath. "Like wanting to be taller, or smarter, or prettier. *Having* one inside you, however, is suddenly very concrete." And concrete was exactly what she felt in her stomach every time she thought about the baby.

* * * *

Something was definitely up with Mel! Joe slammed the door of his Jeep so hard that a couple people passing on the sidewalk jumped and scurried past. Since Mel was off with Hattie, he'd taken advantage of the opportunity to come into town. He'd drop off the books he'd borrowed at the library, then spend some time at the courthouse digging through records. It was amazing the things you could learn from property titles and death certificates.

Right now, though, the most pressing question on his mind was in Hattie Sharp's Mercedes, heading toward Escanaba. Without him! He inhaled deeply, taking a moment to calm himself before striding into the small library building. Mrs. Halloran, the librarian/clerk, gave him a sharp glare as he approached.

"Book returns go in the slot," she snapped, pointing at the clearly labeled opening. "I'll be closing for lunch in ten minutes."

Joe raised one eyebrow. The hours marked on the door hadn't mentioned anything about closing for the lunch hour, but the older woman met his gaze squarely with all the aplomb and dignity of a queen facing down an unruly subject. He had no doubt that if he challenged her edict, she'd have the sheriff's department in here showing him the door. This chilly reception had to be because of his association with Mel. She hadn't been this unwelcoming before, and he couldn't imagine that she treated all the tourists in a similar manner. Not in a town that depended on tourism for most of its economy.

"Fine." He dropped the books into the slot, the resulting thunk echoed through the room, then he nodded politely. "Enjoy your lunch, Mrs. Halloran."

His reception at the courthouse was nearly as cool, though not as direct. The clerk there was a younger woman, without Halloran's years of practiced disapproval. This one merely ignored Joe's presence, except for occasionally wrinkling her nose, as if she smelled something vile that she just couldn't pin down.

Joe ignored her in return, rummaging through the document room, pouring over yellowed pages and faded forms, until he had Mel's family tree established back to 1842. He had marriage licenses, birth and death certificates, and property transfers to support the information.

One thing he learned was that Mel hadn't been exaggerating the stories about her ancestors. For generation after generation, MacRae women had borne illegitimate daughters, usually just one per generation. At least that was all that ever made it to adulthood. The few who had married had been widowed early, except for one whose husband had run off in the 1890's to search for gold in the Yukon and never returned. No wonder Mel was shy of relationships.

While he searched for Mel's past, another segment of his brain was busy pondering her present. Her behavior had taken a hundred and eighty degree turn in the past few days. When he'd first moved in, she'd been warm, inviting, eagerly sexual. The situation had been so domestically cozy that he'd nearly panicked, but had convinced himself to relax, let the future take care of itself. Somehow.

Anyway, they'd been getting along great, both in bed and out. He'd even thought she was okay with his big confession. Then one morning he'd gone out for a walk, only to come back to a different woman. Instead of warm and exuberant, she'd become cold and withdrawn. So far, nothing he'd managed to do had been able to break her out of it. The camaraderie had vanished. She didn't even seem to want to talk to him anymore, and even though they still shared her bed, she wore long pajamas and curled up on the far edge of the mattress. The only time she softened toward him was in her sleep. Once she was out, then he was allowed to cuddle. Joe was getting so damn frustrated he was ready to explode.

Maybe her witchy senses had tipped her off to the fact that there was more he hadn't told her yet. A voice inside his head that couldn't possibly be his conscience began urging him to tell her the *whole* truth. He knew better, of course. Even if she was a witch, that didn't mean she could cope with having a werewolf for a lover. Joe fed dimes into the antiquated copy machine and sighed. That was just too much to expect. His own mother hadn't been able to handle what he was. He couldn't hope for a lover to get past it. No, that was one secret he couldn't share with a woman. Ever.

When he finished up at the records office, Joe decided to make one last stop. Sheriff Mott's office was right here at the courthouse, after all. The man was in, so Joe was ushered into a small Spartan office by a pretty young blonde with glasses and a shy grin. Joe smiled back. She was the first person who'd been friendly since he got into town today.

"My daughter, Veronica." Mott waved Joe into a chair as the girl left and closed the office door behind her. "Hurt her back real bad when she was twelve. Doctors didn't think she'd ever walk again. Martha MacRae showed up on my doorstep, told me the doctors were a bunch of quacks, then she spent the night just sitting by Ronnie's bed. Next morning Ronnie could wiggle her toes. By the end of the week she was back on her feet."

Joe sat on the straight-backed wooden chair facing Mott's desk, and tipped his chin to acknowledge the other man's point. "So you understand that Mel is an exceptional woman."

"No question." Mott leaned backing his own metal chair that had seen better days. The Sanctity county treasury sure didn't waste much money on appearances in here. The office was shabbily functional at best. "She's definitely got the gift, maybe even stronger than her Grandma did."

"So why on Earth are you letting this harassment continue?"

The sheriff placed both hands flat on his desk and leaned toward Joe. "Because all I've seen so far is the kind of petty vandalism that's usually caused by kids on a drinking binge. I don't have any evidence, Mr. Pierce, or anyone to go after."

"But…"

"Find me some solid proof, something that will hold up in a court of law, and I'll have the bastard's ass in a sling before you can blink. Until then, I have no justification for going after one of the biggest taxpayers in the county." He picked up a chewed wooden pencil and toyed with it.

"How about the fact that I've seen him physically assault her?"

The pencil in Mott's hand snapped in two, and he tossed the halves back over his shoulder. His eyes narrowed as he sucked in a breath. "Go on."

"He had his hands on her, sheriff, and he was pushing her further into the barn. She asked him to leave; he said no. Then he told her that she and her land were both going to be his."

"Shit." Mott's curse was quiet but vehement. "Can you talk her into pressing charges?"

"No." Shaking his head, Joe sighed. "She says nobody will believe her. Or me."

"I do," the sheriff admitted. His face sagged. It was as through he'd aged ten years since the beginning of the conversation. "Between you and me, I'd love to arrest that spoiled little shit. Unfortunately, going up against the Talcotts without concrete evidence is pointless. I might just as well pack up and head for Florida now—my career would be over."

"Got it." Joe did understand the man's position, but he was still infuriated. "Just keep your eyes and your mind open then. I'll be sticking to Mel like glue till this is over. Anybody who tries to hurt her is going to have to go through me first, and I guarantee, that isn't going to be pretty."

"Fair enough," the older man acknowledged. "And if you don't mind my saying so, it's about time somebody had the guts to look past that so-called curse. Always thought it was a load of crap, myself, but those MacRae women believe it to the bone. The healing's one thing. That's a talent you can see. Letting a sweet kid like Melissa grow old alone because of words some bitch spewed out a hundred years ago… That always struck me as just plain chicken."

Nodding his agreement, Joe eyed the older man with a new wariness. Just what was his interest in Mel? He wore a wedding ring, had a grown daughter, but still one could never tell.

Mott let out a bark of laughter and leaned back in his seat. "Relax, son. I'm not after your girl. I had a brief thing with her mother Marilyn back in high school. I'm almost sure Melissa isn't my daughter."

"Almost?"

"Marilyn swore she wasn't, even when I offered to marry her. And no, Melissa doesn't look a thing like me. Just in case, though, I've always been just a little protective."

Joe nodded, sending the man a wry smile. Sanctity was turning out to be quite the little Peyton Place. He stood and held out his hand. "Thanks for the information. I'm sure you'll be hearing from me again."

"I sure hope so." Mott stood too, giving Joe's hand a hearty shake. "And Pierce, you be good to Melissa, you hear? I'd hate to have to come after you as well."

"Understood. Though frankly, you don't scare me half as much as Hattie. I've already had this conversation with her."

Mott laughed. "Fair enough. I wouldn't want to face her wrath either. That's one reason I proposed to Marilyn in the first place."

Joe's step was lighter as he left the county building and walked down the street to Rosa's Diner. Was Mott really Mel's father? All Joe's instincts were telling him no. There were no similarities, not in coloring, build, or even the way they moved. Joe's extra senses told him that they didn't even have a similar scent, which was the clincher in his mind. Too bad. If the sheriff really was Mel's dad, maybe he'd do a better job of protecting her. If any child of his was in danger, Joe knew that he'd stop at nothing to protect it. The law wouldn't even be an issue.

Not knowing if a child was his or not, now that must really be a bitch. What had it been like for Mott to look at Mel for all these years and wonder? That had to suck the big one. Joe was glad for the decision he'd made years ago. Kids were okay at a distance, but he never wanted to be responsible for the safety and well-being of another human life. Worse yet, given his genetics, another *mostly* human life!

Still in a funk, he plopped down at the counter in Rosa's, sparing a brief smile for the attractive young waitress. One of Rosa's grand-daughters or nieces, he wasn't quite sure which. She'd sent him unmistakable signals the few times he'd come in here without Mel. She was cute enough, he supposed, but way too young for him, and the truth was, he wasn't even tempted. Being in a remotely exclusive relationship was weird, he'd never even come close before, but odd as it seemed, the only woman he wanted was Mel.

"No-meat burrito," he ordered. "Beans and rice on the side." He didn't even meet her eyes, and she sashayed off as soon as she'd written down his order. He was still lost in thought when a heavy ceramic plate slammed onto the chipped Formica counter in front of his face. This time he looked up.

"So somebody is a famous author, hmmm?"

"Busted." He gazed solemnly into Rosa's black eyes, wondering how she'd found out. He was sure Mel hadn't told anybody.

"Slumming?"

"Lying low," he corrected. "Avoiding over-zealous reporters who think my personal life is more interesting than my books." Of course, for the first time in his life, it was. How odd.

"Melissa know?"

"Isn't that between the two of us?" Rosa just shook her head, and Joe caved. It seemed like everyone in the whole damn town who wasn't out to get Mel was determined to protect her. Including him. "Of course she does."

"That reporter you mentioned, short guy right? Light brown hair, kind of weasely looking?"

All Joe's senses went on instant alert. "Erickson. Yeah. He's the worst of the bunch, all right."

"Well, then." Rosa hunkered down across the counter from Joe. She'd been speaking quietly, but now her voice dropped even lower. "He was in here this morning." Fishing around in her apron pocket, she came out with a partially crumpled business card, and handed it to Joe.

"Andrew Erickson, *Personalities Weekly*." Joe's worst fears were confirmed. Erickson was the slimiest writer for the sleaziest tabloid. Unfortunately, he was also a pit bull, and Joe was his current bone of choice. "Fuck."

"I bought you some time. Didn't think he was a friend of yours, so I sent him on a wild goose chase. Told him I hadn't seen anybody remotely like you. Then I suggested that he might want to try Sanctuary, Wisconsin. People mix up the two all the time, since it's just across the state line, about five hours due west. He lit out in a hurry." She nodded at the door. "I expect he'll be back tomorrow, though next day at the latest. Anyway, you'll at least have enough time to tell Mel goodbye."

To the amusement of all of the other customers in the diner, Joe grabbed Rosa's broad shoulders and planted a loud smacking kiss on her lined forehead. "Rosa, you are truly an angel." He gestured at his plate. "Can you box that up for me? I'll eat it back at the cabin."

She did, watching him with worried eyes all the while. *She thinks I'm out of here.* Suddenly Joe found that notion offensive. He wasn't going to leave Mel in the lurch just because Erickson had traced him to Sanctity.

He should, of course. Winding up in *Personalities Weekly* as J. P. Wolfe's latest conquest probably wasn't going to do Mel any good in the long run. Furthermore, Erickson was just too damn close to uncovering Joe's secret—the big one, not just his real name. Yeah, Joe really ought to hit the road. Australia might be far enough to put the pit bull off the scent.

Instead, he was going home to Mel.

"When he comes back, give me a call." Joe handed Rosa his card with the satellite phone number. "You can reach me at this number if you can't get through at Mel's place."

"Good." Approval radiated from her, as obvious as Mrs. Halloran's disdain or Mott's warning. Interesting town, Sanctity. Everything was everybody's business, and there were no indifferent opinions. Right now, everyone in town was either determined to protect Mel or dead-set against her.

Joe stood, accepted his boxed up dinner, and tried to hand Rosa a ten-dollar bill.

"This one's on me, cowboy." She pushed the bill back toward him, and gestured at a wall displaying a bunch of celebrity photos and autographs. "There's a second burrito in there for Mel. You make sure she eats it. When all this is over, you owe me a picture."

Once again, he leaned over the counter. This time he dropped a kiss on the top of her head. "Deal."

* * * *

Despite her resolution to stay as far from Jonas as possible, Mel was a little disappointed that she didn't find him waiting for her when she returned. She wanted to show off her new minivan, which would haul anything she needed to haul but still be way safer for a car seat. Not that she'd planned to tell him that detail. She was just going to mention that she'd gotten a great deal.

Sheila, Mel's college-student assistant, was waiting in the office though, so Mel demonstrated all the features of her new toy while taking Sheila's report for the afternoon. Sheila's youthful enthusiasm always made Mel smile.

"I got the new family checked into cabin three." They'd both climbed into the front seat of the van, and Sheila played with the buttons on the stereo, cooing her approval at the CD changer. "They've got the world's cutest little girl by the way. Oh, I also got all the glass and stuff swept up in unit one, so we can start the serious cleaning tomorrow."

Thank the gods! Mel rolled her eyes heavenward. Starting the clean-up was the hardest part, and a task Mel had been putting off since the insurance company had given the go-ahead.

"Great work, Shee." They climbed out of the van. Mel took a couple of steps toward her office then stopped. She couldn't wait any longer. It had simply been too long since she'd seen Jonas, and after her talk with Hattie, Mel really felt a need to talk to him, maybe suss out his feelings a bit more. "I see Mr. Pierce's car, but he isn't around, is he?"

"You mean Jonas?" Sheila's brown eyes went bright with feminine approval. "He stuck your dinner in the fridge, then went for a walk. He seemed kind of antsy, kept wondering why you weren't home yet. Nice work, by the way, boss. I don't suppose he's got a younger brother?"

"Nope." Mel grinned and shook her head. "He's an only child."

"Well, shoot." Sheila chuckled and grinned back, loping up the steps. "That rules out nephews, too. Cousins, you think?"

"I don't think so. Jonas Pierce is one of a kind." They both giggled, and Mel gave Sheila an affectionate shove back toward the office.

"Nuts." Sheila wrinkled up her nose as she teased. "This summer isn't going to be nearly as interesting as I had hoped. Only one hot single guest, and you've already snagged him before I even got here."

"If there's nothing to do in the office, you can go start scraping paint off the floors in cabin one. And there's a group of guys coming up from Michigan State in a couple weeks. Maybe they'll be more your speed." She wasn't worried about her young friend. Sheila was way too sensible to get seriously involved before she finished up her studies.

"Sounds good." She ducked into the office and returned in a second with the bucket of cleaning supplies, then with her thick dark braid slapping against her back, Sheila trotted back to cabin one, calling out over her shoulder. "He walked down toward the lake just in case you're interested."

"Damn, am I that transparent?"

She still wasn't sure it was a good idea, but she wanted, no needed, to see Jonas. Would it be too early to start blaming hormones for her idiotic behavior? She set off down the path. *Yeah, It's hormones all right, just not the ones that come from being pregnant.* The hormones urging her to go find Jonas were the same ones that had gotten her into that state in the first place.

Thinking about him, which she seemed to do on the average of about twenty-three and a half hours per day, still made her feel all—well—squishy inside. There was no single word she could think of to describe the way he made her pulse race, her stomach flutter, and her mouth dry up all at the same time. It was completely outside of her frame of reference.

Would their daughter look like him? Would she have Jonas's dark hair or uncanny amber eyes? Mel hoped so. It would be a joy to be able to see his eyes or his smile every day for the next twenty or so years. She needed to get some photos of him soon. She'd want to be able to show her daughter what her daddy looked like, and to be able to assure the child that he was a good man. No daughter of Mel's was going to go through life wondering who had fathered her.

Amber. Mel's thoughts turned dreamy, imagining a curly-haired tot with coppery-brown hair, a few tiny freckles, and Jonas's big golden brown eyes. *I could name her Amber.* There was no law that demanded the MacRae daughters be given names beginning with M. Mel had had it up to here with mindless adherence to family tradition. Amber it was going to be! Even if her eyes turned out to be MacRae green.

A flash of magenta and teal caught her eye, and Mel returned her attention to her surroundings. The bright colors belonged to a swatch of fabric lying off in the grass, and on closer inspection, Mel recognized it as the striped rugby shirt Jonas had been wearing that morning. It was neatly folded in the underbrush, and stacked with his jeans, briefs, and running shoes.

A whisper of sound from behind her had her spinning; her nerves had been on high alert since Sean's attack. She quieted immediately, though. It wasn't Sean's gaze staring back at her but the glowing golden eyes of her friendly neighborhood wolf. Mel sighed in relief, holding out her hand. The wolf stepped closer, allowing her to stroke the silky dark pelt with its one white streak.

One white streak. Smiling with a flash of understanding, Mel took in the wolf's swirling aura and bright amber eyes. Her knees gave out, and she plopped backward onto her bottom, sitting hard on the forest floor. Still smiling, she re-extended her hand.

"Hello, Jonas."

Chapter Twelve

Joe froze.

God damn it, how had she figured it out?

He already had unpleasant news to tell her, but now it was going to be a doozy. Instinctively, he lowered his head and backed away. She couldn't be sure, could she? Maybe he could brazen this out.

"It's the eyes, mostly." Her voice and smile were soft and sweet. There was no trace of the revulsion or horror he'd anticipated, just a tender, aching sadness in her gaze. Joe remained utterly still. "And the white streak. But the aura is even more obvious, now that I'm paying attention. If I hadn't been so distracted, I would have picked up on it weeks ago. Oh, Jonas, why didn't you just tell me?"

When he didn't move, she reached out and he stayed put, allowing her to touch the white streak at his temple. "No wonder we're so attracted to one another. We're two of a kind, aren't we? Both prisoners of our DNA."

Fuck! Not only did she know, she also understood at least a little. There was no point trying to keep up the bluff now. How the hell was he supposed to handle this? He decided it would be easier with clothes on and lips capable of forming coherent words. Settling down on his haunches, he heaved an enormous sigh, and changed.

Despite his hope that she'd avert her gaze and give him some privacy, Mel stared fixedly during the entire transformation. Well, he supposed that someone with as much exposure to the supernatural as she had was bound to be curious. He certainly was; he'd made a career out of it, so he couldn't really blame her. Still, he stared back, less than comfortable sitting on the forest floor buck naked.

As if she'd read his thoughts, she handed him his jockey shorts. "I guess you'll want these." She still refused to look away, but that was okay with him. She'd watched him dress before, and he'd never been particularly modest in the first place. He stood and donned his garments as she handed them to him, one at a time. When he was finally fully clothed, he squatted down beside her, concerned, and laid his hand on her cheek. Her skin was pale, and cool to the touch.

"You okay?"

She blinked, shaking her head. "Yeah." Then she grinned broadly. "Jonas, that was the coolest thing I've ever seen."

His laughter was as much from relief as amusement.

Her grin disappeared. "What's so funny?"

God, she was even cuter when she got prickly. "You. Only you." He sat down and pulled her into his arms, kissing her fiercely. "Any other woman would have been halfway to Detroit by now, screaming her head off. You think it's cool."

"Well, I am a little disappointed if that helps." Her color was returning, so she wasn't about to faint on him, thank God.

"Disappointed? Why?"

"Well, I thought the Preserve was getting a wolf population returning." Her teasing was thawing out areas of his soul that he hadn't even known were frozen. "Instead it was just a four-legged tourist."

"Sorry." Standing, he held onto her hands, and lifted her to her feet beside him. The he pulled one hand away and stroked her cheek, turning her chin up so he could meet her gaze. "There's more, though, isn't there?"

"I guess." She dusted the seat of her jeans off with one hand, but let him keep the other as they turned back toward her cabin.

"What?"

"I might be a little ticked off that you didn't bother to tell me. You should have known I'd understand as soon as I told you about being a witch. I don't like secrets, Jonas." There was a funny look on her face, almost like guilt, but he brushed the idea aside. This was his confession time. Whatever minor secrets Mel was keeping from him could wait.

* * * *

Awestruck, Mel watched as the magnificent wolf transformed in a shimmer of light into the equally impressive form of a man. Jonas. It explained so much. The eyes, the aura, her sense that the wolf both understood and protected her. It hurt, though, that he hadn't told her, and she wondered how she could have missed the obvious for so long.

Her thoughts reeled as they walked along the winding trail back to her cabin. It was hard to be mad at him for keeping secrets while she was keeping a whopper from him.

"Mel?" She could sense his wariness as he waited for her to continue.

She tried to explain. "You knew who I was, *what* I was before we got involved with one another. I trusted you. I guess it didn't work both ways."

"It isn't that simple, Mel. It isn't about trust." He pulled his hand away, and she missed it.

"Isn't it?"

"No." Stuffing both of his hands into the back pockets of his jeans, he pulled away from her and stared off into the trees. "Your witchcraft isn't a secret, Mel. It wasn't told to me in confidence; I knew about that before I even came to Sanctity."

"True." But not necessarily what she'd wanted to hear. "Go on."

"Nobody knows I'm a werewolf. I've only ever shared my secret with one living soul, and he hasn't even told his wife."

"Kent Willoughby." He was the only person Jonas had ever mentioned as a friend with actual affection in his tone. Obviously the relationship was even more important than she'd realized. Kent wasn't just Jonas's best friend, he was his only true friend.

"Right. He'd been my roommate for three years when he found out, and that was under less than ideal circumstances."

"Tell me." She walked over and put her hands on his shoulders. He'd kept so much bottled up for so long. The pain radiating from him was palpable, and her anger evaporated.

"Kent's a doctor, and he was a pre-med student then. There was an—accident one night, and I needed the help of somebody I could trust." She bet he didn't even hear the hurt that laced his voice.

"Don't werewolves have some sort of supernatural healing ability?"

"Don't believe everything you read, please. Do all witches wear black hats and ride around on broomsticks?"

"Touché." Her words must have penetrated his mood, though. He wrapped one arm around her and turned back to the trail.

"But you can heal yourself, can't you? When I scratched you in bed that time, I didn't unconsciously heal you. You did it yourself."

"Yeah." He started moving again, but kept his arm around her waist as she walked alongside.

"So why did you need Kent that night?"

"There are some injuries that don't heal the same." He paused again and pointed to the small scar at this temple that led into the white streak in his hair. "This was one of them. It was the one time in my life I needed stitches."

"How did it happen?"

"It isn't something I like to talk about."

She'd dragged enough out of him for now; she could tell he needed some time to deal with the revelations. She gave him a quick one-armed hug, and nudged him back down the trail. "Okay."

∗ ∗ ∗ ∗

She waited till after they'd eaten to ask more questions. They were drinking tea on her back porch, enjoying the moonlight. A warm breeze carried the scents of the forest onto the deck, and ruffled the ends of their hair.

"Are there many of you?"

He shot her a pointed look and she grinned, that beautiful quirky smile he adored. He could only marvel that she had accepted this so easily. He took a sip of the herbal tea to soothe the lump in his throat.

"Werewolves, I mean. I know there's only one Jonas Pierce."

"I honestly don't know," he replied. "I haven't met any outside my immediate family."

"It's hereditary, then? You parents were werewolves, too?"

"Just my father." He'd promised himself he'd tell her everything she wanted to know. But this, he just didn't know if he could. At least without falling apart.

"And you don't—catch it from being bitten?"

"Nope, that's strictly vampires. So even if I do bite in bed, you're safe on that count." He waggled his eyebrows suggestively, evoking a laugh. God, he loved her laugh.

"That's good to know. It would be a pain being both a werewolf and a witch." She was silent for a minute, her fingers tapping a staccato beat on the arm of her chair. Finally, she sighed and shook her head. "This is it, right? No more surprises? Maybe werewolves are immortal and you're really three hundred and two? I'd really appreciate it if we could get it all out of the way right now."

"Actually, I'm only thirty-nine, but there is one more thing."

Wide eyes that looked silver in the moonlight regarded him warily, but she reached across the arms of their chairs and took his hand. "What?"

"Remember I told you I was hiding?" He laid their clasped hands on the wide wooden arm of her Adirondack chair and gripped her fingers tight. "That there's a reporter from *Personalities Weekly* who's been essentially stalking me? He knows my real name and he's been staking out my apartment and my house in Vermont. From the hints he's dropped in his column, I'm afraid he suspects…"

"The *big* secret."

"Right. The big secret. The I-don't-want-to-become-a-government-sponsored-research-project secret. That's why I chose an out-of-the-way vacation spot, and had my accountant make the reservations. Then I openly bought a first-class ticket to Spain, and had somebody else book a hotel suite in my name. I'd hoped it was enough to throw him off the scent."

"Does your accountant know?"

"Only that I'm obsessed with privacy. Not why. The only people who know are Kent and you." And his father, he supposed, if the old bastard was still alive.

"And maybe this slime ball reporter."

"Maybe. The kicker is that Andy Erickson, the reporter, was in Sanctity this morning."

"Of course he was." He could hear her grit her teeth.

"I don't know how he found me, but the guy's a pit bull. He showed up at Rosa's asking questions."

"That must have been interesting." Her snort was anything but ladylike, but it was kind of cute. She squeezed his fingers.

"I'm sure. Anyway, Rosa didn't tell him anything. She sent him on a wild goose chase to Sanctuary, Wisconsin."

"Good for her!" Mel snickered. Then she sighed. "Too bad he'll probably be back, gunning for bear."

"Probably by tomorrow." Joe wished he could disagree. "Odds are, he'll find me this time."

"Sure." She looked at him with her wry grin and shook her head. "He asks anywhere besides Rosa's, somebody will be only too happy to tell him where you are, who you've been with." Did she have to sound so reasonable about it? It was unsettling that he could never predict her moods. He set his mug down on the deck and slid out of his chair, coming to his knees in front of her. He removed the mug from her hand, and gripped her fingers, so their clasped hands formed a small, intimate circle.

"So I'm going to ask you one more time, Mel, to go away with me. We'll go anywhere you want, even if I have to stay inside the hotel room when I change."

"Jonas, that's sweet, but I can't." Damn, he'd expected that, but he'd had to try. She bent down and brushed a soft kiss on his forehead. "I'll miss you, though."

"Miss me?" That one caught him off guard. "Why?"

"Well, obviously, you have to leave. I can stall your reporter for a day or two, keep him sniffing around here while you disappear."

Her generosity was overwhelming, but he'd already made that decision back at Rosa's. "I'm staying. There's still some jerk-off hassling you, remember? I can't leave you alone to face that and my problems as well. I'll just have to be careful while Erickson's around. I won't be able to change for a while."

"Jonas…"

He let go of one of her hands and stopped her protest with a finger to her lips. "I'm staying. Not forever, you know I can't commit to that, and I think maybe now you're starting to understand why. You should have definitely figured out why I don't want kids. I'm not going to pass this—this curse of mine onto another generation. But I do care about you, and I'm not going anywhere while you could be in danger. Sooner or later, I would have had to face Erickson anyway. It might as well be now."

"I see." Her voice was tiny, enigmatic.

"I just hope you realize that he's probably going to be all over you, too. Even without the werewolf bit, he's going to have a field day reporting that I'm shacked up with a witch."

"Shacking up?" That earned him another snicker, and a poke in the ribs. Her grimace, though, told him she hadn't considered that angle. "What a mess."

"You're sure you wouldn't like to see Scotland? Maybe Africa?" There were wolves in both of those places.

"I'd love to," she admitted. "Unfortunately, I wouldn't have a business to return to if I did. And I can't leave Gladys. Not now."

"No. Of course not." He'd gone with her to visit her friend the day before. She'd been able to take him up on his offer of assistance, and it had been the strangest experience of his life, feeling his own strength flow through Mel, and into the sick woman. He'd been drained afterward, as had Mel, but at least she hadn't made herself ill again. And somehow, it had been one of the most intimate moments of his life. He'd felt the affection between the two women, and he knew there was no way Mel could desert Gladys when the older woman only had a week or two left. He couldn't leave Mel to face that by herself, either.

"So, I suppose I'm going to be famous." Mel cracked a smile, or almost. It came out as more of a grimace. "At least the publicity should be good for business."

"Probably. Your friend Talcott will try to find some way to spin it against you, though. I'm not sure how, but you know he's going to be pissed if your business picks up."

"I'll just send him the overflow." Then she sagged, the forced humor leaving her face. He pulled her off her chair and into his lap, wrapping both arms around her slender frame. "But he's still after my land, and yes, if he can spin this situation to help achieve that goal, he will." She pressed her face into his shoulder, then pulled back and rubbed her eye sockets with the heel of her hand.

"Headache?" He hated that he was even indirectly responsible for her pain.

"A whopper," she confessed.

"And you can't heal yourself, can you?"

"A little. I can focus enough energy to seal a cut, or fix a sprain if I really need to, but it's hard. My gift, talent, whatever you want to call it was meant to work on others. Besides, a tension headache is mostly psychological, isn't it?" Her lopsided grin had his stomach doing flips. "I can't do a damned thing about mental distress."

"The let me have a try," he offered. He shifted, lifting himself back into the chair. Then he pulled her up to sit in the vee of his legs. The position was uncomfortably intimate, but he tried to tune that out, focusing only on her aching muscles, ignoring the usual erotic pull. It was his turn to be the healer.

"Mmm. You're good." She sighed, and her muscles started to relax under his touch. "Where'd you learn to do that?"

He started to hesitate, then confessed. "A Swedish stewardess I used to know."

She chuckled. "Figures."

Not knowing how to respond, he just kept kneading.

"I've read some of your books, you know."

"Really?" He couldn't keep the surprise from his voice. "I wouldn't have thought you were into horror."

"I'm a witch, idiot." She spoke slowly, as if explaining to a slightly dim child. "I'm always interested in the supernatural."

"I know that, but aren't my books a little, well, dark for your taste?" His reputation for bloodcurdling detail and grim endings was well-deserved.

"Yeah," she confessed with a giggle. "I only read two. They were wonderfully written, but the Transylvanian vampire story gave me nightmares."

"Well, they were intended to be creepy," he agreed. "They're based on creepy stuff. It's okay, you know. Actually, I'm sort of glad you're not a fan. The groupie scene gets really old, really fast."

"If you say so." Her back was much looser now, her muscles rapidly turning to Jell-O under his ministrations. Odd how he felt as proud of that as he had his first six-figure advance.

"So, how much of your work is based on fact?"

It was the one question nobody had ever asked. Most people didn't want to. "Maybe twenty percent. Another fifty or so is based on old legends and regional beliefs. The rest is pure bullshit."

"Have you ever written about a werewolf?"

"No."

She yelped as he unconsciously dug his fingers into the tender muscles of her shoulder. "Sorry," she sulked. "Geez it was just a question."

"And a perfectly valid one," he was forced to admit. "But no, that would be just a little too close to home to share with the masses."

"But I would have thought that's why you started. Trying to find out about your own heritage."

"It was. But for some reason, I've only ever come up with bits and pieces. Most of what I know is what the old man told me. I've never managed to get close to another werewolf. I don't even know if there are any others."

She changed the subject. "What about witches?"

"Not like you. I once wrote one about a coven in Ireland, but that was a very different thing." The breeze tossed her curls into his face, and the heady herbal scent hit his already-overloaded libido like a brick.

"Was the coven real? With powers?"

"Real, yes; powers, I don't think so. They were convinced of it though, and so was the local populace." It took a second to get enough blood flowing back to his brain to answer her question. He remembered his time there, remembered tipping off the police just in time to prevent another sacrifice. "Bloodthirsty bunch. Literally."

"Ick!" Mel shuddered under his hands. "Are you going to write a book about me?"

"I already told you I'm not. Sure, your family history would make a great back story, but I won't use it." One of his hands stopped kneading her shoulder to filter through her silky hair. Confession time. Again. "I care about you too much to exploit you like that." Then, to lighten the mood, he bit her lightly on the ear. "But don't be too surprised if my next heroine is a spunky redhead with turquoise eyes and a knack with animals."

"Flattery will get you nowhere."

His lips twitched at the sultry amusement in her tone. "Won't it? How about into your bed?"

"Well, you're already there, aren't you?"

"Yeah, every night." Then he sobered. "But it hasn't been quite as interesting in the last few days, has it? What's been wrong, Mel? Why have you been avoiding me? I've wanted you so badly. I'm liable to explode."

* * * *

She could hear the confusion and hurt in his voice, but she didn't know what to tell him. His reasons for avoiding commitment and marriage made more sense now, and her guilt was even heavier, but she still didn't understand why he considered his heritage such a curse that he didn't want children.

So she asked. "Why did you call it a curse? I'd think being able to change into a wolf was a gift, not a problem."

"It isn't like that. It's not about being able to change, it's about having to."

"You can't choose?"

"Sort of. I have to spend some time in both forms. If I try to go too long without changing, the need sort of builds up. It's like being an alcoholic or something. The instincts take over."

"That must make it hard, living in Manhattan." His hands were working magic on her sore shoulders, and having a noticeable effect on other parts of her as well. She could feel her nipples tighten, and moisture pool between her legs.

"That's why I have the place up in Vermont. I'm only in the city about two weeks out of every month."

"Full moon?"

"Please, we're back to believing in stories again. But, yeah, that one has some basis. The urge is more powerful then, just as it gets more powerful when I'm under any kind of stress."

"Hence the need for Jonas Pierce to always remain in control." She turned sideways, laying her hands on top of his to stop his kneading. All the pieces were falling into place. "So tell me more. Which of the old stories are true? You said you can't turn somebody into a werewolf by biting them. What about silver bullets? Is that really the only way to kill you?" Even the thought made her cringe, but it would be nice to know that Jonas was immune to normal attacks.

He shook his head and kissed her nose. "No. Any bullet, properly placed, can kill me. I'm as mortal as anybody else, but I heal faster, so a shot that misses anything really vital will heal before it kills me. If I ever take a shot to the heart or brain, I won't be able to heal myself fast enough to recover."

"But you said that some injuries don't heal as fast." She ran her hand through the silver streak in his hair, which stood out even in the moonlight. The silky strands slid through her fingers. "Was that from silver?"

"No, silver is just another metal. I'm guessing that the legend of silver bullets comes from the fact that in the old days, guns were notoriously inaccurate. Anyone rich enough to have bullets made from solid silver was probably also wealthy enough to have exceptionally well-made firearms, and the appropriate training to use them. In other words, silver bullets equaled better shots."

"So what gave you this scar?" She felt his whole body tense. His thighs went rigid beneath hers and his hands clenched down on her shoulders almost painfully. She knew this was one secret he hated to tell, which meant that it was one he needed to share. "Jonas."

"Werewolf saliva," he gritted. "The bite from another werewolf seems to cause an allergic reaction or something that causes the wounds to get infected and refuse to heal."

"So you fought another werewolf."

"Yes." It was almost a growl. She was close enough to see that his jaw barely unclenched enough to form the word.

"But you said you'd never met any outside your immediate family."

He turned his head away. "Damn, do you have to remember everything?"

"Your father? Or a brother?"

"My father," he admitted. She could see his eye squeeze shut. "Repeatedly."

She turned into him, wrapped her arms around him and squeezed as tight as she could. "I'm so sorry, Jonas. Please tell me about it." She pulled back just far enough to talk, but kept her arms looped around his neck.

"It was money, as usual. He found me at college, tried to talk me into giving him cash. Lack of money meant lack of booze, and he wasn't about to let that happen. When I refused, he waited outside the dorm and tried to mug me." His voice was as flat as she'd ever heard it, almost as though he were telling one of his own stories.

She kissed his cheek, not caring that tears streaked down her own. "How awful. What happened then?"

"I didn't kill him if that's what you're asking. Damn near, though. Once the killing rage takes over, it's hard to regain control."

"Of course you didn't!" She was shocked he'd even think he was capable of that. She knew better. Then another light bulb went off in her head. "That's why you're a vegetarian. You made a choice not to be a predator. I bet you don't even hunt when you're a wolf, do your?"

He let out a choked sound that she assumed was a strangled laugh.

"It's messy. I don't like changing back with my face covered in rabbit blood."

She laughed back. Sure, that was the reason. She hugged him again and nuzzled the side of his neck. His determination to control his wilder side only added to her respect for this multifaceted man in her arms. "I'm so sorry you had to go through that."

"I haven't seen him since. I have no idea if he's alive or dead."

There was so much raw pain in his voice, she had to offer whatever comfort she could. She placed one hand on each cheek and turned his face, staring directly into his eyes.

"You are a good man, Jonas Pierce. Werewolf or not. I'm sorrier than I can say that your father wasn't." And then she kissed him, letting all the love she felt for him flow through her touch.

He returned the kiss, hesitantly at first, then with increasing hunger. When he finally pulled his lips away from hers, he surged to his feet, easily lifting her with him. He carried her to the door, pausing to let her reach out and work the latch. Once inside he kicked the door shut and carried her to her living room couch, where he laid her down with almost reverential tenderness, then knelt on the floor alongside her.

"Now, about the other thing." Jonas brought his face down to hers, his breath caressing her cheek. "Did I do something to bother you, to turn you off? Because lying in bed with you at night and not having sex is just about killing me."

"It's not that I haven't wanted to." She reached up to loop her arms about his shoulders and sighed. After all he'd just gone through, she owed him some explanation. "It's just that with everything else that's been going on lately, I've been feeling kind of overwhelmed. I've never been involved with anybody before, and it isn't always as easy as I had expected it to be." She hoped lightning didn't strike her through the cabin roof at the enormity of that understatement.

"Okay," he replied with a grim twist of his lips. He used one big thumb to wipe the traces of her tears off her cheeks. His voice was low and husky. "I can respect that. In all honesty, this is new ground for me, too."

"I mean, we both knew this wasn't going to be a long-term thing." She tried to keep the catch of tears out of her voice. Now more than ever she knew she couldn't hang onto him, and it broke her heart. "But when you moved in, it sort of changed the ground rules. I have to protect myself, Jonas. I can't let myself get used to the idea of you being here, of depending on you. I'm sorry if that sounds stupid, but I have to be able to survive on my own once you're gone." It was the most intimate and difficult confession she'd ever made. She only hoped it didn't scare him off completely.

"Of course. I understand perfectly." His tone leveled out, and she couldn't read the expression on his face at all. The last thing she'd ever wanted to do was hurt him. It had really never occurred to her that she could. Of course right now he was so emotionally raw from telling her about himself that he was probably more vulnerable than usual. His voice broke on his next words. "I'll go. Tonight, if you want me to." He turned away, started to rise.

"No!" She clutched his shirt, pulling him down. The one thing she couldn't do was to turn him away tonight. She couldn't let him think that his revelations had turned her against him. "Look, I know this is only for the summer, but that doesn't mean it isn't great. Let's just enjoy it while we can, okay?" The minute she said the words, she knew they were the right ones. The memories she made this summer with Jonas were going to have to last her a lifetime, and she didn't want to waste another minute. She forced herself to calm, smiled up at him through the haze of tears. "Let's just forget about all of it for now. Take me to bed, Jonas. Please."

The wide-eyed expression of shock on his face was swiftly re-placed by relief, and then with pure sexual hunger. He pulled her close with a deep, guttural growl, then lowered his mouth to hers for a long, drugging kiss. Her arms twined themselves around his neck as his clamped tightly about her waist, tugging her off the sofa and onto his lap.

There was nothing soft or gentle about him, not this time. His lips were hard, demanding, possessive, and his tongue plundered ruthless-ly. She moaned when his hands moved around to cup her sensitive breasts, finding her nipples through layers of fabric.

"Too. Damn. Many. Clothes." He bit the words out between kisses.

Mel bit his earlobe sharply. "Yes." She pulled her shirt and sports bra over her head, tossing them aside. Jonas must have approved, he dispensed with his own clothing just as swiftly, while she wiggled out of her jeans and panties. Finally naked, he lay back on the sofa, and dragged her down on top of him as their lips locked again for another hungry kiss.

His erection throbbed between her legs and she shifted forward onto her knees, straddling his thighs. After days without him, she couldn't wait any longer. Using one hand to position him, she slid down, taking all of him in one smooth slide. It almost hurt, he was so deeply seated, and she cried out at the same time, thinking that she'd never be able to get enough. While Jonas kneaded her breasts, which had become even more sensitive over the last week or so, she began to move, quick sharp strokes alternating with long smooth glides.

Jonas was moving too. His hips surged upward meeting her every move, and soon it was he who controlled the rhythm, his fingers digging into the flesh of her hips as he guided her. Each thrust had her breath coming out in soft little cries of rapture so intense she could barely stand it.

"Oh yes, Jonas. Please." Shameless, she begged for release.

"You. Are. Amazing." He grunted out the words as he pumped ever harder, ever faster. Then for just a moment, they both went silent, until Mel screamed her release and Jonas groaned aloud as he stiffened, then poured himself into her body. He clutched her tight to his chest, holding on until the tremors passed for both of them.

Finally, they roused enough to stumble up the stairs and into bed. Mel lay alongside Jonas, leaning up on one elbow to watch him as he slept. She was tired; it seemed like she always was these days, but she was too wired to sleep. Silvery rays of moonlight gleamed off the sharp planes of his face. The stubble of his heavy beard darkened the lower half, making the sharp lines that much more pronounced.

A werewolf. It explained so much. She probably should have guessed earlier, but it had never occurred to her that such a person could actually exist. Kind of hypocritical, she thought with a wry grin. Given that she existed, it only made sense that other types of supernatural beings did too.

Fighting the urge to trace the silver streak in his hair with her fingers, Mel studied it carefully. The white streak and the amber eyes were the two features shared by the wolf she'd befriended, and the man she loved. Those two features and the swirling, shifting aura had finally given him away, and she was so grateful they had.

Jonas stirred in his sleep, and pulled her back down into his arms. Not wanting to wake him, Mel complied. It was no hardship to snuggle against his softly furry, rock-hard chest. Baring his secrets wasn't something that came easily to a man like him, and if holding her in his sleep offered him comfort, she wasn't about to complain. It gave her just one more memory to store away like a souvenir, memories of the man she loved that would have to sustain her for all the lonely nights ahead.

And love him she did, she admitted, ignoring the pangs in her heart as she acknowledged the truth. Her subconscious sounded remarkably similar to Hattie's no-nonsense tone. She loved Jonas and she wanted to be as close to him as she could for as long as she could. Love was an insidious thing, sneaking up on you when you weren't expecting it, infecting you like a virus before you were even aware that you'd been exposed. Her nights after he was gone would be lonely not because she wouldn't be able to find another lover, but because she wouldn't want to. Like it or not, she was in love with Jonas for keeps.

She wondered again about what their daughter would look like. Would she have his hair, or Mel's red curls? Would her eyes be Jonas's amber, MacRae green, or Mel's own blue-green, which were apparently the contribution of her unknown father?

Like Mel, this child wouldn't know her father either, and Mel regretted that fact deeply. She'd tell the child about Jonas, make sure his daughter knew that her father was a good, honorable man, and that she'd been conceived in love on Mel's side at least. Her daughter would have the security she'd lacked as a child. Maybe someday, she'd even tell her his name if it seemed appropriate. She wasn't sure she'd tell the child about Jonas's special abilities, though. Not unless it became necessary.

That thought hit Mel like a punch, and her head swam as her stomach cramped in a sudden, violent bout of nausea. What if… She fought the urge to dash for the bathroom, willing her stomach to settle. What if their daughter was a werewolf like her father? What if she had the powers of both parents? Mel wouldn't have the information necessary to guide her, teach her how to use and control her abilities, and after listening to Jonas talk about his childhood, she knew how important that would be.

She'd keep track of Jonas, she decided, and if their daughter showed any signs of lycanthropy, she'd break her silence, regardless of the emotional cost to herself, and ask him for help. If the baby did turn out to be a shape-shifter, he'd just have to get over his own fears of parenthood and help teach his daughter how to cope.

Even less sure of her predicament than she had been before, Mel lay still in Jonas's arms, reveling in his rich masculine scent and his warm, strong bulk against her back even while she worried. What she wouldn't give to spend every night of her life like this. As fatigue slowly took over, all her tangled up guilt and regret faded into oblivion, and she finally fell asleep, safe in the embrace of the man she'd always love.

Chapter Thirteen

The sun was just rising above the tops of the lodgepole pines as Joe walked silently beside Mel, the pine needles on the path beneath their feet swishing quietly in the cool morning air. When they reached the lake, they paused for a moment, admiring the beauty of the sunrise reflected on the still surface of the water.

"You sure she's ready?" Joe had stopped several yards away, respectful of the power and the skittishness of the bird that rode on Mel's slender forearm. The woman's unexpected strength still awed him; she was so small, yet she'd easily carried the ten pound bird down the quarter-mile trail.

"She's ready." Mel gave the broad feathered back a final affectionate stroke. "I've been watching her fly in the barn. She knows how to hunt again."

She did feel a pang of loss, though; he could see it in her eyes. That was her real curse, her insatiable need to take care of everyone and everything around her. She was so generous with her time and love that she didn't hold enough back for herself. He hoped she could find someone someday who would debunk her so-called curse and give her the love and support she deserved. Well, he tried to anyway. Only problem was, he just couldn't stand to think about her with anybody but himself.

Holding her arm out in front of her, parallel to the ground, Mel slowly unclipped the leather jesses that tethered the eagle's ankles to Mel's wrist. When the bird was free, Mel dropped her arm, forcing the eagle to raise her wings to steady herself. Jonas watched in awestruck silence as Mel stepped back, grinning hugely while the magnificent bird took flight. Woman and eagle were both beautiful, and this was a moment Joe would never forget.

After a few tentative flaps, the eagle's five-foot wingspan caught an air current, and she swiftly soared upward, flying in a spiral above their heads. She circled for a moment or two, still watching them, then dropping one wing in a gesture that could almost have been a salute to her healer, she caught another updraft, before wheeling away, out of their sight.

"Oh, Jonas!" Mel turned to him, her smile wide and tears coursing down her cheeks. "Isn't she gorgeous?"

He didn't take his eyes off Mel as he tugged her into his arms. "She sure is." She didn't even catch the fact that he wasn't talking about the bird.

* * * *

Against Mel's better judgment, Jonas talked her into going into Sanctity that afternoon. She didn't want to see the accusing glares of the people who believed Talcott's lies, or the pitying glances of those who didn't, but she agreed with Jonas on one point. If she didn't face them now, she might just as well pack up and sell. If she wanted Sanctity to remain her home, she had to keep her chin up, and let them know that she was still here. She still had every intention of driving into Escanaba for groceries, however. She wasn't about to patronize Mercer, even if he would allow her into his store.

At Jonas's request, they started off at the library. He was thinking of setting a book in the U. P., and she'd agreed to help him out with some local research. It was an olive branch, and she'd been relieved when he'd taken it. Even though they were sleeping together again, things were still a little strained between them, mostly because she couldn't quite let down her guard. Torn between guilt and joy over her pregnancy, she was having a hard time looking him in the eye. He probably thought her reticence was because of his revelations a few days earlier, and she was trying to reassure him on that score, while still watching her tongue every time she spoke. It broke her heart to think of how deeply wounded he'd been in his past.

"Are we going to Karen's this afternoon?"

He parked his Jeep in the small municipal lot and they walked the few blocks to the library. They'd taken to visiting Gladys on a once-or-twice daily basis. The frequency of the visits, combined with Jonas's additional support, helped keep the sessions manageable for Mel, but even so, this morning's had been brutal.

"Probably." She sighed, squeezing her eyes shut. "It's going to be tonight or tomorrow. I said good-bye to her this morning, but I won't let her suffer any longer than I have to. If she needs me again, I'll go back."

"You'd rather do the suffering yourself." He grabbed her hand, squeezed it tight. "I'm sorry, sweetheart. Did you tell Karen or Doc?"

Nodding, she leaned into his strength as he wrapped a supporting arm about her waist. "Both. I had to. They'll want to get her kids back from their father's in time to say good-bye." It was the best gift she could give the family who had provided her with the only example of normalcy she'd ever known as a child. Gladys would pass away clear-headed and surrounded by the people she loved.

"Do you want to be there?"

Goddess, she loved his thoughtfulness! She quickly brushed that thought away. It wouldn't do to dwell on any thoughts that included both Jonas and the word love. They paused at the top of the library steps to finish the conversation before they went inside.

"No. Enough of their family will be there that I'd just be in the way. Besides, some of the relatives aren't exactly comfortable around me."

"I find that hard to believe. Karen and her dad at the very least know how much you've done, how much you care about Gladys. They'd welcome you, I'm sure."

How did he always know what to say to ease her heart? "They'll call if they need me," she assured him, forcing a smile. "I don't want to cause any more controversy than necessary in their home. Not right now."

"If you're sure," he conceded, his eyes still full of concern.

"Death is part of life, Jonas," she reminded him. "An unhappy one, to be sure, but natural and inevitable. I'm not a religious person, but I do believe to some extent at least in destiny. It's Gladys's time to go. All we can do is make it as peaceful and painless as possible, both for her and for her family. Right now, we have our own lives to deal with, our own fates to face. You need this research to get on with your writing, and I need to face down some of the small-minded busybodies in this town." It was the most intimate conversation they'd had in days, and Mel was glad to feel the wall between them starting to crumble.

"If you say so." He sent her an endearing, crooked smile, then bent down to drop a tiny kiss on the tip of her nose. Taking her hand, he led the way into the dragon's lair.

The dragon herself glared down her pointed nose at the pair of them, but she didn't say a word. Her husband had come to Mel a few days earlier for a slipped disc, and had probably instructed his wife to be polite. They both smiled broadly at Mrs. Halloran as they headed toward the history section, shooting each other conspiratorial grins as they passed her desk. It was all Mel could do to stifle a giggle.

An hour or so later, Mel stretched stiff muscles and groaned quietly. "I still can't see why anyone would want to set a book in this backwater," she grumbled, reshelving the book she'd been going over. She knew Jonas had already read several of the volumes, but she'd been able to provide some assistance, which felt good. They'd located a couple of old journals, along with some maps and other mementos of Sanctity's early days. "It's not like anything ever happens here."

"Nah, of course not," he returned in a whisper, a teasing glint in his eyes. "Who'd believe that things like witches and werewolves were running around up here in the boondocks?"

This time she failed to restrain her giggle, earning them a reproving look as the librarian cleared her throat in that particular way that only librarians had.

"So what are you going to write about?" He'd never mentioned the actual plot of this book he was researching, just reassured her that it wouldn't be about her.

"I'm thinking of focusing on some of the Native American legends. I got a bunch of interesting tidbits off of the Internet, and I thought I'd see if there was any local stuff to back them up."

"That's cool," she agreed. "The little lake on my property was once a sacred site to the Ojibwa," Mel whispered. "There's a journal back at the house you might find interesting."

"Really?"

"Umm-hmm. One of my ancestors married a chief's daughter. When it became apparent that the tribe was going to have to give up the land, my ancestor claimed it as his wife's dowry so that no one could build on that part. The chief went along with it, knowing that his own descendants would then be the guardians of the land. He knew about the MacRae family, knew they'd recognize the magic inherent in the land and take care of it."

"Magic?" His whisper was eager, fascinated. "In the land?"

"Can't you feel it? I'd have thought you were more sensitive than that. There are ley lines, lines of magic that run through the earth like rivers of power. They act as an energy source, and anyone magical can tap into them. I do it every time I heal. My cabin sits on one line, the one you rented sits on another, and they cross right beside the lake. That intersection makes my property an incredibly powerful place. That's a big part of why I can't sell out to Talcott."

They were still whispering, but their conversation had caught Mrs. Halloran's attention, and her pinched expression was growing more irritated by the moment.

"I've heard of ley lines, of course. But since not much of my work has been about magic, per se, I've never paid much attention. I do pick up some sense of power around your place, but I guess I just figured it was you." A shiver coursed up Mel's spine at the open admiration in his gaze.

"I'll show you the difference," she promised huskily. "When we get back."

"So when we made love by the lake, we were practically on top of this magical intersection?" He leaned close, making her skin tingle at the warm puff of his breath on her ear.

"Umm-hmm." They had to get out of here before she jumped him.

"Then I like these ley lines already."

Clasping a hand over her mouth to restrain another nervous giggle, Mel met Barbara Halloran's accusing glare with a guilty flinch. "Let's get out of here." Taking his hand, she tugged him toward the exit. By the time they reached the steps outside, they were both tittering like naughty schoolchildren. They sat on the wide marble steps and laughed.

"I kept expecting to be sent to the principal's office," Mel confessed after the worst of her giggles had subsided.

"At least a spanking," Jonas corroborated. "Though they don't do that in schools anymore, thank heaven."

"No kidding!" She agreed wholeheartedly with that opinion. "Of course, none of my teachers ever had the guts to spank me anyway. Nobody wanted to mess with Gran or Hattie."

"Lucky you!" His voice was suddenly so full of sadness that Mel's heart twisted in her chest.

"One of these days." She laid a hand on his chest. "You're going to tell me about those parents of yours!"

"Not bloody likely," he muttered in response. He stood and held out a hand to help her to her feet.

"Whatever." She'd been enjoying the afternoon too much to get in a fight with Jonas now. She kept hold of his hand and started down the library steps. "I'm starved. Let's go see what Rosa's got for lunch." She was always hungry these days, when she wasn't being nauseous. If she didn't start watching her diet, she'd be gaining weight long before the summer was over, and that would give her some serious explaining to do.

Unfortunately for her waistline, Rosa's three-bean quesadillas were too good to ignore, so she tucked in with relish, while Jonas did the same. The small restaurant was nearly empty with only a few other patrons scattered about. Although they got a couple of dirty looks, no one approached them or said anything openly, and Rosa's cheerful smile more than made up for any chilliness from the general populace.

"You must have an incredible metabolism," Jonas teased as Mel finished the last bite of her lunch.

Mouth full, she nodded guiltily.

"You want dessert?" He stood, smiling indulgently at her second nod. "Good. So do I. Order us something while I go use the rest room."

Rosa was leaning over Mel's table, recommending her brownies and ice cream when the bell over the front door jangled. Mel had her back to the entrance, but she saw Rosa's eyes narrow. "It's that reporter," the older woman hissed, straightening. "You need to go."

"How?"

"Get your man from the restroom. Take him out the back."

Mel nodded, and slipped a ten-dollar bill onto the table while Rosa bustled over to the newcomer, conveniently placing her own ample form between the reporter and his view of the diner's back hallway. Since the restrooms were located down a hallway that also opened onto the kitchen, it was easy for Mel to waylay Jonas on his way out. Holding a finger to her lips, she tugged him through a door labeled, 'Empl-yees On-y,' and into the kitchen.

"What the hell?"

"It's that paparazzi of yours." She tugged him close to whisper. "He's out in the dining room."

"Damn, he's faster than I expected." None of the kitchen staff even looked up as they passed through to the rear exit. Of course, since all of the employees were members of Rosa's family, Mel hadn't expected any trouble. "It won't be long now before he finds out where I am." Still hand-in-hand, they scurried down the street toward his Jeep.

"It's no big surprise." Mel fastened her seat belt as he pulled the Jeep out into traffic. "He'll probably show up at Whispering Pines by tomorrow at the latest." She wasn't thrilled about the idea, but she wasn't about to let him make her run.

"You want me to move my stuff back up to the cabin?" Her great-uncle's old cabin was vacant again, and the repairs in cabin one would be done soon. Jonas could reasonably expect to resume his position as tenant instead of roommate. As much as Mel wanted to be able to maintain some distance in their relationship, that wasn't what she had in mind. She hated the idea of him sleeping anywhere but next to her.

"If you want." She was aiming for nonchalant, but even to her own ears, her tone sounded petulant.

Jonas shook his head and shot her a dirty look. He drove as quickly as was legal through town, a little faster than legal once he hit the state highway. "I didn't say I wanted to move. I offered to move my stuff, to make it look like I was sleeping there. There's still someone out there stalking you. I'm not going to leave you alone."

Maybe it was his matter-of-fact tone, or maybe it was the afternoon they'd spent sneaking around and giggling like truant school kids, but Mel believed him, and it was the first time she'd felt really relaxed in his presence since she'd discovered her pregnancy. She'd never forgotten that she loved Jonas, but for a while there, it had been easy to overlook just how much she *liked* the man.

"Somebody's bound to tell him we're involved anyway. Besides, that part won't make any difference to your readers, will it? Who cares if they think you get lucky in every town you go to? Since he already knows your real name, the only secret we have to hide is…"

"The fact that I grow fur and howl at the moon." Jonas drummed his fingers angrily on the steering wheel. "I couldn't care less if my readers believe I have a girl in every port. I was, believe it or not, concerned about your reputation."

"That's sweet," she cooed, injecting a teasing note. "But as you may have noticed, I have no reputation to protect. Most of Sanctity already assumes that being a witch implies a total lack of traditional family values. What do I care if some tabloid publishes that I'm sleeping with the fabulously wealthy and incredibly handsome author J. P. Wolfe?"

A snort was his only response. He glared through the windshield at the semi crossing slowly through the intersection ahead of them. As soon as it was past, he gunned the accelerator again.

"Besides." Mel laid a hand on his thigh, felt the tension in the muscle. "If the reporter is busy focusing on me and your sex life, maybe he won't have as much time to delve as deeply into other areas."

Tightening his hands on the wheel until his knuckles went white, Jonas simply growled.

"What?" Her logic made perfect sense to her. What was his problem with it?

"Damn it Mel, do you have to take care of everybody? I have a big problem with you trying to get between me and trouble. I don't want anything to happen to you."

Ah, chivalry. How sweet, and how pointless. "Don't worry about it. I really don't care if my name winds up in a few gossip sheets. I can handle my fifteen minutes of infamy. Who knows, it might even be good for business."

Even though she could tell it still didn't sit well with him, he managed to keep his mouth shut. As in so tightly, the skin on his jaw turned pale. Of course, that kind of limited conversation for the rest of the trip, and Mel's sunny mood was beginning to cloud over. She wished he was ticklish. Anything to get rid of this solemn silence!

"I'm going to release Bucky in a week or so." Maybe the change of subject would lighten things up. "Probably down by the lake. I've been feeding him plants from down there so he'll be familiar with the scents and tastes."

"Sounds good." It was a deep rumble. Not exactly effusive, but it was a start.

* * * *

"Tell me about your parents, Jonas. They were back at her house when she finally asked the question he'd been dreading. He had his laptop out on a TV tray in front of an overstuffed chair, and had been thinking about getting some work done. "What happened with them? Couldn't your mother handle the fact that your father was a werewolf?"

"Do we have to talk about this?"

She was sitting cross-legged on the couch across from him, and she tilted her head, her wide blue-green eyes studying him too intently for comfort. "Yes," she answered finally, with a crisp nod. "Yes, I think we do."

"Fine." So much for work. She'd only badger him to death if he didn't give in now. Why was he so categorically unable to say no to this woman? He closed his laptop and leaned back in his chair. "What do you want to know?"

"You said that your father was a werewolf, but your mother wasn't. Is it a male-linked thing, or just dominant-recessive genetics?"

"I have no idea." He'd wondered that himself, but was surprised by her question. Given her witchy ways, it was easy to forget sometimes that Mel had a degree in biology. "My guess is male-linked. The old man never mentioned his mother, but I know his father was a werewolf too. And I know they fought. I could almost swear I remember an uncle when I was little, but my father never mentioned him once I was old enough to make sense of things. He wasn't a big talker, my dad. Not a whole lot of useful information there. But you don't hear very much about female werewolves in folklore."

"Why do you hate it so much?" She twisted one red curl around her finger.

What did this have to do with his parents? "I don't hate it. If I have any hang ups, I'd say it's a control thing, I suppose. Given that I have a very primitive, very *animal* side to my nature, keeping it in balance is important to me."

"Uh-huh." She shook her head and tsked skeptically. "I hate to break this to you, Jonas, but everyone has a primitive side to their personality. Just because yours manifests itself physically once in a while doesn't make you that much different from the rest of us."

He wished it were that simple. If he hadn't watched his father slowly devolve into a savage beast, he might even have believed it. Lord knew he wanted to now more than he ever had before.

He turned, looking out the window. But studying their cars parked next to each other in the drive wasn't going to make it any easier to confess. He turned back to her. There was no censure or horror on her face, just her usual caring curiosity. Mel cared so much about people she had to know what made them tick, and he didn't have it in him to deny her anymore. "There's a reason why werewolves in legends are always evil. There's a certain—attraction to the wild side, or whatever you want to call it. It can take you over if you let it, rob you of any claim at humanity."

"Your dad?" Her eyes widened and she nibbled on her lip.

He shrugged, trying to avoid her gaze.

"What happened with your parents, Jonas?" All the softness he'd ever dreamed of in life was in the warmth of her voice.

"Simple enough. Nice girl marries freak." He heard the bitterness in his own tone, but he couldn't fix it, so he blundered on. "She finds out, she takes off. End of story."

"No, it's not. She left your father, but what about you? Her son?" After a pause, Mel firmed up her voice. "Jonas. Tell me."

Damn, he hadn't heard that tone of voice since he'd had Mr. Racine in third grade. He resisted the urge to shrug again, or to simply run and hide. Instead he spoke in the most simple and general terms possible, trying to distance himself from the pain of the memories. "The first time she took me with her. After that she left me with him."

"What?" Mel's soft modulated voice rose into a high-pitched shriek. "She did what?"

"Once she found out I was a freak too, she figured I ought to be with my own kind." Whatever that had meant. "So she left me with him."

"How horrible! And your dad, was he happy about this?"

"Hell, no. Having a brat around interfered with his drinking and whoring and gambling."

"Have you seen your mother since?" Now Mel had gotten pissed, but he thought she was trying not to show it. Her lips had tightened into a straight line and her bare toe tapped a staccato beat on the rug.

"Sure. Every so often they'd try to get back together. He could be charming when he wasn't drunk or on one of his wild rages. That's how he managed to keep her in the dark in the beginning, anyway. She loved him in her way, I guess. Kept believing he'd stop drinking, stop smacking her around."

She cringed, and he wished he'd kept his mouth shut about that part, but once he'd started telling her, it all just seemed to come out in no particular order.

"He abused her?" Now she wasn't even trying to hide the outrage. Her arms were crossed in front of her chest and her words were shrill and sharp. "Before or after she found out about his abilities?"

"Both."

"And she didn't leave him then? She waited till after you were born?" The foot was tapping even faster now, and Joe watched it, mesmerized.

"Yep." He shrugged again. "It happens all the time."

"That doesn't make it right."

"No, but human emotions are rarely logical, especially anything to do with love." He'd learned that lesson the hard way, and early in life.

"That isn't love." Mel practically spat the words. He was almost leery of disagreeing with her. He'd never seen her this angry before.

"No, in their own twisted way, I believe it was. Why else would she keep coming back to him?"

"Obsession, maybe," was the most she'd concede, but Joe knew better. His mother had loved his father, and it had killed her.

Mel walked over to sit on the arm of his chair and put her hands on both sides of his face. He looked into her eyes and saw that her anger had been banked. All that shone from her gaze right now was a compassion so deep he was afraid he'd drown in it. "Love isn't like that, Jonas. Any woman capable of love wouldn't leave her son with an abusive father, not under any conditions."

"Even after she watched her five-year-old son turn into a wolf cub?"

"Is that how she found out? That had to be difficult." She dropped her hands from his face to clasp both of his. "But no, Jonas, not even then. A parent's love should be unconditional. She should have tried to help you deal with your special abilities, not dump you and run."

"She did what she could." He was too used to placing the whole blame on his father. "Even took me back a time or two."

"She did? When?"

"Whenever the old man took off for long enough for one of the neighbors to notice and call Child Protective Services."

"And how old were you then?"

"I don't know? Seven? Twelve? Fourteen? After she died, I just split when he took off, tried to stay out of the system."

"And how old were you then?"

"Fifteen."

She winced and squeezed her eyes shut, but he saw the tear that beaded in the corner. He hated that once again he'd made her cry. He fought back a lump in his own throat. "I'm sorry, Jonas. Sorry that you were alone, and sorry that both of your parents were too absorbed in their own selfishness to take care of you. But it doesn't reflect on you. You're not your father." She squeezed his hands, and he wanted more than anything in the world to believe her. But the price was just too high. If he let go now, he'd end up giving her what little was left of his soul.

"And your own mother, Mel? Was she such a paragon?" He knew he was out of line, but he was too raw to fight fair.

"No." Her voice was surprisingly steady, and she looked him directly in the eye. "She was a spoiled, selfish child who never grew up. She completely destroyed her own life with sex and booze and drugs, and I'm damned lucky she didn't take mine too. She was probably just too stoned to manage an abortion, or I wouldn't be here at all, and it's a miracle I wasn't born addicted. I can't remember her at all, by the way, but I'll always have her reputation to live down." She drew a deep breath, then smiled with so much tenderness he had to blink back tears of his own. "But Gran and Hattie showed me the other side. I never had to wonder what love was, I always had it from them. I always knew I was treasured and wanted, even though I was the illegitimate daughter of a sixteen-year-old slut. Your parents made choices, Jonas." Straddling his lap, she kneaded the tense muscles of his shoulders and neck, soothing away the physical symptoms of his distress, while her soft, sure words worked on the rest.

"Their choices, good or bad, cannot be blamed on your father's gift. We all start with baggage, believe me. I spent years wishing I could be a normal child who couldn't see auras. What kid wants to know when someone else is lying, or sick, or whose mother is sleeping with someone other than their dad? But what we do with our lives, gifts, curses, and all, that's up to us, and we can't blame it on anyone else."

She leaned down to place a kiss on the top of his head. "I told you before, but it bears repeating. You are a good man, Jonas Pierce. No matter what your father was, who your mother chose to be, you're not like them. You'd never hurt another living soul intentionally, and you'll never let the more primitive side of your nature take control. Believe in yourself. I do."

"Maybe you shouldn't." That husky, choked sound couldn't be his own voice, could it?

"Maybe. But that's my choice to make, and I make it freely. I'm a pretty good judge of human nature. That's part of my gift. Don't be afraid to live your life fully. Let the past stay buried."

He didn't agree with her, couldn't afford to. If he allowed himself to start thinking like that, the next thing he knew, he'd be thinking about possibilities like white picket fences and copper-haired babies. That risk was just too big to take. Endangering himself was one thing, but he could never drag another soul down with him. Far safer to just continue his careful, controlled, solitary existence.

The shrill chirping of his phone startled them both. Mel jumped off his lap, and Joe felt the loss of their physical contact keenly. He unclipped the phone from his belt, and glared at the display.

"My agent," he offered, both relieved and depressed by the interruption. "I have to explain why I haven't sent him any pages in the last couple weeks."

"Go ahead." Her smile was full of understanding and tenderness. "I'm going to run down to the barn and feed Bucky." He followed her as far as the back porch as he switched on the phone and watched her bounce down the steps. While he listened to Bernie's cajoling tones, his eyes followed Mel, admiring the pert sway of her backside as she sauntered down the path.

"No problem, Bern." Conversations with his agent always went like this. If he agreed frequently enough, he could be asleep and Bernie wouldn't know the difference. He really shouldn't let Mel go down to the barn by herself, he thought, listening with half his brain, while his body led him off the porch and down the path. There was still a stalker around, after all.

His longer legs ate up the path till he was only about thirty yards behind her when she stopped to unlock the barn door. "Sure thing," he mumbled into the phone, his attention still on Mel, who hadn't noticed him behind her. "I can get to New York in a week or so, two at the most." Surely this situation would be resolved by then. If not, he'd find another excuse to stall. Or he'd haul her butt with him.

He was just rounding the last curve of the path when Mel stepped into the barn. At the sound of her earsplitting scream, he dropped the phone and ran.

Chapter Fourteen

"Here, drink this."

Mel accepted the glass of water with shaky hands. "Thanks," she managed. One of her juvenile tenants had heard her screams, and had, bless him, run to fetch his mother. The other woman had arrived on the scene just in time to witness Mel puking her guts out into the underbrush with Jonas standing guard alongside her. When she was done throwing up, he'd carried her to her back deck and installed her in a chair, while the tenant, a nurse, apparently, had fetched the water from Mel's kitchen. The woman's husband and two children stood nearby on the deck, along with Sheila, who'd been manning the office.

Mel closed her eyes, wishing she could banish the memory of the fawn lying disemboweled on the barn floor. Fighting another bout of nausea, she sipped gingerly at the water.

"Sheriffs on his way." Sheila switched off the cordless phone, and perched lightly on one of the wooden railings.

"Good." Mel's voice was shaky, but she managed to sit upright and keep her eyes open without her head swimming.

"Damn straight. Maybe this time he'll actually do something." Jonas was angrier than she'd ever seen him.

"Jonas, the barn. You need to make sure no one goes in there till the sheriff gets here." There were children in several of the units, as well as the two sitting on Mel's steps. She had a horrified vision of one of them walking in, seeing what she'd just seen.

"Mike, you go with him." The nurse jerked her head at her husband. "We'll be fine here till the cops show up."

The husband turned to Jonas and gave him a wry masculine grin, holding out a strong ebony hand. "Guess we've got our orders. I'm Mike Wilcox, by the way. That's my wife, Eileen."

"Joe Pierce." Jonas jumped a little at being addressed, but he shook the other man's hand. "You know Mel." He didn't look happy about leaving her, but apparently he wasn't going to argue, thank goodness. His burning amber gaze encompassed all the women on the deck as he started down the path. "If you see anything suspicious, yell."

Mike nodded at the two young children. "Wait here with your mother."

As soon as the men had headed down the trail, Eileen Wilcox gave Mel a critical once-over with a trained eye.

"So how far along are you?"

Mel ignored Sheila's startled gasp, and slumped back into her chair. So much for secrets. "How did you know?" She kept her voice pitched low enough that the children couldn't hear.

"When you're upset, you cover your belly with your hand."

Did she really? That would have to stop.

"Besides, I saw you heaving the other morning behind your cabin."

"Fantastic." Good grief, was she that obvious?

"Have you seen your doctor yet?"

"Of course." She almost managed a smile at the nurse's persistence. It wasn't really a lie, either. She'd had a brief chat with Karen's father just yesterday.

Eileen sat down in the second deck chair, the one Jonas usually favored. She reached over and patted Mel's hand. "I hate to ask, but just exactly what did you find in your barn?"

Sheila started to chime in—Jonas had given her enough information for her to call the sheriff—but just then Mel heard the sirens beginning to approach. "I can't..." She broke off with s shudder and inclined her head toward the children. "Just take your kids inside for a while, okay?"

Eileen appraised Mel's face intently, then nodded. "Okay, but I'll expect a full report later if Mike doesn't get all the details from your man." She stood and herded her two children into Mel's kitchen.

He's not my man. She wanted to say it aloud but the words wouldn't come out. She didn't have the strength to argue semantics. She could also tell by the expression in Sheila's eyes that she was going to have some serious explaining to do in that quadrant later. The three women waited in silence as Mott and his deputy approached.

"Melissa." Mott didn't let Harkness open the conversation this time. "There's been another break-in?"

"In the barn this time." Sheila swung her legs from her perch on the railing.

"What kind of damages?" Mott flashed Sheila a reproving look, but accepted her answer.

"The fawn," Mel began, sobs choking her voice.

"Seems like you might want to go look for yourself." Eileen had let herself back out the door, and regarded the men coolly. "You being the sheriff and all."

"And you are…" Harkness inquired snidely, notebook poised as usual.

"Eileen Wilcox, R. N." She pointed toward the kitchen window, through which the two children were watching the officers with rapt fascination. "Those are my children, Lucinda and Matthew. You'll find my husband Michael down by the barn with Mr. Pierce. They'll be able to tell you what you need to know."

Harkness started to speak, but Mott quelled him with a sharp gesture. "Are you a guest here, Mrs. Wilcox?"

"Cabin two," Mel affirmed, pushing against the arms of her chair to give herself the leverage to stand. Her limbs felt like lead, but she had to do something. This wasn't about her guests. "Thanks for your help, Eileen. Why don't you and Sheila hang out with the kids in the kitchen. Sheila knows where the cookies are stashed. I'll walk these gentlemen down to the barn."

Mott and Eileen exchanged appraising looks, then Eileen broke eye contact and nodded at Mel. "You know where I'll be if you need me." She threw a warning look over her shoulder. "You be careful, now."

"I will," Mel promised. At least her new friend had kept the admonition nonspecific. She wasn't ready for the whole town to know she was pregnant.

As they rounded the house, they turned at the sound of a car in the drive. Another vehicle skidded to a halt just inches shy of the sheriff's cruiser, and a short, auburn-haired man climbed out, a camera slung around his neck.

"Shit!"

Mott stiffened at Mel's curse. He'd probably never heard her swear before. "Who's he?"

"Andrew Erickson. He's a reporter for *Personalities Weekly*."

"What's he doing here?"

"Long story. Jonas Pierce is actually a famous author, J. P. Wolfe. Apparently this guy's been after him for some time, trying to get some kind of exposé."

"Shit." The sheriff's sentiments echoed her own. He motioned her down the trail ahead of him, then stood to face the journalist.

"Excuse me sir, but this is private property. Are you aware that you're trespassing?"

"This is a resort, right? I'm just here to inquire about a room."

"We're all booked up," Mel lied. "Now please leave."

"Why? Is there something going on that the public might want to know about?"

"Yes."

"No."

"Not at all."

The three replies were simultaneous, but only Harkness had answered in the affirmative. Mel wouldn't want to be in his shoes when Mott got him back to the office.

"I believe you've been asked to vacate the premises," Mott continued smoothly. "Now please do so before I'm forced to arrest you for trespassing."

Grumbling about redneck officials, Erickson climbed back into his car. They all watched silently as he drove down the lane and disappeared.

Mott shook his head. "He'll probably just pull over then sneak back in on foot."

Once the reporter was gone, Mel led the way down the path. Joe and Mike Wilcox stood in front of the closed barn doors. They each leaned on one of the door panels, and wore matching grim expressions on their faces. Mel was glad the winding path had shielded them from the reporter's view. One look and he'd have definitely known something was wrong.

Jonas greeted Mott politely, ignoring Harkness to introduce Mike.

"Well, somebody needs to let me in." Mott gave Harkness a disgruntled look. "Bill, hand me the digital camera, so you can stay out here and watch for that reporter."

"Mel doesn't need to see this again." Jonas stood in front of Mott, arms crossed and refused to budge. "She should be back at the house."

"I'm fine." There was no real enthusiasm in her voice. Truth was, she didn't want to see it again.

Mott raised one eyebrow, but apparently trusted Jonas's judgment. That was an interesting development, one she'd think about later. "Melissa, I could sure go for a cup of coffee. I can get your statement just as easily from your kitchen table."

"Men." She gave what she hoped was a disgusted snort. "Typical. Send the little woman for beverages." She wasn't really too unhappy though, so she tossed her hair and whirled back up the path. After only a few steps, she heard the click of the latch and Mott's horrified epithets.

When she got back to her cabin, fresh tears streamed down her cheeks. Since Sheila and Eileen already had the coffee preparations underway, Mel found herself pulled into her own kitchen and ordered into a chair.

"There's herbal tea in that tin on the counter." Mel wiped her nose with a tissue. "Chamomile and peppermint."

"You sit. I'll fix it," Eileen instructed. Sheila, on the phone with one of Whispering Pines' suppliers, just nodded and gave Mel a compassionate smile. The sound of the television coming from the living room let Mel know where the children had been sent.

The nurse, about Mel's own age, or just a couple years older, moved about the kitchen with professional efficiency. "So how far along are you?"

"Officially, about five weeks," Mel answered. She'd done enough midwifing to know that doctors like to count from the beginning of your last period. "So just three, really."

"You just found out then."

"It's been a few days."

"You told your man yet?"

The woman's insight was a little unsettling. "No."

"You gonna?"

"No."

Eileen poured the scalding water over the dried herbs in Mel's teapot, adding the sweet scent of mint to the pungent aroma of coffee that filled the room. A plate of Mel's homemade brownies had been set in the center of the table alongside a stack of paper napkins.

"That's a shame. A blind woman could see he's a keeper. Strong, smart, protective. That, and he's nuts about you. Sounds like prime daddy material if you ask me."

"Well, I didn't." Mel rubbed her eyes, immediately regretting her outburst. "Sorry."

"No, you didn't ask, and that's the truth. But I offered my opinion and I'll stand by it. I believe a man has a right to know if he's going to be a father, not to mention the responsibilities that go along with the knowledge."

"It's complicated." And it would be easier if Mel didn't whole-heartedly agree. She sipped slowly at the mug the other woman handed her. "I would appreciate it if you wouldn't say anything to anybody. I haven't really had time to assimilate it myself yet."

"And with all this shit going down, you've had other things to worry about."

"No kidding." Her voice broke, and she laid her face down on her folded arms. Eileen whisked the half-full mug aside before it could spill. "I'm going to have to close Whispering Pines this time. I can't take the risk that he'll hurt someone else to get to me."

"Understandable." Neither Eileen's voice nor her face betrayed any concern that she might have about her own family, or the outcome of her vacation.

"I'm sure Talcott has rooms available for anybody who wants to stay in the area. I'll make up the difference in price, of course." Heck, that was probably Sean's plan in a nutshell.

"Stop fretting for five minutes and wait." Eileen handed her a tissue. "It isn't good for either you or the baby for you to keep stressing out like this. Maybe the sheriff can take care of things."

"Maybe." She didn't believe it for a minute, but she knew when to quit fighting and follow directions. A lifetime with Hattie and Gran had taught her that much. She sipped her tea quietly till they heard the clomping of booted feet on the back porch.

All four men tromped into the kitchen. Sheila, who had hung up the phone, bustled around with Eileen pouring coffee and glaring at

Mel whenever she made a move to stand up. If the next eight months were like this with everyone telling her what not to do, she was liable to strangle someone before her second trimester.

"I'm sorry, Melissa." Warren Mott removed his Smokey the Bear hat and sat down beside her at the table. "Obviously we've got a real sicko on our hands, and not just kids screwing around. Are you still convinced it's Sean Talcott?"

"Not completely."

There was a growl from Jonas, who didn't sit. Arms crossed, he just leaned on the countertop behind Mel. His fierce glare was a warning to anyone who dared mess with her. While his protectiveness thrilled her, she cautioned herself not to read too much into it. Whether Jonas believed it or not, there was a lot of the knight-errant in his makeup. He'd instinctively defend anyone he thought needed it.

"We'll have to question all your renters, of course," Harkness inserted in his usual condescending tone. "Since we've never had a problem like this in Sanctity before, it only makes sense that it's someone from Down Below." He glared at the Wilcoxes, who stood side-by-side near the sink.

"Down below?" Jonas glared at Harkness but tipped his head at Mel for the explanation.

She gave him a smile. She forgot sometimes that he didn't speak Yooper. "Lower Michigan, or below the Mackinac Bridge. Actually that's the polite term. Usually we call them trolls.

"Can it, Harkness," Mott ordered.

Mel's jaw dropped; she'd never heard him castigate his flunky openly before. The sight on the barn floor must have shaken even the world-weary sheriff.

"I've got a suggestion for you, Melissa," Mott offered. "I'd like you to hire some full time security till this is over."

That was an option she hadn't considered, and a lot more appealing than the idea of closing Whispering Pines. "Who?" she asked. "I don't know anyone who does that kind of thing."

"I've got a friend in the Soo who operates a security firm. Does business for a couple of the casinos. I'll give him a call, have him get in touch. Meanwhile, I've got a wet-behind-the-ears new deputy I'll send over for tonight. Do him some good to stand out in the cold and keep an eye on things."

As much as she hated the idea of having a fulltime watchdog, Mel had to admit it made sense. Sean, or whomever it was, had crossed the line from harassment into violence, and there was no telling what he'd do next. She would sleep a lot better knowing her guests were protected.

Mott smirked and added. "He can keep that pain in the ass reporter out of your hair while he's at it."

* * * *

Mott's words reminded Joe that Erickson was still a very pressing problem. He'd heard the altercation between Mott and Erickson earlier, of course, but showing Mott the carnage and giving his statement had driven the other matter from his mind. His rage over Talcott's depredation and his worry for Mel had pretty much eclipsed every other concern.

But Erickson, in his way, could be an even bigger problem. He liked Mott's suggestion of hiring security; he was more convinced than ever that Talcott was a serious threat. At the same time it galled him that he couldn't take care of her all by himself.

As far as his personal concerns went, the rent-a-cop shouldn't be a problem. Joe had changed enough in the last few weeks that he could hold off on doing so, or if necessary, dodge one guard. Dodging Erickson might prove more difficult. The man had the nose of a bloodhound, and the determination of a frigging pit bull.

"What about the cleanup, Sheriff?" He spoke to Mott in an undertone. "Should I bury the umm, remains, or will somebody official be removing the evidence?"

"I called the state crime lab," Mott returned with the heavy sigh of a small-town cop who liked his work slow and uncomplicated. "They're sending somebody over. Seems the DNR also might have jurisdiction, since slaughtering a white-tail is technically poaching, along with the B. and E. and vandalism. I'm going to try to add stalking to the list of charges, but the D. A. will probably get that one thrown out, even assuming, of course, that we actually catch this yahoo."

"It strikes me as odd that this sort of behavior cropped up out of the blue," Joe mused. "Usually there's a certain progression. Had any incidents of animal dismemberment, or anything like that before?"

"Ah, the famous writer showing his stripes." Harkness had apparently been eavesdropping. His sneer and snide tone left no doubt as to his opinion of Joe's profession. "I suppose you would be an expert on psychotic behavior, wouldn't you, Pierce?"

"I've read a bit about the pathology of serial killers." Less for research and more because true crime novels were what he read for relaxation. Harkness's comment had caught the attention of the rest of the group, and he checked their faces for reactions. Neither of the Wilcoxes seemed overly shocked by the revelation, and Sheila just raised one eyebrow and grinned. Maybe having his secret out wouldn't be that big of a deal in Sanctity. *That* secret, anyway.

"So have there been any incidents?"

"Nothing documented." Mott's words were measured, careful. "But, yeah, there've been one or two."

"Little things, not too scary taken one at a time, right? Swept under the rug so that Daddy wouldn't be embarrassed?"

"Bullshit!" Harkness exploded up out of his chair till Mott's glare forced him back down. "Keep that up, Pierce, and I'll arrest you for libel."

"Slander," Joe countered. "Libel's in print. And then only if it can't be substantiated."

"Shut *up*, Bill." Mott's tone was lethal. "Nobody's arresting anybody at the moment." He turned to Joe. "You're right, of course. But there hasn't been so much a hint of any pathological behavior in at least ten years. Damn, I really thought he'd outgrown these shenanigans."

"And instead he's progressed." Shenanigans, his ass! "You've got to treat him as a stalker, you know. His next act of violence could well be against a human."

"I know. But without any evidence, my hands are still tied. His daddy's lawyers would have him out in five minutes flat."

"Right." Cold shivers ran down Joe's spine. The guy had potential serial killer written all over him, and Joe's woman was his target. He could take care of the problem himself. A wolf attack would be surprising, but it wouldn't cast any suspicion on himself or on Mel. He looked over and caught her eye, her tired smile hitting him like a punch in the gut. It astounded him that she could know who he was, what he was, and still smile at him in a way that turned his insides to jelly. He didn't like his sudden powerful urge to live up to her faith in him, but he couldn't fight it, which meant he probably wasn't going to get to rip Talcott's throat out. He didn't know which scared him more, his desire to please Mel, or his sudden, visceral need to hurt someone. What he'd always believed had just been verified. Caring too much about another person *did* bring the beast in him to the surface. All the effort he'd put into controlling his nature had been futile.

Despite his brooding, he managed to be polite to the crowd gathered in Mel's kitchen. Mott hauled Mel into her office to get her statement, and when she returned she was even paler than when she'd left. It was tough to be civil when he wanted to chew the sheriff a new one for distressing her, but one look in Mott's tired, sickened eyes reminded Joe that the man had his own reasons for wanting Mel safe. If her statement helped put Talcott away, he had to admit it was worth temporarily upsetting her.

"The deputy I've assigned will be here before I take off," Mott informed Joe after hauling his butt into the office for a formal statement. "He knows he's to check in with you or Melissa on a regular basis."

"Your other deputy seems to think I'm the guilty party." Joe paced while Mott sprawled in Mel's office chair. "Why is it you don't?"

"Bill can be an idiot." Mott's answer was calm, equable. "It's pretty clear you care about Melissa. Besides, I saw your face in the barn. It was green. Either you were as sickened as I was, or you're the best damn actor I've ever met."

Joe nodded in acceptance. It was good to have the law on your side.

A knock at the locked outside door interrupted his thoughts, and Joe automatically moved to answer it.

"Right at home here, aren't you, son?"

Joe couldn't tell if Mott was amused or pissed off at the idea, but he didn't much care. "Bite me," he tossed over his shoulder as he opened the door. Someone, probably Mott, had pulled down the blind, blocking the glass window that made up the upper half. The guests from cabin five stood there, looking grim and determined.

"We need to know what's going on," the husband announced. "Why are there police cars here?"

"Just some vandalism down at the barn." Joe tried to project calm and assurance. "Nothing that will impact the guests at all."

"That's right." Mott walked up beside him and used his best good old boy grin. "Nothing to worry about. By the time you folks go to town and have a nice dinner, it will be all over with."

"Well, it better be!" The wife's tone was shrill as she tapped her foot on the decking. "If it isn't we're going to expect a full refund! This was supposed to be a peaceful, relaxing vacation, and all this," she waved at the two police cruisers in the parking area. "Is very stressful!"

"Only if you've got something against cops," Joe muttered under his breath. Mott must have the ears of a cat, though, because he shot Joe an amused glance.

"You folks go on into town and have some dinner." He handed the man a business card. "Tell Rosa at the diner that your desert is on me. Best food in the county."

The pair of yuppies in their matching L. L. Bean khakis cast him a skeptical glance, but they nodded and accepted the card. As soon as they were out of earshot, Mott expelled a long breath.

"There'll be more of that, I expect."

"Most likely." Joe nodded. "Probably all five cabins will show up sooner or later wanting reassurance that all's right in their little vacation wonderland."

"Yep. Except for the group that's already involved. I'll talk to Sheila about handling the others. Send her in next, would you?"

Joe did. Over the next hour, the cabin turned into a three-ring circus. More tenants pounded on the office door, Hattie showed up, having heard something suspicious on her police scanner, the state police arrived, and Karen called. While Sheila handled the other customers, the Wilcoxes gave their statements and returned to their cabin, and Mott led the state cops down to the barn. Joe watched as the circles under Mel's eyes grew darker and darker. He'd tried to talk her into going upstairs and lying down for a while, but she'd refused until Hattie whispered something in Mel's ear. Whatever the older woman had said must have worked, because Mel dragged herself to her feet.

"Fine. I'm going upstairs. Is everybody happy now?"

He resisted the urge to go with her, largely because Hattie was already headed in that direction. He did follow her to the stairs though, and reached out to touch Mel's cheek as she hesitated on the first step. "Sweetheart, you look absolutely wiped. Try to get some sleep, okay? I'll hold the fort down here, then come up when it's over."

He tucked a strand of her hair behind her ear as she nodded. "Okay." Then she leaned down and kissed him. "Thanks for being here, Jonas."

He was still leaning on the stair rail a few minutes later when the bleeping of his satellite phone started him out of his introspective funk. Hadn't he dropped it? No, he remembered, one of the deputies had found it on the ground and returned it to him. He pulled it off his belt. "Hello, Bernie."

"What the hell is going on up there?" Bernie Michaelson was not a sweet, touchy-feely agent, and his gruff demeanor carried over to his clients as well as their publishing houses. "Are you all right? I've been trying to reach you for hours." Exaggeration was another part of his stock-in-trade, but Joe was too used to him to be bothered.

"There's been some…unpleasantness at the place I'm staying." Joe hesitated, deciding how much to reveal. "Some asshole is stalking my landlady."

"Well then haul your lily-white ass back to New York where it's safe," Bernie barked.

Joe chuckled. Only Bernie would think of New York as safe. "No can do, Bern."

"Bullshit! You're weeks behind schedule, pal. Your editor is hounding me for your pages. I don't care if you're getting some redneck tail up there in the sticks, it isn't worth it if you're not getting work done. You haven't even signed and returned the contract I sent you last week. The one for the witch book."

"I'm not doing the witch book, Bernie, I told you that. I'll have a new proposal to you in a week or so." Squeezing his eyes shut to ease the throbbing in his skull, Joe sat down on the steps and waited till Bernie's tirade wound down.

"Give it up, Bernie. The witch book is simply not going to happen. You'll get your pages, you'll get a new proposal, and I'll be in New York in a week or two."

The profanity that issued from the other end of the phone line was so loud Joe held the phone away from his ear till it was over.

"Cope," he growled back. "That's why I pay you your freaking fifteen percent. And while you're at it, brace yourself to do damage control on some unexpected publicity. Erickson is here in Sanctity. He knows my real name, knows where I'm staying, and I'm sure if he doesn't find anything sleazy enough to print, he'll make something up."

"Get the hell out of there, Joe! Why can't you go screw beach bimbos like all my other writers do on their vacations?"

"Cause I'm not on vacation, Bern. I'm trying to meet a deadline."

"So glad you remembered. You've got half a manuscript, and less than two months to finish it. Quit fooling around with your little country cutie, and get to work. Don't make me fly out to Michigan to personally kick your ass."

"Kiss it instead, Bernie. Now hang up the phone so we can both get back to work."

"Get me pages, Joe," Bernie threatened one last time. "And sign the damned contract." Then he slammed the receiver down hard enough to make Joe's ear ring. Only Bernie. Joe knew the man kept an old-fashioned rotary-style phone on his desk for just that purpose,. Flicking the power button on a modern phone just didn't have the same effect, according to Bernie.

He glanced up the stairs, wondering how Mel was doing, and wondered why Hattie hadn't come down yet. There was something odd going on there, something he couldn't quite put his finger on. Mel had been through a lot in the past few weeks, granted, but she was one strong lady, and he couldn't quite figure out why all of a sudden all the women were treating her like she was made out of glass.

Unable to sit still any longer, he let himself out the back door and started down the path to see what the cops were up to. He made it most of way to the barn before meeting up with Mott, who was on his way back to the house.

"They haven't found any prints," the sheriff announced without preamble. "No hairs, no footprints, no fibers, nothing. The weapon was a hunting knife, most likely. Probably a common model. No help there."

"Whoever cut open that deer knew what he was doing." Joe turned to follow Mott back to the house. "It was done with a steady, deliberate hand. Since this is hunting country, I suppose most of your residents know how to field-dress a deer."

"Probably down to the average fourth-grader."

"You'll watch Talcott? He's got motive, and I know he's come after her before."

"Yeah, I'll watch him. I'll also grill Harkness, find out just how much he's been covering up for Sean in the last few years." Mott's expression was grim and set, but Joe didn't have it in him to feel sorry for the deputy. If he'd been covering for Talcott, he deserved whatever he got.

"I'll keep an eye on Sean." Mott nodded slowly, let out a ponderous breath. "You keep yours on Melissa."

Chapter Fifteen

Overcast skies and a brisk, clammy breeze lent the impression that nature herself was in mourning. Standing beside Mel in the dressiest clothes he'd packed, black chinos, a blue Oxford-cloth shirt, and his black leather jacket, and with his hair tied neatly at the back of his neck, Joe wrapped his arm around Mel's waist, feeling her shiver even through her raincoat and linen blouse. She'd taken Gladys's death hard, even though she'd known it was coming. The older lady had died in her sleep the same night they'd found the deer butchered in the barn.

With everything hitting her all at once, Mel had changed, and Joe was worried. He didn't like the pallor of her skin, the dark circles under her eyes, or the fact that she wasn't eating enough to keep a goldfish alive. Her passivity was the worst, though. It was like some vampire had sucked all the brightness and life out of Mel, leaving nothing but a husk behind. She didn't smile, but she didn't argue either. And while she didn't resist his touch, she'd stopped seeking it out, and he missed that too. He didn't mind so much that they hadn't had sex…well he minded a lot, but if he'd asked, he was sure she would have obliged him. Obligatory sex wasn't what he wanted, though. He wanted the sad eyed-waif to turn back into his eager and enthusiastic Mel. He wanted to watch her catch fire in his arms, but most of all, he wanted to see her really, truly smile again.

Karen tossed a bouquet of flowers into the grave, following her dad, then her two children tossed smaller sprays. Before the minister began his closing prayer. Joe felt Mel flinch, and tucked her just a little closer to his side, wishing he could do more to ease her grief. This had to bring back memories of her grandmother's passing. Hattie, who had of course been a friend of Gladys's as well, stood on the other side of Mel, grim but dry-eyed, and looking older than Joe had realized she was.

As the service closed, a misty rain began to fall, and a crowd formed around Karen and her father. Mel made no move to join them, so Joe stood where he was, taking his cues from her. "Do you want to go home, now?" he asked, his lips brushing her ear. "I don't think Karen would mind."

"No," she demurred in a ragged whisper. "I'll stay for the luncheon. Gladys was important to me, and I'm not going to let the narrow minded hypocrites run me off."

"Good!" It was the first real spark he'd seen in days. Then, "Aww, shit!"

"What?" Her head whipped around.

"Erickson."

"Of course."

Tightening his grip around her waist, Joe whispered, "Want to make a run for it?"

Her grin was faint and fleeting, but it was genuine, and for that, he could have kissed Erickson or the devil himself. "No. It isn't worth it. At least now we *know* he's watching us, and we don't have to wonder which shrubbery he's hiding behind."

As the crowd around Karen's family started to thin, they began to drift in that direction, pointedly ignoring the reporter's watchful gaze. Well, what could he get from this anyway? That Joe was so smitten with his landlady he'd attended the funeral of her third grade teacher? Somehow he didn't think even Erickson could get much mileage out of that one.

"Thanks so much for coming, Jonas." Karen embraced him warmly while Mel hugged both children at once, and Hattie was in quiet conversation with Dr. Clark.

"No problem." It wasn't exactly a lie, even though he hadn't felt quite so out of place in years. The truth was he wanted to be wherever Mel was. "I'm sorry about your mom."

"I know." Karen was subdued but not despondent, thank heavens. Then again, she'd had plenty of time to prepare for this moment. He couldn't help remembering his own mother's death, and wishing it had been more like Gladys's.

"Thanks to Mel, she was able to go peacefully at home," Dr. Clark interjected. "Instead of in a hospital pumped full of drugs. That meant a lot to her. To all of us."

"Thanks to you, too, Jonas," Karen added. "Not everyone would volunteer to help a stranger the way you did. Not even to impress a girl like Mel."

He looked away. His behavior hadn't been altruistic. It had been selfish. Hadn't it? After all he'd done it for Mel. If she was happier and healthier, he got laid more often. Right?

"I don't believe that *you* have the effrontery to show your face!"

The shrill insult pierced the low buzz of the general conversation. Joe instinctively gathered Mel close, whirling around to appraise the new threat.

"This is a *Christian* ceremony, in a *Christian* cemetery, for a *Christian* woman. How dare you defile that with your heathen presence?"

Mel's already wan complexion paled to ash, and she sagged against Joe's arm. "I'm sorry," she offered weakly. At least she wasn't apologizing to the harridan. She'd turned her face to Karen and Dr. Clark.

"Don't be." Clark's voice was firm and pitched to carry to the gathered crowd. "You haven't done a thing wrong. Edna, I'd appreciate it if you would keep your opinions to yourself. This is a solemn occasion, and Melissa is a dear friend of the family, as well as an invited guest."

Edna Mercer, the grocery store owner's wife. Joe hadn't placed the face at first. She glared daggers at Mel. "It was probably her witchcraft that killed Gladys in the first place. You're a fool, Bill Clark, for trusting that devil-worshipping harlot in the first place, and I only hope she doesn't drag all your souls to hell along with her!"

"Come along, Edna." This time it was the reverend who interrupted her, possibly figuring she was encroaching on his turf, or possibly wanting to protect her from contamination by the likes of them. He took the woman's arm, his pitying glance at Mel making Joe long to rearrange his gaunt, pallid face. "This isn't the time or place for recriminations. The lord will judge each of us on his own schedule, rest assured."

Phil Mercer followed his wife, scowling fiercely. The other mourners stared, in either shame or fascination. Probably both. Looking over his shoulder, Joe groaned inwardly. Sure enough, Erickson had watched the whole incident, and now scribbled furiously into his notebook.

Karen, bless her heart, enveloped Mel in an enormous hug, not even bothering to tug her out of Joe's grip. She just wrapped him up in it too. "What a bitch! I don't even know why she showed up; Mom never liked her anyway."

* * * *

Over the course of the next few hours, Mel didn't say another word about the incident, but it was clear to Joe that the woman's cruel outburst had stung. The funeral luncheon was held in the elementary school cafeteria rather than the church basement, probably in honor of Gladys's years of teaching. Joe couldn't have cared less, but he was glad that Mel didn't risk censure from some self-important clergyman for attending. The tables and benches were a little small for someone his height, but at least there was plenty of food. Everyone had kicked in, and Joe had a plateful of food in front of him, with Mel's veggie pasta filling half of it. Apparently everyone in town had contributed.

So far, the luncheon hadn't been unpleasant. There were probably two hundred people in the cafeteria, many of whom had been polite. A few had asked for his autograph, but he'd shrugged that off, since today wasn't about him. All his attention was fixed on Mel. Though most of the locals didn't seem to share Edna Mercer's open hatred, there were still several cold shoulders being shown. Hattie must have shared his concern, because she was sticking to Mel like glue almost as much as he was. They sat at one end of a long narrow lunch table, with Mel squished between Joe and Hattie, Sheila and some friends of hers facing them across the table. When Mel stood, Joe automatically rose to follow, as did Harriette.

"Cut it out you two." Hands on her hips, Mel shook her head at both of them. She was gorgeous in a slim black skirt and short-sleeved lavender blouse. Her unruly curls were pulled back by a simple black barrette. "I'm just going up to the buffet for a piece of pecan pie. I don't need a pair of mismatched bodyguards dogging my every step."

"I'm not following you." Joe lied casually, without so much as a blink. "I was just going after another brownie."

"Right." Crossing her arms over her chest, Mel turned her glare at Hattie. "What's your excuse?"

"Don't have one. But since I'm up, I think I'll go talk to someone." With that, the silver-haired woman disappeared into the crowd.

"Honestly, Jonas. I'm delighted with your company and grateful for your support, but I don't need a babysitter. Do you intend to follow me to the bathroom next?"

"Nope. Since Hattie debunked, that job falls to Sheila." A quick nod at Mel's young assistant had her on her feet.

"Good grief," Mel sputtered. She sank back onto the bench with her feet still out into the aisle and thrust her heavy ceramic plate up into his hands. "Here. Since you're going up for dessert anyway, grab me a piece of pecan pie. A big one. With lots of whipped cream."

He repressed a grin. Maybe the attack at the cemetery had been enough to shock her out of her lethargy. She was cute as hell when she got pissed, but his strong sense of self-preservation kicked in before he could say so. He hesitated, debating the wisdom of leaving her here alone, when a sharp-heeled foot slammed down on his instep.

"Go. I'm fine."

Sheila was still there, so he did. When he returned with their desserts two minutes later, however, the young woman was nowhere to be seen. Instead, Joe's seat was being filled by Warren Mott.

"Need anything, Sheriff?" Joe sat the plates on the table and stood behind Mel, one hand resting possessively on her shoulder.

"No, I'm all set." The older man stood and shook Joe's hand. "I was just asking Melissa how the new security firm was working out."

"They're doing fine." The three men assigned to provide Whispering Pines with round-the-clock protection all seemed competent enough. He hadn't caught any of them slacking off. Yet.

"They haven't seen anything in the past few days." Mel nodded her agreement. "There's been no new damage, no crank phone calls either." She'd finally fessed up about the harassing phone calls, but apparently those had stopped as soon as Joe had moved in.

"Crime lab hasn't gotten anything either." Mott kept his voice low, so the general buzz of conversation would cover their conversation. "No prints, no DNA, nothing."

"So we just wait for him to strike again? What if somebody gets hurt this time?"

"Then we have a case. Meanwhile, I've got my best deputy trailing Sean Talcott. Since Benson's from down state, he doesn't have any reason to overlook things that one of the local boys might."

"Good." Joe had to admit the sheriff was doing all he possibly could. "I'm surprised the Talcotts aren't here today," he mused. "The rest of the town sure is." To Joe's relief, however, Erickson was not present at the luncheon. It was the first bright spot in a miserable day.

"Byron and Sean both sent their apologies."

Joe jumped at the sound of Karen's voice. He hadn't heard her come up behind him. He was definitely going to have to do something about his distraction level.

"Thanks, Warren." Mel squeezed the sheriff's hand. "Stay in touch."

"Will do, Melissa." As he turned to leave, Mott looked Joe straight in the eye. "Heard any more from that reporter?"

"He was at the cemetery, taking notes, but he hasn't approached either of us directly, or been harassing anyone else, as far as I know."

"Hear he picked up a parking ticket yesterday." Mott's broad, ruddy face held just the suggestion of a smile. "Strangest thing about small towns. Turns out it doesn't pay to stick your nose places it doesn't belong."

"So I've heard." Joe dropped his voice another notch so Mel and Karen wouldn't hear. "Which would explain why I'm not welcome at the library and Mel can't shop at the local grocery store."

"Oh really?" The sheriff's eyes narrowed. "We'll see about that."

After Mott walked away, Joe turned his attention back to the conversation between Karen and Mel, just in time to hear Mel ask Karen, "Where'd the kids go?"

"Some of the high schoolers gathered up all the little kids, took them outside to play. I'm stealing Sheila from you tonight if that's okay. She offered to take the rugrats so Dad and I can crash for a while."

"No problem." Mel's selfless response was instantaneous and unsurprising.

"We'll manage," he heard himself say at the same time, which was a surprise. Where the heck had that *we* come from? Man, he really had to get out of this town.

They left shortly thereafter. Karen was busy with everybody else, and Mel was visibly drooping. "Make sure she gets some sleep." Hattie gave him the instructions as she said good-bye. "She hasn't been, has she?"

Joe shook his head. She'd been restless, exhausted for days. He was worried about how much the stress seemed to be affecting her physically, but she refused to discuss the matter.

"I'm fine, Hat." Mel hugged the older woman, then climbed into Joe's Jeep.

"Tell it to your mirror." Hattie shook her silver head. "Are you sure you shouldn't close down for the season? Maybe take a vacation yourself?"

"No!" There was steel in her heated response. "Both of you knock it off! I'm not closing down, not unless it looks like I have to for my guests' safety. This is my livelihood, and I'm not letting that slimy toad take it away from me."

"Putting yourself in danger is risking somebody else." Mel's spine stiffened, then relaxed as Hattie explained. "Collateral damage happens."

"It's not going to come to that."

"It isn't?" Joe and Hattie asked in unison.

"No." Mel projected a world of determination, and closed her door.

Joe shrugged at Hattie, who shook her head. There were undercurrents he was missing, but he understood both Mel's independence and Hattie's need to protect the girl she'd helped raise.

"Might as well try to drain Lake Superior with a drinking straw as get that girl to listen." Hattie's disgusted remark came through the open window as Joe put the Jeep in gear and waved.

Mel waved and grinned.

Joe just rolled his eyes.

* * * *

Mel sent a smile at the young security guard who had been left behind while she and Jonas were at the funeral. She'd told the tenants that the office would be closed, but apparently they'd expected poor

Derek to play tour coordinator in her absence. The flustered young man sat in a chair on the front porch, where he'd been waiting on their return. Mel paused on her way into the house, and leaned against the porch rail, with Jonas just a few steps away, his arms crossed over his chest.

"I sent all the couples to the casinos," he admitted. Native American gaming enterprises had become a big part of the U. P.'s economy in recent years and were a good rainy-day choice. "I just handed out a bunch of brochures from your office to the ones with kids."

"Perfect. We'll make an innkeeper out of you yet, Derek."

He stood and smiled back, even white teeth gleaming against his ebony skin. "Fat chance, Ms. MacRae. I start at the State Police Academy in September, remember?"

"I know." She stifled a yawn with her hand. Damn, she was always so tired lately. If that didn't change soon, Jonas was bound to figure it out. The man was altogether too perceptive.

"Thanks, Derek." Jonas shook the guard's hand then wrapped his left arm around Mel's waist, steering her toward the front door. "Keep up the good work. And be extra cautious today. Talcott didn't show up at the funeral. He may be up to something."

'Yes, sir, Mr. Pierce." With a quick salute, Derek strode down the steps and toward the cabins.

"Were we ever that young?"

"No," Jonas replied with a chuckle, propelling her into her living room. He helped her out of her raincoat and hung it on the hook by the door. "Somehow, I don't think we ever were."

"Because of what we are?" He hated personal conversations, but she could tell he'd needed to talk all day. She curled her legs up on the couch, kicked off her high-heeled pumps, and patted the space next to her.

"Yeah." He plopped down beside her and tugged his tie loose. "That's part of it."

"And who our parents were."

"Same thing, isn't it?"

"No. You're not your father any more than I'm my mother, or my grandmother for that matter. But they did have an impact on who we are, what we had to deal with."

"Our experiences aren't exactly the same, Mel." He ran his hands through his hair, loosening the leather thong that tied back his ponytail. "Your gifts are just that. Gifts. My heritage is more…"

"More what?" She touched his hand as his voice trailed off. "Powerful? Maybe. But you've only witnessed some of what I can do. My powers are definitely more versatile."

"That's what I meant. Your abilities are useful. My so-called power is more of a handicap. It doesn't serve any useful purpose and it's a day-to-day struggle just to keep the beast under control. That isn't a blessing, or a gift, by any stretch of the imagination."

"Ever stop to think that if you wasted less energy fighting your power, you might not have so much trouble with control? Life is about balance. It's hard to maintain any kind of equilibrium when you spend so much time hating a big part of yourself."

"I don't hate myself, Mel. But I've seen what this so-called gift can do, and it isn't pretty. My mother may not have been the most devoted parent in the world, but she didn't deserve…"

"Didn't deserve what? A difficult husband? A troubled son?" They were getting close to the heart of the matter. Whatever he'd almost blurted out was important, and she couldn't let him freeze up on her now.

"She didn't deserve to die." His tone was stark, his expression utterly blank except for the massive pain lurking in the back of his amber eyes.

"Tell me."

He fought it, but she watched his resolution crumble. Burying his face in his hands, he sighed. "She brought me back to him one night when I was fifteen. He'd been on a bender, he was drunk, high, maybe both. She interrupted his party and threw his current bimbo out the door. They screamed at each other for a while, threw things. That was all pretty normal. But this time, something in him snapped. He changed, right in front of her. And then he went for her throat."

Mel gripped both of his wrists in hers. She pulled his hands away from his face and raised them to her lips. "I'm so sorry, Jonas. Sorry that you had to witness that."

His laugh was bitter. "Witness, hell, I joined in. I was still young enough to believe I was a superhero instead of a monster. I changed too, tried to get between them."

"What happened?"

"He was older, stronger, and stoned on top of it. I got knocked out, didn't come to for hours. When I did, he was long gone, and she was dead."

"What did you do?"

"Dragged her body out into the woods, cleaned up the mess, and took off."

"Was she ever found?"

"Sure." He shrugged. "But since it had clearly been an animal attack of some sort, there was no investigation or anything."

"And your father?"

"He popped up now and again. Usually asking for money."

"And you gave it to him."

"Sometimes. It was worth it to make him go away. But I haven't heard from him since he gave me this." He pulled one hand from hers and touched the white streak in his hair. "Maybe he's really dead this time. Or maybe he stayed a wolf for long enough that he hasn't bothered to change back. Either way, I hope to God I never see him again."

"You're not your father, Jonas." Her heart bled for all he'd been through. No wonder he was afraid of his power, of himself. She crawled into his lap so she could wrap her arms around him. "Don't punish yourself for his weaknesses."

"If I'm so damn good, why do I still want to rip Talcott's throat out?"

"Because you're protective of the people you care about. That's not a bad thing, Jonas. You couldn't save your mother, but it wasn't your fault she died. You can't save me either, no matter how hard you try. I could be hit by lightning or a bus tomorrow, and it wouldn't be your fault. You can only save yourself. And for that to happen, you need to believe that you're worth saving. You are, Jonas. No matter what you believe, what you try to pretend, you are a decent, caring person. I see it, Hattie sees it, and Karen sees it. You have to believe in yourself and live your own life outside of the shadow of your father."

"Look who's talking." His voice was low and laced with bitterness. "The lone witch. You're determined to make the same mistakes as your ancestors did, when any idiot can tell you'd make some lucky guy a fantastic wife. Quit wasting your time with me and go find a man who can give you the home and kids you deserve."

"I'm not my mother, Jonas. I'm not addicted to drugs and sex.

And I'm not my grandmother. I think we've proven my preferences definitely run toward men."

He smiled at that. Good.

"And who knows, maybe sometime down the road, I will decide to take the risk and settle down. Even if I don't, it doesn't make me less of a person. Outside circumstances can happen to anybody. Some people get blue eyes, some get a genetic tendency toward cancer, some get a family curse, and some might even get werewolf genes. Those things can affect what we do. They don't make us who we are."

"If you say so." He didn't sound convinced, but he'd quit arguing. That was progress. Not having the faintest idea of what to say next, she kissed him.

* * * *

The minute she kissed him, all bets were off. They hadn't had sex in days, he was as edgy as a wolf in a bear trap to begin with, and this conversation had strung him out completely. Forgetting he'd intended to be gentle, he ground his lips against hers with fierce possession, gratified that she was kissing him back just as hard.

Her plain black skirt rode up her thighs as she wriggled on his lap. Without even thinking about it, he slid his hands up underneath then groaned.

"You're not wearing pantyhose." How had he missed noticing her bare legs at the funeral?

"Don't own any," she sighed, her lips caressing his neck. "Can't stand them."

He shifted her, stripping away the scrap of soaking wet silk that passed as panties while she fumbled with his belt and zipper, freeing him from the constriction of his trousers. Her skirt was shoved up around her waist as she straddled him, both knees planted on the couch. Slowly she lowered herself onto his aching cock.

"It's been too long." Her sigh echoed his thoughts.

"No kidding." It felt like forever. He worked the tiny pearl buttons of her blouse, but left it hanging from her shoulders as he buried his face between her lace-covered breasts. He hoped she was having fun, because there was no way he was going to last.

"Hurry!"

Like he had a choice! It was over in seconds for both of them. She lay on his chest, panting, limp, and boneless. His arms were locked around her, holding her as close as he possibly could. And he wondered how he was ever going to let her go.

"I've missed this." Her whisper tickled his throat with her breath. "I'm sorry."

"For what?" His sated brain was too muzzy to make sense of what she said.

She gave a soft chuckle against his chest. "That it's been so long, silly."

Oh, that. So was he. But that probably wasn't what she needed to hear. "Don't be." Oddly enough, he understood, and that was a novel experience for him. She'd been so leveled by her grief in the two days since Gladys died, he hadn't even tried to do anything more than hold her at night. He'd never been so deeply involved before, and he felt strangely honored to be the one standing by her through a rough time. She turned her face up to him with a contented smile and it made him feel like a hero.

In an instant, though, the rosy post-coital flush drained from her face. Clapping a hand over her mouth, she dashed to the bathroom.

Zipping his trousers, he followed at a slower pace. "You okay?" He leaned against the sink, and handed her a damp washcloth as soon as she finished bringing up her lunch.

"Fine." She stayed on her knees, but looked up at him and obviously tried to smile.

"Liar. Green isn't the best color for your skin." Looking for mouthwash, he opened the medicine cabinet. Most of their toiletries were in the upstairs bathroom, he'd never needed to look in this one before.

It was mostly empty. There was a tin of bandages and a bottle of aspirin. Then he caught sight of a large medicine bottle with bold pink lettering, and his own stomach lurched. "Prenatal vitamins?"

He closed his eyes as Mel began another round of heaves. He may have even stopped breathing, he wasn't sure. Nothing registered except those damned pink letters that seemed burned into his brain.

Once the world stopped tilting on its axis, a million thoughts jumbled into his head. It all made sense now, her fatigue, her mood swings, even her erratic appetite over the last few weeks. He tried to speak, but no sound came out until the third try. His mouth was drier than it had ever been, and his hand shook as the closed the cabinet.

Finally a brittle rasp emerged from his throat. "You're pregnant?" There had to be some other explanation.

"Uh-huh." She wiped her mouth with the cloth and slumped back on her heels.

The impact of her simple answer was a greater blow than one of his father's punches. He literally reeled, his back slamming into the doorjamb behind him. For the first time in his life he'd allowed himself to trust. What a fucking stupid move that had been.

While he was still processing the extent of her betrayal, he knew he couldn't leave her there on the bathroom floor, weak as a kitten, no matter what she'd done. Fighting back the vicious curses and the lump in his throat, he lifted her in his arms, and carried her upstairs. He laid her on her bed and stood there watching, till he finally found the words he'd been searching for.

"When, Mel? And who?" Nothing since his mother's death had made him feel like his heart had been ripped out of his chest, until now. All he could think to do was howl at the moon. But he couldn't stop himself from asking. "Wasn't I enough for you? And when did you find the time to sleep with somebody else?"

CHAPTER SIXTEEN

Jonas was gone.

Numb, Mel tried to process that simple fact. She leaned against the outside wall of her barn and stared into the woods.

Gone.

Sure, he claimed it was just a quick business trip to talk to his agent, and sure, he hadn't taken all his stuff, but she really didn't expect him to come back. He thought she'd slept with somebody else.

Well, that answered one of her lingering questions. She no longer doubted that he'd actually had the vasectomy. Had the MacRae curse really been powerful enough to override the surgery? Apparently so. So much for Hattie's belief that it had faded over time.

"Are you okay, Ms. MacRae?"

"I'm fine, Derek," she lied, then nodded to the second guard as he passed by on his rounds. "I just wish they'd hurry up in there." At least it wasn't raining today, but it was still gray and overcast, an accurate reflection of Mel's mood. Sheriff Mott was showing the barn to her insurance representative. She'd be damn lucky if they didn't cancel her policy after this. At the very least, her rates were going to go through the roof.

She was grateful to Warren, however, who'd volunteered for this particular duty. Apparently Jonas had called him this morning to let him know he was leaving town, and Warren had stopped by to check on her just before the agent arrived. Even as angry and hurt as he was, Jonas hadn't left her unprotected. He'd also called the security company and doubled the guard. Derek was now Mel's personal shadow, while his partner patrolled the grounds. Somehow, though, Jonas's consideration made her feel worse, not better. She knew he felt betrayed, and she couldn't bring herself to blame him. She had betrayed him, in a way, by exposing him to her curse. Just not with another man.

Yuck. Just the thought of sleeping with somebody else made her nauseous.

"Why don't we go inside?" Derek urged. "You're pale as a ghost. Mr. Pierce will skin me alive if I let you make yourself sick while he's gone."

"I'm fine," she repeated, but she did compromise a little, sitting down on a nearby tree stump. "Besides, I don't think you need to worry about Mr. Pierce. He's not coming back."

The young guard snorted. "Whatever you say. You're the boss." His wide grin told her he wasn't buying it.

"Melissa, I thought you were waiting up at the house." Mott and the insurance adjuster emerged from the barn. Even though the remains of the fawn had been removed by the DNR, it must have been a pretty nasty sight in there, judging by the green tinge on the adjuster's pale face. Only Harkness, trailing Mott as usual, seemed unaffected.

"Don't you start, Warren." She turned to the man in the rumpled blue suit. "Well?"

"There doesn't seem to be too much physical damage," the man began, flipping through forms on his clipboard. "The refrigerator will have to be replaced, and some of your other equipment, but the structure is still basically intact. Most of it can be fixed with a thorough cleaning and a fresh coat of paint. Collect three estimates for the painting and submit them to our office."

"Three!" She'd be lucky to find one contractor willing to work for her.

"We'll take care of it," Mott interjected. He glared at Harkness, who had started to speak, but then seemed to think better of it.

"I also have to warn you," the adjuster continued. "Your policy is under review. At the very least, we're going to have to move you into the high-risk category, but it's likely that your coverage will be discontinued entirely. We expect a certain amount of replacement and maintenance claims from anyone in the hospitality industry, but lately your business seems to attract the sort of destructive element that we really can't condone."

Ignoring the scowls of both Mott and Derek, the smaller man stepped up to Mel, one finger poking her accusingly in the chest. "This is simply not the kind of operation we prefer to do business with, madam. You'll be hearing from us." With that, he turned and stalked up the path to his car.

"Prick." Derek glared at the agent's retreating back.

"You said it," Mott agreed. "Too bad it's his uncle who owns the business. We'll see what he thinks about Junior's little snit fit next poker game."

Derek grinned widely. "Dude, I like the way you think."

"Way too much testosterone around here." Mel rolled her eyes in disgust. "Now I'm gonna need someone to clean all that up!"

It was probably for the best that both men ignored her.

"When's Pierce coming back?"

Mel wasn't sure exactly why Mott and Harkness followed her to the house, but she guessed it had more to do with cookies than official business.

"Never," she snarled.

"Two days," Derek corrected. "He's in New York on an emergency business trip."

Again they ignored her grumbled response as they trailed her into her kitchen like a row of ducklings. She'd started coffee brewing as soon as she'd seen the sheriff's cruiser pull up, and the rich aroma pervaded the kitchen, reviving her nausea. Plopping down in a chair, she waved at the counter.

"Help yourselves. Cookies are in the tin by the coffee maker."

Grabbing cups and plates, they accepted her offer. Soon, Derek and Mott were seated with her at the table while Harkness, mug in hand, hovered by the back door.

"You and Pierce have a fight, Mel?" Mott's line of questioning was anything but subtle.

"I guess you could call it that."

"You okay?" His implication, his expression as he scanned her exposed arms and neck for possible bruises almost made her laugh. Jonas hadn't done a thing. She'd been the one to cause the damage.

"I'm fine." She seemed to be saying that a lot lately, and nobody seemed to believe her. "He didn't *do* anything, Warren. He just left."

"You don't believe he had anything to do with the trouble you're having, do you?"

"Hell, no!"

Mott grinned. "Me either. Just checking." He reached across the table and patted Mel's hand. "He'll be back."

"That's what I told her, too," Derek added. Then he filled Mott in on the beefed-up security patrol.

"Well, if you gentlemen are through arranging my life, I've got a business to run." Glaring, she pushed away from the table and stood. "If you need me, I'll be in my office." Normally she hated doing her monthly accounting, but today it would be a welcome distraction. Columns of numbers would keep her too busy to think about anything else. Any*one* else.

"Right behind you, Ms. M." Derek topped off his coffee mug, then followed Mel to her office. "See you around, Sheriff. Deputy."

"Keep up the good work, Monroe," Mott replied. "I'm always looking for quality deputies. You let me know if you ever need work."

"Male bonding." Mel scowled and logged into her accounting software. "Ugh!"

Ignoring her again, Derek pulled a magazine out of his backpack and sat down with surprising grace for such a large young man. He'd positioned his chair so that he could see both entrances to the room, as well as being within arm's reach of Mel. She had to smile. He was good at his job, and if she had to have a watchdog, she was glad it was at least somebody pleasant.

* * * *

The only way he'd been able to get to New York this morning had involved a series of short flights and a lengthy cab ride. Considering he had started the trip in a pissed-off mood, the tiresome delays were driving Joe abso-freaking-lutely nuts.

Pregnant.

He couldn't get that word out of his head.

How on Earth could Mel be pregnant?

It just didn't make any sense. After putting her to bed last night, he'd sat in her kitchen for hours staring at the wall and trying to figure it out. And failing. Pregnant. It was as if someone had yanked the ground right out from under his feet.

Who? He hadn't noticed her spending any time with another man. And it couldn't have been before she got involved with him. Her virginity had been too physically obvious. So when? Since they'd been together, he didn't think she'd been out of his sight long enough to have slept with anybody else. He could not come up with a single possible scenario for how this could have happened.

Unless it was his.

Which was the scariest damn thought he'd ever had.

Joe swallowed hard as the small plane dipped in the wind. It couldn't be his, he reminded himself. He'd taken care of that possibility years ago. Still, the niggling doubt persisted. She was a witch. Just how strong *were* her healing powers? He didn't know which eventuality hurt more, the idea that she'd cheated on him, or the idea that she might have taken it upon herself to reverse his vasectomy. Either way, she'd betrayed him, thus proving the lesson he'd learned from his mother. Women just couldn't be trusted.

The possibility of fatherhood raised another whole set of issues. What if the baby had Joe's—abilities? Could he then simply walk away? Leaving another child to flounder like he had, unsure of his powers and how to handle them? Of course, if he believed in Mel's supposed curse, then the child would be a girl. And a witch. Could one child possibly be both? He had no idea if his werewolf gene was sex-linked or not. The amount of raw power possible in a child of his and Mel's was staggering. A werewolf/witch? Witch/wolf? Joe experienced a surge of responsibility not just toward the baby but to the world. A child with that kind of power would need to be taught responsibility and control right from the cradle.

Maybe he should sue for custody. He was rich. He could afford to get better lawyers than Mel. Her local reputation as witch would work against her in court. A judge wouldn't accept that her powers were real. He'd just see her as an unstable young woman playing with the occult. She might get visitation rights, but if Joe took the child to New York or Vermont, how often would he actually have to deal with her?

Of course, if the baby was a witch, he or she would need Mel to learn about that part of his or her heritage. God, what a tangled up mess!

The shrill beeping of his satellite phone brought him back to Earth.

"What?" he snarled into the receiver. "I'm landing in ten minutes."

"I got you a meeting with your publicist at two," Bernie announced, unfazed by Joe's surliness. "Did you bring the pages for Doro?"

"Yeah." Well, mostly. His editor wouldn't be happy, but Joe had enough pages for her to get started with.

"Good. You're having lunch with her. There's a car waiting for you at the airport to bring you into Manhattan. Next time use a real airline."

"Bite me." So what if the puddle-jumper he'd arranged was landing at a smaller airstrip out on Long Island, rather than LaGuardia or JFK? Of course, to Bernie's mind, leaving Manhattan Island was an enormous undertaking, akin to trekking across the Sahara, or scaling Everest.

"There's a new piece in *Personalities* this morning," Bernie warned. "Shows you at a funeral with some hot little redhead. He gives your real name, Joe."

"Shit!" He'd been expecting it, but it was still a nuisance. "What does he say about Mel?"

"Who?"

"Melissa MacRae. The redhead."

"Oh." Speculation dripped from Bernie's tone. "Says you're boinking her. Doesn't mention her by name, just calls her a local innkeeper who's reputed to be a witch."

"Christ!" The fasten seat belts light came on, indicating their imminent landing. "Talk to you later, Bern. Gotta go."

He'd spoken to Bernie's assistant first thing that morning, told her to cram his day as full as possible of the meetings he'd been putting off since he'd left for Sanctity. He needed activity, needed to stay busy, almost as much as he needed this time away from Michigan, away from Mel. He wasn't going to feel guilty about that, he told himself as the wheels of the plane touched down. He'd made sure she was safe while he was gone, what more could she expect?

The limo was waiting by the tarmac as Joe exited the plane, and he pushed all thoughts of Mel firmly from his mind. Today was about business. Business and distance. He'd worry about the other stuff tomorrow. Climbing into the limo, he pulled out his PDA, mentally and physically leaving Mel behind.

* * * *

Mel was really, really tired of being cosseted. Twenty minutes after Mott left, Sheila showed up for work, deliberately cheerful and quick to take on any task more physical than typing. She hadn't yet said a word to Mel about knowing she was pregnant. She just delegated all the cleaning and maintenance tasks to herself, leaving Mel sitting in the office with her bodyguard, feeling crabby and superfluous.

"Am I allowed to go to the bathroom by myself?" She couldn't seem to stop herself from snapping at Derek after Sheila left to clean the coin-operated laundry room.

"Ms. MacRae…"

Mel sighed and rubbed her eyes. "Sorry, Derek. None of this is your fault."

"What's not his fault?"

Great! Now Hattie was here to baby-sit her too.

"Warren Mott told me that Jonas left for New York this morning." Hattie let herself in through the screen door. "When's he coming back?"

"Two days."

"He's not." Derek and Mel spoke simultaneously. Hattie arched one silver eyebrow, and helped herself to a chair facing Mel's desk.

"He *said* it's just a short trip." Mel tried to keep her voice calm and level, but a tiny crack snuck in anyway. "But even if he does come back, he won't be sticking around."

"Derek," Hattie asked sweetly with a wide smile for the guard. "Would it be possible for you to do your job from right outside on the porch?"

"Sure thing, Ms. Sharp." The young man's smile showed he was clearly relieved to be excused from their personal conversation. He shut the storm door behind him, giving him a clear view of the two women, but blocking the sound of their voices.

"What happened, dear?"

"He found out."

"About the baby?" Hattie's blue eyes were wide with compassion. She walked around the desk to envelop Mel in a warm, motherly hug.

"Yes." Mel nodded against Hattie's shoulder.

"You poor thing!" After a moment, Hattie drew back and leaned against the desk, still gripping Mel's hands in hers. "I take it he was less than thrilled?"

"That's an understatement." Mel sniffed, and Hattie withdrew one of her hands to reach for the tissue box.

"So he stormed out?" Now the blue eyes glittered.

"Not exactly." Mel didn't want Hattie angry at Jonas. None of this was his fault. "He waited till this morning, doubled the security patrols, and let Warren know he was leaving."

"And he said he'd be back in a day or two?"

"Yeah. He didn't even pack."

"Hmm." Hattie paused, and Mel recognized her friend's thoughtful look. Finally Hattie spoke. "Maybe he just needed time to think, to absorb the news. It had to be quite a shock."

No kidding! Mel gave a reluctant nod. "Maybe. I'm sure he wanted time to cool off, anyway. Control is important to him." More like an obsession, but if she tried to get into that, she'd have to explain, and Joe's secrets weren't hers to share. Twin tears leaked down her cheeks. "It's over, Hattie. He's not going to be able to forgive me for this."

Hattie pursed her lips and narrowed her eyes, clearly not making sense of the situation. "Even though he was a willing participant in the conception?"

"Was he? Not in his mind. He thinks I slept with somebody else."

Hattie's sharp burst of laughter came as something of a shock. "I'm sure he knows better than that." She patted Mel's hand and gave her what was probably meant as an encouraging smile. "Give the boy some breathing room, sweetie. He'll have his head together by the time he comes back."

* * * *

Karen, who showed up a couple hours later, shared Hattie's conviction. "He'll be back."

Mel hit the save button on her computer and closed the software window. Then she shook her head. "You're here, too? Does the entire damn town have to have an opinion on the status of my love life?"

"Of course," Karen replied breezily, sliding into the same chair Hattie had occupied earlier. "Duh. This is Sanctity, after all. By the way, Dad wanted me to remind you to take your vitamins."

Mel leaned her forehead on the heels of her hands. "Don't mention those damned things! Jonas found them."

"That's how he found out?" Karen's delicate dark brow arched.

"Yep."

"Ouch!" Karen grimaced empathetically. "That had to suck!"

"For both of us." Mel nodded, her shoulders slumped. "He doesn't believe it's his."

Karen waved her hand and shook her head breezily. "He'll get over it. Geez, Mel, it's not like he's going to believe you're promiscuous. He'll figure things out, and then he'll be back."

"Am I that predictable?"

"Well, yeah." Karen's honesty had always been one of the reasons Mel liked her so much, but right now it was irritating. At Mel's scowl, her friend held up a paper bag and grinned. "Don't throw me out; I brought you food. Rosa sends her best."

Of course she did. The whole town was either trying to get rid of her, or trying to take care of her, and right now she wasn't sure which group was bugging her more. After seeing Karen off, Mel stared at the boxed salad and veggie lasagna. One portion. Even Rosa knew Jonas had left her. Still grumpy at the world, she glared at the food. She had to eat. It wasn't fair to the baby not to. Rosa's cuisine was wasted on her though. Today everything tasted like sawdust.

"You can't go in there." Derek's booming voice outside her door startled her. Who the heck was it this time?

"Who is it?"

"He says he's a reporter, Ms. MacRae."

"Andrew Erickson." It was an unfamiliar voice. "From *Personalities Weekly*."

Great. That was all she needed today. "Let him in, Derek." She was going to have to talk to him sometime, she reasoned, sighing. Why not now?

"I don't think so, ma'am." Derek's tone was apologetic but determined. "Mr. Pierce left specific instructions about this guy. He said…"

"Mr. Pierce isn't here right now." It probably wasn't fair to snarl at Derek, but she couldn't help it. Mel was sick of everyone trying to run her life. "And you might want to remember that he isn't the one who hired your company in the first place. Let him *in*, Derek."

The thin, reedy young man who stepped inside didn't look like a particularly formidable opponent. Not until you looked past the horn-rimmed glasses and into his eyes. And his solid, unwavering aura. Mel swallowed hard. Jonas had been right. Erickson *was* a pit bull.

Derek had followed the other man in and was standing in the doorway, arms crossed over his chest, glowering. Mel smiled at her bodyguard, then turned her most businesslike manner on the reporter.

"Have a seat, Mr. Erickson. I'm afraid that all of my cabins are occupied at the moment. Is there something else I can do to help you?"

"You could start by cutting the crap. You know perfectly well why I'm here." His gaze remained steady on Mel as he sat across from her and reached into his pocket. Derek had moved inside behind the other man, and kept a wary watch on the reporter's movements.

"I do have some idea," she acknowledged. "But why don't you fill me in on the details."

"Fine, if that's how you want to play it." He set a compact cassette recorder down on the desk, openly pressing the record button. "Ms. MacRae, I'd appreciate it if you'd tell me about your relationship with J. P. Wolfe."

"J. P. Wolfe is a pseudonym, Mr. Erickson." She kept her gaze leveled on his, schooling her features to show as little emotion as possible. "Jonas Pierce, however, is a tenant of mine for the summer."

"Just a tenant? Word around town is that you're living together."

"Really? Well, small town gossip is notorious for exaggeration. That certainly isn't the case." Not after yesterday, anyway. "It is true that we've dated a few times. He's a very attractive man."

Erickson pulled a folded up newspaper from his backpack and handed it to Mel. Unfolding it, she saw that it was an issue of his tabloid, dated the day before. On the front cover was a photograph of Jonas and Mel, standing together in the rain at Gladys's funeral.

"Well, it's not a very flattering picture." She forced a tiny laugh. "But my hair always looks awful when it's raining."

"Ms. MacRae, I hear you call yourself a witch. Any truth to that?"

"Depends on your definition of witch, Mr. Erickson. I'm something of an herbalist."

"With a degree in botany to prove it."

She nodded. "You've done your homework."

"I always do. Don't you find it odd that a noted horror writer would be staying at a low-budget resort when the owner just happens to be a witch? Has it occurred to you that you're nothing more than his latest research project?"

The question echoed her own earlier fear, but so much had happened in the meantime that that it simply didn't bother her anymore. No, now she was pissed. She and Jonas might not be a couple anymore, but this little weasel had no business degrading him. Her tone was clipped and icy. "Not particularly. Since he was up front about his curiosity from the beginning, he didn't need to take me out to get me to talk to him."

"Oh." Her adamant defense of Jonas seemed to take him back a bit. Then his expression hardened. "So Pierce is pursuing his research here in Michigan with your full cooperation." His sneering tone made the simple words sound somehow dirty, but she refused to take the bait.

She tipped her head a fraction of an inch. "That's correct."

"And you two are also, 'dating' as you put it?"

"Also correct."

"He escorted you to a funeral. That's hardly a casual date."

"Jonas is a nice man. He offered to provide moral support at a very difficult time."

"So you're really just friends?"

"Just what are you insinuating, Mr. Erickson?"

"Well, rumor around town is that you and Pierce are way more than friends, more than just casual lovers. Word is that you, Ms. MacRae, are pregnant, and the Jonas Pierce, a.k.a. J. P. Wolfe, is the baby's father."

CHAPTER SEVENTEEN

"That's ridiculous!" Mel had to fight to keep her jaw from dropping. How the hell had he heard about that?

"You're telling me I'm wrong?" One sandy eyebrow rose in disbelief.

"I'm telling you that Jonas Pierce is an exceptionally responsible man. He would never put his partner at risk. You're barking up the wrong tree."

Erickson shrugged. "All right. So you're not carrying Wolfe's love child. That was only going to be a small part of the article anyway." His aura was unpleasant, which Mel supposed was mainly a result of his seedy profession. An innate determination showed through; she had no doubt that he *was* a pit bull when it came to a story, but there was also an inner core of honesty that she doubted he could completely suppress. She didn't think he'd print anything that he didn't think was at least possibly true. "I've got way bigger fish to fry."

"Yes?" She knew her tone was guarded, wary. She didn't trust that snake-oil-salesman voice of his, not for a minute.

"You're supposedly a witch, Ms. MacRae. I'm sure my readers could find that very interesting, but it isn't you that I'm after. Help me out, and neither your face or your name will ever appear in my publication again."

"Help you how?" She really hoped her rising nausea didn't show on her face.

"J. P. Wolfe, or Jonas Pierce, is a famous man. Talented, good-looking, wealthy, and in a profession where a certain amount of public exposure is expected. Yet until this morning's publication, the reading public has never even known his real name."

"So the man likes his privacy. It may be unusual, but it's certainly not extraordinary."

"My readers feel they have the right to know about the celebrities whose careers they support. My employers mutter something about the first amendment. My interest, however, goes a little deeper. You claim to be a witch. Surely that means you believe in the supernatural?"

"What do my beliefs have to do with anything, Mr. Erickson?"

"Have you noticed anything unusual about your boyfriend?"

"Besides being attractive, intensely private and a very nice man?" She shrugged with as much faux nonchalance as she could muster. "Well, he is a vegetarian, and he likes the Three Stooges. I've always thought that was kind of odd."

"I meant anything of a paranormal nature."

"He writes horror novels for a living. I'd say he has a pretty powerful interest in things that go bump in the night." She hoped lightning didn't strike her for the way she was bending the truth, but she had a fierce need to protect Jonas in any way she could. She'd hurt him so much. He deserved what help she could give him.

A twitch appeared above Erickson's right eyebrow, and his foot tapped a rapid beat against the leg of his chair. "How about moonlight, Ms. MacRae?" he growled.

Dropping her voice to what she hoped was a seductive purr, she chuckled. "Oh, he likes moonlight well enough. Moonlight, sunlight, candlelight, he really isn't picky." Maybe that would give him something to speculate about, and he'd back off. Hopefully before she threw up on his shoes.

She should have known better. "Allow me to be blunt. Have you ever had any indication that Pierce might be something other than human? Tell me the truth, and I'll make sure your name is left completely out of it."

Looking him straight in the eye, she flattened her palms on her desk and lied through her teeth without any hesitation whatsoever. "I have no idea what you are implying, but I'm pretty damned sure I don't like it. Print whatever you like about me, I really don't care. I'm a witch, and I've never tried to hide it. You can print your silly rumors about a love child, but that will only make you look stupid nine months from now, so I don't think you'll bother. And I don't give a damn whether you print that I'm sleeping with Jonas Pierce, J. P. Wolfe, Elvis Presley, or a whole shipload of little green aliens."

"About Jonas, however, you are way out of bounds. He spends his life studying things that scare most of us to death, then fictionalizing his research for the amusement of the more literate masses. That doesn't mean he is supernatural. He's very much a man, Mr. Erickson, and an awfully good one, in my opinion. He has his strengths and his faults, his good days and his crummy ones, just like everybody else. Of course, since he's smart, kind and gorgeous, I can see why other, lesser men would be only too happy to tear him down. Don't. And if you must, don't use me to do it."

"Ms. MacRae…" Erickson stood, seeming to be at a loss for words.

She glared him down. "Good bye, Mr. Erickson."

At her nod, Derek, who had been a silent witness to the entire conversation opened the door and held it with his shoulder while he escorted the reporter out of the building. Erickson showed enough of a survival instinct to comply, but he was yelling questions over his shoulder until the moment Derek gently closed the door of his rental car behind him.

"What a pain in the ass." Mel was still sitting at her desk shaking when Derek returned to the office after watching Erickson's car disappear down the road. He settled back into his chair and shook his head with a frown on his normally pleasant face. "Do I have to let him in again?"

"No." Slumping over her desk, she buried her head in her hands to hide the tears. "Next time, feel free to toss him in the lake."

* * * *

According to his watch, this meeting had only been going for an hour. It felt like days.

Trying to focus on his editor's words, Joe stared at her blankly, ignoring her sleek, high-tech office. All he could think about was waiting back in Michigan.

"Joe!" Dorothea Cox slapped some papers on the desk in front of him. "You with me here?"

He blinked, bringing her face back into focus. "Yeah, just jet lag, I guess. Sorry, Doro."

"Jet lag, my ass. You didn't even change time zones. What's up?"

Doro was a fifty-something brunette who looked thirty-five and knew it. She was a fireball, as stubborn as they came, and a fantastic editor. Looking into her wide brown eyes, Joe realized she wasn't just asking what was wrong, she actually cared. When had that happened? It had been the same with Bernie, and Joe was stupefied by his own ignorance. How had he made all these friends and not even noticed? And why on Earth was he just noticing now? It was terrifying to discover there were several people in the world who mattered to him.

"Joe, what the hell is wrong?" Doro repeated.

"Woman trouble." He figured she deserved the answer, though he'd rather have eaten ground glass than admit it.

"In Michigan?" Her raw snort of laughter contrasted with her ultra-feminine image. "You have got to be kidding. Is that why you're so far behind on pages?"

Embarrassed beyond belief, he nodded.

"The girl in the picture, huh?" He should have known Doro wouldn't let it go. Should have known she'd seen the article, too. "Red hair, ugly rain coat?"

"Yeah." He'd already been through this inquisition once today with Bernie. How many more times was he going to have to explain himself?

"Good!"

He looked across her desk in horror, startled by her gleeful exclamation. "Huh?" That was him, Mr. Articulate.

"It's about time you got a life, pal. Good thing you're a bestseller though. If you were a newbie, I wouldn't be extending your deadline by a month. Are you really sure you can't do the witch book, though? It sounded fantastic."

"Uh, no. I'm sure." Even if it was over between him and Mel, he couldn't, wouldn't exploit their relationship like that. Especially after her appearance in the tabloid, everyone would see a book about a witch, and know he was talking about her. She had enough trouble with the locals—he wasn't going to expose her to national scrutiny.

Maybe, though, it was time he took a closer look at his own demons.

"How about a story about a werewolf in New York City?"

* * * *

"I'll pick up the grocery order."

Sheila had been restless all day, and Mel smiled. Picking up supplies meant a trip to Escanaba, where the younger woman would no doubt find an excuse to do some shopping of her own.

"Okay." Whatever Sheila's reason for volunteering, Mel was happy to be rid of the chore. "It'll give me more time to work on the books." She hadn't gotten much done since her earlier encounter with Andy Erickson.

"Take the minivan, you'll need it for all the supplies. And don't worry about when you get back, as long as you take a cooler for the milk and stuff." Sheila's beat up VW wouldn't hold a box of paper towels, let alone the large order of cleaning supplies they needed.

"Sweet! Thanks Mel, you're the greatest boss ever." Sheila caught the keys Mel tossed her and bounced out of the office with a wave over her shoulder, while Derek watched hopelessly out the window.

"Enjoying the scenery, Derek?" His crush on her assistant was really kind of sweet.

"I sure am." He sent her a sheepish grin. "You've got great scenery around here. Just great."

"So ask her out, silly." They were both young, attractive, and unattached. Shaking her head, Mel turned her attention back to her accounts. Even without further interruptions, she wasn't getting anywhere. Bookkeeping was never a favorite task, but today, trying to focus on numbers was making her head swim more than usual.

Maybe she should just sell out to Talcott. Byron would give her a reasonably fair price, so she'd have enough money to live on for a while, even support herself as a stay-home mom for a couple years while she figured out what to do next. She could go anywhere she wanted, somewhere far from here where no one had ever heard of the MacRae family witches.

She'd left Sanctity once before, and she thought about what it had been like to go away to college. For four years she hadn't been the witch, hadn't been the focus of gossip and speculation like she'd always been at home. She'd never been outgoing and popular, but she hadn't been singled out as a freak, either. In that sense, college had been wonderful.

But when each semester had ended, she couldn't wait to get home. The unfortunate truth of it was that Sanctity always had been, always would be her home. She'd missed it terribly, the house, the garden, the land, and the animals. And, most of all, surprisingly enough, she'd missed the people.

Sure, there were a few, like Sean Talcott, and Edna Mercer who didn't like her, but there were so many more who were always there for her, like Rosa, Hattie, the Clarks and even Warren Mott. Sancti-ty might not be much of a town, but it was *her* town. She wasn't about to let Sean Talcott chase her out of it. This was her place, where she wanted to grow old and her daughter would grow up. This was *home*.

The shrill ringing of the telephone caused her to jump. It had only been twenty minutes since Sheila left. Obviously she wasn't going to get any work done today.

"Whispering Pines, can I help you?"

"Melissa, this is Warren Mott. There's been an accident."

"Is anybody hurt?"

"Not too badly, but your new van is totaled. Doc Clark's on his way to see Sheila, but I think you might want to come as well."

"Sheila? What happened?" She didn't care a fig about the van, as long her friend was all right.

"She's just banged up a little," Mott assured her. "She'll be fine. We're at the intersection of the state highway and Long Lake Road. See you in a bit."

"I'm on my way!"

Except, she realized as she darted out the door, she didn't have a car.

"Derek, you have a car." She smiled in relief at the guard who was right behind her, as usual. "Thank goodness. You're driving!"

"Okay." He seemed to take everything in stride. "Where're we going?"

Mel gave him the directions as they scurried to his car. She fidget-ed constantly on the short trip, more worried than she wanted to admit.

A light drizzle had started up, and the sky was as gloomy as Mel felt. Flashing lights greeted their arrival, and her stomach churned as she spotted her new minivan—upside down in the muddy ditch beside the road.

"Sheila!" she cried, hopping out of Derek's car even before he'd completely stopped.

"Over here." Sheriff Mott stepped out from behind a blue pickup. "Settle down, Melissa. She'll be fine."

Taking her arm, the sheriff led Mel across the two-lane highway to his cruiser, where Dr. Clark sat in the back seat beside a very pale and shaken Sheila.

"How bad?" Mel automatically assessed her friend's injuries, noting the bruises on her pale forehead and a bloody gouge along her left arm.

"Not very," assured the doctor. "Thank God for seat belts and airbags. She's got a few cuts, lots of bruises, and a concussion."

"Sorry about the van, Mel." Sheila whispered with a sniffle.

Fighting back her own tears, Mel traded places with the doctor. "Don't. I couldn't care less about the van." Grasping Sheila's hands in hers, Mel closed her eyes and called on her powers, sensing the energy that flowed out of her skin and into Sheila. She could feel each of the wounds as her own skin briefly tore and then almost instantaneously repaired itself. Her head pounded ferociously for a moment, then eased back to a dull throb.

"Are you sure this is a good idea?" Sheila's voice steadied but was still weak as her concussion cleared. "What about the baby?"

"She's fine." Mel forced her eyes open. "Your uncle was right, your injuries were all pretty minor. We'll just sit here for a minute, though, I think." In truth, she felt weak and shaken, as much from the emotional impact of seeing her friend hurt as from the energy expended in healing. Seeing the van upside down had scared the daylights out of her. "What happened?"

"I was coming down the hill pretty fast." Sheila bit her lip and closed her eyes like she was visualizing the accident. "The light was red, and there was traffic coming the other way, so I slammed on the brakes."

"And then?"

Sheila shook her head. "Then nothing. No brakes at all. It was either hit the ditch, or plow into the oncoming traffic. I picked the ditch. I must have been going too fast, though, because the van rolled." Tears trickled down her pale cheeks. "Lord, Mel, I've never been so scared in my life."

"I'll bet." Tears stung at Mel's eyes too, and she shuddered then hugged her young friend hard. She closed her eyes against a wave of nausea. "Thank heavens you're okay!"

"Most of the other cars stopped," Sheila added. "The guy in the blue pick-up helped me get out of the van. Somebody else called the sheriff, and my uncle."

Breathing deeply, Mel got her tears and her stomach under control. "And Warren called me. Now, we should probably go see what we need to do next."

It took her a minute to be sure her feet were steady underneath her, but Mel was able to walk away from the police car under her own steam.

Doc Clark eyed her with professional caution, but she flashed him a reassuring smile, and he responded in kind.

"Thanks, Mel," he offered quietly. "You're better than any medicine I could prescribe. She's okay?"

Sheila answered for herself. "Right as rain, Uncle Bill. Scared spitless and pissed as hell, but physically fine."

"Did somebody call a tow truck?" Mel's insurance company was not going to be pleased.

Mott nodded. "Wayne's on his way. He's taking it to the county impound lot; I want somebody to have a look at those brakes."

The wait was nerve-wracking. She stood with Sheila, while Derek and Dr. Clark hovered nearby. Mott and his deputies were taking the witnesses' statements and directing the tow-truck crew as they righted the van and dragged it from the ditch.

The drizzle evolved into a misty rain, which had them all crowding into Dr. Clark's sedan for cover, the close confines further exacerbating already stretched nerves. By the time the witnesses and tow-truck left, Mel was ready to strangle the bunch of them.

"We need to go." She jerked her head at Derek. Then she turned to Sheila. "You take tomorrow off. Hattie can run me into Escanaba for the supplies."

"You need some rest, too, Mel." Doc Clark sent her a reproachful look. "I don't like those circles under your eyes. You need to remember to take care of yourself, especially now."

"I'm fine, Doc." She darted a glance at Derek, reminding the doctor that her condition was still a secret.

One look at Derek's wide grin, however, informed her that it was already too late. "Oh, I know you're expecting. Mr. Pierce told me before he left."

"He would." The rat. No wonder her bodyguard had been treating her like glass. Along with everyone else in town.

* * * *

It was just before dinnertime when Joe knocked on Kent and Nora Willoughby's door. He hadn't called, hadn't provided any warning to expect him, but after the day he'd had, Joe felt a powerful need to connect with his closest and oldest friend, the one other man who knew his secrets.

Clutching a bunch of flowers and a big box of candy to apologize for his intrusion, he stood at the security entrance to their building, praying they were home.

"Joe!" Nora's cheerful voice was surprised, but welcoming. "Come up, come up!"

She buzzed open the door, and he made his way up to their tenth-story apartment, a large, airy flat filled with kids and laughter. Nora greeted him at the door with a bear hug.

"I didn't even know you were in town!" She accepted the flowers and candy just in time for Kent to bound out of his study and across the room to clasp Joe's hand in his.

"Hey, dude, what's up?" One good look at Joe's expression, and Kent's smile dimmed. "We'll talk after dinner," he promised, his intuition acute, as always. "Nora's got steaks…"

"In the fridge," Nora interjected. "Tonight it's broccoli alfredo."

"You don't need to change your menu for me." Joe didn't want to be a nuisance. "I just came from a dinner meeting."

"Baloney!" Nora was a sweetheart, an earth mother who assumed it was her duty to feed anyone who entered her domain. She was also stubborn as a rock. Joe gave in and ate another dinner.

* * * *

Mel was still cranky at nine that evening, when the sheriff's cruiser pulled into her driveway. She stepped out onto her front porch to meet him, her faithful shadow Derek close behind her.

"Isn't your shift over?"

"Nope." He didn't elucidate.

"Men!" She snorted under her breath before affixing a polite smile to her face. "What's up, sheriff?"

"Melissa. Monroe." He greeted them quietly, his voice and expression entirely neutral. Mel was surprised to note that he had also driven himself. Harkness was nowhere in sight.

"Come on in, Warren." Mel's offer was only a little bit grudging. "There's coffee if Derek here hasn't finished it."

She'd derived a small spiteful pleasure from feeding Jonas's expensive Kenyan coffee beans to his paid watchdogs all day. The two men followed her to the kitchen.

"Heard from Pierce yet?" Mott accepted a steaming mug and seated himself at the kitchen table.

"No." Mel handed Derek a cup then poured a glass of water from the tap and sat down between the two men.

"He'll be back, tomorrow or the day after." Derek's faith was sweet, but was beginning to wear on Mel's nerves.

"You staying on till then?"

"Yes, sir. I stick to her like glue, and there will be two men on the outside tonight."

"Glad somebody bothered to inform me." Mel wanted to strangle somebody. "I wouldn't object to a bit of privacy, you know."

The men rolled their eyes at one another, as though humoring her feminine foolishness. If they wanted to see a tantrum they were on the right track. If one more person started telling her what to do, she was liable to start throwing things.

Mott gave her a serious look. "Thing is, Melissa, I was right to be concerned. I had the mechanics at the impound lot look over your van. Your brakes didn't fail. They were deliberately cut."

CHAPTER EIGHTEEN

After dinner, of course, Joe had to play with the kids for a while. At three, five and seven, they were an energetic and inquisitive handful. By the time Nora gathered them up to get ready for bed, Joe was exhausted.

"How do you do it?" he asked Kent when the two men were finally alone in Kent's study. Joe sprawled on the beat-up old couch that was going to be his bed tonight. "How do you balance all your different responsibilities and stay sane?"

"You just do." Kent swiveled around in his computer chair and shrugged. "It helps that I love my job, love my kids even more, and love my wife more than anything. Some days, sure it's more work than fun, but you just slog through those. The good days more than make up for the bad ones."

Busy absorbing that response, Joe didn't reply. He supposed, if he'd really thought about it, he should have been able to predict Kent's answer.

"What's going on, Joe? You can't tell me you're finally thinking about settling down?"

"Don't turn your bedside manner on me, pal." He sipped at his Coke, while Kent nursed a light beer. After a long pause, Joe looked back at his friend. "Do you believe in magic?"

The blond man raised one eyebrow. "Well, I believe in were-wolves, so why not?"

"You're a doctor. Is it… Do you think it's possible for a spell to negate an operation?"

"Don't know, I've never thought about it. What kind of surgery?"

"How about a vasectomy?"

Kent eyed Joe shrewdly then laughed. "Is that it? That's what has you more stressed out than I've ever seen you except when your dad was nearby?"

Squeezing the bridge of his nose to quell his aching head, Joe nodded.

Kent's eyes narrowed. "Oh, hell, you're serious, aren't you? This isn't just speculation."

"Bingo." Joe nodded, his jaw clenched so tightly it hurt.

"Sure it's yours?"

"I don't see how it could be, unless she used some kind of a spell. But she was a virgin three weeks ago, and we've been together almost constantly since then."

"This is Melissa MacRae we're talking about, right? Owner of Whispering Pines, witch, gorgeous red-head, your landlady?"

"Right." Of course Kent would put two and two together. He'd probably been matchmaking when he recommended Whispering Pines in the first place.

"You're sure she was a virgin?"

"Yeah, the physical evidence would be a little hard to fake."

"You've only been in Michigan for what, three weeks? Four? You must work fast, pal. She probably couldn't even be sure yet."

"She's sure. For that matter, so am I. She's a witch, remember? A *healing* witch. Besides, all the symptoms are there, fatigue, nausea, the works."

"Great time for you to split town." Kent tapped his foot and sipped his beer. Joe could practically hear the gears turning inside his friend's brilliant mind. "Sounds like a time she could use some support."

He was right, Joe acknowledged mentally, wracked with guilt. And Kent didn't even know the half of it. Joe hadn't mentioned Erickson, or Mel's stalker yet. But still, there was his side of the story to be considered. "Look, I'm still not even sure it's mine, and if it is, then it means she cast a spell on me, deliberately using me to father a kid I never wanted. You know better than anybody else that I'm not exactly daddy material."

"I know that you *think* you shouldn't have children," Kent corrected. "But I don't agree with you. Never have. You're not your old man, Joe. If you were, believe me, I'd never let you in the same room with my kids."

"But the genes are still there."

"I see. We're back to the old nature versus nurture argument. Get over it, Joe. Just because you're a little different doesn't make you evil, and it doesn't mean that your kids will be. You know, it really pisses me off. We've been friends for twenty years. Do you really think so little of my judgment that I'd have a murderous lunatic for a best friend? That I'd name my son after him, for God's sake?"

Joe winced. Kent's three-year-old was called Matthew Jonas. It had been years since he'd seen Kent lose his temper, and he had to admit that it was at least partially justified.

"Anyway," Kent continued in a more moderate tone of voice. "There's another possibility you don't seem to have considered."

"What's that?"

"Your vasectomy may have failed on its own."

"You admitting to possible malpractice?"

"Not in a hundred years." Kent laughed wryly. "But your circumstances are a bit outside my usual ballpark. Melissa may be able to cast spells, but I know you're a werewolf. To be honest, I've wondered for years if your body would eventually repair itself."

Joe's eyes narrowed. "And you didn't mention this sooner because…"

"Because I figured you were intelligent enough to be careful, anyway. I warned you to use back-up protection. Did her spell magically make a condom disappear?"

"No. That was a mistake on my part." One he'd never made with another woman.

"Well, let's go see." Kent stood up with a sigh. "My office should be empty by now."

After a quick word with Nora, they were on their way. As Kent had predicted, the office was empty, except for the night security guard who patrolled the hallways. Their footsteps echoed in the dim corridor.

"In there." Kent handed Joe a specimen bottle and pointed to a rest room. "I can probably round up a magazine if you need it. Meanwhile, I'll be in my office, catching up on paperwork."

"I think I can manage." All he had to do was think about Mel; he didn't need porno. A few minutes later, he carried the container into the lab, where Kent wordlessly prepared a slide, then checked out the contents under a microscope.

"Take a look." Kent pulled back from the scope and offered Joe a wide grin. The bottom fell out of Joe's stomach as he did. Even his untrained eye could detect the mass of movement in the sample.

"Fuck."

"Yeah, that would be what got you into this mess. Whether it was a spell, or your own regenerative ability, it definitely wasn't a one-time thing. I'd recommend at least double protection in the future. Like spermicide-coated rubbers *and* a partner who's on the pill."

"Fuck." He sounded like a parrot, but it bore repeating. Celibacy had never looked so good.

He owed Mel an apology, big time. While he still wasn't certain that she hadn't cast some sort of spell, Kent's comments had raised a whole bunch of doubts. Maybe surgery *had* been a poor option for a werewolf. At the very least, he was now convinced that the baby was his. That realization caused the breath to leave his chest and his knees to buckle. Kent grabbed him, steadied him for a moment.

"Congratulations, Dad. You okay?"

"Yeah." Breathing carefully, he got his legs and lungs working again.

"Reality just bit you on the ass big time, didn't it?"

While he would have loved to wipe the smug grin off his friend's face, right now he was too busy trying to breathe. He just grunted an affirmative and glared.

"It'll pass," Kent assured him. "It always does."

"I take it you know the feeling." He forced the words through clenched teeth.

"Four times now." He didn't have to sound so damned cheerful about it.

Wait a minute!

"Four?" Kent and Nora only had three kids.

"Due in December," Joe confirmed, beaming. "By the way, I'd hazard a guess that you're looking at the end of February."

"I can't do this, Kent." He'd remember to congratulate his friend later, right now he was busy panicking.

"You don't have to. Believe me, she'll be doing all the work. Besides, you could just write her a check and disappear if that's what you really want." Kent's tone had gone frigid, and he turned from Joe to tidy up the lab. "But you'd be missing out on some of the best stuff life has to offer."

"That's not what I meant and you know it!" Oh, hell, even he didn't know what he was saying, how could he expect Kent to? The chirping of his satellite phone was a welcome interruption. "Hello?"

"Hi, Mr. Pierce. This is Derek Monroe, the security guard."

"Hi, Derek." He'd requested daily check-ins. Even in his anger, he couldn't, wouldn't have walked away leaving Mel unprotected. "How's it going?"

"Not so good, Mr. Pierce. We had a little trouble today."

When the call ended, Joe turned to Kent. "I've got to go. Now."

In the cab on the way to the airport, he filled Kent in, telling him all about Talcott, the vandalism, and everything. "This time he really tried to hurt her." Joe's stomach was wracked with guilt at having left her. "Or worse."

"Call if there's anything I can do," Kent demanded as Jonas exited the cab.

"Sure." Not in a million years. "Give my love to Nora and the kids. Oh, and congratulations on the new one." Joe shuddered. "Even though I think you're crazy."

"Say hi to Mel for us. And congratulations to both of you, too." Then the cab was history, and Joe was at the desk, arranging for transportation and furious at the inevitable delays. This was all his fault. He never should have left her.

＊ ＊ ＊ ＊

Her bedroom was the only place she could escape her watchdogs. Not that she didn't like Derek, mind you. He was a great kid. But it had been twenty-four hours since Jonas's departure, and the only time she'd had to herself was while she slept. Derek had camped on the couch.

She finished dressing and brushed her teeth. Jonas wasn't coming back. No matter how many times she repeated it, her brain couldn't quite convince her heart to believe it. Her love for him, unintentional though it might have been, had become such a tangible part of her being that she found it hard to accept that on some level, he didn't love her back. She knew he'd told her things, shared his feelings in a way he'd never done with anybody else, not even his friend Kent. That had to mean something. Didn't it?

For thirty-four years she'd believed that her family's curse meant she could never have a man in her life, and she'd always told herself that she could have a full, rewarding existence without one. It was still true. She was strong, smart, independent. She'd spent the night wrestling with her emotions, and had come to the conclusion that if Jonas didn't come back, she was perfectly capable of leading a fulfilling life, and providing a happy, loving home for her daughter. Without Jonas, however, there would always be an empty place in her heart.

Why had she wasted so much time worrying about the stupid curse? Hattie and Karen had been trying to tell her for years to ignore it, but she hadn't listened. Life was precious, life was short, and life was for *living*. If, by some miracle, she ever got the chance to make things up to Jonas, she was going to jump all over it. Besides, even if the curse was still in force, it had never had to deal with a werewolf before. If anyone could stand up to the curse, Jonas was it.

If only he wanted to.

That was the crux of the problem. Jonas didn't want a long-term relationship and never wanted to have children. He had his own issues to deal with, his own burdens to bear. She'd betrayed him, however unwittingly, and she just didn't know if he would ever be able to forgive her for that.

With all her heart she hoped he could. She loved him so much, and even though he didn't think so himself, he would make a terrific father.

Her stomach growled and she laid her hand over it. It was going to be one of those mornings, was it? The days she woke up nauseous were alternating with the must-eat-everything-in-sight mornings. Well, Derek probably wouldn't object if she went downstairs and made a big batch of French toast. A glance at her watch informed her that Andy Erickson would be here in a half hour as well. She didn't know why she'd agreed to another meeting, but something about his earnest request had made it too much effort to say no. Well, hopefully he liked French toast too.

Closing her eyes, she inhaled deeply, a big cleansing breath, then let it out slowly through her nose. It was a beautiful morning—she had work to do, friends who loved her, and a baby on the way. Focusing on the positives would get her through today, and tomorrow would take care of itself. She'd tell herself that every day if she had to, until the pain of Jonas's absence started to fade.

A determined smile fixed on her face, she started down the stairs toward the kitchen. "Derek?" She was surprised not to find the guard waiting for her. Maybe he'd stepped outside to confer with his partner. Opening the back door, she stepped out onto her back porch, inhaling deeply of the fresh, pine-scented air. It really was going to be a beautiful day.

"Derek?" She couldn't spot either of the guards. "Rich? You guys want breakfast?"

Something was wrong. Stepping down off the porch, the hairs on the back of her neck stood upright. Thinking she spotted movement in the underbrush, she took a step forward.

There was a soft whooshing noise behind her head. She started to spin around. "Derek?"

That's when the lights went out, and everything faded to black.

Chapter Nineteen

Where the hell was she?

His footsteps echoed in the stillness of the empty cabin. "Mel?" He'd checked the office first. It was empty too. "Derek?" Nothing.

Joe went back through the office to the outside, heading down the path to the rental cabins. She wasn't in the laundry area, the shed, or either of the barns. Nothing. Finally, he started knocking on cabin doors, which also proved futile. Only a couple of the guests were in, and none of them had seen their landlady since the previous day. None of them had seen the guards, either. Catching the sound of a vehicle coming up the road, he waited at the end of the drive.

"Erickson." He shot the reporter a stare that should have sent him running for the nearest airport. "What the hell are you doing here?"

"Oddly enough, not looking for you. I have an appointment with Ms. MacRae."

"Stay away from Mel," Joe growled. "Or all your paper's fancy lawyers won't be able to find enough pieces of you to put back together."

One eyebrow lifted. Damn, the cocky little bastard refused to be intimidated. Under other circumstances, Joe could have admired that.

"Are you really a werewolf, Pierce?"

"What?" Damn, it, he didn't have time for this. "Are you nuts?"

"Just checking. Your girlfriend admits to being a witch. Why shouldn't you be a werewolf."

"Get a life, Erickson. And quick poking your damn nose into mine."

"Poking my nose into things is my life, Pierce," the reporter shot back with a grin. "You write bestsellers and make millions of dollars. That makes you a celebrity. Celebrities have to deal with the press. Get over it."

"You're not the press, you're a freaking vampire," Joe muttered. "What time was your appointment with Mel?"

Checking his watch, Erickson frowned. "Ten minutes ago. Why, where is she?"

"I wish I knew," Joe murmured, even more worried now. "I'll have her call you."

Erickson shook his head and strode toward the house. "You don't scare me, Pierce. Grow fur and fangs, and maybe I'll run away. Maybe."

"She's not in the house."

Erickson halted halfway up the steps. "You really don't know where she is, do you?"

"No." Darting a glare at his nemesis, Joe stalked around the side of the cabin. "If you won't go away, make yourself useful and help me look for her."

With a shrug, the reporter complied, starting around the far side of the house from Joe. Well, he was still a pit bull, Joe grumbled to himself, but maybe he wasn't a total asshole. At least he was willing to help in a pinch.

"Pierce!" Now Erickson sounded scared. His voice was high pitched with panic. "Over here!"

Sprinting around the building, Joe prayed for maybe the first time in his adult life. *Please don't let her be dead.* He sent up a silent plea to any deity who might be listening. He didn't want her hurt or raped either, but they could get past those. She couldn't heal herself from being dead.

It wasn't Mel. Relief warred with renewed fear as he bent over the two unconscious forms in the bushes beside the building.

"Are they dead?" Erickson's face went ashy white beneath his freckles, but he helped Joe haul the two guards out of the brush.

"No." Both pulses were strong. "But they're both going to have massive headaches for a while."

"Amen to that," Derek muttered, his eyes flickering open. He looked up at Joe in alarm. "Mr. Pierce! Where's Ms. MacRae?"

"I was hoping you could tell me. Did you see who hit you?"

"No." Derek's succinct answer was full of self-reproach. "I stepped outside to talk to Rich and next thing I knew the lights went out."

"Damn." Joe reached out a hand to assist Derek into a sitting position. Then he did what he should have done when he'd first noticed Mel was missing. With unsteady hands, he tugged his phone from his belt and called the cops.

After a quick conversation with Mott, he turned back to Derek and Erickson. "Mott's on his way. Anybody have any idea who took her or where?"

Derek groaned and shook his head. "No. She was still upstairs, last I remember."

Erickson bent over the other guard, shaking the man and apparently tried to talk him awake. Joe ignored him with a disgusted shake of his head.

"What time was that?" How long had Talcott had Mel? It had to be him. Well, one of them at least. Joe's nose was telling him that either Byron or Sean had been around. Recently.

Derek checked his watch. "Twenty, thirty minutes. Not long. I have a hard head; I was only out for a while." He struggled to stand. Joe reached out to help.

"Did you see a car, or hear one?" Through the fear that knotted his stomach, Joe tried to focus on his senses. It was no use. He couldn't hear a thing out of the ordinary, and if he wanted to track by scent, he needed a longer nose.

"No." Derek was vertical, but he reached over the bush with one long arm to lean against the wall for support. "He must've come by foot. There wasn't any traffic."

"Well, that means they left on foot, so they might be close. Erickson, Derek, you two wait here for the sheriff, and keep an eye on Rich. I'm going to go check out some of the footpaths."

The reporter started to argue, but he must have realized it was pointless. Joe left them there, sprinting around the house, all his hopes for the future pinned on one possibility. As soon as he was out of sight of the others, he kicked off his shoes, then stripped off his clothes, not caring when he heard a seam rip in his urgency. The instant he was naked, he kicked the pile into the brush beside the path, and willed himself to change.

"Holy shit!" Joe's sharpened hearing picked up the whispered expletive and he mentally echoed it. Erickson. He'd been so focused on Mel, he hadn't even heard the reporter coming up behind him.

Fixing Erickson with a menacing stare, Joe growled.

"Damn, I was right all along!" Erickson shook his sandy hair, his face showing equal parts astonishment and jubilation. "Are you following her scent, or what?"

The wolf nodded.

"Cool. I'll be right behind you. Want me to bring your pants?"

Fine. He nodded again, tilting his head toward the pile of clothes. Let the idiot follow him if he had to. Right now all that mattered was Mel. *Christ!* What a time for him to realize he was in love with her. He could only hope he found her in one piece. If he didn't, he was liable to kill somebody. He just couldn't conceive of a world without Mel in it.

Sniffing the ground near the back steps, he quickly picked up traces of Mel's scent, overlaid with Sean Talcott. Following his nose, Joe bounded down the path with Andy Erickson jogging along behind.

* * * *

"Let me go, Sean."

Mel kept her voice level, hoping he couldn't see how badly she was shaking. "If we both walk out of here now, it isn't kidnapping. That's a Federal crime, Sean. Your dad won't be able to get you out of that one."

"Just shut up, bitch!" He backhanded her across the mouth, slicing open her lip. Mel fell, sitting down hard on the front step of her great-uncle's cabin, the one recently vacated by Jonas. Her eyes remained firmly fixed on the matte black automatic pistol in Sean's other hand. His were trembling almost as much as hers. Her skull throbbed fiercely. He'd probably used that same gun to hit her over the head and knock her out.

"What did you do to Derek and Rich?"

Keep him talking, she reminded herself. That's what you were supposed to do, right? Buy whatever time you can.

"Same thing I did to you, only harder. Then I left them lying in the brush beside the house, for the cops to find."

"Why?"

"Because they were in my way." He shook his head and sneered. "Duh!"

Despair twisted in her belly. He'd snapped. Completely divorced himself from reality, from any culpability over his actions.

"Did you kill them?"

"I don't think so." Then he shrugged. "I probably should have. Should have dressed them both out like I did the deer."

Nausea crawled up her throat, but she had to keep him talking. "Why?"

"Because they kept you away from me." His bright blue eyes regarded her with frightening solemnity, and she could see the pulse throb in his throat. "They were in the way. I want you, so you're mine, and anybody who tries to stop me has to be punished."

"It doesn't work like that Sean. You can't make me want to be with you."

"That's where you're wrong, Melissa." He punctuated this correction with a stern shake of the gun in his hand. His voice was flat and cold. "I *can* make you be with me. I already have."

"But wouldn't it be nicer if I was with you because I wanted to be?" She kept her voice soft, coaxing, and hoped he wouldn't notice her shake. "Wouldn't it be nicer without the gun?"

"No." He gave her a tired sounding sigh. "I'm not quite that stupid, Mel. I know you can't really do magic, but I'm not taking any chances. You've been a very, very bad girl already. You always tell me no, always run away from me. And we can't have that anymore now, can we?"

"I won't run away, Sean," she lied. "You're so much bigger and faster than me anyway, you'd catch me in no time. No, I promise, I'll do anything you ask, anything you want." Anything that wouldn't put her baby in greater danger.

"You'll do whatever I want anyway, bitch." He waved the gun at her negligently. "You can start by taking your clothes off."

"Sean, please don't do this!" Tears pricked the corners of her eyes.

"Too late. Take them off." He aimed the gun more carefully at her chest.

If he killed her, her baby would die too. She'd suffer any indignity to protect her child. Swallowing hard against the acid taste of the bile that filled her mouth, Mel bent over and as slowly as she could manage, untied her hiking boots. Her trembling fingers kept dropping the laces.

"Faster!" He still sounded bored, but some emotion had crept in there. Was that a good sign or bad?

"I'll sell you the land," she offered, rolling off her heavy white socks and tucking them neatly into the toes of her boots, anything to drag things out. "You can name the price, any price, and I'll sign the papers. Then I'll leave Sanctity, and you'll never have to see me again."

"It's too late for that, pretty Melissa."

"But if you kill me, you'll never get your hands on the land. My will names the Nature Conservancy as my beneficiary." She grasped at any straw she could think of to buy time.

"They'll find a newer will in your office. Everybody will understand that you left all your worldly possessions to your loving and heartbroken fiancé."

That confused her. "Jonas?"

"No!" His face flamed and his composure broke. Obviously her instinctive response had infuriated him. "Me, you stupid bitch!"

He narrowed his gaze and gestured with the gun again. She gulped and began to slowly work her arms out of the sleeves of her sweatshirt. What now? She didn't know any spells for this situation. She looked over into the woods she loved, praying for a miracle. *Wait!* Was that a flicker of movement she saw over by the path? Sean was blocking her view, but for a moment, she thought she'd caught a glimpse of black fur. The breath whooshed from her lungs, and she almost fell off the step. *Jonas!*

More time. With a deep breath and suddenly steadier fingers, she shimmied out of her sweatshirt, wanting to keep Sean's attention focused completely on her. "Of course. That makes perfect sense. I've always had a crush on you, Sean, and most of the town knows it. They'll find it totally believable that we were engaged." *Not!*

"Damned right! Now take off the rest of your fucking clothes!"

"Can I stand up?" she asked, her fingers on the waistband of her jeans.

Head cocked to one side, his gaze narrowed with suspicion, he considered her request. "I guess so," he allowed. "But don't try anything funny."

"I won't, I promise." Baloney. She'd say anything, do anything, to protect herself and her baby. Jonas's baby. Hoping to buy time as well as hold his attention, she moved slowly, doing an impromptu striptease as she unbuttoned her jeans, then slid down the zipper.

There was another movement behind Sean, closer this time, and away from the path. Jonas stood, bare-chested in the trees pulling on his own denims. Either her face gave her away, or her movements must have faltered.

"What?" Sean looked around, panicked. Jonas had melted back into the forest, where Talcott couldn't see him. "Who's there?"

When nobody answered, Sean snaked out the arm not holding the gun and yanked Mel off the step and into his grip. Pressing the barrel of the pistol to her temple, he yelled. "Come out, damn you. I know somebody's there."

Dead silence filled the clearing.

"I swear, I'll shoot her." His voice cracked.

"It's probably just an animal." Mel tried desperately to stay calm. "You know they tend to follow me around."

"I don't believe you." Sean's voice rose into a shriek. "You're nothing but a lying bitch. Now somebody had better show his face right this minute, before I blow your fucking head off!"

"Don't shoot."

Slowly, hands held high, Jonas stepped into the clearing. He was barefoot, wearing only a pair of jeans, and Mel had never seen a more beautiful sight.

"Pierce!" Sean spit out the name like a curse. "Or should I call you Wolfe, instead? I know who you are, you know, even though you've been hanging around in our little backwater banging the witch. I bet that's how you get all your stories."

Jonas didn't reply, just studied Mel with that intense amber gaze. "You all right?"

"Ducky." Her voice shook along with the rest of her body. "Well, at least so far." Especially now that Jonas was here. The splitting headache hardly counted.

"Shut up!" Sean commanded. "How did you find us?"

"Accident," Jonas answered. "I was just going for a walk in the woods, and thought I heard somebody. Since there's nobody staying in this cabin this week, I thought I'd better check it out."

"Are you alone?"

"Yep. Just me."

Sensing Sean's hesitation, Mel considered her options. She'd tried every verbal tactic she could think of, and she still had a gun to her head. She couldn't break away and risk getting shot. Taking a chance, she forced her body to relax, sagging limply against Sean.

"I think I'm going to be sick." She groaned, bringing one hand up to cover her mouth. Her other hand clutched her stomach.

Sean shoved her roughly back to the step. "Don't move. And if you're going to puke, puke that way. Don't do it on my shoes."

Which wouldn't have been a bad idea, all things considered.

She had no idea how long the stalemate lasted. It felt like hours but was probably only seconds. She sat on the step with her head in her hands, trying not to throw up for real. Sean stood next to her. Sean's eyes were focused on Jonas but he kept the gun pointed at Mel's skull, as if waiting for Jonas to make a move. Jonas stood still as a statue, fifteen feet in front of them.

"You don't want to kill her." Jonas spoke in a deep rumble that even at this inappropriate moment sent shivers of love and desire down Mel's spine.

"Of course I don't want to." Sean glared and snarled, more the wild animal than Jonas in his fur. "But I'm going to have to. After I'm done with her of course." Raising the pistol, he pointed it toward Jonas. "But I think I'll take care of you first."

"No!" Mel heard herself cry out.

Jonas took a step forward. Mel knew he was trying to keep the gun focused on him, hoping that Sean would shoot him in some non-vital area. But even given his extraordinary ability to heal himself, Mel remembered his admission that it didn't take a silver bullet. A shot to the brain or heart and he'd be just as dead as the next guy. Sean had been hunting since he could walk, and Mel didn't doubt for minute that he'd loaded his gun with hollow points for maximum damage. Jonas was too smart not to make those assumptions. He was deliberately risking his own life for hers.

"Stop right there!" Sean's voice rose to a screech. Jonas paused, only ten feet away now, and the standoff resumed.

Watching Jonas intently, she saw his eyes flicker a moment before she heard the sounds of other people coming up the path.

"Damn it." Sean lowered his arm to shove the gun back into Mel's temple. "Who the fuck is it this time?"

"It's me, son." Byron Talcott stepped slowly into view, hands held out in a pleading gesture. "Put the gun down now. We'll work this out."

"But I want her, Dad." Now Sean whined. "She always acts like she's too good for me, and that just isn't right. She should be honored that I want to fuck her before I kill her."

"Don't be a fool, Sean. Let her go."

"But Daaad." Apparently the appearance of his father had altered the course of his delusions, sending him back into his childhood in some respects. "I want her."

"You can't have her son. Not like that. She's your sister."

* * * *

Not a word, hardly even a breath disturbed the glade. Joe stood poised, barely breathing himself, as both Sean and Mel stared at Byron Talcott.

"What?" Both voices chorused in unison, their stunned expressions nearly identical. How had he missed the resemblance? They shared the same sleek bone structure, the same native grace. Looking at them now, the relationship was obvious.

"It's true." Byron took a step forward. If the gun hadn't still been pressed to Mel's head, Joe would have taken advantage of Sean's temporary paralysis and jumped him, but pulling the trigger would be just too easy of a reflexive action. Instead, he waited, hoping the older man could get through to his troubled son.

"I slept with Marilyn MacRae. Melissa is my biological daughter."

"No!" Once again Mel and Sean cried out in unison. Joe heard a low hiss in the woods off to his right. Apparently Warren Mott didn't think too highly of the idea either. Joe had heard Mott moving into place, knew the sheriff's rifle was aimed and ready to fire.

He heard others, too. Harkness, probably, Erickson definitely. There were two or three others on the path, spectators of some nature. Whoever they were, they didn't move like cops. Great. This was turning into a freaking three-ring circus!

Keeping secrets wasn't even the issue right now. For maybe the first time in his life, he couldn't care less who saw what, or what Erickson would publish. Everything he cared about was sitting on the cabin steps with a gun to her head. He couldn't lose her, not now, not like this. He couldn't stand to lose either of them. Shock hit him like a physical punch. He loved Mel, really, truly loved her and their baby. Somehow, he had to save them both.

"But you were married." Mel looked sick to her stomach.

"To my mother!" Sean added, his expression losing focus. The arm holding the gun sagged a little, but not enough.

"Yes, I was. But your mother had some health problems after you were born, son. We couldn't be—together much. A man has needs, after all. Marilyn was a pretty little thing, and she was as easy as they come. Things happened."

"She was sixteen," Mel cried out. "She wasn't even legal!"

Talcott shrugged. "She knew what she was doing. Not like I was the only one, or anything. I gave her money, after the blood tests showed the kid was mine. It's not my fault she spent it all on drugs."

"You despicable bastard!" Mel started to surge to her feet, but Sean pushed the gun against her head. She sagged back onto the steps.

"It isn't true." Sean's voice broke. "You're lying, Dad. She isn't my sister. She can't be!"

A loud snap disturbed the stillness of the clearing, drawing all eyes to the woods behind Joe. Immediately following the crack was a crash, a curse, and then a brilliant flash of light. Shit! Erickson!

"Who's there?" Sean screamed, pulling the gun away from Mel. Joe leaped across the grass in his bare feet and tackled the other man just as a shot echoed through the glade.

Chapter Twenty

Chaos ensued.

Hearing the shot, Mel wondered why she didn't feel any pain. Was she already dead?

Before the last echoes of the gunshot had died away, there was another, and Sean slumped, just as Jonas leaped over Mel and tackled him.

"Jonas!" Adrenaline coursed through muscles that just seconds earlier had been frozen in shock. Her hands reached instinctively for Jonas, but he was still tangled up with Sean. "Did he shoot you?"

"No." The single word was all he spared as he wrestled a writhing Sean into submission on the porch. Others ran in from the cover of the woods, but Mel didn't notice who they were—the whole crowd was just a blur.

Jonas subdued Sean, who was bleeding from a graze on his upper arm. The sheriff must have shot him, she realized, shuddering. Thank goodness he hadn't hit Jonas or her instead.

As soon as Sean was immobilized, still sputtering curses and threats, Mott slipped a pair of handcuffs on his wrists, and read him his rights. Byron stood with his hand on his son's shoulder, face impassive as he used a handkerchief to blot at the blood streaming from the bullet wound.

"Let me." She held out her hands toward her half-brother. Byron—she swallowed hard—her father stepped back so she could reach Sean.

"Mel, don't!" Jonas had materialized behind her, his strong hands gripping her shoulders. Resisting the urge to lean back into him and let him wrap her in his arms, she wriggled out of his grasp and turned to lay her hand on his chest and stare up into his beautiful eyes.

"I have to."

His eyes burned into hers for a moment, then he nodded, and let her go. While Mott and Byron held Sean still, she laid her hands on his wound and healed him.

"Thank you," Byron managed.

"Save it," Mott barked as Jonas caught Mel's swaying body in his arms. Mott shoved Sean toward the path, shooting dire looks at each of the people gathered in the clearing. "I'll need *all* of you to come downtown and give statements. Harkness, let's get moving!"

"Uh, sheriff, you'd better come over here," the deputy called from the woods. "We need an ambulance, fast."

"Erickson," Joe cried hoarsely, releasing Mel to dart into the woods after the sheriff. "Shit!"

Mel followed them as quickly as her shaky legs would allow. She found Jonas and Harkness kneeling over the still body of the tabloid reporter, a black pool of blood saturating the pine needle carpet.

"Is he dead?"

"Damn near," Harkness reported to his boss. "Bullet wound right through the chest, definitely got the lung, maybe nicked the heart."

Dropping to her knees, she grabbed his wrist, searching desperately for a pulse. She didn't detect one at first, but probing deeper, she found it. The faintest, weakest sign of life she'd ever tried to work with.

"Mel, he's too far gone." Hattie's voice. Where had she come from?

"Don't," Jonas echoed. "Please."

"He saved me, Jonas." It might not have been intentional, but when Erickson had snapped the twig and his flash had gone off, Sean had shot at the sound, giving Jonas time to pounce. She begged for his understanding, while never totally diverting her focus from the man on the ground. Scrambling around, she sat cross-legged, tugging the sandy head into her lap. "I have to try."

Laying her hands on the paper-white cheeks, she felt it when Jonas moved up behind her, engulfing her body with his, as he had when he'd helped her with Gladys. Gratefully, she included him in the link, absorbing his strength into hers.

Then, focusing all of her energy onto Erickson, she gasped. The damage was enormous. Heart, lungs, ribs. The bullet had even nicked the spinal cord before exiting in a huge, craterous wound. He'd stopped breathing, she noted. The blood was even now slowing in his veins.

Still, she couldn't just give up. He'd saved her life, distracting Sean at a critical moment. If he died, the news would bring in even more reporters, which nobody in Sanctity wanted. Most of all, he was a fellow human being, despite his sordid profession, and she just couldn't let him die. Not if she could help it.

It took everything she had, and more. Feeling Jonas sag beside her, she lightened the link with him. She could feel the injured organs begin to heal, but there was so much damage, so much pain. She focused slowly, methodically, one organ at a time. Heart. Lung. Spine. Arteries. Veins. Bone. Muscle. Nerves. Sinew. Skin. She hadn't quite gotten to that last one when she slumped sideways onto the forest floor, unconscious.

* * * *

"Mel!" Other voices echoed his hoarse cry, as Joe gathered her into his arms, fighting to retain his own upright position. She was barely breathing, her skin as pale as the moon they'd watched together over the lake.

"Come back to me, Mel." His voice was broken, but he didn't care. Were those tears coursing down his cheeks, blurring his vision? Frantic, he grasped her wrist and searched for a pulse. "Don't you dare die on me, damn it!"

"What the hell?" Erickson sat up groggily, looking around in abstract confusion. "What the fuck just happened?"

"She saved your life." Mott answered the reporter, his eyes never leaving Mel.

"How?"

"It's her gift," Hattie chimed in, kneeling beside Joe, heedless of her chic suit and pantyhose. Gently she brushed a strand of hair out of Mel's face. "But it cost her."

"Will she be okay?" The reporter was probably still dazed from his own brush with death and confused by his first real encounter with the paranormal.

"She has to be." Joe cradled his woman in his arms, then found the strength to stand. "She just has to."

He carried her to the cabin, and found that Mott had handcuffed Sean to the porch railing. Byron, gray faced, stood next to his son. Derek had arrived, supporting his still woozy partner Rich, and Mott, Hattie, Harkness, and Erickson followed along behind Mel like a funeral procession as he mounted the steps. Derek had the foresight to open the door in front of them.

Striding to the sofa in the living room, Joe laid his precious burden down with infinite tenderness, draping a plaid wool throw over her inert form. Then he sank to his knees on the floor beside her, burying his face in her hair.

In the distance, Joe heard Erickson. "What did she do?" Several minutes went by in virtual silence. "Will somebody please explain this to me?"

"Magic," Mott answered simply. He'd sent Harkness and his other deputies to escort the prisoner to town. Byron, of course, had followed his son. The rest were still gathered in the small cabin, holding vigil. "She used her own energy to heal you."

"Too much of it," Hattie added, echoing Joe's thoughts. "You were so far gone…"

Erickson examined the hole in his chest, noted the matching perforation in his polo shirt.

"There's a bigger one in back," Mott told him. "Exit wounds are a lot messier."

"Is she going to be okay?" Erickson walked up beside the couch. To Joe's surprise, his voice sounded anxious, genuinely concerned.

"She's still breathing." Joe looked up at the others. He could sense just a touch of hope entering his heart, his voice. "She's got a pulse."

"I heard this happened once with Gladys." Hattie crowded close, laid a small hand on Joe's shoulder. "Was it this bad before?"

"No." She hadn't been this pale, this still when she'd passed out at the Clarks'. "But she'd just healed Sean, and I think the pregnancy drains her reserves too."

Mott's eyebrows raised, as did Erickson's, but nobody said a word.

"How long was she unconscious before?" Hattie asked Joe.

"Ten minutes." He couldn't let go of her. He clutched her hand, stroked her face. "Don't leave me," he whispered. "Don't either of you leave me."

"Then I guess we wait." Hattie moved over to the table, pulled out a chair and plunked herself into it. Mott and the guards followed suit. Erickson just slid down to sit on the floor nearby. Part of Joe wished they'd go away, leave him alone with Mel. Another part, one he hadn't even known he possessed, was grateful for their support. He doubted it would be enough to hold him together if she didn't make it, but their unquestioning acceptance of his place in her life meant a lot.

* * * *

Her world swam slowly into focus. She'd made it. Mel knew exactly how close she'd come to dying, even before the conversation she'd just had with her grandmother. Martha's spirit had let Mel know in no uncertain terms that it wasn't her time to go yet, and that she'd better haul her metaphysical butt back to Earth. She'd even grudgingly admitted that Jonas was a reasonably decent specimen, for a man, and encouraged her granddaughter to hold onto him if she could.

"But what about the curse?" Mel had asked, even though she'd already decided to disregard it.

The answer she'd been shown had filled her heart with joy. Fighting for all she was worth, she'd forced her spirit back to her drained, exhausted body, relieved and thrilled to know that the baby was still with her.

As reality began to seep back in, the first thing she felt was Jonas's hand on her face, and his lips against her hair.

"Mmm," she sighed. "Nice." Her eyelids were still too heavy to lift.

"Mel?" The catch in his voice warmed her heart. He'd come back for her, she remembered joyfully.

A tear splashed onto her cheek, and her eyes flew open. "Don't cry."

He hugged her tight, his arms squeezing the breath from her still-limp body. "Thank God! Don't ever, ever scare me like that again!"

Shivering, she snuggled into the warmth of his embrace. "Okay."

There was a shuffle from behind Jonas, and Mel tried to look over his shoulder. Understanding, he lifted her in his arms, then sat on the sofa, cradling her in his lap.

Jonas gave her a crooked smile. "I'm not the only one who was worried."

The first face she saw was Andy Erickson. "You okay? I didn't quite finish."

"You did fine," he replied with a deep swallow. "All that's left are a couple of scratches. Hey, they say chicks dig scars, right?"

"You going to write about all of this?"

The reporter looked nervously at Jonas, then down at his toes. "Nah. Who'd believe it anyway?"

Everyone nodded thoughtfully. Mel looked over at Derek and Rich. "What happened to you two?"

"Conked over the head," Derek replied with the guilty look of a schoolboy caught in some mischief.

"You okay?" Without thinking, she extended her hand toward her would-be-protectors. Derek jumped back guiltily, as Jonas snatched her hand and held it tight with his own.

"Stop that!"

"We're okay!" Rich had also stood and was backing away as he spoke. "Honest. Couple aspirin, a good night's sleep, we're good as new."

"Okay." Sinking back into Jonas's arms, she sighed. She wouldn't have been able to do anything, anyway. Her powers were as exhausted as the rest of her.

Hattie walked over and placed a steaming cup of chamomile tea into Mel's hand. The others all had coffee, she noticed. She'd been out longer than she'd realized. Good thing she kept this cabin stocked even when it was vacant.

"Is Byron Talcott really my father?"

Mott shrugged, but Hattie nodded. "He is. Marilyn admitted it to me before she died. I'd promised her I wouldn't tell, but maybe I should have. If it could have prevented Sean…"

"It wouldn't have. I think on some level, maybe he did know." Which made his obsession with her all the sicker. "Maybe I did too. That's why his advances repulsed me so much, and why he couldn't stop resenting me. He didn't want me for sex, not really. Just for the subjugation of it."

The grip on her shoulders tightened, and Jonas growled deep in his chest. Mel patted his arm. "It's weird, and I don't suppose I'll ever be able to think of him as my father, but that was his choice. At least now I can stop wondering."

Jonas exchanged an odd glance with Warren Mott that was almost sympathetic. She'd have to ask for an explanation of that later.

"You okay about that?" Hattie asked. "As a counselor, I can assure you that Sean's issues aren't genetic."

Mel gave Jonas a squeeze. It was just like she'd been trying so hard to convince him. "I'm okay. It isn't what we start with that matters in the end. It's what we do with it."

Jonas groaned and squeezed her back. She hoped that meant he finally got it.

Mel took a deep breath and smiled out at the people she loved. "But it's over now. Now we can all move on with our lives."

* * * *

And that's just what they were going to do, she thought happily, glad to be back in her own cabin. Home had never looked so good. The others had gone, to file reports, or take care of business. The Whispering Pines office was being manned by Hattie and Derek, and Mel and Jonas were finally alone.

"Are you sure you're okay?" He'd carried her up the stairs, then helped her out of the clothes that had stiffened with Erickson's blood.

"I'll be fine. But you could shower with me, just to be on the safe side."

He tilted his head into what she'd come to think of as his thoughtful pose, then sent her a broad grin and unsnapped the jeans that were still all he wore. She'd have to ask about that. Later.

Holding her close under the warm, cleansing spray, he gently soaped away the blood and the grime. Watching his face, her fear and pain seemed to seep slowly away as well. When they were both clean, she sighed and turned, leaning with her back pressed against his front.

"The baby?" Jonas's voice was shaky and uncertain as he cupped both his hands reverently over her abdomen. "Is she okay?"

"The baby is fine." She clasped her hands over his. "And this is your child, Jonas." She had to explain, prayed he'd understand.

"I know." His lips brushed the top of her head, then he turned off the water. Handing her out of the tub, he dried her gently with a fluffy, lavender-scented towel. Then he guided her to her bed, tugged a soft nightshirt over her head, and pulled a pair of running shorts on over his own nakedness.

Damn, she'd really been enjoying the view. After a few hours of sleep, she was going to have to drag those off of him. She sat on the bed, leaning back against the headboard.

"I didn't cast any spells on you."

"I know." He sat at the foot of the bed, close to her, but far enough away that she couldn't touch him. That wasn't good. But he smiled.

Why wasn't he upset? Now she was really confused.

"I saw my friend Kent while I was in New York." His gentle smile twisted into a wry grimace. "He seems to be of the opinion that surgery was a poor choice of birth control for a werewolf."

"You mean…" She bit her lip, afraid to hope.

"I do." His smile was broad and thrilling to behold. "It's a damned good thing I always used back-up till you came along."

"Then you're not mad anymore?" Her heart was thumping against her ribs. "You don't mind about the baby?"

"Oh, I'm still terrified," he confessed, with that lopsided grin she loved so much. "But I guess I'm excited, too." His eyes burned with intensity. "When I thought I'd lost you earlier, both of you, it was the single worst moment of my life. I love you, Melissa MacRae. And I can't wait to hold our daughter in my arms."

Using every bit of strength she could muster, she launched herself across the bed and into his arms. "Oh, Jonas! I love you so very much!"

"You're going to have to marry me, you know." He dropped tiny kisses on her cheeks and forehead. "I don't give a damn about your stupid curse."

"Well, actually…"

"It's never had a werewolf to deal with before. I'm not going to be that easy to kill."

"There's something I need to…"

"We can live where ever you want. I can write books here, in New York, or anywhere else. As long as you're with me."

"Jonas!" She still couldn't get a word in edgewise, but she'd never been happier in her life.

"Say yes, Mel. Please. Promise me we can be a family, all three of us."

"Of course!"

Standing, he whooped, and lifted her off the bed, spinning her around till she was dizzy.

"Jonas! I'm going to throw up on you if you don't stop. Right now!"

He stopped instantly, falling back on the bed with her on top, arms and legs tangled together.

"She'll be beautiful like her mother." Jonas was still grinning like an idiot, and Mel's heart almost shattered. Her idiot. "I hope she gets your powers. But without any stupid curse."

"Actually, there's something I've been trying to tell you for the last five minutes." Mel gave a little laugh and plopped her hand over Jonas's beautiful, talented mouth. "Now shut up and listen."

He did. Finally. Still cuddled in his arms, Mel told him about her near-death experience, including the conversation with her grandmother.

"Wow." No kidding. He believed her. What a guy!

"She likes you by the way. Says if I *have* to be with a man, she guesses you'll do."

"High praise."

"From Gran? It's a freaking Nobel Prize. Then I asked her about the curse."

"And?" She felt him stiffen as he braced for the news.

"Well, you know that part of the curse was that MacRae women would only have daughters?"

He nodded.

"While I was talking to Gran, I was standing, and I had the baby in my arms, wrapped in a blanket. Gran didn't say a word about the curse, just reached over and pulled back the blanket."

"Go on."

"Jonas, we're having a boy! The first son born of a MacRae witch in over a hundred years. I don't know if it just wore off, or if it somehow tested us and we beat it, or if it never existed in the first place. But it's gone. The curse, if there ever was one, is really and truly gone!"

* * * *

He hugged her tight, relieved and yet terrified. Relieved that his child wouldn't have to grow up under the shadow of the MacRae curse, terrified because… His intuitive witch must have sensed his tension.

"Jonas, what's wrong?'

"Nothing, really."

"What is it?" She rolled them both, pinning him beneath her. Knowing how weak she still was, he didn't struggle. "What is wrong?"

"What if he's like me, Mel?"

Smiling broadly, she kissed his nose. "Then we'll have to beat the neighborhood girls away with a stick."

"You know what I mean."

She did. She always seemed to understand his fears. How had he gotten so lucky?

"If he's a werewolf, you'll teach him." Her shining gaze bespoke her complete confidence. She placed one hand on each of his cheeks and stared right into his eyes. "And if he has my powers, we'll teach him how to handle those. And if he has both sets, I imagine he'll run us ragged!"

Her sweet laugh soothed away the last of his fears.

"He won't be like you were, Jonas, with parents who can't see past *what* he is to *who* he is. Our son will have all the love and support and training he needs to deal with whatever gifts he's given."

"You amaze me." He whispered the words, tears pricking his eyelids again. "You're everything I never dreamed I could have."

"I know. It's the same for me." Twin tears leaked out from between her lashes, sparkled on her cheeks. He leaned his head up, kissed them away. "Thank you, Jonas. You've made me happier than I ever thought I could be."

"Thank you," he countered huskily, wrapping his arms tightly around her.

A little later he rolled, snuggled her close with one arm, and drew a light blanket up around them both with the other.

"Now get some sleep, my love," he whispered as her beautiful eyes fluttered shut. "We've got the rest of our lives to work out the details."

EPILOGUE

"Are we forgetting anything?"

"No," Mel replied, securing and testing the strap of her one-year-old daughter's car seat. "Not a thing." The brand-new minivan was fully loaded with toys and luggage.

"Well then. Disneyworld, ho!" Jonas slammed shut the tailgate while Mel checked on Amber's almost three-year-old brother Robbie, who bounced enthusiastically in his own built-in child seat.

"I still can't believe we're driving to Florida," Mel grumbled as she strapped herself into the front, shaking snowflakes out of her hair. "I don't mind taking Robbie to Disneyworld for his birthday, but couldn't we just fly like normal people?"

Jonas had been so determined to make this a family road-trip, however, that she hadn't been able to deny him. He'd worked so hard on his last book, as well as helping her with the kids and Whispering Pines. He deserved this chance to create the kind of family memories neither of them had ever had as a kid.

They'd stayed in Sanctity, for the most part. They maintained his flat in New York, and spent several weeks there every year, as well as a few months here and there on Jonas's research. Jonas had even, finally, met other werewolves. They'd been at a jazz club in Chicago when Mel had noticed that the owner's aura swirled like Jonas's. He'd been in frequent contact with him and his pack, and had learned a lot.

But Sanctity was home. Hattie was here, the doting great-grandma. Warren Mott and Rosa helped spoil the two Pierce children, along with other residents of their tiny community.

The Talcotts were gone. Sean was in a maximum-security mental institution in another state, and Byron had moved to be closer to his son. Sanctity had settled back to normal, more or less. Even the Mercers had given up hating Mel after the truth about Talcott had come out. They'd never be her best friends, even though they were her cousins, but at least they sold her groceries again.

The rest of the community had accepted Jonas with relatively little fuss. Especially after he and Mel had purchased Talcott's resort, installing a top-notch, environmentally friendly management team. The resort staff helped out at the Pines, too, covering when Mel and Jonas traveled. They'd gone to Scotland this summer for Jonas's research, and Mel had loved it, just as she was sure she'd love this trip to Orlando. She loved coming home even more, though. Coming back to their family and friends, and their newly-expanded cabin.

Good thing they'd added several more bedrooms, as well as an office for Jonas. Mel put her hand on her tummy, glancing over at Jonas as he negotiated the snow-dusted gravel road. He didn't know about baby number three yet. She hadn't wanted to dim his enthusiasm for this trip, and he got kind of over-protective when she was pregnant, even though she never had a bit of trouble.

Another boy, she thought, but it was still too early to tell for sure, even with her special senses. Robbie was a witch like his mother, while Amber had her father's golden eyes as well as his gifts, shooting down Jonas's theory that the werewolf heritage was a guy thing. Their daughter hadn't changed yet, wouldn't for a few years, but when she did, she'd have a beautiful cinnamon-brown pelt, and her father by her side.

As for the new baby, Mel could already sense power, enormous power, but she had no idea what form that power would take. It didn't matter. She and Jonas would love and protect their child no matter what. All their kids would always know that their family had been blessed.

"You okay, babe? You look tired." Jonas kept his voice soft, so

Robbie wouldn't hear as they drove through town to the highway. Mel sighed with contentment and closed her eyes. Early pregnancy always made her sleepy.

"Too busy last night to sleep much, I guess," she fibbed, squeezing his hand. "I love you, Jonas."

"Love you too, Mel." There was a devilish glint in his golden eyes. "Did I mention that I booked a suite for tonight outside of Cleveland?" He waggled his eyebrows. "Two bedrooms. Maybe we can get started on kid number three."

She laughed and closed her eyes again. Maybe she'd tell him tonight. After she jumped his bones. With a smile on her face, she drifted off to sleep, her entire world secure around her.

A WORD ABOUT THE AUTHOR...

Multi-award-winning author Cindy Spencer Pape firmly believes in happily-ever-after and brings that to her writing, which blends fantasy, adventure, science fiction, suspense and romance. Author of 19 novels and more than 40 shorter works, Cindy lives in southeast Michigan with her family and a houseful of pets. When not hard at work writing she can be found restoring her 1870 home, dressing up for steampunk parties and Renaissance fairs, or with her nose buried in a book. For more about Cindy and her books, you can find her on her website, www.cindyspencerpape.com.

www.ingramcontent.com/pod-product-compliance
Lightning Source LLC
Chambersburg PA
CBHW070627100726
47907CB00007B/1884